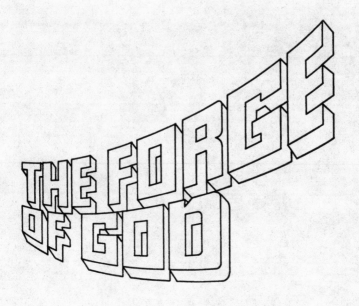

GREG BEAR

THE FORGE OF GOD

TOR

THE FORGE OF GOD

Copyright © 1987 by Greg Bear

A TOR Book

Published by Tom Doherty Associates, Inc.
49 West 24 Street
New York, N.Y. 10010

Jacket art by Alan Gutierrez
Jacket design by Carol Russo

Printed in the United States of America

For Alan Brennert, who gave me hell on TV.

INTROIT: KYRIE ELEISON

June 26, 1996

Arthur Gordon stood in the darkness by the bank of the Rogue River, having walked a dozen yards away from his house and family and guests, momentarily weary of company. He stood six feet two inches in height, losing no more than an inch to a slight stoop. His hair was a dusty brown color, his eyebrows a lighter shade of the same. He had a well-proportioned frame and a sufficient amount of muscle, but he lacked any trace of fat; his muscles showed clearly beneath the skin, giving him an appearance of thinness.

The same leanness added intensity and, falsely, a hint of villainy to his face. When he smiled, it seemed he might be thinking something unpleasant or planning mischief. But when he spoke or laughed, that impression was quickly dispelled. His voice was rich and even and calm. He was and always had been—even in his year and a half in Washington, D.C.—the gentlest of men.

The clothes Arthur Gordon owned tended to the professorial. His favorite outfit was an old brown pair of corduroy pants—he wore them now—a matching jacket, and a blue checked long-sleeved shirt. His shoes were few and sturdy, running shoes for wear around the house, and for work solid brown or black leather wing tips.

His only ostentation was a wide rectangular belt buckle showing a turquoise Saturn and silver stars set in rosewood above brass and maple mountains. He had done little actual astronomy for five years, but he kept that job description close to his heart and quick to his lips, still thinking it the noblest of professions.

Kneeling in the starshadow of ash and maple, he dug his fingers into the rich, black leaf-crusted cake of humus. Closing his eyes, he sniffed the water and the tealike tang of rotting leaves and the clean soapy scent of moist dirt. To be alone was to reappraise. To be alone and know that he could go back, could return at any moment to Francine and their son, Marty, was an ecstasy he could hardly encompass.

The wind hissed through the branches overhead. Looking up, peering between the black silhouettes of maple leaves, Arthur saw a thick spill of stars. He knew every constellation, knew how the stars were born (as much as anyone did) and how they grew old and how a few died. Still, the stars were seldom more than lights on deep blue velvet. Only once in a great while could he make them fill out and see them for what they were, far participants in an intricate play.

Voices carried over the woods. On the broad single-story cabin's porch, vaulting on sturdy concrete pillars above the fern- and tree-covered bluff, Francine talked about fishing with her sister Danielle and brother-in-law, Grant.

"Men love hobbies full of guts and grease," Danielle said, her voice high and sweet, with a touch of North Carolina that Francine had mostly abandoned.

"Nonsense," Grant countered cordially, pure Iowa. "The thrill lies in killing God's innocent creatures."

Below Arthur, the river flowed with a whispering rumble. Still squatting, he slid down the bank on the heels of his thoroughly muddy running shoes and dipped his long-fingered hands into the cold water.

All things are connected to a contented man. He looked up again at the sky. "God damn," he said in awe, his eyes moistening. "I love it all."

Something padded close to him in the dark, snuffling. Arthur tensed, then recognized the eager whine. Marty's three-month-old chocolate Labrador, Gauge, had followed him down to the river. Arthur felt the pup's cold nose against his outstretched palm and rumpled the dog's head and ears between his hands. "Why'd you come all the way down here? Young master fickle? Not paying attention?"

Gauge sat in the dirt, rump wriggling, tail swishing through the damp leaves. The pup's moist brown marble eyes reflected twin star-glints. "Call of the wild," Arthur said on the pup's behalf. "Out here in the savage wilderness." Gauge leaped away and pounced his forepaws into the water.

Arthur had owned three dogs in his life. He had inherited the first, a ragged old collie bitch, when he had been Marty's age, on the death of his father. The collie had been his father's dog heart and soul, and that relationship had passed on to him before he could fully appreciate the privilege. After a time, Arthur had wondered if somehow his father hadn't put a part of himself into the old animal, she had seemed so canny and protective. He hoped Marty would find that kind of closeness with Gauge.

Dogs could mellow a wild boy, or open up a shy one. Arthur had mellowed. Marty—a bright, quiet boy of eight, spectrally thin—was already opening up.

He played with his cousin on the sward below and east of the patio. Becky, a pretty hellion with more apparent energy than sense—excusable for her age—had brought along a monkey hand puppet. To give it voice she made high-pitched chattering noises, more birdlike than monkeylike.

Marty's giggle, excited and girlish, flew out through the tops of the trees. He had a hopeless crush on Becky. Here, in isolation—with nobody else to distract her—she did not spurn him, but she often chided him, in a voice full of dignity, for his "boogy" ways. "Boogy" meant any number of things, none of them good. Marty accepted these comments in blinking silence, too young to understand how deeply they hurt him.

The Gordons had lived in the cabin for six months, since the end of Arthur's stint as science advisor to the President of the United States. He had used that time to catch up on his reading, consuming a whole month's worth of astronomical and scientific journals in a day, consulting on aerospace projects one or two days a week, flying north to Seattle or south to Sunnyvale or El Segundo once a month.

Francine had gladly returned from the capital social hurricane to her studies of ancient nomadic Steppes peoples, whom she knew and understood far more than he understood the stars. She had worked on this project since her days at Smith, slowly, steadily accumulating her evidence, pointing toward the (he thought, rather obvious) conclusion that the great ecological factory of the steppes of central Asia had spun forth or stimulated virtually every great movement in history. Eventually she would turn it all into a book; indeed, she already had well over two thousand pages of text on disk. In Arthur's eyes, part of his wife's charm was this dichotomy: resourceful mother without, bulldog scholar within.

The phone rang three times before Francine could travel from the patio to answer it. Her voice came through the open bedroom window facing the river. "I'll find him," she told the caller.

He sighed and stood, pushing on the corduroy covering his bony knees.

"Arthur!"

"Yeah?"

"Chris Riley from Cal Tech. Are you available?"

"Sure," he said, less reluctantly. Riley was not a close friend, merely an acquaintance, but over the years they had established a pact, that each would inform the other of interesting developments before most of the scientific community or the general media had heard of them. Arthur climbed the path up the bank in the dark, knowing each root and slippery patch of mud and leaves, whistling softly. Gauge bounded through the ferns.

Marty watched him owlishly from the edge of the lawn, under the wild plum tree, the monkey puppet hanging loose and grotesque on his hand. "Is Gauge with you?"

The dog followed, ears and eyes locked on the monkey, which he wanted passionately.

Becky lay on her back in the middle of the yard, luminous blond hair fanned over the grass, gazing solemnly at the sky. "When can we get the telescope out, Dad?" Marty asked. He grabbed Gauge's collar and bent down to hug him fiercely. The dog yelped and craned his neck to nip air as the monkey's plastic face poked him in the withers. "Becky wants to see."

"A little later. Tell Mom."

"She'll get it?" Marty was passing through a stage of doubting his mother's technical skills. This irritated Arthur.

"She's used it more than I have, buddy."

"All *right!*" Marty enthused, releasing the dog, dropping the puppet and running for the steps ahead of Arthur. Gauge immediately grabbed the monkey by the throat and shook it, growling. Arthur followed his son, turned left in the hallway past the freezer chest, and picked up his office extension.

"Christopher, what a surprise," he said affably.

"Art, I hope I'm the first." Riley's voice was a higher tenor than usual.

"Try me."

"Have you heard about Europa?"

"Europe?"

"Europa. Jupiter's sixth moon."

"What about it?"

"It's gone."

"I beg your pardon?"

"There's been a search on at Mount Wilson and Mauna Kea. The *Galileo*'s still going strong out there, but it hasn't been aimed at Europa for weeks. JPL turned the cameras to where Europa should be, but there's nothing big enough to photograph. If it were there, it would come out of occultation again in about ten minutes. But nobody expects to see it. Calls from amateurs have been flooding JPL and Mount Palomar for sixteen hours."

Arthur couldn't shift gears fast enough to think how to react. "I'm sorry . . . ?"

"It's not painted black, it's not hiding, it's just *gone*. Nobody saw it go, either."

Riley was a rotund, crew-cut, plaid sports–coated kind of scientist, shy in person but not on the phone, deeply conservative. He had always been critically deficient in the humor department. He had never pulled Arthur's leg on anything.

"What do they think happened?"

"Nobody knows," Riley said. "Nobody's even venturing a guess. There's going to be a press conference here in Pasadena tomorrow."

Arthur pinched his cheek speculatively. "Did it explode? Something hit it?"

"Can't say, can we?" He could almost hear Chris's smile in his voice. Riley did not smile unless he was faced with a truly bizarre problem. "No data. I've got about seventy other people to call now. Keep in touch, Arthur."

"Thanks, Chris." He hung up, still pinching his cheek. The smoothness of the moment by the river had passed. He stood by the phone for a moment, frowning, then walked into the master bedroom.

Francine reached high to rummage through the top shelf of the bedroom closet, Marty and Becky at her heels.

In their seventeen years together, his wife had moved over the line from voluptuous to *zoftig* to plump. The physical contrast between Arthur and Francine, all curves and fulfilling grace, was obvious; equally obvious was the fact that what others saw in them, they did not see in each other. She tended to wear folk art print dresses, and much of her wardrobe was a stylish acquiescence to matronliness.

Yet in his thoughts, she was eternally as he had first seen her, walking up sunny white-sanded Newport Beach in southern California, wearing a brief one-piece black swimsuit, her long black hair loose in the breeze. She had been the sexiest woman he had ever known, and she still was.

She pulled down the bulbous canvas Astroscan bag. Bending over, she rummaged for the box of eyepieces under a pile of shoes. "What did Chris want?" she asked.

"Europa's disappeared," Arthur said.

"Europe?" Francine smiled over her shoulder and straightened, passing the bag to him.

"Europa. Sixth moon of Jupiter."

"Oh. How?"

Arthur made a face and shrugged. He took the telescope and its painted gray metal base and carried them outside, Gauge snorting at his heels.

"Uh-oh, kids. Dad's in robot mode," Francine called from the bedroom. "What did Chris really say?" She followed him down the stairs and onto the lawn, where he pressed the telescope base into the soft grass and soil.

"That's what he really said," Arthur replied, dropping the big red ball of the reflector gently into the three hollowed branches of the base.

Gray, dignified Grant and lithe blond Danielle stood by the railing on the east side of the rear deck, overlooking the yard and the plum tree. "It's a lovely night," Danielle said, holding Grant's arm. Arthur thought they most resembled models in upscale real estate ads. Still, they were good people. "Stargazing?"

"It's not secret or anything, is it?" Francine asked.

"I truly doubt such a thing can be kept secret," Arthur replied, peering into the eyepiece.

"One of Jupiter's moons has disappeared," Francine called up to them.

"Oh," her sister said. "Is that possible?"

"We have a friend. An acquaintance, really. He and Arthur keep each other up-to-date on certain things."

"So he's looking for it now?" her sister asked.

"Can you see Jupiter from here? I mean, tonight?" Grant asked.

"I think so," Francine replied. "Europa is one of the Galilean moons. One of the four Galileo saw. The kids were going to—"

Arthur had Jupiter in view, a bright spot in the middle of the blue-gray field. Stars formed a resolving fog in the background. Two pointlike moons, one bright and one quite dim, were clearly visible on one side of the brighter planet. The dim one was either Io or Callisto, the bright probably Ganymede. The third was either in transit across the planet or in Jupiter's cone of shadow, eclipsed —or behind the planet, occulted. He tried to remember Laplace's law regarding the first three Galilean moons: *The longitude of the first satellite, minus three times that of the second, plus twice that of the third, is always equal to half of the circumference . . .* He had memorized that in high school, but it did him a fat lot of good now. He murmured the consequences of the law to himself: "The first three Galileans—that includes Europa—can never be all eclipsed at once, nor can they all be in front of the disk at once. If Io and Europa are eclipsed or occulted simultaneously, or in transit simultaneously . . . Ah, hell." He couldn't remember the details. He would just have to sit and wait for the four to be visible all at once, or for only three to make an appearance.

"Can we see?" Marty asked.

"Sure. I'm going to be out here all night, probably," Arthur said.

"Not Becky," Danielle said.

"Oh, Mooommm! Can't I see?"

"Go ahead," Arthur encouraged, leaning back. Marty squatted next to the telescope and showed his cousin how to look into the eyepiece. "Don't knock it," Arthur warned. "Francine, can you get me the field glasses?"

"Where are they?"

"In the hall cupboard, above the camping gear, in a black leather case."

"What would cause a moon to disappear? How big a moon is it?" Grant asked.

"It's quite large as moons go," Arthur said. "Rock and ice, probably with a liquid water layer under an ice shell."

"That's not like our moon, is it?" Danielle asked.

"Very different," Arthur said. Francine handed him the glasses and he trained them on the sky in the general vicinity of Jupiter. After a few moments of sweeping and focusing, he found the dot of light, but couldn't hold the glasses still enough to make out moons.

8 • Greg Bear

Becky pulled away from the telescope, rubbing her eye and making a face. "That's hard," she said.

"All right. Let me use it again," Arthur said.

Marty asked his cousin if she had seen it.

"I don't know. It was hard to see anything."

Arthur applied his eye to the eyepiece and found a third moon visible, also comparatively dim. Callisto, Io, and bright Ganymede. No sign of a fourth.

The rest of the family soon tired of the vigil and went inside, where they played a noisy game of Scrabble.

After two hours of straining his eyes, Arthur stood up. He felt dizzy. His legs tingled painfully from the knees down. Francine returned to the backyard around ten o'clock and stood next to him, arms folded.

"You have to see for yourself?" she asked.

"You know me," Arthur said. "It should be visible, but it isn't."

"Pretty big thing to lose, a moon, isn't it?"

"Unheard-of."

"Any idea what it means?"

Arthur looked up at her. "There's only three. I know I should have seen four by now."

"What does it mean, Arthur?"

"Damned if I know. Somebody's collecting moons, maybe?"

"It scares me," Francine said. "If it's true." She looked at him plaintively. He said nothing. "Then it's true?"

"I suppose it is."

"Doesn't it scare you?"

Arthur stretched to relieve cramped muscles and took his wife's hands in his. "I don't know what it means yet," he said.

Francine moved almost as easily and blissfully in the sciences as he, albeit on a more instinctive level. He valued her insights, and the thought of her fear sobered him further. "Why are you scared?"

"A moon is bigger than a mountain, and if a mountain, or the river, disappeared without a trace, wouldn't you be afraid?"

"I might," he conceded. He picked up the telescope and replaced its aperture cover. "That's enough for tonight."

Francine wrapped her arms around herself. "Bed?" she asked. "Grant and Danielle and the children are asleep. Gauge is with Marty."

Arthur's mind raced as he lay next to Francine. The wide bed's flannel winter sheets hadn't been changed to the regular percale spring and summer sheets. He was glad for their fuzzy comfort. His emotions had caught up with him.

Europa had been around for billions of years, silently orbiting Jupiter. Some scientists had thought there might be life there, but that had never been proved or disproved.

If a mountain or the river disappears, that's much closer to home . . .

Arthur dreamed of fishing with his best friend, Harry Feinman. They sat in a boat on the river, lines trailing in the current, wearing wide-brimmed hats against a sun that was not all that bright. In the dream, Arthur remembered Harry playing with Martin at the house, lifting the boy high in the air and making an airplane noise as he ran around the tree in the backyard. Harry's wife—tall, stately Ithaca—had watched in this dream memory, her smile carrying a slight edge; she was barren, and had never given Harry the child he wanted. Only occasionally did Harry seem to regret the missed opportunities. *I haven't seen Harry in over eight months,* Arthur thought. *Yet here he is.*

How are you doing, fellah? Arthur asked Harry in the boat. *Any nibbles?* It was curious to realize that the figure of Harry, sitting with hat slouched over his face, was part of a dream. Arthur wondered what the dream Harry would say. *You asleep?*

He reached over to lift the hat.

The Earth's moon lay under Harry's hat, bright and full. Harry's face was in the craters and seas of its surface. *Wow,* Arthur said. *That's really beautiful.*

But he worried for the merest instant that he was not dreaming, and awoke with a start.

QUID SUM, MISER!
TUNC DICTURUS?

PERSPECTIVE

AP/Home Info Service, September 2, 1996:
WASHINGTON, D.C.-Scientists are convening at
the American Association for the Advancement
of Science (AAAS) Conference to listen to
speakers presenting papers on subjects ranging from "Lack of Proof for Supermassive In-
tergalactic Gravitational Lenses" to "Dis-
tribution of Wild Rodent Plague Through
Ground Squirrel Fleas *(Diamanus Montanus)* in
Southern California." Yesterday, one of the
most hotly debated papers was presented by Dr.
Frank Drinkwater of Balliol College, Oxford
University. Dr. Drinkwater maintains that
there are no intelligent extraterrestrial
civilizations. "If there were, we would certainly have seen their effects by now." Dr.
Drinkwater maintains that one civilization,
creating self-reproducing planet-visiting
spacecraft, would permeate the galaxy in less
than a million years.

No conclusion was reached by conference scientists regarding the recent disappearance
of Jupiter's sixth moon, Europa. Professor
Eugenie Cook of the University of Washington,
Seattle, maintains that the moon has been dis-
placed from its orbit by collision with a mas-

sive and heretofore unknown asteroid. Famed astronomer Fred Accord maintains that such a collision would have "shattered the moon, and we would still be able to see the orbiting fragments." No such sightings have been reported. Many scientists remarked on public apathy over such an unprecedented event. After a month, the story of Europa has almost vanished from the media. Accord commented, "Obviously, more provincial difficulties, like the U.S. presidential election, loom larger."

1——

September 28–29

Camped beside the mountain that should not have been there, wrapped in cold desert darkness, Edward Shaw could not sleep. He heard steady breathing from the still forms of his two companions, and marveled at their ease.

He had written in his notebook:

The mound is approximately five hundred meters long and half as wide, perhaps a hundred meters high, (apparently) the basaltic cinder cone of a dead volcano, covered with boulder- and cobble-sized chunks of dark black scoria and surrounded by fine white quartz sand. It is not on our maps nor in the 1991 Geosat directory. The flanks of the cone are steeper than the angle of repose, as much as fifty and sixty degrees. The weathering is haphazard at best—some parts open to the sun and rain are jet black, shiny, and other areas are only mildly rusty. There are no insects on the mound—specifically, lift any rock and you will *not* find a scorpion or millipede. There are no beer cans.

Edward, Brad Minelli, and Victor Reslaw had journeyed from Austin, Texas, to combine a little geology with a lot of camping and hiking across the early autumn desert. Edward was the eldest, thirty-three; he was also the shortest and in a close race with Reslaw to lose his hair the fastest. He stood five feet nine inches in his hiking boots, and his slender frame and boyish, inquisitive features made him seem a lot younger, despite the thinning hair. To see objects closer than two feet from his round nose, he wore gold wire-framed round-lensed glasses, a style he had adopted as an adolescent in the late seventies.

Edward lay on his back with his hands clasped behind his head and stared up at the clear steady immensity of the sky. Three days before, dark and gravid clouds had conspired in the flaming sunset to drop a true gully-washer into Death Valley. Their camp had been on high ground, but they had seen basketball-sized boulders slide and roll down freshly gouged channels.

The desert seemed once again innocent of water and change. All around the camp hung a silence more precious than any amount of gold. Not even the wind spoke.

He felt very large in the solitude, as if he might spread his fingers over half the land from horizon to horizon, and gather a mica coat of stars on his fingers. Conversely, in his largeness, he was also a little frightened. This inflated magnitude of self could easily be pricked and shrink to nothing, an illusion of comfort and warmth and high intellectual fever.

Not once in his six-year career as a professor of geology had he found a major error in the U.S. Geological Survey Death Valley charts. The Mojave Desert and Death Valley were the Mecca and Al Medina of western U.S. geologists; they had tramped over the regions for well over a century, drawn by the nakedness and shameless variety of the Earth. From its depths miners had hauled borax and talc and gypsum and other useful, unglamorous minerals. In some places, niter-lined caves wedged several hundred feet into the Earth. A spelunker need descend only twenty or thirty feet to feel the heat; creation still lay close under Death Valley.

There were hundreds of dead volcanoes, black or sullen red on the tan and gray and pink desert, between the resort at Furnace Creek and the small town of Shoshone, yet each one had been charted and was likely featured in some graduate research paper or another.

This mountain was an anomaly.

That was impossible.

Reslaw and Minelli had shrugged it off as an interesting if unique error on the maps; a misplacement, like the discovery of some new island in an archipelago, known to the natives but lost in a shuffle of navigators' charts; a kind of Pitcairn of volcanic mounds.

But the cinder cone was too close to routes traveled at least once or twice a year. Edward knew that it had not been misplaced. He could not deceive himself as his friends did.

Neither could he posit any other explanation.

They walked once again around the base of the mound at mid-morning. The sun was already high in the flat, still blue sky. It was going to be a hot day. Red-haired, stocky Reslaw sipped coffee from a green-enameled Thermos bottle, a serviceable antique purchased in a rock-and-junk shop in Shoshone; Edward chewed on a granola bar and sketched details in a small black cloth-bound notebook. Minelli trailed them, idly chipping at boulders with a rock pick, his loose, lanky form, unkempt black hair, and pale skin giving him the appearance of a misplaced urban scrounger.

He stopped ten yards behind Edward. "Hey," he called out. "Did you see this?"

"What?"

"A hole."

Edward turned back. Reslaw glanced back at them, shrugged, and continued around the mound to the north.

The hole was about a meter wide and slanted upward into the mass of the mound. Edward had not seen it because it began in deep shadow, under a ledge illuminated by the warm rays of the sun. "It's not a flow tube. Look how smooth," Minelli said. "No collapse, no patterns."

"Bad geology," Edward commented. *If the mound is a fake, then this is the first mistake.*

"Hm?"

"It's not natural. Looks like some prospector got here before us."

"Why dig a hole in a cinder cone?"

"Maybe it's an Indian cave," Edward offered lamely. The hole disturbed him.

"Indians with diamond drills? Not likely," Minelli said with a faint edge of scorn. Edward ignored his tone and stepped on a lava boulder to get a better look up into the darkness. He pulled a flashlight from his belt and squeezed it to shine a beam into the depths. Smooth-bored matte-finish lava walls absorbed the light beyond eight or ten meters; to that point, the tunnel was straight and featureless, inclining upward at about thirty degrees.

"Do you smell something?" Minelli asked.

Edward sniffed. "Yeah. What is it?"

"I'm not sure . . ."

The odor was faint and smooth and sweet, slightly acrid. It did not encourage further investigation. "Like a lab smell," Minelli said.

"That's it," Edward agreed. "Iodine. Crystalline iodine."

"Right."

Minelli's forehead wrinkled in a mock fit of manic speculation. "Got it," he said. "This is a junkie rock. A sanitary junkie cinder cone."

Edward ignored him again. Minelli was infamous for a sense of humor so strange it hardly ever produced anything funny. "Needle mark," Minelli explained in an undertone, realizing his failure. "You still think this isn't a map mistake?"

"If you found a street in New York City, not on any map, wouldn't you be suspicious?"

"I'd call up the mapmakers."

"Yeah, well, this place is as crowded as New York City, as far as geologists are concerned."

"All right," Minelli conceded. "So it's *new*. Just popped up out of nowhere."

"That sounds pretty stupid, doesn't it?" Edward said.

"Your idea, not mine."

Edward backed away from the hole and suppressed a shiver. *A new mole and it won't go away; a blemish that shouldn't be here.*

"What's Reslaw doing?" Minelli asked. "Let's find him."

"This-a-way," Edward said, pointing north. "We can still catch up."

They heard Reslaw call out.

He had not gone far. At the northernmost point of the mound's base, they found him squatting on top of a beetle-shaped lava boulder.

"Tell me I'm not seeing what I'm seeing," he said, pointing to the shade below the rock. Minelli made a face and hurried ahead of Edward.

In the sand, two meters from the boulder, lay something that at first glance resembled a prehistoric flying creature, a pteranodon perhaps, wings folded, canted over to one side.

It was not mineral, Edward decided immediately; it certainly didn't resemble any animal he had seen. That it might be a distorted plant, a peculiar variety of succulent or cactus, seemed the most likely explanation.

Minelli edged around the find, cautiously giving it a berth of several yards. Whatever it was, it was about the size of a man, bilaterally symmetric and motionless, dusty gray-green with touches of pastel flesh-pink. Minelli stopped his circling and simply gaped.

"I don't think it's alive," Reslaw said.

"Did you touch it?" Minelli asked.

"Hell no."

Edward kneeled before it. There was a definite logic to the thing; a kind of head two feet long and shaped rather like a bishop's miter, or a flattened artillery shell, point down in the sand; a knobby pair of shoulder blades behind the fan-crest of the miter; short thin trunk and twisted legs in squat position behind that. Stubby six-digit feet or hands on the ends of the limbs.

Not a plant.

"Is it a corpse, maybe?" Minelli asked. "Wearing something, like a dog, you know, covered with clothes—"

"No," Edward said. He couldn't take his eyes away from the thing. He reached out to touch it, then reconsidered and slowly withdrew his fingers.

Reslaw climbed down from the boulder. "Scared me so bad I jumped," he explained.

"Jesus Christ," Minelli said. "What do we do?"

The snout of the miter lifted from the sand and three glassy eyes the color of fine old sherry emerged. The shock was so great that none of the three moved. Edward finally took a step back, almost reluctantly. The eyes in the miter-head followed him, then sank away again, and the head nodded back into the sand. A sound issued from the thing, muffled and indistinct.

"I think we should go," Reslaw said.

"It's sick," Minelli said.

Edward looked for footprints, hidden strings, signs of a prank. He was already convinced this was no prank, but it was best to be sure before committing oneself to a ridiculous hypothesis.

Another muffled noise.

"It's saying something," Reslaw said.

"Or trying to," Edward added.

"It isn't really ugly, is it?" Minelli asked. "It's kind of pretty."

Edward hunkered down and approached the thing again, edging forward one booted foot at a time.

The thing lifted its head and said very clearly, "I am sorry, but there is bad news."

"What?" Edward jerked, his voice cracking.

"God almighty," Reslaw cried.

"I am sorry, but there is bad news."

"Are you sick?" Edward asked.

"There is bad news," it repeated.

"Can we help you?"

"Night. Bring night." The voice had the whispering quality of wind-blown leaves, not unpleasant by itself, but chilling in context. A waft of iodine smell made Edward recoil, lips curled back.

"It's morning," Edward said. "Won't be night for—"

"Shade," Minelli said, his face expressing intense concern. "It wants to be in shade."

"I'll get the tent," Reslaw said. He jumped down from the boulder and ran back to the camp. Minelli and Edward stared at each other, then at the thing canted over in the sand.

"We should get the hell out of here," Minelli said.

"We'll stay," Edward said.

"Right." Minelli's expression changed from concern to puzzled curiosity. He might have been staring at a museum specimen in a bottle. "This is really, wonderfully ridiculous."

"Bring night," the thing pleaded.

Shoshone seemed little more than a truck stop on the highway, a café and the rock shop, a post office and grocery store. Off the highway, however, a gravel road curved past a number of tree-shaded bungalows and a sprawling modern one-story house, then ran arrow-straight between venerable tamarisk trees and by a four-acre swamp to a hot-spring-fed pool and trailer court. The small town was home to some three hundred permanent residents, and at the peak of the tourist season—late September through early May—hosted an additional three hundred snowbirds and backpackers and the occasional team of geologists. Shoshone called itself the gateway to Death Valley, between Baker to the south and Furnace Creek to the north. To the east, across the

Mojave, the Resting Spring, Nopah and Spring ranges, and the Nevada state line, was Las Vegas, the closest major city.

Reslaw, Minelli, and Edward brought the miter-headed creature into Shoshone after joining California state highway 127 some fifteen miles north of the town. It lay under moistened towels in the back of their Land Cruiser on the spread fabric of the tent, where once again it seemed dead.

"We should just go into Las Vegas," Minelli said. He shared a front seat with Reslaw. Edward drove.

"I don't think it would last," Edward said.

"How can we find help for it here?"

"Well, if it really *is* dead, there's a big meat locker in that grocery."

"It doesn't look any more dead than before it spoke," Reslaw said, glancing back over the seat at the still form. It had four limbs, two on each side, but whether it stood or walked on all four, none of them knew.

"We've touched it," Minelli said mournfully.

"Shut up," Edward said.

"That cinder cone's a spaceship, or a spaceship is buried underneath, obviously—" Minelli blurted.

"Nothing's obvious," Reslaw said calmly.

"I saw that in *It Came From Outer Space.*"

"Does that look like a big eye floating on a tentacle?" Edward asked. He had seen the movie, too. Its memory did not reassure him.

"Meat locker," Minelli responded, his hands trembling.

"There's a phone. We can call ambulances in Las Vegas, or a helicopter. Maybe we can call Edwards or Goldstone and get the authorities out here," Edward said, defending his actions.

"What'll we tell them?" Reslaw asked. "They won't believe the truth."

"I'm thinking," Edward said.

"Maybe we saw a jet plane go down," Reslaw suggested.

Edward squinted dubiously.

"It spoke English," Minelli commented, nodding.

None of them had mentioned that point in the hour and a half since they had hauled the creature away from the base of the cinder cone.

"Hell," Edward said, "it's been listening to us out there in space. Reruns of *I Love Lucy.*"

"Then why didn't it say 'Hey, Ricky!'?" Minelli asked, covering his fear with a manic grin.

Bad news. Like a mole that shouldn't be there.

Edward pulled the truck into the service station, its heavy-duty tires tripping the service bell. A deeply tanned teenage boy in jeans bleached to nondescript pale gray and a Def Leppard T-shirt walked out of the garage attached to one side of the grocery and approached the Land Cruiser. Edward warned him back with his hands. "We need to use a phone," he said.

"Pay phone right there," the boy drawled suspiciously.

"Anybody got quarters?" Edward asked. Nobody did. "We need to use the store phone. This is an emergency."

The boy saw the towel-shrouded shape through the Land Cruiser windows. "Somebody hurt?" he asked curiously.

"Stay back," Minelli warned.

"Shut up, Minelli," Reslaw whispered through gritted teeth. "Yeah."

"Dead?" the boy asked, one cheek jumping with a nervous tic.

Edward shrugged and entered the grocery. There, a short and very wide woman clerk in a muumuu adamantly refused to let him use the phone. "Look," he explained. "I'll pay for it with my credit card, my phone card," he said.

"Shoa me the cahd," she said.

A tall, slender, attractive black-haired woman came in, dressed in unfaded jeans and a white silk blouse. "What's wrong, Esther?" she asked.

"Man's givin' us a royal payin," Esther said. "Woan use the pay phone ahtside, but sayes he's gaht a credit cahd—"

"Jesus, thanks, you're right," Edward said, glancing between them. "I'll use my card on the pay phone."

"Is it an emergency?" the black-haired woman asked.

"Yeah," Edward said.

"Well, go ahead and use the store phone."

Esther glared at her resentfully. Edward sidled behind the counter, the clerk moving deftly out of his way, and punched a button for an open line. Then he paused.

"Hospital?" the black-haired woman asked.

Edward shook his head, then nodded. "I don't know," he said. "Maybe the Air Force."

"You've seen an airplane go down?" the woman asked.

"Yeah," Edward said, for the sake of simplicity.

The woman gave him an emergency hospital number and suggested he use directory assistance for the Air Force. But he did not dial the emergency number first. He dithered, glancing nervously around the store, wondering why he hadn't planned a clear course of action earlier.

Goldstone, or Edwards, or maybe even Fort Irwin?

He asked directory assistance for the number of the base commander at Edwards. As the phone rang, Edward hunted for an excuse. Reslaw was right: telling the truth would get them nowhere.

"General Frohlich's office, Lieutenant Blunt speaking."

"Lieutenant, my name is Edward Shaw." He tried to be as smooth and calm as a television reporter. "I and two of my friends —colleagues—have seen a jet go down about twenty miles north of Shoshone, which is where I'm calling from—"

The lieutenant became very interested immediately, and asked for details.

"I don't know what kind of jet," Edward continued, unable to keep a slight quiver from his voice. "It didn't look like any I'm familiar with, except maybe . . . Well, one of us thinks it looked like a MiG we've seen in *AvWeek.*"

"A *MiG?*" The lieutenant's tone became more skeptical. Edward's culpable squint intensified. "Did you actually see the plane go down?"

"Yessir, and the wreckage. I don't read Russian . . . But I think there were Cyrillic markings."

"Are you positive about this? Please give me your name and proof of identity."

Edward gave the lieutenant his name and the numbers on his license plate, driver's license, and, for good measure, his MasterCard. "We think we know where the pilot is, but we didn't find him."

"The pilot is alive?"

"He was dangling on the end of a chute, Lieutenant. He seemed alive, but he went down in some rocks."

"Where are you calling from?"

"Shoshone. The . . . I don't know the name of the store."

"Charles Morgan Company Market," the black-haired woman said.

Edward repeated the name. "The town's grocery store."

"Can you lead us to where you saw the aircraft?" the lieutenant asked.

"Yessir."

"And you realize the penalty for giving false information about an emergency of this sort?"

"Yessir, I do."

Both women regarded him with wide eyes.

"A *MiG?*" the slim, black-haired woman asked after he hung up. She sounded incredulous.

"Listen," Edward said. "I lied to them. But I'm not going to lie to you. We might need your meat locker."

Esther looked as if she might faint. "What's happenin' heah?" she asked. "Stella? What's this awl abauht?" Her drawl had thickened and her face was sweaty and pasty.

"Just you," Edward said to Stella.

She examined him shrewdly and pointed to his belt and rock hammer, still slung in its leather holder. "You're a rock hound?"

"A geologist," he said.

"Where?"

"University of Texas," he said.

"Do you know Harvey Bridge from—"

"U.C. Davis. Sure."

"He comes here in the winter . . ." She seemed markedly less skeptical. "Esther, go get the sheriff. He's at the café talking to Ed."

"I don't think we should let everybody in on this," Edward suggested. *Bad feeling.*

"Not even the sheriff?"

He glanced at the ceiling. "I don't know . . ."

"Okay, then, Esther, just go home. If you don't hear from me in a half an hour, go get the sheriff and give him this man's description." She nodded at Edward.

"You'll be okay heah?" Esther asked, short thick fingers rapping delicately on the counter.

"I'll be fine. Go home."

The store had only one customer, a young kid looking at the paperback and magazine rack. With both Stella and Edward staring at him, he soon moved out through the door, shrugging his shoulders and rubbing his neck.

"Now, what's going on?" Stella asked.

Edward instructed Minelli to drive the Land Cruiser around to the back of the store. He motioned for Stella to follow him through the rear door. "We'll need a cool dark place," he told her as they waited.

"I'd like to know what's happening," she repeated, her jaw firm, head inclined slightly to one side. The way she stood, feet planted solidly on the linoleum and hands on her hips, told Edward as plain as words she would stand for no more evasion.

"There's a new cinder cone out there," he said. Minelli parked the vehicle near the door. Talking rapidly to keep his story from crashing into splinters, Edward opened the Land Cruiser's back gate, pulling aside the tent and moist towels. "I mean, not fresh . . . Just new. Not on any charts. It shouldn't be there. We found this next to it."

The miter-head lifted slightly, and the three sherry-colored eyes emerged to stare at the three of them. Reslaw stood by the store's far corner, keeping a lookout for gawkers.

To her credit, Stella did not scream or even grow pale. She actually leaned in closer. "It's not a fake," she said, as quickly convinced as he had been.

"No, ma'am."

"Poor thing . . . What is it?"

Edward suggested she stand back. They unloaded it and carried it through the delivery door into the refrigerated meat locker.

PERSPECTIVE

East Coast News Network interview with Terence Jacobi, lead singer for the HardWires, September 30, 1996:
ECNN: Mr. Jacobi, your group's music has consistently preached-so to speak-the coming of the Apocalypse, from a rather radical Christian perspective. With two songs in the Top 40 and three records totaling ten million sales,

you've obviously hit a nerve with the younger generation. How do you explain your music's popularity?

Jacobi (*Laughing, then snorting and blowing his nose*): Everybody knows, between the ages of fourteen and twenty-two, you've got only two best friends: your left hand and Christ. The whole world's out to get you. Maybe if the world went away, if God wiped the slate clean, we could get on with just being ourselves. God's a righteous God. He will send his angels to Earth to warn us. We believe that, and it shows in our music.

2——

October 3

Harry Feinman stood near the back of the boat untangling line from the spindle of his reel. Arthur let the boat drift with the slow-moving water. He dropped anchor a dozen yards south of the big leaning pine that marked the deep, watery hollow where, it was rumored, fishermen had pulled in so many big ones the past few years. Marty played with the minnows in the bait bucket and opened the cardboard containers full of dirt and worms. The sun was a dazzle outlined by thin high clouds; the air smelled of the river, a fresh, pungent greenness, and of coolness, of the early fall. In the calm backwater of the hollow, orange and brown leaves had collected in a flat, undulating clump.

"Do I have to bait my own hook?" Marty asked.

"That's part of the game," Harry said. Harry Feinman was stocky and muscular, six inches shorter than Arthur, with premature ash-gray hair receding on all fronts but his neck, where it ventured as stiff fuzz below the collar of his black leather jacket. His face was beefy, friendly, with small piercing eyes and heavy dark eyebrows. He reeled in loose nylon vigorously and propped the pole between the bait can and a tackle box. "You don't earn your fish without doing the whole thing."

Arthur winked at Marty's dubious glance.

"Might hurt the worms," Marty said.

"I honestly don't know whether they feel pain or not," Harry said. "They might. But that's the way of things."

"Is that the way of things, Dad?" Marty asked Arthur.

"I suppose it is." In all the time they had spent living by the river, Arthur had never taken Marty fishing.

"Your dad's here to break things easy to you, Marty. I'm not. Fishing is serious business. It's a ritual."

Marty knew about rituals. "That means we're supposed to do something a certain way so we won't feel guilty," he said.

"You got it," Harry said.

Marty put on the vacant look that meant he was hatching an idea. "Peggy getting married . . . is that a ritual, because they're going to have sex? And they might be guilty?"

In the morning, Francine and Martin would drive to Eugene to attend her niece's wedding. Arthur would have accompanied them, but now there were far more important things.

Arthur raised his eyebrows at Harry. "You've done all the talking so far," he said.

"He's your son, fellah."

"Getting married is celebration. It's a ritual, but it's joyous. Not at all like baiting a hook."

Harry grinned. "Nobody's guilty about having sex anymore."

Marty nodded, satisfied, and took a hooked line from Arthur. Arthur gingerly pulled a worm out of the carton and handed it to his son. "Twist it around and hook it several times."

"Blecchh," Martin said, doing as he was told. "Worm blood is yellow," he added. "Squishy."

They fished in the hollow for an hour without luck. By nine-thirty, Martin was ready to put the pole down and eat a sandwich. "All right. Wash your hands in the river," Arthur told him. "Worm juice, remember."

"Bleechh." Marty bent over the gunwale to immerse his hands.

Harry leaned back, letting his knees grip the pole, and locked his hands behind his neck, grinning broadly. "We haven't done this in years."

"I don't miss fishing much," Arthur said.

"Sissy."

"Dad's not a sissy," Marty insisted.

"You tell him," Arthur encouraged.

"Fishing's gross," Marty said.

"Like father, like son," Harry lamented.

Harry's floppy fisherman's cap cast a shadow over his eyes. Arthur suddenly remembered the dream, with Harry's head a full moon, and shuddered. The wind rose cool and damp in the tree shadows of the hollow with a beautiful, mourning sigh.

Marty ate his sandwich, oblivious.

October 4

Beyond the wide picture windows and a curtain of tall pines, the river eddied quiet and green around a slight bend. To the west, white clouds rolled inland, their bottoms heavy and gray.

In the kitchen, amid hanging copper pots and pans, Arthur cracked eggs into an iron skillet on the broad gas stove.

"We've known each other for thirty years," he said, bringing out two plates of scrambled eggs and sausage and laying one on the thick oak table before his friend. "We don't see nearly enough of each other."

"That's why we've been friends for so long." Harry tapped the end of his fork lightly on the tabletop. "This air," he said. "Makes me feel like thirty years ago was when I last ate. What a refuge."

"You're cramping my sentimentality," Arthur said, returning to the kitchen for a pitcher of orange juice.

"The sausages . . . ?"

"Hebrew National."

"God bless." Harry dug into the fluffy yellow pile on the round stoneware plate. Arthur sat down across from him.

"How do you ever get any work done here? I prefer concrete cells. Helps the concentration."

"You slept well."

"I *snore*, Arthur, whether I sleep well or not."

Arthur smiled. "And you call yourself an outdoorsman, a fisherman." He cut the tip from a sausage and lifted it to his mouth. "Between consulting and reeducating myself, I've been trying to write a book about the Hampton administration. Haven't even seriously started on chapter one. I'm not sure how to describe what happened. What a wonderful tragic comedy it all was."

"Hampton gave science more credibility than any President since . . . Well," Harry said, "since." He lifted one hand and splayed his fingers.

"I'm hoping Crockerman—"

"That name. A president."

"May not be so bad. He's part of the reason I invited you out here."

Harry raised a bushy eyebrow. The two were as much a contrast as any classic comedy team—Arthur tall and slightly stooped, his brown hair naturally tousled; Harry of medium height and stocky to the edge of plumpness in his middle years, with a high forehead and a friendly, wide-eyed expression that made him seem older than he was. "I told Ithaca." Ithaca, the lovely, classically proportioned wife, whom Arthur hadn't seen in six years, was a decade younger than Harry.

"What did you tell her?"

"I told her you used the tone of voice that means you have some job for me."

Arthur nodded. "I do. The bureau is being revived. In a way."

"Crockerman's reviving Betsy?"

"Not as such." The Bureau of Extraterrestrial Communication— BETC or "Betsy" for short—had been Arthur's last hurrah in Washington. He had served as Secretary of BETC for three years under Hampton, who had appointed him after the Arecibo Incident in 1992. That had turned out to be a false alarm, but Hampton had kept Arthur on until his assassination in Mexico City in August of 1994. Vice President William Crockerman had been sworn in on a train in New Mexico, and had immediately moved to place his own stamp on the White House, replacing most of the Cabinet with his own choices. Three months after the swearing-in, the new chief of staff, Irwin Schwartz, had told Arthur, "No little green men, no lost ships off Bermuda . . . might as well go home, Mr. Gordon."

"Is he going to make you science advisor?" Harry asked. "Kick out that idiot Rotterjack?"

Arthur shook his head, grinning. "He's forming a special presidential task force."

"Australia," Harry said, nodding sagely. He put down his glass of orange juice without taking a sip, braced as if for an assault, his eyes fixed on the salt and pepper shakers in the center of the table. "Great Victoria Desert."

Arthur was not surprised. "How much do you know?" he asked.

"I know it was found by opal prospectors and that it's not supposed to be there. I know that it could be a virtual duplicate of Ayers Rock."

"That last part isn't quite true. It differs substantially. But you're right. It's recent, and it shouldn't be there." Arthur was relieved to know that Harry hadn't heard of the incident much closer to home.

"What do we have to do with it?"

"Australia is finally asking for advice. The Prime Minister is going public with a report in three days or less. He's under some pressure."

"Little green men?"

"I can't even comment on that until I've asked you the questions, Harry."

"Then ask," Harry said, still braced.

"The President has put me in charge of the civilian science investigation team. We work with the military and with State. You're my first choice."

"I'm a biochemist. That means . . ."

Arthur shook his head slowly. "Hear me out, Harry. I need you for biochemistry, and as my second-in-command. I'm pushing for Warren from Kent State for geology, and Abante from Malibu for physics. They've agreed, but they have to go through political examination."

"You think I'd pass Crockerman's political pop quiz?" Harry asked.

"You will if I insist, and I will."

"You need a biochemist . . . really?"

"That's the rumor," Arthur said, his grin widening.

"It would be lovely." Harry pushed his chair back with only half his eggs and one sausage eaten. "Old friends, working together again. Ithaca would agree. Hell, even if she didn't . . . but . . ."

"There will never be another chance like this," Arthur said, emphasizing each word as if he were putting some essential point across to a dunderhead student.

Harry wrinkled his forehead, staring up at Arthur. "Dupres at King's College?"

"I've asked for him. He hasn't answered yet. We may not be able to get extranationals on the team."

"I wouldn't turn you down lightly," Harry said. Arthur saw his friend's eyes were red. He appeared close to tears. "You need somebody reliable."

"What does that mean?"

Harry looked out the window, hand tensing on a fork handle, relaxing. "I just told Ithaca three weeks ago."

Arthur's face became placid, clear of all the excitement he had exhibited seconds before. "Yes?"

"Chronic leukemia. I've got it. It has me."

Arthur blinked twice. Harry would not look straight at him.

"It's not good. In a few months, I'll be spending most of my time fighting this. I can't see how I'll be anything but a hindrance."

"Terminal?" Arthur asked.

"My doctors say perhaps not. But I've been reading." He shrugged.

"These new treatments—"

"Very promising. I have hope. But you must see . . ." Harry turned his bright gaze on Arthur. "This thing's as big as Ayers Rock, and it's been there how long?"

"No more than six months. Survey satellites mapped that area just over six months ago and it wasn't there."

Harry grinned broadly. "That's wonderful. That's truly wonderful. What the hell is it, Arthur?"

"A piece of Europa, perhaps?" Arthur's voice was far away. His friend still wouldn't meet his gaze.

Harry laughed out loud and flung his napkin on the table. "I'll not be sad and weepy. Not with this."

Arthur's throat tightened. He had practically grown up with Harry. They had known each other for thirty years. He couldn't possibly be dying. Arthur coughed. "We'll become adults with this one, Harry. The whole human race. I need you very much—"

"Can you take on a might-be invalid?" Now their eyes met, and this time Arthur glanced away, shoulders stiff. With an effort, he looked back. "You'll make it, Harry."

"Lord, speak of will to live."

"Join the team."

Harry wiped his eyes with the forefinger of his right hand. "Travel? I mean, much—"

"At first, but you can stay in Los Angeles if you wish, later."

"I'll need that. The treatment is at UCLA."

Arthur offered his hand. "You'll make it."

"After this, maybe it won't be so bad," Harry said. He took the offered hand and squeezed it firmly.

"What?"

"Dying. What a thing to see . . . Little green men, Arthur?"

"Are you with us?"

"You know I am."

"Then you get the big picture. It's not just Australia. There's something in the Mojave Desert, Death Valley, between a resort called Furnace Creek and a little town called Shoshone. It resembles a cinder cone. It's new. It doesn't belong there."

Harry grinned like a little boy. "Wonderful."

"And yes, there's an LGM."

"Where?"

"For the moment, Vandenberg Air Force Base."

Harry glanced at the ceiling and lifted both arms, tears spilling from his eyes. "Thank you, Lord."

PERSPECTIVE

WorldNet USA Earthpulse, October 5, 1996:
Almost all's well with the world today. No earthquakes, no typhoons, no hurricanes approaching land. Frankly, we'd say today was bright and glorious, but for early light snows in the northeastern United States, rain by tonight in the Pacific Northwest, and the confirmation last week that the ever-popular El Niño current has returned to the South Pa-

cific. Australians are bracing for another long drought in the face of this warm-water oceanic scourge.

3——

When Trevor Hicks told Shelly Terhune, his publicist, that the morning interview with KGB was on, she paused, snickered, and said, "Vicky won't like you turning traitor." Vicky Jackson was his editor at Knopf.

"Tell her it's FM, Shelly. I'm going to be squeezed between the surf report and the morning news."

"The KGB do a surf report?"

"Look, it was on your list of stations," he said, mock-exasperated. "I'm not responsible."

"All right, let me look," Shelly said. "KGB-FM. You're right. You've confirmed the slot?"

"The news manager says ten or fifteen minutes, but I'm sure it'll end up about thirty seconds."

"At least you'll reach the surfers. Maybe they haven't heard of you."

"If they haven't, it's not for want of your trying." He tried to put on a petulant tone. He was in fact quite tired; he was sixty-eight years old, after all, and while comparatively hale and hearty, Hicks was not used to such a schedule anymore. Ten years ago, he could have done it standing on his head.

"Now, now. Tomorrow we have you set up for that morning TV talk show."

"Confirmed, tomorrow morning. Live so they can't edit."

"Don't say anything rude," Shelly admonished him. This was hardly necessary. Trevor Hicks gave some of the most polite and erudite interviews imaginable. His public image was bright and stylishly rumpled; he resembled both Albert Einstein and a middle-aged Bertrand Russell; what he had to say was consensus technocracy, hardly controversial and always good for a short news item. He had founded the British chapter of the Trojans Society, devoted to space exploration and the construction of huge orbiting space habitats; he was a forty-seven-year member of the British Interplanetary Society; he had written twenty-three books, the most recent being *Starhome*, a novel about first contact; and last but not least, he was the most public spokesman in the so-called "civilian sector" for manned exploration of space. His was not quite a household name, but he was one of the most respected science journalists in the world. Despite spending twelve years in the United States, he had not lost his English accent. In short, for both radio and television he was a natural. Shelly had taken advantage of this by booking him on a generic "whirlwind" tour of seventeen cities in four weeks.

This week, he was in San Diego. He had not been in San Diego since 1954, when he had covered the flight trials of the first jet fighter seaplane, the *Sea Dart*, in San Diego Bay. The city had changed greatly since then; it was no longer a sleepy Navy town. He had been booked in the new and stylish Hotel Inter-Continental, on the harbor, and from his tenth-story window could see the entire bay.

In those years, he had been a wire service reporter with Reuters, concentrating on science stories whenever possible. The world, however, had seemed to fall into a deep and troubled sleep in the 1950s. Few of his science stories had received much attention. Science was equated with H-bombs; politics was the sexier and more easily encompassed subject of the time. Then he had flown to Moscow to cover an agricultural conference, as part of the background for a planned book on the Russian biologist Lysenko and the Stalinist cult of Lysenkoism. That had been in late September.

The conference had dragged on for five excruciatingly dull days, with no meat for his book and worse, no stories to convince Reuters he even had a clue as to why he was there. On the last day of the conference, news of the launch of the world's first artificial moon, a 184-pound silvery metal ball called *Sputnik*, had come just in time to save his career. *Sputnik* had returned science to the forefront of world journalism. Trevor Hicks had suddenly found his focus: space. He had buried his book on Lysenkoism and forged ahead without a backward glance.

He had shed a wife—there really was no kinder word for it—in 1965, and had lived with and broken up with three women since.

Currently, he was a confirmed bachelor, though he had fancied the reporter from *National Geographic* he had met at the *Galileo* flyby celebration in Pasadena last year. She had not fancied him.

Trevor Hicks was not just accumulating a greater store of historical memories; he was growing old. His hair was solidly gray. He kept in shape as best he could, but . . .

He drew the draperies on the bay and the glittering, Disney-landish conglomeration of shops and restaurants called Seaport Village.

His portable computer sat silent on the room's maple-veneer desk, its unfolded screen filled with black characters on a cream background. The screen looked remarkably like a framed sheet of typing paper. Hicks sat on the chair and gnawed a callus on the first knuckle of his middle finger. He had gained that callus, he thought idly, from thousands of hours with pencil in hand, taking notes that he could now just as easily type on the lap-sized computer. Many younger reporters did not have calluses on their middle fingers.

"That's it," he said, turning the machine off and pushing the chair back. "Nothing for it. Chuck it." He closed the screen and put on his shoes. The evening before, he had seen an old sailing ship and a maritime museum on the wharf, just a short hike.

Whistling, he locked the hotel room behind him and walked on powerful short legs down the hallway.

"What do you expect mankind to find in space, Mr. Hicks?" asked the news manager, a young, bushy-haired man in his late twenties. The microphone on its tilting arm and sling suspension poked up under Hicks's nose, forcing him to lift his chin slightly to speak. Hicks dared not adjust it now; it was live. The interview was being taped on an ancient black and gray reel-to-reel deck behind the news manager.

"The war for resources is hotting up," Hicks said. More romance than that. "The sky is full of metals, iron and nickel and even platinum and gold . . . Flying mountains called asteroids. We can bring those mountains to Earth and mine them in orbit. Some of them are almost pure metal."

"But what would convince, say, a teenage boy or girl to study for a career in space?"

"They have a choice," Hicks said, still cold to the microphone and the interviewer, his mind elsewhere. Call it a reporter's instinct, but he had been feeling uneasy for days. "They can elect to stay on Earth and live an existence, a life, very little different from the lives their parents led, or they can try their wings on the high frontier. I don't need to convince the young folks out there who are really going into space in the next ten or twenty years. They know already."

"Preaching to the choir?" the news manager asked.

"Rather," Hicks said. Space was no longer controversial. Hardly the sort of topic likely to get much airtime on a rock-and-surf radio station.

"Did fears of 'preaching to the choir' lead you to write your novel, perhaps in hopes of finding a wider audience?"

"I beg pardon?"

"An audience beyond science books. Dabbling in science fiction."

"Not dabbling. I've read science fiction since I was a lad in Somerset. Arthur Clarke was born in Somerset, you know. But to answer your question: no. My novel is not written for the masses, more's the pity. Anyone who enjoys a solid novel should enjoy mine, but I must warn them"—oh, Lord, Hicks thought—not just cold; bloody well frozen—"it's technical. No ignoramuses admitted. Dust jacket locks tight on their approach."

The manager laughed politely. "I enjoyed it," he said, "and I suppose that means I'm not an ignoramus."

"Certainly not," Hicks allowed.

"Of course you've heard of the Australian reports—"

"No. Sorry."

"They've been coming in all day."

"Yes, well, it's only ten o'clock in the morning and I slept late." His neck hair was standing on end. He regarded the news manager steadily, eyes slightly protruding.

"I was hoping we could get a comment from you, an expert on extraterrestrial phenomena."

"Tell me, and I'll comment."

"The details are sketchy now, but apparently the Australian government is asking for advice on dealing with the presence of an alien spacecraft on their soil."

"Pull the other one," Hicks said reflexively.

"That's what's been reported."

"Sounds loony."

The manager's face reddened. "I only bring the news, I don't make it."

"I have been waiting all my life for a chance to report on a true extraterrestrial encounter. Call me a romantic, but I've always held out hope as to the possibility of such an encounter. I have always been disappointed."

"You think the report's a hoax?"

"I don't know anything about it."

"But if there *were* alien visitors, you'd be among the first to go talk with them?"

"I'd invite them home to meet my mum. My mother."

"You'd welcome them in your house?"

"Certainly," Hicks said, feeling himself warming. Now he could show his true wit and style.

"Thank you, Mr. Hicks." The manager addressed his microphone now, cutting Hicks out. "Trevor Hicks is a scientist and a science reporter whose most recent book is a novel, *Starhome,* dealing with the always-fascinating subjects of space colonization and first contact with extraterrestrial beings. Coming next on '90's News: another attempt to capture drift sand in Pacific Beach, and the birth of a gray whale at Sea World."

"May I see these Australian reports?" Hicks asked when the news manager had finished. He thumbed through the thin sheaf of wire service printouts. They were sketchy at best. A new Ayers Rock in the middle of the Great Victoria Desert. Geologists investigating. Anomalous formation.

"Remarkable," he said, returning the sheaf to the news manager. "Thank you."

"Anytime," the manager said, opening the door.

A bright yellow cab awaited him in the station parking lot. Hicks climbed into the back seat, neck hair still prickling. "Can you find a newsstand?" he asked the driver.

"Newsstand? Not in Clairemont Mesa."

"I need a paper. A good paper. Morning edition."

"I know a place on Adams Avenue that sells the New York *Times,* but it's going to be yesterday's."

Hicks blinked and shook his head. His technological reflexes were slow. "To the Inter-Continental, then," he said. Large parts of his brain still lived twenty years in the past. On his desk in the hotel was a device that could get him all the news he needed: his computer. With its built-in modem, he could access a dozen big newsnets within the hour. He could also peek into a few esoteric space bulletin boards for information the newspapers might not deem reliable enough to print. And there was always the enigmatic *Regulus*. Hicks hadn't accessed *Regulus* during his periodic ramblings through the boards and nets, but he had been given the number and ID code by a friend, Chris Riley at Cal Tech.

Regulus, Riley had told him, knew unholy things about space and technology.

To hell with promoting a book. Hicks hadn't felt this charged since 1969, when he had covered the lunar landing for *New Scientist*.

4———

Arthur lay in bed, arms folded behind his head. Francine sat against bunched pillows beside him. She and Martin had returned the day before, to find him preoccupied with deep secrets. A preliminary task force scheduling and planning book was spread open but unread in his lap.

He was assessing a life without Harry. It seemed bleak, even when charged with mystery and events of more than historic significance.

Francine, black hair loose around her shoulders, glanced at her husband every few minutes, but did not interrupt his reverie. Arthur intercepted these glances without reacting. He almost wished she would ask.

He had spent all of his adult life knowing that Harry was available for discussion, by phone or letter; available for visits on a day's notice, whenever they weren't both too involved in work. They had matured together, double-dated (quaintly enough); Harry had approved wholeheartedly of Francine when a much younger Arthur had introduced them. "I'll marry her if you don't," Harry had said, only half joking. Together, for ten years, Francine and Arthur had arranged meeting after meeting of various eligible and sensible women and Harry, but Harry had always politely drifted away from these good matches. It had surprised everybody when he met and married Ithaca Springer in New York in 1983. The marriage, against all predictions, had prospered. Young socialite banker's daughter and scientist; not a likely success story, yet Ithaca had proved remarkably adept at keeping up with the rudiments of her husband's work, and had brought Harry a most useful dowry: loving, persistent training in the social graces.

Both had kept a stubborn independence, but Arthur had sensed early on that Harry could no longer do without Ithaca. How would Ithaca get along without Harry?

Arthur hadn't told Francine yet. Somehow, the news seemed Harry's property, to be dispensed with his permission alone, but that prohibition was silly and Arthur's wall of resistance was wearing thin.

Tomorrow morning he would fly to Vandenberg and be introduced to the "evidence." That would be the biggest moment of his life, bar none, and yet here he was on the edge of tears.

His best friend might be dead within a year.

"Shit," he said softly.

"All right," Francine said, putting down her own book and rolling to lay her head on his shoulder. He closed the notebook and stroked her forehead. She wound her fingers through the thick salt-and-pepper patch of hair on his chest. "Are you going to tell me? Or is it more security stuff?"

"Not security," he said. He ached to tell her about that. Perhaps in a few weeks he could. News was leaking rapidly; he suspected that soon even the Death Valley find would be public knowledge. Everybody was too excited.

"What, then?"

"Harry."

"Well, what about him?"

The tears started to come.

"What's wrong with Harry?" Francine asked.

"He has cancer. Leukemia. He's working with me on . . . this project, but he might not see it through to the end."

"Jesus," Francine said, laying her palm flat on his chest. "Isn't he getting treatment?"

"Of course. He just doesn't think it will save him."

"Five more years. We keep on hearing five more years, and it won't be a killer anymore."

"He doesn't have five years. He may not have one."

Francine hugged him closer and they lay together in silence for a moment. "How do you feel?" she finally asked.

"About Harry? It makes me feel . . ." He thought for a moment, frowning. "I don't know."

"Betrayed?" she asked softly.

"No. We've always been very independent friends. Harry doesn't owe me anything, and I don't owe him anything. Except the friendship, and . . ."

"Being there."

"Yeah. Now he's not going to be there."

"You don't know that."

"He does. You should have seen him."

"He looks bad?"

"No. He looks pretty good, actually." Arthur tried to imagine one's entire body a battleground, with cancer spreading from point to point, or through the blood, unchecked, a kind of biological madness, a genetic suicide aided by mindless, lifeless clumps of protein and nucleic acid. He hated all errant microscopic things with a sudden passion. Why could not God have designed human bodies with seamless efficiency, that they might face the challenge of everyday life feeling at the very least internally secure?

"How was the visit?" Francine asked.

"We had a good couple of days. We'll see each other tomorrow, too, and that's all I can tell you."

"A week, two weeks?"

"I'll call if it's longer than a week."

"Sounds like something big."

"I'll tell you just one more thing," he said, aching with greater intensity to reveal it all, to share this incredible news with the person he loved most on Earth. (Or did he love Francine less than Harry? Different love. Different niches.)

"Don't spill the beans," she warned him, smiling slightly.

"No beans, no cats, just this. If it wasn't for Harry, right now I'd be the happiest man on Earth."

"Jesus," she said again. "Must be something."

He wiped his eyes with a corner of the flannel bed sheet. "Yup."

5———

Edward Shaw swirled the spoon in the cup of coffee and stared at the glass port mounted at head level in the sealed chamber door. He had slept soundly during the night. The chamber was as quiet as the desert. The clean white walls and hotel-style furniture made it reasonably comfortable. He could request books and watch anything he wished on the TV in one corner: two hundred channels, the chamber supervisor informed him.

By intercom, he could speak with Reslaw or Minelli or Stella Morgan, the black-haired woman who had given him permission to call from the grocery store in Shoshone, seven days before. In other rooms, Minelli had told him, were the four Air Force enlisted men who had investigated his call and seen the creature. All of them were undergoing long-term observation. They might be "in stir" for a year or more, depending on . . . Depending on what, Edward was not sure. But he should have known the creature would mean enormous trouble for all of them.

The threat of extraterrestrial diseases was sufficiently convincing that they had submitted to the rigorous two-day round of medical tests with few complaints. The days since had been spent in comparative boredom. Apparently, nobody was quite sure what their status was, how they should be treated or what they should be told. Nobody had answered Edward's most urgent question: What had happened to the creature?

Four days ago, as they were being led to the sealed chambers by men in white isolation suits, Stella Morgan had turned to Edward and asked, conspiratorially, "Do you know Morse code? We can tap out messages. We're going to be here for a long time."

"I don't know any code," Edward had answered.

"It's okay," an attendant had said from behind his transparent visor. "You'll have commlink."

"Can I call my lawyer?" Stella had asked.

No answer. A shrug of heavily protected shoulders.

"We're pariahs," Morgan had concluded.

Breakfast was served at nine o'clock. The food was selected and bland. Edward ate all of it, at the recommendation of the duty officer, an attractive woman in a dark blue uniform with short, bobbed hair. "Any drugs in it?" He had asked the question before; he was becoming boring, even to himself.

"Please don't be paranoid," she said.

"Do you people *really* know what you're doing?" Edward asked. "Or what's going to happen to us?"

She smiled vaguely, glanced to one side, then shook her head no. "But nobody's in any danger."

"What if I start growing fungus up my arm?"

"I saw that one," the duty officer said. "The astronaut turns into a blob. What was its name?"

The Creeping Unknown, I think," Edward said.

"Yeah. 'Creeping' or 'Crawling.' "

"Goddammit, what will you do if we actually get sick?" Edward asked.

"Take care of you. That's why you're here." She didn't sound convinced. Edward's intercom panel buzzed and he pushed the tiny red button below a blinking light. There were eight lights and eight buttons in two corresponding rows on the panel, three of them live.

"Yeah?"

"This is Minelli. You owe us another apology. The food here is terrible. Why did you have to call the Air Force?"

"I thought they'd know what to do."

"Do they?"

"Apparently."

"They going to shoot us up on a shuttle?"

"I doubt it," Edward said.

"I wish I'd majored in biology or medicine or something. Then I might have some idea what they're planning."

Edward wondered aloud whether they had isolated all of Shoshone, blocking off the highway and the desert around the cinder cone.

"Maybe they've put a fence around California," Minelli suggested. "And maybe that's not enough. All of the West Coast. They're building a wall across the plains, not letting fruits and vegetables through."

The intercom system was wired so they could all talk at once or privately.They could not exclude the watch or the chamber duty officers. Reslaw joined them. "There's only four of us, plus the four investigators—they didn't isolate that clerk, what's her name."

"Esther," Edward said. "Or the kid at the service station."

"That must mean they're holding only those people who might have touched it, or came close enough to breathe microbes in the air."

Morgan joined in. "So what are we going to do?" she asked.

Nobody answered.

"I'll bet my mother is frantic."

None of them had been allowed to make calls out.

"You own the store?" Edward asked. "I've been wanting to thank you . . ."

"For letting you call? Really smart of me, wasn't it? My family owns the store, the café, the trailer court, propane distributorship, beer distributorship. It's not going to be easy keeping this quiet. I hope she's okay. God, I hope she hasn't been arrested. She's probably called our lawyer already. I sound just like a spoiled rich kid, don't I? 'Wait'll my mommy hears about this.'" She laughed.

"Well, who else here has connections?" Edward asked.

"We're supposed to be gone for two more weeks," Reslaw said. "None of us is married. Are you . . . Stella?"

"No," she said.

"There it is," Minelli concluded. "You're our only hope, Stella."

"Don't be so glum," the chamber supervisor intruded. He was fortyish, a lieutenant; most of the watch personnel were majors or lieutenant majors.

"Are we being bugged?" Edward asked, angrier than he had any real right to be.

"Of course," the supervisor replied. "I'm listening. Everything's being recorded on audio and video."

"Are you running security checks on us?" Stella asked.

"I'm sure they are."

"Damn," she said. "Count me out, guys. I was a student radical."

Edward cut through his anger and frustration and forced a laugh. "You and me both. Minelli?"

"Radical? Hell, no. First time I voted it was for Hampton."

"Traitor," Reslaw said.

"Speak not ill of the dead," Edward cautioned. "Hell, he was good for science. He boosted the space program."

"And cut the hell out of domestic spending," Morgan added. "Crockerman's no better."

"Maybe we'll meet the President," Minelli said. "Get on TV."

"We're going to be here for the rest of our lives," Reslaw predicted with Vincent Price intonation. Edward couldn't tell whether he was being serious or melodramatic.

"Who's the oldest?" Edward asked, deliberately asserting leadership and moving them on to less timely subjects. "I'm thirty-three."

"Thirty," Minelli said.

"Twenty-nine," Reslaw said.

"Then I'm the oldest," Stella said.

"How old are you?" Edward asked.

"None of your business."

"*They* know," Reslaw said. "Let's ask."

"Don't you dare," Morgan warned, laughing.

All right, Edward thought, *we're in good spirits, or as good as can be expected. We're not being tortured, beyond a few pinpricks. No sense learning everything about each other right away. We might be here for a long time.*

"Hey," Minelli shrieked. "Supervisor! Supervisor! My face . . . My face. There's something growing on it."

Edward felt his pulse quicken. Nobody spoke.

"Oh, thank God," Minelli said a few moments later, milking the situation for all it was worth. "Just a beard. Hey! I need my electric razor."

"Mr. Minelli," the supervisor said, "no more of that, please."

"We should have warned you about him," Reslaw said.

"I'm known to be something of an asshole," Minelli explained. "Just in case you might be having second thoughts about keeping me here."

PERSPECTIVE

AAP/NBS WorldNet, Woomera, South Australia,
October 7, 1996 (October 6, USA):
Despite Prime Minister Stanley Miller's decision to "go public" with news of extraterrestrial visitors in South Australia, scientists at the site have heretofore released
very little information. What is known is
this: The object discovered by opal prospectors in the Great Victoria Desert is less than
eighty miles from Ayers Rock, just over the
border into South Australia. It lies some 210
miles due south of Alice Springs. Its appearance has been disguised to resemble the three
great granite tors of the region, Ayers Rock
and the Olgas, although it is apparently
smaller than these well-known formations.
The Department of Defense has surrounded the
site with some 90 miles of razor wire in three
concentric circles. Current investigations
are being carried out by scientists from the
Ministry of Science and the Australian Academy of Science. Help has been offered by offi-
cials at the Australian Space Research Center
at Woomera and NASA's Island Lagoon tracking
facility, although scientific and military
cooperation with other nations is by no means
certain at present.

6———

The dark gray Mercedes bus took Arthur Gordon and Harry Feinman from the small Air Force passenger jet through a heavily guarded gate into the Vandenberg Space Operations Center. Through the window, over a concrete hill about a mile north, Arthur could see the top half of a space shuttle and its mated rust-orange external tank and white booster rockets poised beside a massive steel gantry.

"I didn't know you were prepared for this sort of thing, I mean, to bring specimens here," Arthur said to the blue-uniformed officer sitting beside him, Colonel Morton Hall. Hall was about Arthur's age, slightly shorter, husky and trim, with a narrow mustache and an air of quiet patience.

"We aren't, speaking frankly," Hall said.

Harry, seated in front of them next to a black-haired lieutenant named Sanborn, turned and peered around the neck rest. Each member of the civilian group was accompanied by an officer. "Then why is everything here?" Harry asked.

"Because we're the closest, and we can improvise," Hall said. "We have some isolation facilities here."

"What are they used for, under normal circumstances?" Harry asked. He glanced at Arthur with an expression between roguishness and pique.

"I'm not at liberty to discuss that," Hall said, smiling slightly.

"It's what I thought," Harry said to Arthur. "Yes, indeed." He nodded and faced forward.

"What were you thinking, Mr. Feinman?" Colonel Hall asked, still smiling, albeit more tightly.

"We're moving biological weapons research into space," Harry said tersely. "Automated modules controlled from Earth. Bring them back here, and they'll have to be isolated. Son of a bitch."

Hall's smile flickered but, to his credit, did not vanish completely. He had sprung his own trap. "I see," he said.

"We all have the highest clearances and presidential authorization," Arthur reminded him. "I doubt that there's anything we can be kept from knowing, if we press hard enough."

"I hope you appreciate our position here, Mr. Gordon, Mr. Feinman," Hall said. "This whole thing was tossed into our laps just a week ago. We haven't straightened out all of our security procedures, and it'll be some time before we decide who needs to know what."

"I would think this takes priority over practically everything," Arthur said.

"We're still not sure what we have here," Colonel Hall admitted. "Perhaps you gentlemen can help us clear up our priorities."

Arthur grimaced. "Now the ball's in *our* court," he said. *"Touché,* Colonel."

"Better your court than mine," Hall said. "This whole thing has been an administrative nightmare. We have four civilians and four of our own men in isolation. We have no warrants for arrest or any other formal papers, and there is no—well, you can imagine. We can only stretch national security so far."

"And the LGM?" Harry asked, turning back again.

"He's—it's—our star attraction. You'll see it first, then we'll interview the men who found it."

" 'It,' " Arthur said. "We'll have to find a less ominous name for that soon, certainly before 'it' becomes common knowledge."

"We've been calling it the Guest, with a capital g," Hall said. "It almost goes without saying, we'd like to avoid any leaks."

"Not likely to avoid it for long, with the Australians having gone public," Harry said.

Hall nodded, facing up to practicalities. "We still don't know whether they have what we have."

"What we have, the Russians probably already know about," Harry said.

"Don't be cynical, Harry," Arthur admonished.

"Sorry." Harry grinned boyishly at the officer beside him, Lieutenant Sanborn, and then at Hall. "But am I wrong?"

"I hope you are, sir," Sanborn said.

On a concrete apron a mile and a half from the shuttle runway stood an implacable concrete building with inward-sloping walls, covering about two acres of ground. The tops of the walls rose three stories above the surrounding plain of concrete and asphalt.

"Looks like a bunker," Harry said as the bus approached a ramp inclining below ground level. "Built to withstand nuclear strike?"

"That's not really a priority here, sir," Lieutenant Sanborn said. "It would be next to impossible to harden the launch sites and runway."

"This is the Experiment Receiving Lab," Colonel Hall explained. "ERL for short. ERL holds our civilian guests and the specimen."

In a broad garage below ground level, the bus parked beside a rubber-buffered concrete loading dock. The front passenger door opened with a hiss and their escorts led Harry and Arthur out of the bus, across the dock, and into a long, pastel green hallway lined with sky-blue blank-faced doors. Each door was described by numbers and cryptic acronyms on an engraved plastic plaque mounted in a small steel holder. Somewhere, air conditioners hummed quietly. The air smelled faintly of antiseptic and new electronics.

The hall opened into a reception area equipped with two long brown vinyl-upholstered couches and several plastic chairs spaced around a table covered with magazines—scientific journals, *Time* and *Newsweek,* and a lone *National Geographic.* A young alert-looking major sat behind a desk equipped with a computer terminal and a card identification box. One by one, the major cleared all four of them and then punched a code into the keypad lock of a broad double door behind his desk. The door opened with a sucking hiss.

"The inner sanctum," Hall said.

"Where is it?" Harry asked.

"About forty feet from where we are right now," Hall said.

"And the civilians?"

"About the same distance, on the other side."

They entered a half-circular room equipped with more plastic chairs, a small wash-up area and lab table, and three shuttered windows mounted in the long curved wall. Harry stood by the bare lab table and rubbed his hand along the shiny black plastic top, examining his fingers briefly for dust—the gesture a professor might make in a classroom. Arthur's mouth twitched in a brief smile. Harry caught the twitch and lifted his eyebrows: So?

"Our Guest is behind the middle window," Hall said. He spoke into an intercom mounted to the left of the middle window. "Our inspectors are here. Is Colonel Phan ready?"

"I am ready," a soft, almost feminine voice replied over a speaker.

"Then let's get started."

The shutters, mounted on their side of the window, clacked and began to rise. The first layer of glass behind was curtained in black. "This is not a one-way mirror or anything fancy," Hall said. "We're not concealing our appearance from the Guest."

"Interesting," Harry said.

"The Guest has requested a particular environment, and we've done our best to meet its requirements," Lieutenant Sanborn said. "It is most comfortable in conditions of semidarkness, at a temperature of about fifteen degrees Celsius. It seems to enjoy a dry atmosphere with approximately the same mix of gases found in our own air. We believe it exited its normal environment at about six o'clock on the morning of the twenty-ninth of September to explore . . . well, frankly, we don't know why it left, but it was caught by daylight and apparently succumbed to the glare and heat by about nine-thirty."

"That doesn't make sense," Harry said. "Why would it leave its . . . environment . . . without protection? Why not make all the necessary precautions and plan the first excursion carefully?"

"We don't know," Colonel Hall said. "We have not interrogated the Guest or caused it any undue strain. We supply it with whatever it requests."

"It makes its requests in English?" Arthur asked.

"Yes, in quite passable English."

Arthur shook his head in disbelief. "Has anyone called Duncan Lunan?"

"We haven't 'called' anybody but people with an immediate need to know," Hall said. "Who is Duncan Lunan?"

"A Scottish astronomer," Arthur explained. "He made a fair mess of a controversy about twenty-three years ago when he claimed to have evidence of an alien space probe orbiting near the Earth. A probe he thought might be from Epsilon Bootis. His evidence consisted of patterns of anomalous returned radio signals that seemed to have been bounced from an object in space. Like a great many pioneers, he had to face disappointment and recant, after a fashion."

"No, sir," Hall said, again with his enigmatic smile. "We haven't spoken to Mr. Lunan."

"Pity. I can think of a hundred scientists who should be here," Arthur said.

"Eventually, perhaps," Hall allowed. "Not right now."

"No. Of course not. Well?" Arthur gestured at the dark window.

"Colonel Phan will give us a direct view in a few minutes."

"Who is Colonel Phan?" Harry asked.

"He's an expert in space medicine from Colorado Springs," Hall said. "We couldn't find anyone better qualified on such short notice, although I doubt we could find a better man for the job even if we searched all year."

"You didn't ask us," Harry said. Arthur nudged him gently in the arm.

The lights in the viewing room dimmed. "I hope someone's making videotapes of our Guest," Harry whispered pointedly to Arthur as they pulled their seats close to the window.

"We have a digital recorder and three high-resolution cameras working around the clock," Lieutenant Sanborn explained.

"All right," Harry said.

Harry was obviously nervous. For his own part, Arthur felt both alert and vaguely anesthetized. He could not quite accept that an age-old question had been answered affirmatively, and that they were about to see the answer.

The black curtain drew aside. Beyond another thick pane of glass framed in stainless steel, they saw a small, dimly lighted, almost empty square room, watery green in color. In the middle of the room was a low platform draped with what appeared to be blankets. A plastic beaker of clear water sat in one corner. In the right-hand corner nearest their window was a meter-tall transparent cylinder, open at the top. Arthur took all this in before focusing on what lay under the blankets on the low table.

The Guest moved, raised a forward limb—clearly a kind of arm, with a three-fingered hand, each finger divided in two above the middle joint—and then sat up slowly, the blanket falling free of its wedge-shaped head. The long "nose" of its head pointed at them and the golden brown eyes emerged from the blunt end, withdrew, emerged. Arthur, mouth dry, tried to see the being as a whole, but for the moment could only concentrate on whether the eyes were lidded, or actually withdrew within "pools" of pale gray-green flesh.

"Can we speak to it?" Harry asked Hall over his shoulder.

"There's two-way communication with the room."

Harry sat in a seat near the window. "Hello. Can you hear us?"

"Yes," the Guest said. Its voice was sibilant and weak but clearly understandable. It lowered itself to the floor and stood uncertainly beside the low table. Its lower limbs—legs—were jointed in reverse, yet not like a dog's or horse's hind legs, where the "knee" is the analog of a human wrist. The Guest's articulation was quite original, each joint actually reversed, with the limb's lower half dropping smoothly, gracefully, to split into three thick extensions, the tip of each extension splayed into two broad "toes." The legs made up much of its height, its rhinoceros-hide "trunk" occupying only about half a meter of its full meter and a half. The end of the long head, thrust forward on a thick, short neck, dropped a few centimeters below the juncture of legs and trunk. The arms rose from each side of the trunk like the folded manipulators of a mantis.

Harry scowled and shook his head, temporarily unable to speak. He waved a hand in front of his mouth, glancing at Arthur, and coughed.

"We don't know quite what to say to you," Arthur finally managed. "We've been waiting a long time for someone to visit the Earth from space."

"Yes." The Guest's head swung back and forth, the jewel-bright, moist, sherry-colored eyes fully revealed. "I wish I could bring better words on such an important occasion."

"What . . . ah, what words do you bring?" Harry asked.

"Are you related?" the Guest asked in turn.

"I'm sorry—related?"

"There is a question about my communication?"

"We are not of the same family—not siblings, brother or father and son or . . . whatever," Arthur said.

"You have a social relationship."

"He's my boss," Harry said, pointing to Arthur. "My hierarchical superior. We're friends, also."

"And you are not the same individuals in different form as the individuals behind you?"

"No," Harry said.

"Your forms are steady."

"Yes."

"Then . . ." The Guest made a sharp, high-pitched whistling noise, and the long crest above the level of the shoulders appeared to inflate slightly. Arthur could not see a mouth or nose near the eyes, and surmised such openings might be on the head below the neck and facing the chest, in the area corresponding—if such correspondences were at all useful—to a long "chin." "I will relate my bad news to you, as well. Are you placed highly in your group, your society?"

"Not the highest, but yes, we are highly placed," Harry said.

"The news I bring is not happy. It may be unhappy for all of you. This I have not spoken before in detail." Again the whistling noise. The head lifted and Arthur spotted slitlike openings on the underside. "If you have the ability to leave, you will wish to do so soon. A disease has entered your system of planets. There is little time left for your world."

Harry pulled his chair a few inches forward, and the Guest, with an awkward sidling motion, came closer to the thick glass. Then it sat on the floor, leaving only its upper arms and long head visible. The three eyes pointed steadily at Harry, as if wishing to establish some unbreakable and facile rapport, or as if commiserating . . .

"Our world is doomed?" Harry asked, somehow avoiding all melodrama, giving the last word a perfectly straightforward and unstrained emphasis.

"Unless I sadly misknow your abilities, yes. This is bad news."

"It does seem so," Harry said. "What is the cause of this disease? Are you part of an army of conquest?"

"Conquest . . . Uncertain. Army?"

"Organized group of soldiers, fighters, destroyers and occupiers. Invaders."

The Guest was silent and still for a few minutes. It might have been a statue but for the almost invisible throbbing of its upper crest. "I am a parasite, a happen-by voyager."

"Explain that, please."

"I am a flea, not a soldier or a builder. My world is dead and eaten. I travel here within a child of a machine that eats worlds."

"You've come on a spaceship?"

"Not my own. Not *ours.*" The emphasis there was striking.

"Whose, then?" Harry pursued.

"Its forebears made by very distant people. It controls itself. It eats and reproduces."

Arthur trembled with confusion and fear and a deep anger he could not explain. "I don't understand," he said, blocking Harry's next words.

"It is a traveler that destroys and makes the stars safe for its builders. It gathers information, learns, and then eats worlds and makes new younger forms of itself. Is this clear?"

"Yes, but why are *you* here?" Arthur almost shouted.

"Shh," Harry said, holding up one hand. "It just said that. It's hitched a ride. It's a flea."

"You didn't build the rock, the spaceship or whatever it is, in the desert? That's not your vehicle?" Colonel Hall asked. Obviously, they had heard none of this before. Young Lieutenant Sanborn was visibly shaken.

"Not *our* vehicle," the Guest affirmed. "It is powerful enough not to fear our presence. We cannot hurt it. We sacrifice . . ." Again it whistled. "We survive only to warn of the death our kind has met."

"Where are the pilots, the soldiers?" Harry asked.

"The machine does not live as we do," the Guest said.

"It's a robot, automatic?"

"It is a machine."

Harry pushed his chair back and rubbed his face vigorously with both hands. The Guest appeared to observe this closely, but otherwise did not change position.

"We have a couple of names for that kind of machine," Arthur said, facing Colonel Hall. "It sounds like a von Neumann device. Self-replicating, without outside instructions. Frank Drinkwater thinks the lack of such machines proves there is no intelligent life besides our own in the galaxy."

"Playing devil's advocate, no doubt," Harry said, still massaging the bridge of his nose. "What scientist would want to *prove* intelligence was unique?"

Colonel Hall regarded the Guest with an expression of mild pain. "It's saying we should be on war alert?"

"It's saying . . ." Harry began angrily, and then controlled his tone, "it's saying we haven't got the chance of an ice cube in hell. Art, you read more science fiction than I do. Who was that fellow—"

"Saberhagen. Fred Saberhagen. He called them 'Berserkers.' "

"I am not being spoken with," the Guest said. "Have you become aware of the results of this information?"

"I think so," Arthur replied. They had not asked a perfectly obvious question. Perhaps they didn't want to know. He appraised the Guest in the silence that fell over them. "How long do we have?"

"I do not know. Perhaps less than an orbit."

Harry winced. Colonel Hall simply gaped.

"How long ago did your—did the ship land?" Arthur continued.

The Guest made a small hissing sound and turned away. "I do not know," it replied. "We have not been aware."

Arthur did not hesitate to ask the next question. "Did the ship stop by a planet in our solar system? Did it destroy a moon?"

"I don't know."

A short, powerfully built Asiatic man with close-trimmed black hair, dark pockmarked skin, and broad cheekbones entered the room. Arthur slapped his hands on his knees and glared at him.

"I beg your pardon, gentlemen," he said.

Sanborn cleared his throat. "This is Colonel Tuan Anh Phan." He introduced Arthur and Harry.

Phan greeted each with a reserved nod. "I've just been informed that the Australians are releasing news photos and motion pictures. I believe this is important. Their visitors are not like our own."

PERSPECTIVE

InfoNet Political News Forum, October 6, 1996, Frank Topp, commentator:
President Crockerman's rating in the World-News public opinion polls has been a rock-steady 60 to 65 percent approval since June, with no signs of change as Election Day approaches. Political pundits in Washington doubt that anything can derail the President's easy victory in November, not even the hundred-billion-dollar trade imbalance between the Eastern Pacific Rim nations and Un-

cle Sam . . . or the enigmatic situation in Australia. I, for one, am not even wearing campaign buttons. It's going to be a dull election.

QUARENS ME,
SEDISTI LASSUS

7——

Hicks, bleary-eyed, clothing rumpled, sat on the straight-backed hotel desk chair and scanned the contents of the file he had marked "Hurrah." "Hurrah" contained the choicest bits of information from twenty-two hours and perhaps three hundred dollars' worth of accessing specialist bulletin boards around the world. He did not care about costs. He was still high.

Australia did indeed have an artifact in their Great Victoria Desert, something apparently disguised to resemble a huge chunk of red granite. The Australian government had kept the find secret for about thirty days, until leaks through investigating military and scientific agencies threatened to scoop them on the greatest story of all time. This much and more—speculation, rumors—had been repeated again and again on all the networks he had accessed. While the government had not released full details, they were expected to do so any day.

The *Regulus* bulletin board was used solely by radio astronomers belonging to the 21cm Club, of which he was an honorary member. After searching through the general and special interest messages, in a small area headlined "Irresponsible Murmurs," Hicks had found a cryptic and unsigned note: "Ham fanatic, right? Say no more about identity. Picked up unscrambled transmission to AF1"—that, Hicks decided, must be *Air Force One*, the President's plane—"concerning 'our own bogey in the Furnace.' The Man's heading west to Vandenberg. Could this be . . . ?"

Hicks frowned again, reading that. He knew several shuttle

pilots currently flying out of Vandenberg. Dare he call them up and ask if anything untoward had been happening? Dare he mention "our own bogey in the Furnace"?

A knock interrupted his reverie. He was heading for the door when it opened and a young Asian woman in lime-green blouse and slacks backed in. "Housekeeping," she announced, seeing him. "Okay?"

Hicks looked over his room abstractedly, relieved that he had chosen to wear a robe. He often worked in the buff, paunch, gray chest hairs, and all—the habit of a bachelor of long standing. "Please, not yet."

"Soon?" she asked, smiling.

"Soon. An hour."

She shut the door behind her. Hicks paced back and forth from curtained window to bathroom door, chin in hand, face as clear and guileless as an infant's. "I cannot think straight," he muttered. Turning on the television and selecting a twenty-four-hour news station, he sat on the corner of the bed.

For a moment, he thought he had tuned to a movie channel by mistake. Three shiny silver objects, shaped like long-necked gourds, hovered above arid sandy ground. Nearby squatted a large van topped by an array of electronic sensing equipment. The van gave the objects scale; each was as tall as a man. Hicks reached over to turn up the volume, joining a male announcer in mid-sentence:

"—from four days ago, shows the three mechanical remote devices which the Australian government claims emerged from a disguised spacecraft. The government says these devices have communicated with their scientists."

The video of the silvery gourds and van was replaced by a typical press conference scene, with a slender, thirtyish man in a brown suit standing behind a clear plastic podium, reading a prepared statement: "We have communicated with these objects, and we can now affirm that they are not living creatures, but robots, representing the builders of the spacecraft—it is now confirmed to be a spacecraft—buried within the rock. While the actual communications are still being analyzed and will not be released immediately, the substance of the information supplied was positive, that is, not threatening or alarming in any fashion."

"Jesus bloody Christ," Hicks said.

The image of the hovering gourds returned. "They're flying,"

Hicks said. "What's holding them up? Come on, you bastards. Do your job and say what the bloody hell's going on."

"Commentary from world leaders, including the Pope, after these messages—"

Hicks flung his arms out and swore, kicked the cabinet holding the television, and punched the set off. He could spend another three hundred dollars chasing rumors across all the networks and bulletin boards in the world, or—

Or he could stop being a novelist wallah and start being a journalist again by finding the news behind the news. Certainly not in Australia. The Great Victoria Desert, by now, had representatives of the media three-deep, trying to interview every grain of sand.

A faint memory of some obligation suddenly flared into consciousness. He had had an appointment this morning. "Damn." That single word, said almost happily, adequately expressed his slight irritation at having forgotten the local television interview. He should have been at the studio five hours ago. It hardly seemed to matter. He was on to something.

The "Furnace" . . . Where in hell would that be? Somewhere near Vandenberg, apparently. He had visited Vandenberg seven times in his career, twice covering important combined civilian-military shuttle launches to polar orbit. Hicks pulled out his pocket compact disk player from a suitcase and hooked it into the computer. He indexed the World Atlas sector on his reference disk and searched through the F's in the gazetteer. "Furnace, furnace, furnace—"

He quickly found several Furnaces, the first in Argyll County, Scotland. There was also Furnace, Kentucky, and Furnace L ("What is L, lake?") in County Mayo, Ireland. Furnace, Massachusetts . . . And Furnace Creek, California. He entered the map number and coordinates. In less than two seconds, he had a detailed color map of an area a hundred kilometers square. A flashing icon in the lower left-hand corner indicated a comparative satellite photograph was available. His eye searched the map until an arrow appeared, flashing next to a tiny dot.

"Furnace Creek," he said, smiling. "On the edge of Death Valley proper, not far from Nevada actually . . ." But not very close to Vandenberg—across the state from it, in fact. He switched disks and keyed in a request for Automobile Club of Southern California information. The computer found a year-old listing. "1995L Brief:

Furnace Creek Inn. 67 units. Golf, riding. Long-established, picturesque location overlooking Death Valley. Three stars."

Hicks thought for a moment, very much aware that the facts were not coming together perfectly. Operating solely on instinct, he picked up the phone, punched a button for an outside line, and requested the area code for Furnace Creek. It was the same as San Diego's although it was hundreds of miles north-northeast. Shaking his head, he called information and asked for the number of Furnace Creek Inn. A mechanical voice informed him, and he jotted it down, whistling.

The phone rang three times. A sleepy-voiced, young-sounding girl answered. Hicks checked his watch again, for the fourth time in ten minutes. For the first time, he actually paid attention to the dials. One-fifteen P.M. He hadn't slept all night. "Reservations, please."

"That's me," the girl said.

"I'd like to book a room for tomorrow."

"I'm sorry, sir, we can't do that. We're completely full."

"Can I make a reservation for your dining room, then?"

"The inn is closed for the next few days, sir."

"Big traveling party?" Hicks asked, his smile broadening. "Special reservations?"

"I can't tell you that, sir."

"Why not?"

"I'm not allowed to give out that information now."

Hicks could almost see the girl biting her lip. "Thank you." He hung up and fell back on the bed, suddenly exhausted.

Who else would have tracked this down?

"Can't sleep," he resolved, sitting up again. He called room service and asked for coffee and a substantial breakfast—ham, eggs, whatever they had. The clerk offered a three-egg concoction with ham and bell peppers mixed in—a Denver omelet, as if pigs and peppers might be special to that city. He agreed, held down the button, and called the downstairs travel agency listed in the hotel directory.

The agent, an efficient-sounding woman, informed him that there was a private airstrip near Furnace Creek, but the closest he could fly in commercially would be Las Vegas.

"I'll take a seat on the next flight out," he said. She gave him the flight number and departure time—about an hour from now, cutting it close—and the gate number at Lindbergh Field, and asked if he would need a rental car.

"Yes, indeed. Unless I can fly directly in."

"No, sir. Only small airfields out that way, no commuter flight service. The drive between Vegas and Furnace Creek will take about two or three hours," she said, adding, "if you're like everybody else who drives on the desert."

"Madmen all, eh?" he asked.

"Madwomen, too," the agent said briskly.

"Mad, all mad," Hicks said. "I'd like a hotel room for the night, as well. Quiet. No gambling." It would be late afternoon by the time he arrived in Las Vegas, and he would not be able to make it to Death Valley before dark. Best to get a good night's sleep, he thought, and start out in the morning.

"Let me confirm your reservations, sir. I'll need your credit card number. You're a guest at the Inter-Continental?"

"I am. Trevor Hicks." He spelled the name and gave his American Express number.

"Mr. Trevor Hicks. The writer?" the agent asked.

"Yes, indeed, bless you," he said.

"I heard you on the radio yesterday."

He pictured the travel agent as a well-tanned blond beach bunny. Perhaps he had been unfair to KGB-FM. "Oh, indeed?"

"Yes. Very interesting. You said you'd take an alien home to meet your mum. Your mother. Even now?"

"Yes, even now," he said. "Feeling very friendly toward extraterrestrials, aren't we all?"

The agent laughed nervously. "Actually, it frightens me."

"Me, too, dear," Hicks said. Delicious, lovely fright.

8————

Harry stood before the glass, hands in his pockets, staring at the Guest. Arthur conferred with two officers at the rear of the room, discussing how the first physical examination was going to be conducted. "We won't be entering the room this time," he said. "We have your photographs and . . . tissue samples from the first day. They'll keep us busy."

Harry felt a small flush of anger. "Idiots," he said under his breath. The Guest, as usual, was curled beneath the blankets on the low platform, only a "foot" and "hand" sticking out from the covers.

"Beg pardon, sir?" asked the current duty officer, a tall, muscular Nordic-looking fellow of about thirty.

"I said 'idiots,' " Harry repeated. "Tissue samples."

"I wasn't there, sir, but we didn't know whether the Guest was alive or dead," the Nordic man said.

"Whatever," Arthur broke in, waving his hand at Harry: slack off. "They're useful, however they were taken. Today, I'm going to ask the Guest to stand up, allow us to photograph it . . . him—"

"It," Harry said. "Don't coddle our prejudices."

"It, then, from all sides, in all postures, while active. I'll also ask if it will submit to further examinations later—"

"Sir," the Nordic man said, "we've discussed this, and considering the warning the Guest has delivered, we believe absolute caution is called for."

"Yes?"

"We're revealing a great many things about ourselves. It could be an information conduit to the object in Death Valley, and how we carry out our examinations, X rays, whatever, could tell them a lot about how advanced we are and what our capabilities are."

"For God's sake," Harry said. He ignored Arthur's sharp glance. "They've been listening to our broadcasts for who knows how many decades. They know everything there is to know about us by now."

"We don't believe that's necessarily so. A lot of information is simply not conveyed in civilian broadcasts, and certainly not in military broadcasts."

"They can type us down to our toenails just by the fact that we still broadcast analog radio waves," Harry said, not moving from the window.

"Yes, sir, but—"

"Your warnings are well taken, Lieutenant Dreyer," Arthur said. "But we can't get anywhere unless we examine the Guest. If this means some two-way exchanges, so be it. If the Guest is a conduit to the ship, we might be able to learn how through the exams."

"It's an interesting idea," Harry conceded in an undertone.

"Yes, sir," Dreyer said. "I've been told to pass these on to you—your itineraries for the Commander in Chief's visit. We're at your disposal."

"All right. Let's have two-way back on." Arthur walked down the slightly sloping floor to the window and stood beside Harry. He pushed the button activating the intercom to the Guest's chamber.

"Excuse me. We'd like to continue our questions and examinations."

"Yes," the Guest said, pushing aside the blankets and standing slowly.

"What is the state of your health?" Arthur asked. "Are you feeling well?"

"Not altogether well," the Guest said. "The food is adequate, but not sustaining."

The Guest had been allowed to choose between a variety of carefully prepared "soups." The first tissue samples had revealed that the Guest could conceivably digest dextro-rotary sugars and proteins generally found in Earth life forms. Purified water was being supplied in beakers passed through with the "food." Thus far, the Guest had not excreted anything into the wide stainless-steel sample tray left open in another corner. The Guest had eaten sparingly, and without apparent enthusiasm.

"Can you describe substances that would please you?"

"In space, we hibernated—"

Harry emphasized the "we" in his notepad.

"And our nutrition was provided by synthesizing machines throughout the voyage."

Arthur blinked. Harry scribbled furiously.

"I am not aware of the names of substances in this language to describe them. The food you provide seems adequate."

"But not enjoyable."

The Guest didn't respond.

"We'd like to conduct another physical examination," Arthur said. "We are not going to take any more tissue samples."

The Guest withdrew its three brown eyes and then produced them again, but said nothing, standing in what might have been a dejected posture—if the Guest could feel dejected, and if body language was at all similar . . .

"You do not have to cooperate," Arthur said. "We don't want to force anything on you."

"Difficulties with speaking, with language," the Guest said. It stepped sideways in one fluid motion to the far right corner of the room. "There are questions you do not ask. Why?"

"I'm sorry, I don't understand."

"You do not ask questions about interior thoughts."

"You mean, what you are thinking?"

"Interior states are far more important than physical construction, are they not? Is this not true for your intelligences?"

Harry glanced at Arthur. "All right," Harry said, putting down his notes. "What is your interior state?"

"Disorganized."

"You're confused?" Harry asked.

"Not at ease. Mission is completed. We will not survive this incident."

"You won't . . ." Arthur searched for clear words. "When the ship leaves, you won't be aboard?"

"You are not asking proper questions."

"What questions should we ask?" Harry tapped his pencil on a chair arm. The Guest appeared to focus its three sherry-colored eyes on this gesture. "What questions should we ask?" he repeated.

"Process of destruction. Past deaths of worlds. How you fit into the scheme."

"Yes, you're right," Arthur said quickly. "We haven't been asking those questions. We experience fear, a negative emotional state, and we do not really want to know. This may be irrational—"

The Guest lifted its "chin" high, revealing the two slits and a shadowed, two-inch-wide depression on the underside of the miter. "Negative emotions," it repeated. "When will you ask these questions?"

"Some of our leaders, including our President, will be joining us tomorrow. That might be a good time," Harry said.

"I think we'd better hear it now, first." Arthur was uneasy at the thought of blindly springing information on Crockerman. He had no idea how the man would react.

"Yes," the Guest said.

"First question, then," Arthur began. "What happened to your world?"

The Guest began its story.

OFFERTORIUM

9

"You're privileged, folks," the new duty officer, a young, slender black woman in gray blouse and slacks, told her four isolated charges.

Ed Shaw sat up on his bunk and blinked.

"The President's coming here this evening. He wants to talk with you and commend you all."

"How long until we get out of here?" Stella Morgan asked, her voice hoarse. She cleared her throat and repeated her question.

"I have no idea, Miss Morgan. We have a message from your mother. It's in your food drawer. We can relay any message from you to her that does not carry information as to your whereabouts or why you are here."

"She's putting on the pressure, isn't she?" Minelli said. They had been discussing Stella's mother, Bernice Morgan, a few hours earlier. By now, Stella was convinced, Mrs. Morgan would have marshaled half the lawyers in the state.

"She is indeed," the duty officer said. "You've got quite a mother, Miss Morgan. We hope to get this all straightened out quickly. Labs are running tests around the clock. So far, we haven't found any foreign biologicals on you or the Guest."

Edward lay back on his bunk. "What's the President going to do here?" he asked.

"He wants to talk to the four of you. That's all we've been told."

"And see the alien," Minelli said. "Right?"

The duty officer smiled.

"When are you going to tell the press?" Reslaw asked.

"Lord, I wish we could do it right now. The Australians have told just about everything, and their case is even weirder than our own. They have *robots* coming out of their rocks."

"What?" Edward sat on the edge of the bunk. "Is it on the news?"

"You should watch your TVs. There are newspapers in your food drawers now. Starting tomorrow, you'll be getting CD machines. Infonet players. We don't want you to be ignorant when the President gets here."

Edward pulled open his food drawer, a stainless-steel tray that shuttled through the walls of the isolation unit, and pulled out a folded newspaper. There were no personal messages for him. His off-and-on girlfriend in Austin didn't expect him back for a month or two; he hadn't spoken to his mother in months. Edward began to regret his fancy-free life-style. He unfolded the newspaper and quickly scanned the headlines.

"Jesus, are you reading what I'm reading?" Reslaw asked.

"Yeah," Edward said.

"They look like chrome-plated gourds."

Edward flipped through the pages. The Australian Armed Forces had gone on alert. So had the United States Air Force and Navy. (Not the Army? Why not the Army?) Shuttle launches had been canceled, for reasons not clearly spelled out.

"Why robots?" Minelli asked after a few minutes of silence. "Why not more creatures?"

"Maybe they found out they can't take the atmosphere and the heat," Minelli suggested. "So they send remotes."

That seemed to make the most sense. But if there were two disguised spacecraft—and why disguised?—then there could certainly be more.

"Maybe it's an invasion," Stella said. "We just don't know it yet."

Edward tried to recall the various science fiction scenarios he had read in books or seen in television and movies.

Motivations. No intelligent beings did things without motives. Edward had always sided with the scientists who thought Earth too puny and out of the way to be of interest to potential spacefarers. Of course, that was geocentrism in reverse. He wished he had read more on SETI, the Search for Extra-Terrestrial Intelligence. Nearly all of his science reading was in geology now; he seldom read magazines like *Scientific American* or even *Science* unless he needed to catch up on relevant articles.

Like most experts, he had grown insular. Geology had been his life. Now he doubted whether he would ever again have a private life. Even if the four of them were released—and that question worried him more than he wanted to admit—they would all be public figures, celebrities. Their lives would change enormously.

He shut off the player and turned to the comics page of the Los Angeles *Times*. Then he lay back on the bunk and tried to sleep. He had slept enough. His anger was getting to the point where he didn't think he could control it. What would he tell Crockerman? Would he rattle the bars of his cage and hoot miserably? That seemed the only appropriate response.

"But look at the big picture," he murmured to himself, not caring whether anybody else heard. "This is history."

"This is *history!*" Minelli yelled from his cell. "We're *history!* Isn't everybody thrilled?"

Edward heard Reslaw clapping slowly, resolutely. "I want to see my agent," Minelli said.

10————

Harry looked over the President's itinerary—and their own, neatly appended with a plastic clip—and sighed. "The big time," he said. "You're used to it. I'm not. Stifling security and appointments timed by the minute."

"I've grown accustomed to being away from it," Arthur said. They shared a room in the Vandenberg Hilton, as the blocky, elongated, three-story concrete officer's quarters had been dubbed by the shuttle pilots who generally occupied the austere rooms. Harry handed him the paper and shrugged.

"Mostly, I'm just tired," he said, lying back and clasping his hands behind his neck. Arthur regarded him with some worry. "No, not because I'm ill," Harry said testily. "It's all this thinking. Coming to grips."

"Tomorrow's going to be very busy. Are you sure you're up to it?" Arthur asked.

"I'm sure."

"All right. Tonight we brief the President and whichever members of his staff and Cabinet he's brought along, and then sit in on the President's interviews with the Guest and the citizens."

Harry grinned and shook his head, still dubious.

Arthur put the papers down on the table between their beds. "What will he do when he hears the story?"

"Christ, Art, you know the man better than I."

"I never even met him before I was canned. When he was Veep, he stayed in the background. To me, he's a riddle wrapped in an enigma. You read the papers; what do you think?"

"I think he's a reasonably intelligent man who doesn't belong in the White House. But then, I'm a radical from way back. I was a communist when I was three years old, remember. My father put me in red sweaters—"

"I'm serious. We have to soften the blow for him. And it *will* be a blow, however much he's prepared by his staff. Seeing our Guest. Hearing from its own lips, or whatever . . ."

"That Earth is doomed. Lambs to the slaughter."

It was Arthur's turn to grin. The grin almost hurt. "No," he said.

"You don't believe it?"

Arthur stared up at the ceiling. "Don't you feel something's not right here?"

"Doom is never right," Harry said.

"Questions. Lots and lots of questions. Why does this spacecraft allow 'fleas' to ride on its back and warn the populace before it can destroy their home?"

"Smugness. Absolute assurance of power. Assurance of our weakness."

"When we have nuclear weapons, for Christ's sake?" Arthur asked sharply. "A fighter pilot down in some jungle should show respect for the natives' arrows."

"It probably—it *should* have weapons and defenses we know nothing about."

"Why hasn't it used them?"

"Obviously, it used *something* to land huge rocks without being detected by radar or satellites."

Arthur nodded agreement. "If what landed wasn't something small, to start with . . . But that would contradict our Guest's story."

"All right," Harry said, propping himself up against the wall with a pillow as a cushion. "It doesn't make sense to me either.

This Australian statement that *their* aliens have come in peace for all mankind. Same group of invaders? Apparently; same tactics. Bury themselves in a duck blind. One ship has 'fleas,' the other doesn't. One ship has robot publicity agents. The other keeps silent."

"We haven't seen the complete text from the Australians."

"No," Harry admitted. "But they seem to have been candid so far. What's the obvious answer?"

Arthur shrugged.

"Maybe the powers behind these ships are incredibly unorganized or inconsistent or just plain callous. Or there's some sort of dispute within their organization."

"Whether to eat the Earth or not."

"Right," Harry said.

"Do you think Crockerman will make this public?"

"No," Harry said, fingers wrapped on his ample stomach. "He'd be crazy if he did. Think of the disruption. If he's smart, he's going to sit back and wait until the very last minute—he's going to see how people react to the Good News spaceship."

"Perhaps we should be bombing Death Valley right now." Arthur stared at a painting over the nightstand between the two single beds. It showed four F-104 fighters climbing straight up over China Lake. "Cauterize the whole area. Act without thinking."

"Make them madder than hell, right?" Harry said. "If they are being incredibly arrogant, then it means they have some assurance we can't hurt them. Not even with nuclear weapons."

Arthur sat in a straight-backed chair, facing away from the windows and the painting. High-tech fighters and bombers. Cruise missiles. Mobile laser defenses. Thermonuclear weapons. No better than stone axes.

"Captain Cook," he said, and then gently bit his lower lip.

"Yes?" Harry encouraged.

"The Hawaiians managed to kill Captain Cook. His technology was at least a couple of hundred years more advanced than theirs. Still, they killed him."

"What good did it do them?" Harry asked.

Arthur shook his head. "None, I guess. Some personal satisfaction, perhaps."

* * *

President William D. Crockerman, sixty-three, was certainly one of the most distinguished-looking men in America. With his graying black hair, penetrating green eyes, sharply defined, almost aquiline nose, and lines of goodwill around his eyes and mouth, he might be equally the revered head of a corporation or some teenager's favorite grandparent. On television or in person, he projected self-confidence and a trenchant wit. There could be no doubt that he took his job seriously, but not himself—this was the image portrayed, and it had won him election after election along his twenty-six-year career in public office. Crockerman had only lost one election: his first, as a mayoral candidate in Kansas City, Missouri.

He entered the Vandenberg isolation laboratory accompanied by two Secret Service agents, his national security advisor—a thin, middle-aged Boston gentleman named Carl McClennan—and his science advisor, David Rotterjack, soporifically calm and thirty-eight years of age. Arthur knew the tall, plump blond-haired Rotterjack well enough to respect his credentials without necessarily liking the man. Rotterjack had tended toward science administration, rather than doing science, in his days as director of several private biological research laboratories.

This entourage was ushered into the combination laboratory and viewing room by General Paul Fulton, Commander in Chief of Shuttle Launch Center 6, West Coast Shuttle Launch Operations. Fulton, fifty-three, had been a football player in his academy days, and still carried substantial muscle on his six-foot frame.

Arthur and Harry awaited them in the central laboratory, standing by the Guest's covered window. Rotterjack introduced the President and McClennan to Harry and Arthur, and then introductions were made in a circle around the chairs. Crockerman and Rotterjack sat in the front row, with Harry and Arthur standing to one side.

"I hope you understand why I'm nervous," Crockerman said, concentrating on Arthur. "I haven't been hearing good things about this place."

"Yes, sir," Arthur said.

"These stories . . . these statements about what the Guest has been saying . . . Do you believe them?"

"We see no reason not to believe them, sir," Arthur said. Harry nodded.

"You, Mr. Feinman, what do you think of the Australian bogey?"

"From what I've seen, Mr. President, it appears to be an almost exact analog of our own. Perhaps larger, because it's contained within a larger rock."

"But we haven't the foggiest notion what's in either of the rocks, do we?"

"No, sir," Harry said.

"Can't X-ray them, or set off blasts nearby and listen on the other side?"

Rotterjack grinned. "We've been discussing a number of sneaky ways to learn what's inside. None of them seem appropriate."

Arthur felt a twinge, but nodded. "I think discretion is best now."

"What about the robots, the conflicting stories? Some folks in my generation are calling them 'shmoos,' did you know that, Mr. Gordon, Mr. Feinman?"

"The name occurred to us, sir."

"Bringers of everything good. That's what they've been telling Prime Minister Miller. I've spoken to him. He's not necessarily convinced, or at least he doesn't let us think he is, but . . . he saw no reason to keep everybody in the dark. It's a different situation here, isn't it?"

"Yes, sir," Arthur said.

McClennan cleared his throat. "We can't predict what kind of harm might come if we tell the world we have a bogey, and it says doomsday is here."

"Carl takes a dim view of any plans to release the story. So we have four civilians locked up, and we have agents in Shoshone and Furnace Creek, and the rock is off limits."

"The civilians are locked up for other reasons," Arthur said. "We haven't found any evidence of biological contamination, but we can't afford to take chances."

"The Guest appears to be free of biologicals, true?" Rotterjack asked.

"So far," General Fulton said. "We're still testing."

"In short, it's not happening the way we thought it might," Crockerman said. "No distant messages in Puerto Rico, no hovering flying saucers, no cannon shells falling in the boondocks and octopuses crawling out."

Arthur shook his head, smiling. Crockerman had a way of coercing respect and affection from those around him. The President cocked one thick dark eyebrow at Harry, then Arthur, then briefly at McClennan. "But it *is* happening."

"Yessir," Fulton said.

"Mrs. Crockerman told me this would be the most important meeting of my life. I know she's right. But I am scared, gentlemen. I'll need your help to get me through this. To get *us* through this. We are going to get through this, aren't we?"

"Yes, sir," Rotterjack said grimly.

Nobody else answered.

"I'm ready, General." The President sat straight-backed in the chair and faced the dark window. Fulton nodded at the duty officer.

The curtain opened.

The Guest stood beside the table, apparently in the same position as when Arthur and Harry had left it the day before.

"Hello," Crockerman said, his face ashen in the subdued room light. The Guest, with its light-sensitive vision, could see them perhaps more clearly than they saw it.

"Hello," it replied.

"My name is William Crockerman. I'm President of the United States of America, the nation you've landed in. Do you have nations where you live?"

The Guest did not answer. Crockerman looked aside at Arthur. "Can he hear me?"

"Yes, Mr. President," Arthur said.

"Do you have nations where you live?" Crockerman repeated.

"You must ask important questions. I am dying."

The President flinched back. Fulton moved forward as if he were about to take charge, clear the room, and protect the Guest from any further strain, but Rotterjack put a hand on his chest and shook his head.

"Do you have a name?" the President asked.

"Not in your language. My name is chemical and goes before me among my own kind."

"Do you have family within the ship?"

"We are family. All others of our kind are dead."

Crockerman was sweating. His eyes locked on the Guest's face, on the three golden-yellow eyes that stared at him without blinking. "You've told my colleagues, our scientists, that this ship is a weapon and will destroy the Earth."

"It is not a weapon. It is a mother of new ships. It will eat your world and make new ships to travel elsewhere."

"I don't understand this. Can you explain?"

"Ask good questions," the Guest demanded.

"What happened to your world?" Crockerman said without hesitating. He had already read a brief of Gordon and Feinman's conversation with the Guest on this subject, but obviously wanted to hear it again, for himself.

"I cannot give the name of my world, or where it was in your sky. We have lost track of the time that has passed since we left. Memory of the world is dimmed by long cold sleeping. The first ships arrived and hid themselves within ice masses that filled the valleys of one continent. They took what they needed from these ice masses, and parts of them worked their way into the world. We did not know what was happening. In the last times, this ship, newly made, appeared in the middle of a city, and did not move. Plans were made as the planet trembled. We had been in space, even between planets, but there were no planets that attracted us, so we stayed on our world. We knew how to survive in space, even over long times, and we built a home within the ship, believing it would leave before the end. The ship did not prevent us. It left before the weapons made our world melted rock and gaseous water, and took us with it, inside. No others live that we are aware of."

Crockerman nodded once and folded his hands in his lap. "What was your world like?"

"Similar. More ice, a smaller star. Many like myself, not in form but in thought. Our kind was many-formed, some swimming in cold melt-seas, some like myself walking on ground, some flying, some living in ice. All thought alike. Thousands of long-times past, we had molded life to our own wishes, and lived happily. The air was rich and filled with smells of kin. Everywhere on the world, even in the far lands of thick ice, you could smell cousins and children."

Arthur felt his throat catching. Crockerman's cheek was wet with a single tear. He did not wipe it away.

"Did they tell you why your world was being destroyed?"

"They did not speak with us," the Guest said. "We guessed the machines were eaters of worlds, and that they were not alive, just machines without smells, but with thoughts."

"No robots came out to speak with you?"

"I have language difficulties."

"Smaller machines," Rotterjack prompted. "Talk with you, deceive you."

"No smaller machines," the Guest said.

Crockerman took a deep breath and closed his eyes for a moment. "Did you have children?" he asked.

"My kind were not allowed children. I had cousins."

"Did you leave some sort of family behind?"

"Yes. Cousins and teachers. Ice brothers by command bonding."

Crockerman shook his head. That meant nothing to him; indeed, it meant little to anybody in the room. Much of this would have to be sorted out later, with many more questions—if the Guest lived long enough to answer all their questions.

"And you learned to speak our language by listening to radio broadcasts?"

"Yes. Your wasting drew the machines to you. We listened to what the machines were gathering."

Harry scribbled furiously, his pencil making quick scratching noises on the notepad.

"Why didn't you try to sabotage the machine—destroy it?" Rotterjack asked.

"Had we been able to do that, the machine would never have allowed us on board."

"Arrogance," Arthur said, his jaw tightening. "Incredible arrogance."

"You've told us you were asleep, hibernating," Rotterjack said. "How could you study our language and sleep at the same time?"

The Guest stood motionless, not answering. "It is done," it finally replied.

"How many languages do you know?" Harry asked, pencil poised.

"I am speaker of English. Others, still within, speak Russian, Chinese, French."

"These questions don't seem terribly important," Crockerman said quietly. "I feel as if a nightmare has come over us all. Who can I blame for this?" He glanced around the room, his eyes sharp, hawklike. "Nobody. I can't simply announce we have visitors from other worlds, because people will want to see the visitors. After the Australian release, what we have here can only demoralize and confuse."

"I'm not sure how long we can keep this a secret," McClennan said.

"How can we hold this back from our people?" Crockerman seemed not to have heard anybody but the Guest. He stood and approached the glass, grimly concentrating on the Guest. "You've brought us the worst possible news. You say there's nothing we can do. Your . . . civilization . . . must have been more advanced than ours. It died. This is a *terrible* message to bring. Why did you bother at all?"

"On some worlds, the contest might have been more equal," the Guest said. "I am tired. I do not have much more time."

General Fulton spoke in an undertone with McClennan and Rotterjack. Rotterjack approached the President and put a hand on his shoulder. "Mr. President, we are not the experts here. We can't ask the right questions, and clearly there isn't much time remaining. We should get out of the way and let the scientists do their work."

Crockerman nodded, took a deep breath, and closed his eyes. When he opened them again, he seemed more composed. "Gentlemen, David is correct. Please get on with it. I'd like to speak to all of you before we go out to the site. Just one last question." He turned back to the Guest. "Do you believe in God?"

Without a moment's hesitation, the Guest replied, "We believe in punishment."

Crockerman was visibly shaken. Mouth open slightly, he glanced at Harry and Arthur, then left the room on trembling legs, with McClennan, Rotterjack, and General Fulton following.

"What do you mean by that?" Harry asked after the door had closed. "Please expand on what you just said."

"Detail is unimportant," the Guest said. "The death of a world is judgment of its inadequacy. Death removes the unnecessary and the false. No more talk now. Rest."

11———

Bad news. Bad news.

Edward awoke from his dreaming doze and blinked at the off-white ceiling. He felt as if somebody very important to him had died. It took him a moment to orient to reality.

He had had a dream he couldn't remember clearly now. His mind shuffled palm leaves over the sand to hide the tracks of the subconscious at play.

The duty officer had told them an hour before that nobody was sick, and no *biologicals* had been discovered in their blood or anywhere else. Not even on the Guest, which seemed as pure as the driven snow. Odd, that.

In any ecology Edward Shaw had heard of, which meant any *Earth* ecology, living things were always accompanied by parasitic or symbiotic organisms. On the skin, in the gut, within the bloodstream. Perhaps ecologies differed on other worlds. Perhaps the Guest's people—wherever they came from—had advanced to the point of *purity:* only the primaries, the smart folks, left alive; no more little mutating beasties to cause illness.

Edward sat up and drew himself a glass of water from the lavatory sink. As he sipped, his eyes wandered to the window and the curtain beyond. Slowly but surely, he was losing the old Edward Shaw, and finding a new one: an ambiguous fellow, angry but not overtly so, afraid but not showing his fear, deeply pessimistic.

And then he remembered his dream.

He had been at his own funeral. The casket had been open and somebody had made a mistake, because within the box was the Guest. The minister, presiding in a purple robe with a huge medallion on his chest, had touched Edward on the shoulder and whispered into his ear, "This is Bad News indeed, don't you think?"

He had never had dreams like that before.

The intercom signaled and he shouted, "No! Go away. I'm fine. Just go away. I'm *not sick.* I'm not dying."

"That's okay, Mr. Shaw." It was Eunice, the slender black duty officer who seemed most sympathetic to Edward. "You go ahead and let it out if you want. I can't shut off the tapes, but I'll shut down my speaker for a while if you wish."

Edward sobered immediately. "I'm all right, Eunice. Really. Just need to know when we're going to get out of here."

"I don't know that myself, Mr. Shaw."

"Right. I don't blame you."

And he didn't. Not Eunice, not the other duty officers, not the doctors or the scientists who had spoken to him. Not even Harry Feinman or Arthur Gordon. The tears were turning to laughter he could barely suppress.

"Still all right, Mr. Shaw?" Eunice asked.

"*'I'm a victim of coicumstance,'*" Edward quoted Curly, the plump and shave-pated member of the Three Stooges. He punched the intercom button for Minelli's room. When Minelli answered, Edward imitated Curly again, and Minelli did a perfect *"Whoop hoop ooop."* Reslaw joined in, and Stella laughed, until they sounded like a laboratory full of chimpanzees. And that was what they became, chittering and eeking and stomping the floor. "Hey, I'm scratching my armpits," Minelli said. "I really am. Eunice will vouch for me. Maybe we can get the sympathy of Friends of the Animals or something."

"Friends of Geologists," Reslaw said.

"Friends of Liberal Businesswomen," Stella added.

"Come on, you guys," Eunice said.

At eight o'clock in the evening, Edward glanced at his face in the shaving mirror over the sink. "Here comes the Prez," he murmured. "I won't even vote for the man, but I'm primping like a schoolgirl." They wouldn't be shaking hands. Yet the President would look in upon Shaw and Minelli and Reslaw and Morgan, would see them—and that was enough. Edward smiled grimly, then checked his teeth for food specks.

12——

The Secretary of Defense, Otto Lehrman, arrived at seven-fifteen. After Crockerman had had a half hour alone with him and Rotterjack—sufficient time to gather his wits, Arthur surmised—they entered the laboratory around which the sealed cubicles were arranged, and onto which their windows all opened, a larger version of the central complex that held the Guest. Colonel Tuan Anh Phan stood before the isolation chambers' control board.

Crockerman shook the doctor's hand and slowly surveyed the laboratory. "One more civilian witness and they'd have had to double up with the military, right?" he asked Phan.

"Yes, sir," Phan said. "We did not plan to incarcerate entire towns." This was evidently a struggling attempt at humor, but the President was not in a bantering mood.

"Actually," Crockerman said, "this isn't funny in the least."

"No, sir," Phan said, crestfallen.

Arthur came to his rescue. "We couldn't ask for better facilities, Mr. President," he said. Crockerman had been behaving strangely since the meeting with the Guest. Arthur was worried; that conversation had upset them all on a deep psychological level, but Crockerman seemed to have taken it particularly to heart.

"Can they hear us?" Crockerman asked, nodding at the four steel shutters.

"Not yet, sir," Phan said.

"Good. I'd like to get my thoughts in order, especially before I talk to Mrs. Morgan's daughter. Otto, Mr. Lehrman here, was delayed by his duties in Europe, but Mr. Rotterjack has briefed him on what we've already heard."

Lehrman took a shallow but obvious breath and nodded. Arthur had heard many things about Lehrman—his rise from microchip magnate to head of the President's Industrial Relations Council, and only two months before, his confirmation as Secretary of Defense, replacing Hampton's more hawkish appointee. He appeared to be a philosophical twin to Crockerman.

"I have a question for Mr. Gordon," Lehrman said. He looked at Arthur and Harry, standing beside each other near the lab's hooded microbiologicals workbench.

"Ask away," Arthur said.

"When are you going to authorize a military investigation of the Furnace?"

"I don't know," Arthur said.

"That's your area, Arthur," the President said in an undertone. "You make the decision."

"Nobody has put the issue to me before now," Arthur said. "What sort of investigation did you have in mind?"

"I'd like to find the site's weaknesses."

"We don't even know what it is," Harry said.

Lehrman shook his head. "Everybody's guessing it's a disguised spaceship. Do you disagree?"

"I don't agree or disagree. I simply don't know," Harry replied.

"Gentlemen," Arthur said, "I think this isn't quite the time. We should discuss this after the President has talked with the four witnesses and we've all seen the site together."

Lehrman conceded this with a nod and gestured for them to continue. General Fulton entered the lab carrying a thick sheaf of papers in a manila folder and sat to one side, saying nothing.

"All right," Crockerman said. "Let's have a look at them."

Eunice's voice came over Edward's intercom speaker: "Folks, you're going to meet the President now." With a hollow humming noise, the window cover slid down into the wall, revealing a transparent panel about two meters wide and one high. Through the thick double layers of glass, Edward saw President Crockerman, two men he didn't recognize, and several other faces he knew vaguely from television.

"Excuse me for intruding, gentlemen and Ms. Morgan," Crockerman said, bowing slightly. "I believe we know each other, even if we haven't been introduced formally. This is Mr. Lehrman, my Secretary of Defense, and this is Mr. Rotterjack, my science advisor. Have you met Arthur Gordon and Harry Feinman? No? They're in charge of the presidential task force investigating what you've discovered. I suspect you have a few complaints to pass on to me."

"Pleased to meet you, sir," Minelli said. Crockerman changed his angle. Edward realized they were all facing into the central laboratory. In the farthest window, at the opposite end of the curved wall, he could see Stella Morgan, face pale in the fluorescent lighting.

"I'd shake your hands if I could. This has been hard on all concerned, but especially hard on you."

Edward mumbled something in agreement. "We don't know what our situation is, Mr. President."

"Well, I've been told you're in no danger. You don't have any . . . ah, space germs. I'll level with you, in fact—you're probably here more for security reasons than for your health."

Edward could see why Crockerman was called the most charming of presidents since Ronald Reagan. His combination of dignified good looks and open manner—however illusory the latter was —might have made even Edward feel better.

"We've been worried about our families," Stella said.

"I believe they've been informed that you are safe," Crockerman said. "Haven't they, General Fulton?"

"Yes, sir."

"Ms. Morgan's mother has been giving us fits, however," Crockerman said.

"Good," was Stella's only comment.

"Mr. Shaw, we've also informed the University of Texas about you and your students."

"We're assistant professors, not students, Mr. President," Reslaw said. "I haven't received any mail from my family. Can you tell me why?"

Crockerman looked to Fulton for an answer. "You haven't been sent any," Fulton said. "We have no control over that."

"I just wanted to stop by and tell you that you haven't been forgotten, and you won't be locked away forever. Colonel Phan informs me that if no germs are discovered within a few more weeks, there will be no reason to keep you here. And by that time . . . well, it's difficult to say what will be secret and what won't be."

Harry glanced at Arthur, one eyebrow lifted.

"I have a question, sir," Edward said.

"Yes?"

"The creature we found—"

"We're calling it a Guest, you know," Crockerman interrupted with a weak smile.

"Yes, sir. It said it had bad news. What did it mean by that? Have you communicated with it?"

Crockerman's face became ashen. "I'm afraid I'm not allowed to tell you what's happening with the Guest. That's irritating, I know, but even I have to dance to the tune when the fiddler plays. Now I have a question for you. You were the first to find the rock, the cinder cone. What first struck you as odd about it? I need impressions."

"Edward thought it was odd before we did," Minelli said.

"I've never seen it," Stella added.

"Mr. Shaw, what struck you most?"

"That it wasn't on our maps, I guess," Edward answered. "And after that, it was . . . barren. It looked new. No plants, no insects, no graffiti new or old. No beer cans."

"No beer cans," Crockerman said, nodding. "Thank you. Ms. Morgan, I plan on seeing your mother sometime soon. May I take any personal message to her? Something uncontroversial, of course."

"No, thank you," Stella said. *Atta woman,* Edward thought.

"You've given me something to think about," Crockerman said after a moment's silence. "How strong Americans are. I hope that doesn't sound trite or political. I mean it. I need to think we're strong right now. That's very important to me. Thank you." He waved at them, and turned to leave the laboratory. The curtains hummed back into place.

13——

October 7

The sky over Death Valley was a leaden gray and the air still carried the chill of morning. The presidential helicopter landed at the temporary base set up by the Army three miles from the false cinder cone. Two four-wheel-drive trucks met the party and drove them slowly over the paved roads and unpaved Jeep trails, and then off the trails, lurching and growling around creosote bushes and mesquite and over salt grass, sand, chunks of lava, and desert-varnished rocks. The false cinder cone loomed a hundred yards beyond their stopping point, the edge of a bone-white desert wash that had been filled with water just ten days before. The perimeter of the mound was cordoned off by Army troops supervised by Lieutenant Colonel Albert Rogers from Army Intelligence. Rogers, short, wiry, swarthy-skinned, and gentle-eyed, met the presidential party of eight, including Gordon and Feinman, at the cordon perimeter.

"We've had no activity," he reported. "We have our surveillance truck on the other side now, and a survey team on the top. There's been no radiation of any sort beyond the kind of signature we expect from sun-heated rock. We've inserted sensors on poles up into the hole the three geologists found, but we haven't sent anybody past the bend. Give us the order, and we will."

"I appreciate your eagerness, Colonel," Otto Lehrman said. "I appreciate your caution and discipline more."

The President approached the cinder cone's tall black north face, accompanied by two Secret Service agents. The Marine officer who carried the "football"—presidential wartime codes and emergency communications system in a briefcase—stayed by the truck.

Rotterjack dropped back a few paces to snap a series of pictures with a Hasselblad. Crockerman ignored him. The President seemed to ignore everybody and everything but the rock. Arthur worried about the expression on his face; tense yet slightly dreamy. *A man informed of a death in the immediate family,* Arthur thought.

"This is where the alien was found," Colonel Rogers explained, pointing to a sandy depression in the shadow of a lava overhang. Crockerman walked around a big lava boulder and knelt beside the depression. He reached out to touch the sand, still marked by the Guest's movements, but Arthur restrained him. "We're still nervous about biologicals," he explained.

"The four civilians," Crockerman said, not completing his thought. "I met Stella Morgan's granddaddy thirty years ago in Washington," he mused. "A real country gentleman. Tough as nails, smart as a whip. I'd like to meet Bernice Morgan. Maybe I could reassure her . . . Can we arrange something for tomorrow?"

"We go to Furnace Creek Resort, after this, and tomorrow you're meeting with General Young and Admiral Xavier." Rotterjack looked over the President's schedule. "That's going to fill most of the morning. We're to have you back at Vandenberg and aboard the Bird at two P.M."

"Make a slot for Bernice Morgan," Crockerman ordered. "No more arguments."

"Yes, sir," Rotterjack said, pulling out his mechanical pencil.

"They should be here with me, those three geologists," the President said. He got to his feet and walked away from the overhang, brushing his hands on his pants. The Secret Service agents watched him closely, faces impassive. Crockerman turned to Harry, still clutching his black notebook, and then nodded at the cinder cone. "You know what my conference with Young and Xavier is all about."

"Yes, Mr. President," Harry said, matching Crockerman's steady gaze.

"They're going to ask me if we should nuke this whole area."

"I'm sure that's going to be mentioned, Mr. President."

"What do you think?"

Harry considered for a moment, eyebrows meeting. "The entire situation is an enigma to me, sir. Things don't fit together."

"Mr. Gordon, can we effectively retaliate against this?" He indicated the cinder cone.

"The Guest says we cannot. I tend to accept that statement for the time being, sir."

"We keep calling him the Guest, with a capital G," Crockerman said, coming to a halt about twenty yards from the formation, then turning to face south, examining the western curve. "How did that come about?"

"Hollywood's absorbed just about every other name," McClennan observed.

"Carl has been an avid watcher of television," Crockerman explained candidly to Arthur, "before his duties made that impossible. He says it lets him keep in touch with the public pulse."

"The name obviously evolved as a way to avoid other, more highly colored words," McClennan said.

"The Guest told me he believes in God."

Arthur chose not to correct the President.

"From what I understand," Crockerman continued, his face drawn, eyes almost frantic above a forced calm, "the Guest's world was found wanting, and eliminated." He seemed to be searching the faces of Arthur and those nearest to him for sympathy or support. Arthur was too stunned to say anything. "If that's the case, then the agency of our own destruction awaits us inside this mountain."

"We *must* have more cooperation from Australia," McClennan said, clenching one fist and shaking it in front of him.

"They're telling quite a different story down there, aren't they?" The President began walking back to the trucks. "I think I've seen enough. My eyes can't squeeze truth out of rocks and sand."

"Making tighter arrangements with Australia," Rotterjack observed, "means telling them what we have here, and we're not sure we can risk that yet."

"There's a possibility we're not the only ones who have 'bogeys,' " Harry said, giving the last word an almost comic emphasis.

Crockerman stopped and turned to face Harry. "Do you have any evidence for that?"

"None, sir. But we've asked for the NSA and some of our team to check it out."

"How?"

"By comparing recent satellite photographs with past records."

"More than two bogeys," Crockerman said. "That would be something, wouldn't it?"

14——

Trevor Hicks slowed the rented white Chevrolet as he approached the small town of Shoshone—little more than a junction, according to the map. He saw a cinder-block U.S. post office flanked by tall tamarisk trees and beyond it, a stark sprawling white building housing a gas station and grocery store. On the opposite side of the highway was a coffee shop and attached to it, a spare building with neon beer advertisements in its two small square windows. A small sign spelled out "Crow Bar" in flickering light bulbs—a local tavern or pub, obviously. Hicks had always been partial to local pubs. This one, however, did not seem to be open.

He pulled into the post office's gravel parking lot, hoping to ask someone if the coffee shop was worth a visit. He didn't trust local American eateries any more than he liked most American beer, and he did not think the appearance of the coffee shop—or café, as it styled itself on an inconspicuous sign—was very encouraging.

It was almost five o'clock and the desert was already chilly. Twilight was an hour or so away and a mournful wind blew through the tamarisk trees beside the post office. His morning and afternoon had been frustrating—a rental car breakdown fifty miles outside Las Vegas, a ride in the tow truck, arranging for another car, and as a lagniappe, a heated conversation with his publisher's publicist when he thought to call and explain his missed interview . . . Delay after delay. He stood near the car for a moment, wondering what sort of idiot he was, then chose the glass door on his right. As it happened, that led him into the local equivalent of a branch library—two tall shelves of books in a corner, with a child-sized reading table squatting before them. A counter stood opposite the shelves, and beyond it the furniture and apparatus—so a small plaque read—of the Charles Morgan Company. The door on the left led into a separate alcove that was the post office proper. The air of the office was institutional but friendly.

Beyond the counter, seated before an old desktop computer, was a stately woman of about seventy-five or eighty years, wearing jeans and a checked blouse, her white hair carelessly combed back. She spoke into a black phone receiver cradled between her neck and shoulder. Slowly, she swiveled on her chair to glance at Hicks, then raised one hand, requesting patience.

Hicks turned to examine the books in the library.

"No, Bonnie, not a word," the woman said, her warm voice cracking slightly. "Not a word since the letter. I'm just about at my wits' end, you know. Esther and Mike have quit. No. I'm doing fine, but things are kind of sliding here . . ."

The library held a fair selection of science books, including one of his own, an early popular work on communications satellites, long since out of date.

"It's all crazy," the woman said. "We used to worry about Gas Buggy, and all the radiation from the test site, and now this. They closed down our meat locker. It's enough to scare the hell out of me. Frank came in with Tillie yesterday and they were so nice. They worried about Stella so much. Well, thank you for calling. I've got to start closing up now. Yes. Jack is in the warehouse and he'll walk me down to the trailer park. Thanks. Goodbye."

She replaced the phone and turned to Hicks. "Can I help you?"

"I didn't mean to interrupt. I was wondering about the coffee shop across the street. Is it recommended?"

"I'm not the one to ask," the woman said, standing.

"I'm sorry," Hicks said politely. "Why?"

"Because I own the place," she answered, smiling. She approached the counter and leaned on it. "I'm prejudiced. We serve good solid food there. Emphasis sometimes on the solid. You're English, aren't you?"

"Yes."

"On your way to Las Vegas?"

"From, actually. Going to Furnace Creek."

"Might as well turn back. Everything's sealed up that way. The highway's closed. They'll just turn you around."

"I see. Any idea what's happening?"

"What's your name?" the woman asked.

"Hicks. Trevor Hicks."

"I'm Bernice Morgan. I was just talking about my daughter. She's being held by the federal government. Nobody can tell me why. She writes to say she's well, but she can't say anything about where she is, and I can't talk to her. Isn't that crazy?"

"Yes," Hicks said, his neck hair prickling again.

"I've got lawyers all over the state and in Washington trying to find out what's going on. They might think they're tangling with some small-town yo-yos, but they're not. My husband was a county supervisor. My father was a state senator. And here I am, talking your ear off. Trevor Hicks." She paused, examining him more closely. "Are you the science writer?"

"Yes, actually," Hicks said, pleased at being recognized twice in as many days.

"What brings you out this way?"

"A hunch."

"Mind if I ask what sort of hunch?" Clearly, Bernice Morgan, for all her warm voice and hospitable manner, was a tough-minded woman.

"I suppose it could connect with your daughter," he said, deciding to go for broke. "I'm following a very thin trail of clues to Death Valley. Something important has happened there—important enough to draw your President to Furnace Creek Resort."

"Maybe Ester isn't hysterical," Mrs. Morgan mused.

"I'm sorry?"

"My store clerk. She says some men talked about a MiG crashing in the desert."

Hicks's heart fell. Was that all it was, then? Some sort of unusual defection? No connection with the Great Victoria Desert?

"And Mike, he's a young fellow who worked in our service station, he says some men came to the store in a Land Cruiser and talked to my daughter. They had something covered up in the back. Mike sneaked a look when they took it around the rear and he thought it was something green—dead-looking, he said. Then the government comes in here and sprays this awful stuff all over the inside of my meat locker, closes it off, and says we can't use it . . . We lost five hundred dollars in meat. They carted it away, said it was spoiled. Said the locker was contaminated with salmonella."

Hicks's intuition made his skin crawl. "Where were you when this happened?"

"In Baker visiting my brother."

Bernice Morgan gave not the slightest impression of frailty, despite her years. Nor did she appear leathery or "grizzled." She was the last sort of person Hicks expected to find in a small American desert town. But for her manner of speech, she might have been the elderly wife of an English lord.

"How long has your daughter been missing?"

"A week and a half."

"And you're certain she was taken by federal authorities?"

"Air Force types, I've been told."

Hicks frowned. "Have you heard of anything odd in the area—around Furnace Creek Inn, perhaps?"

"Only that it's closed off temporarily. I called about that, and nobody knows anything. The phone service went out this afternoon."

"Do you think that's where your daughter is?"

"It's a possibility, isn't it?"

He pursed his lips.

"I don't think they're holding her so she can talk to the President about business. Do you?" She raised a skeptical eyebrow.

An old, battered primer-gray Ford truck pulled off the road and into the parking lot with a spray of dust and gravel. Two young men in straw cowboy hats jumped from the back, while a third boy and a heavy-paunched, bearded man with oversized wire-framed MacArthur sunglasses stepped down from the driver's seat. They all came through the glass door. The bearded man nodded at Hicks, then faced Mrs. Morgan. "We've been out and back. Road's still closed. George is out there, like Richard said, but he doesn't know what's going on."

"George is one of our highway patrol boys," Mrs. Morgan explained to Hicks.

"Ron, here, thinks his Lisa is still in Furnace Creek," the bearded man continued. A doe-eyed, thin young man nodded wearily. "We're going to take the plane and fly over. Find out what the hell's going on."

"They've probably got the airstrip out there closed," Mrs. Morgan said. "I'm not sure that's smart, Mitch."

"Smart, hell. I never let no government folks push me around before. Kidnaping and shutting down public roads for no good reason—it's time somebody did something." Mitch stared pointedly at Trevor Hicks, surveying his suede jacket, slacks, and running shoes. "Mister, we haven't met."

Mrs. Morgan did the favor. "Mitch, this is Mr. Trevor Hicks. Mr. Hicks, Mitch Morris. He's our maintenance man and drives the propane truck."

"Pleased to make your acquaintance, Mr. Hicks," Morris said in a formal tone. "You're interested in this?"

"He's a writer," Bernice said. "Pretty well known, too."

"I have an idea something is happening near Furnace Creek, something important enough to bring the President here."

"President like from the White House?"

"The same."

"He thinks Stella might be at Furnace Creek," Mrs. Morgan said.

"All the more reason for us to fly over there and find out," Morris said. "Frank Forrest has his Comanche ready to go. We have room for five. Mr. Hicks, are you interested in coming with us?"

Hicks realized he was becoming much too involved. Mrs. Morgan continued her protest about the risks, but Morris paid her only polite attention. His mind was made up.

There was no other way to see what was happening in Furnace Creek. He would be stopped on the highway as everybody else had been.

"There's too many of us here, with a pilot, already," Hicks said.

"Benny doesn't fly," Morris said. "He gets terrible airsick."

Hicks took a shallow, spasmodic breath. "All right," he said.

"It's not far at all. A few minutes there and back."

"I don't like it. Don't do this just for Stella," Mrs. Morgan said. "I'm still trying other ways. Don't get foolish and . . ."

"No heroics, no daring rescues," Morris assured her. "Let's go. Mr. Hicks . . . ?"

"Yes," Hicks said, following them out the glass door. Mrs. Morgan laid her hands on the countertop and watched them grimly as they climbed into the truck, Benny giving up his shotgun seat to Hicks and sitting in the back.

He had never done anything so stupid in his life. The Piper Comanche's wheels pulled free of the dirt runway and the twin-engine aircraft leaped into the air, leaving the weathered asphalt landing strip and corrugated metal hangar far behind and below.

Mitch Morris turned to regard Hicks and Ron Flagg in the back seat. Frank Forrest, in his mid-sixties and as burly as Morris, banked the plane sharply and brought them around to an easterly direction, then banked again before they had time to catch their breath. Morris hung on to Forrest's seat with a huge, callused hand. "You all right?" he asked Hicks, with barely a glance at Ron.

"Fine," Hicks said, swallowing an anonymous something in his gullet.

"You, Ron?"

"Ain't flown much," Flagg said, his skin pale and damp.

"Frank's an expert. Flew Super Sabres during the war. Korean War. His daddy flew Buffaloes at Midway. That's where he died, wasn't it, Frank?"

"Goddamn planes were flying coffins," Forrest said.

Hicks felt the Comanche shudder in an updraft from the low hills below. They were flying under five hundred feet. A cinder-covered hill near Shoshone passed below them with breathtaking closeness.

"I hope you don't think we're impetuous," Morris said.

"Perish the idea," Hicks returned, concentrating on his stomach.

"We owe a lot to Mrs. Morgan. We like Stella just fine, and Ron's Lisa is a great girl. We want to make sure they're okay, wherever they are. Not like they've been spirited off to the Nevada test site to be used as guinea pigs or something, y'know?"

Whether Morris was suggesting this or dismissing it as a possibility, Hicks couldn't decide.

"So what do you think they've got in Furnace Creek?" Forrest asked. "Mike the garage boy says they've got a dead Russian pilot. That why you're here—to scoop everybody on a dead Russian pilot?"

"I don't think that's what they have," Hicks said.

"So what is it, then? What would bring ol' Crockerman out here?"

Hicks thought for a moment about the possible unpleasant effects of discussing visitors from space with these men. He could almost sympathize with any government efforts to keep such things secret.

Yet Australia was loaded with men like these: tough, resourceful, valiant, but not particularly imaginative or brilliant. Why would Australia trust public reaction, and not the United States?

"I'm not sure," he said. "I've come out here on a hunch, pure and simple."

"Hunches are never pure and simple," Forrest shot back. "You're a smart man. You've come out here for a reason."

"Mrs. Morgan seems to think you're important," Morris said.

"Well . . ."

"You a doctor?" Flagg asked, looking as if he might need some medical assistance.

"I'm a writer. I have a Ph.D. in biological science, but I'm not an M.D."

"We get all sorts of Ph.D.'s in Shoshone," Morris said. "Geologists, archaeologists, ethnologists—study Indians, you know. Sometimes they come into the Crow Bar and sit down and we get into some real interesting conversations. We're not just a bunch of desert rats."

"Didn't think you were," Hicks responded. *Oh?*

"All right. Frank?"

"Coming up on Furnace Creek shortly."

Hicks looked through the side window and saw tan and white

sand and patches of scrub, HO-scale dirt roads and tracks. Then he saw the highway. Forrest banked the Comanche again. Hicks's stomach kept its discipline, but Flagg moaned. "You got a bag?" he asked. "Please."

"You can keep it down," Morris assured him. "Hold up on the aerobatics, Frank."

"There it is," Forrest said. He inclined the plane so Hicks was staring practically straight down at a cluster of buildings spread among rust-brown rocks, copses of green trees and low hills. He could make out a golf course spreading lush green against the waste, a tiny airstrip and an asphalt parking lot filled with dark cars and trucks, and rising from the parking lot, a green two-seat Army Cobra helicopter.

"Shit," Forrest said, pulling back sharply on the wheel. The plane's engines screamed and the Comanche swung around like a leaf in a strong wind.

The helicopter intercepted them and kept pace with the Comanche no matter what twists and turns Forrest executed. Flagg threw up and his vomit struck the side windows and Hicks and seemed to have a life of its own, bobbling about between surfaces and air. Hicks wiped it away frantically with his hands. Morris yelled and cursed.

The Cobra quickly outmaneuvered them. A uniformed and helmeted copilot in the rear seat gestured for them to land.

"Where's your radio?" Hicks demanded. "Turn it on. Let them talk with us."

"Hell no," Forrest said. "I'd have to acknowledge—"

"Goddammit, Frank, they'll shoot us down if you don't go where he says," Morris said, beard curling up and then back with the aircraft's motion.

The helicopter's copilot meticulously pointed down to the road below. Green cars and camouflaged trucks raced along the highway.

"We'd better land," Forrest agreed. He peeled away from the helicopter, descended with astonishing speed, pitched his Comanche nose-high, and brought the aircraft down with at least four hard jounces on the gray asphalt airstrip.

Quietly heaving without issue, Hicks tried to control himself. By the time they were surrounded by what he took to be Secret Service men—in gray suits and brown—and military police in dark blue uniforms, he had his nausea largely under control. Flagg had bumped his head and lay stunned in his seat.

"God damn," Morris said, none the worse for wear.

15——

Arthur, stooped even more than usual, walked down the inn's flagstoned hallway, barely glancing at the adobe walls and black, white, and gray Navajo carpets hung above antique credenzas. He knocked on Harry's door and stepped back, hands in pockets. Harry opened the door and swung his arm impatiently for him to come in. Then he returned to the bathroom to finish shaving. They were all joining the President for dinner in the resort's spacious dining room within the hour.

"He's not taking it well," Arthur said.

"Crockerman? What did you expect."

"Better than this."

"We're all staring down the barrel of a gun."

Arthur glanced up at the bright open doorway of the bathroom. "How are *you* feeling?"

Harry came out lifting one ear to poke the razor beneath it, his face lined with remnants of shaving cream. "Well enough," he said. "I have to leave in two days for treatment. Warned you."

Arthur shook his head. "No problem. It's scheduled. The President's leaving day after tomorrow. Tomorrow he confers with Xavier and Young."

"What's next?"

"Negotiations with the Australians. They show us theirs, we show them ours."

"Then what?"

Arthur shrugged. "Maybe our bogey is a liar."

"If you ask me," Harry said, "the—"

"I know. The whole thing stinks."

"But Crockerman's swallowed the message. It's working on him. Young and Xavier will have seen the site . . . Ah, Lord." Harry wiped his face with a towel. "This is not nearly as much fun as I thought it would be. Isn't it a bitch? Life is always a bitch. We were so excited. Now it's a nightmare."

Arthur raised his hand. "Guess who was captured riding an airplane with three desert types?"

Harry blinked. "How the hell should I know?"

"Trevor Hicks."

Harry stared. "You're not serious."

"The President is reading his novel now, which is trendy enough, and not quite pure coincidence. He obviously felt it was research material. The three desert types have been returned to Shoshone with a stiff reprimand and the loss of their plane and license. Hicks has been invited to dinner tonight."

"That's insane," Harry said, turning off the bathroom light and picking up his dress shirt from the corner of the bed. "He's a journalist."

"Crockerman wants to talk things over with him. Get a second opinion."

"He has a hundred opinions all around him."

"I last met Hicks," Arthur mused, "three years ago, at Cornell."

"I've never met him," Harry said. "I suppose I'd like to."

"Now's your chance."

Arthur left his friend's room a few minutes later, feeling worse than ever. He could not shake the sensibilities of a disappointed child. This had been a wonderful early Christmas present, bright and filled with hope for an unimaginable future, a future of humans interacting with other intelligences. Now, by Christmastime, the Earth might not even exist.

He took a deep breath and squared his shoulders, not for the first time hoping by physical effort to shake the gloom.

The waitresses and cooks behind the white walls and copper-paneled pillars of the dining room had come up with a formal repast of prime rib, wild rice, and Caesar salad, the salad greens a trifle wilted because of the halt in deliveries, but all else quite acceptable. Around a rectangular table assembled from four smaller tables sat the principals of the action at the "Furnace," plus Trevor Hicks, who acted as if he were taking it all in stride.

I have stumbled into a jackpot, he thought as the President and the Secretary of Defense entered and took their seats. Two Secret Service agents ate at a small table near the doorway.

Crockerman nodded cordially at Hicks, seated beside the President and across from Lehrman.

"These people have really done a fine job, haven't they?" the President said after the main course had been served and the dishes cleared. By a kind of silent and mutual decree, all talk during dinner had been of trivial things. Now coffee was brought out in an old, dented silver service, poured into the owner's personal Wedgwood bone china cups, and served around the long table. Harry declined. Arthur loaded his coffee with two cubes of sugar.

"So you are acquainted with Mr. Feinman and Mr. Gordon," Crockerman said as they sat back with cups in hand.

"I know them by reputation, and met Mr. Gordon once when he was in command of BETC," Hicks said. He smiled and nodded at Arthur as if for the first time this evening.

"I'm sure our people have asked you what moved you to come to Furnace Creek Inn."

"It's an ill-kept secret that something extraordinary is happening here," Hicks said. "I was working on a hunch."

The President gave another of his weak, almost discouraged smiles, and shook his head.

"I am amazed I was brought here," Hicks continued, "after the way we were initially treated. And I am truly astounded to find you here, Mr. President, even though I had deduced you would be, by a chain of reasoning I've already described to your Army and Secret Service agents. Let us say, I am astounded to find my hunch proving out. What *is* happening here?"

"I'm not sure we can tell you that. I'm not sure why I've invited you to dinner, Mr. Hicks, and no doubt the other gentlemen here are even more unsure than I. Mr. Gordon? Do you object to the presence of a writer, a reporter?"

"I am curious. I do not object."

"Because I think we are *all* out of our depth," Crockerman said. "I would like to solicit outside opinions."

Harry winked without humor at Arthur.

"I am in the dark, sir," Hicks said.

"Why do you think we are here?"

"I have heard—never mind how, I will not tell—that there is a bogey here. I presume it has something to do with the Australian discovery in the Great Victoria Desert."

McClennan shaded his eyes with one hand and shook his head.

"The unscrambled transmission from *Air Force One*. This has happened before. They should all be shot."

Crockerman dismissed this with a wave of his hand. He pulled a cigar from his pocket, then asked by an inclination of eyebrows whether anyone would share his vice. Politely, all around the table declined. He clipped the cigar and lit it with an antique silver Zippo. "I trust you've been cleared to enter military bases and research laboratories."

"Yes," Hicks said.

"You're not a United States citizen, however."

"No, Mr. President."

"Is he a security risk, Carl?" Crockerman asked McClennan.

The national security advisor shook his head, lips pursed. "Other than being a foreign national, he's got a good record."

Lehrman leaned forward and said, "Mr. President, I believe this conversation should end now. Mr. Hicks has no formal clearance, and—"

"Dammit, Otto, he's an intelligent man. I'm interested in his opinion."

"Sir, we can find and clear all sorts of experts for you to talk to," McClennan said. "This sort of thing is counterproductive."

Crockerman slowly looked up at McClennan, lips drawn tight. "How much time do we have until this machine starts dismantling the Earth?"

McClennan's face reddened. "Nobody knows, Mr. President," he said.

Hicks stiffened his back and glanced around the table. "Excuse me," he said, "but—"

"Then, Carl," Crockerman continued, "isn't the time-consuming, formal way of doing things counterproductive?"

McClennan stared pleadingly at Lehrman. The Defense Secretary held up both hands. "You're the boss, sir," he said.

"Within limits, I am," Crockerman affirmed peevishly. "I have chosen to bring Mr. Hicks into our confidence."

"Mr. Hicks, if I may say so, is a media celebrity," Rotterjack said. "He has done no research, and his qualifications are purely as a journalist and a writer. I am amazed, sir, that you would extend this kind of privilege to a *journalist.*"

Hicks, eyes narrow, said nothing. The President's gentle, dreaming smile returned.

"Are you finished, David?"

"I may very well be, sir. I agree with Carl and Otto. This is highly irregular and dangerous."

"I asked if you were finished."

"Yes."

"Then allow me to repeat myself. I have decided to take Mr. Hicks into our confidence. I assume his security clearance will be processed immediately?"

McClennan did not meet the President's eyes. "I'll get it started."

"Fine. Mr. Gordon, Mr. Feinman, I am not expressing any doubts about your capabilities. Do you object to Mr. Hicks?"

"No, sir," Arthur said.

"I have nothing against journalists or writers," Harry said. "However wrong Mr. Hicks's novel has turned out to be."

"Fine." Crockerman mused for a moment, then nodded and said, "I believed we turned down Arthur's request for a Mr. Dupres, simply because he is a foreign national. I hope none of you mind a little inconsistency now . . .

"We do indeed have a bogey, Mr. Hicks. It released an extraterrestrial visitor we call the Guest. The Guest is a living being, not a robot or a machine, and it tells us it rode a spaceship from its world to this one. But—" The President told Hicks most of the story, including his version of the Guest's dire warning. Again, nobody corrected him.

Hicks listened intently, his face white. When Crockerman finished, puffing at the cigar and blowing out an expanding globule of smoke, Hicks leaned forward, placing his elbows on the table. "I'll be damned," he said, his voice low and deliberately casual.

"So will we all if we don't decide what to do, and soon," Crockerman said. All others kept their counsel. This was the President's show, and few if any were happy with it.

"You're speaking with the Australians. They know about this, of course," Hicks said.

"They haven't been told yet," Crockerman said. "We're worried about the effect the news might have on our people if it leaks."

"Of course," Hicks said. "I . . . don't know quite what to make of it myself. I seemed to have stepped into a real hornet's nest, haven't I?"

Crockerman stubbed out his cigar half smoked. "I'll be returning to Washington tomorrow morning. Mr. Hicks, I'd like you to come with me. Mr. Gordon, you also. Mr. Feinman, I understand you won't be able to accompany us. You have an important medical appointment in Los Angeles."

"Yes, Mr. President."

"Then if you will, after your treatment—and my sincere good wishes go with you there—I would like you to recommend a group of scientists to meet with the Guest, conduct further interrogations—that doesn't sound good, does it? Ask more questions. This team will be our liaison with the Australian scientists. Carl, I'd like you to arrange with the Australians for one of their investigators to be flown to Vandenberg and sit in on these sessions."

"Are we sharing with the Australians, sir?" Rotterjack asked.

"I think that's the only rational approach."

"And if they're reluctant to go along with our stance on security?"

"We'll climb that wall when we come to it."

A tired-looking young man in a gray suit entered the dining hall and approached Rotterjack. He handed the science advisor a slip of paper and stood back, eyes darting nervously around the table. Rotterjack read the paper, the lines around his mouth and on his forehead deepening.

"Colonel Phan sends us a message," he said. "The Guest died at eighteen hundred hours this evening. Phan is conducting an autopsy at midnight. Mr. Feinman and Mr. Gordon are requested to attend."

Silence around the table.

"Mr. Gordon, you are free to do so, and then please come to Washington as soon as you can," Crockerman said. He put his napkin next to his plate, backed his chair away from the head of the table, and stood. He appeared very old in the dining room's subdued light. "I'm retiring early tonight. This day has been exhausting, and there is much to think about. David, Carl, please make sure Mr. Hicks is comfortable."

"Yes, sir," McClennan said.

"And Carl, make sure the staff here realizes how much we appreciate their service and the hardship."

"Yes, sir."

PERSPECTIVE

AAP/UK Net, October 8, 1996; Woomera, Local Church of New Australia:
The Reverend Brian Caldecott has proclaimed the Australian extraterrestrials to be "patent frauds." Caldecott, long known for his fiery harangues against all forms of government, and for leading his disciples in a return to "the Garden of Eden," which he claims was once located near Alice Springs, came to Woomera in a caravan of thirty white Mercedes-Benzes to hold a tent rally this evening. "These 'aliens' are the Country Party's attempt to mislead the citizens of the world, and to make the Australian Government, under Prime Minister Stanley Miller, the center of a world government, which I of course deplore." Caldecott's crusade suffered a public relations setback last year when it was discovered he was married to three women. The Church of New Australia promptly declared bigamy to be a religious principle, stirring a legal stew as yet unsettled.

AGNUS DEI

16———

October 8, 12:15 A.M.

Colonel Tuan Anh Phan, wearing a white helmeted suit with self-contained breathing apparatus, stood beside two assistants in similar garb in the isolation chamber once occupied by the Guest, and now by its corpse. Harry Feinman entered the chamber in his own suit, stepping with some awkwardness around the others. With four in the chamber, and equipment brought in for the autopsy, there was little room for maneuvering. Arthur sat in the laboratory beyond the glass and observed.

The Guest lay on its back on the central table, now elevated a meter above the floor. Its long head extended full length with "chin" paralleling the tabletop. The four limbs were splayed outward, held against a natural resilience by plastic straps.

Phan indicated with a sweep of one plastic-gloved hand the three video cameras behind their protective plastic plates. "Beginning twelve-seventeen A.M., October eighth, 1996. I am Colonel Tuan Anh Phan, and I am beginning an autopsy of the extraterrestrial biological specimen found near Death Valley, California. The specimen, also called the Guest, died at eight fifty-eight P.M., October seventh, in isolation room three of the Vandenberg Emergency Retrieval Laboratory, Shuttle Launch Center Six, Vandenberg Air Force Base, California.

"There is no evidence of physical injury or any apparent sign of internal trauma." Phan removed a scalpel from a tray proffered by an assistant. "I've already collected external culture samples from the Guest when it was alive. I will now take samples from sites along its limbs and on its body and head to see if terrestrial micro-organisms have begun to multiply on its external tissues." Using the scalpel to abrade the skin, and swabs to pick up the samples, he carried out this task. Each swab was dropped into a tube which was then stoppered. "As you can see, the body exhibits no signs of lividity, or indeed of any decay or change, external or internal." Phan lifted a forward limb. "There is resilience, but no stiffness. Indeed, the only visible evidence of death is a lack of movement and no reaction to stimuli.

"There is no sign of electrical activity within the Guest's cranium, or anywhere else in the body. As such activity existed before, we can only assume that this is another indicator of death. The Guest has not moved in ten hours and thirty-one minutes. Dr. Feinman, do you concur that the Guest is now dead, by any measurements we can make?"

"I concur," Harry said. "There are no reflexes. The Guest's body previously exhibited a living tension when touched. In its present state, there is no living tension in evidence."

"Obviously, this is more in the nature of an exploratory dissection than a true autopsy," Phan continued, his voice weary. "We have already conducted a thorough examination of the Guest through external means, including X ray, ultrasound exploratory, and NMR imaging. We have located several shapes which might be organs, a few small cavities, some fluid-filled and some apparently empty, within the Guest, and using these printouts as maps" —he pointed a scalpel at several sheets of paper hung on the outside of the viewing windows—"I will investigate the Guest's interior more directly.

"The Guest's thoracic skeletal structure differs substantially from our own. It appears to be made of a series of spines—in the porcupine sense of the word—connected by collagenous flexible joints, all wrapped around the internal cavity. There are no hollow lungs. In fact, there are few hollows of any kind." Phan drew the scalpel along a pronounced ridge running the length of the "breast" and revealed a clean gray-green surface with the sheen of bathroom tile. The sliced edges of skin were coppery blue-green in color.

"Here is the central breast 'bone' or 'process' we first saw in our X rays." He peeled back the skin, cutting delicately at adhering tissue, until one side of the thorax was exposed. "These joined processes provide a flexible but efficient cage around the thoracic organs. As you can see, the cage is fairly rigid in one direction"—he pushed with his finger toward the Guest's head, producing no movement—"but flexible in another." He pressed down and the cage sank slightly. "There is an obvious similarity between the Guest and ourselves at this point, with a protective cage around the thorax, but the similarity ends there."

Phan took a small electric circular saw and cut through the processes on the Guest's left side, facing the window. Working the saw twenty centimeters across the top, then down on two sides another twenty centimeters, then across the bottom, he was able to lift free a glutinous section of the thoracic cage. Below lay a pearly membrane.

Arthur sat rooted in his chair, fully focused on the opening to the Guest's thorax. Phan maneuvered past Feinman and the assistants around the table, pausing for a moment to glance at the printouts. He then reached for a syringe and inserted it into the pearly membrane, withdrawing a sample of fluids. Harry pushed a slender biopsy core sampler through the membrane a little lower and removed a long, slender tube of tissue.

This he passed to an assistant, who sealed it in a glass phial and passed it with the other samples to the outside through a stainless-steel drawer.

"The temperature is now twelve degrees centigrade. We are reducing that to several degrees above zero, to inhibit terrestrial bacterial growth. The core and fluid samples will be analyzed and the autopsy will continue at a later hour. Gentlemen, it is time I rested. My assistants are going to make further measurements and take core samples from the limbs. Later this morning we will begin on the head."

Hicks sat at the table across from the President, smiling at the waitress as she poured him a cup of coffee. They were alone in the dining hall; it was early, just past seven in the morning. The President had called him at midnight and requested his presence at breakfast for a private discussion. "What's your pleasure, Mr. Hicks?" Crockerman asked him.

"Toast and scrambled eggs, I think," he said. "Can you make a Denver omelet?"

The waitress nodded.

"The same for me," Crockerman told her. As she left, Crockerman pushed his chair back a few inches and bent to pull papers from an open valise beside him. "I'll be meeting with a distraught mother at nine o'clock, and with an admiral and a general at eleven. Then I fly back to Washington. I've been making notes all night long, trying to put my thoughts in order. I hope you don't object to my bouncing a few ideas off you."

"Not at all," Hicks said. "But first, I must make my situation clear. I'm a journalist. I came here for a story. All this—your request that I stay here, instead of being booted out with the others —is . . . well, it's extraordinary. I must honestly say that under the circumstances, I . . ." He ran out of words, looking into Crockerman's rich brown eyes. Lifting his hand, he gestured vaguely at the door of the dining room. "I'm not trusted here, nor should I be. I'm an outsider."

"You're a man with imagination and insight," Crockerman said. "The others have expertise. Mr. Gordon and Mr. Feinman have imagination and expertise, and Mr Gordon has been very close to this kind of problem, as administrator of BETC. Perhaps he's been too close, I don't know. I've been wondering whether or not we're dealing with extraterrestrials, as he would have us believe. You have a distance, a fresh perspective I could find very useful."

"What is my official capacity, my role?" Hicks asked.

"Obviously, you can't report this story now," Crockerman said. "Stay here, work with us until the story is about to be released. I suspect we'll have to go public soon, though Carl and David strongly disagree. If we do go public, you have your exclusive. You get first crack."

Hicks frowned. "And our conversations?"

"For the time being, what we say to each other is not to be discussed elsewhere. In the fullness of history, in our memoirs or whatever . . ." Crockerman nodded to the far walls. "Fine."

"I'd like some more details," Hicks said, "especially if Mr. Rotterjack and Mr. McClennan or Mr. Lehrman have control over me or my story. But for the time being, I'll agree. I will not report what we say to each other privately."

Crockerman put the papers on the table in front of him. "Now, here are my thoughts. Either we've been invaded twice in the last year, or somebody is lying to us."

"The choice seems to be between doom and a hands-across-space policy," Hicks said.

The President nodded agreement. "I've made some logic diagrams." He held up the first sheet of paper. "Venn diagrams. Scant remnants of my college math days." He smiled. "Nothing complicated, just drawings to help me sort the possibilities out. I'd appreciate your criticisms."

"All right." Hicks glanced at the piece of paper before the President. Brief notations of possible scenarios lay within nested and intersecting and separated circles.

"If these two spacecraft have similar origins, I see several possibilities. First, the Australians are dealing with a splinter group of extraterrestrials, some kind of dissident faction. But our information is correct, and the primary aim of the overall mission is to destroy the Earth, and the Guest does indeed represent survivors of their last conquest. With me so far?"

"Yes."

"Second," the President continued, "we are dealing with two separate events, which by some literally astronomical chance are happening simultaneously. Two groups of aliens, unacquainted or only marginally acquainted with each other. Or third, we are not dealing with aliens at all, but with emissaries."

Hicks raised an eyebrow. "Emissaries?"

"I'm not completely comfortable with the vastness of the universe." Crockerman said nothing for ten or fifteen seconds, staring at the table, his face passive but his eyes darting back and forth between the candle and his cup of coffee. "I suppose that you are."

"I'm human," Hicks said. "I'm limited, too. I accept the vastness without truly understanding it or feeling it."

"That makes me feel better. I'm not doing too badly, then, am I?" Crockerman asked.

"No, sir."

"I wonder if, perhaps, in charting our universe from a scientific perspective, we haven't lost something . . . an awareness of . . ." Again he paused, searching for words. "Transgressions. If we think of God as a superior intelligence, not human, but demanding certain obediences . . . Do you follow me?"

Hicks nodded once.

"Perhaps we are no longer satisfying this superior intelligence. He, or more accurately, It, sends Its emissaries, Its angels if you will, to brandish the kind of sword we understand. The end of the Earth." Crockerman raised his eyes to meet Hicks's.

The waitress brought their breakfast and asked if they wanted more coffee. Crockerman refused; Hicks accepted a warm-up. When she had gone, Hicks investigated his omelet with a fork, no longer very hungry. His stomach knotted, acid. He could feel a kind of panic coming on.

"I've never been comfortable with religious interpretations," he said.

"Must we classify this as a religious interpretation? Couldn't this just as easily be an alternative to theories of conflicting aliens, or factionalized invaders?"

"I'm not sure what your theory is."

" 'The moving finger, having writ.' That."

"Ah. *'Mene, mene, tekel, upharsin,'* or whatever."

"Precisely. We've screwed up. Polluted, overarmed. The twentieth century has been a mess. The bloodiest century in human history. More needless human death than at any other time."

"I can't argue with that," Hicks said.

"And now, we move outward. Perhaps we've been suffered only so long as we remained on Earth. Now—"

"It's an old idea," Hicks interrupted, his unease converting rapidly to irritation.

"Does that mean it's invalid?"

"I think there are better ideas," Hicks said.

"Ah," Crockerman said, his own breakfast still untouched. "But none of them convince *me.* I am the only judge I can truly rely upon in this situation, am I not?"

"No, sir. There are experts—"

"In my political career, I have ignored the advice of experts many times, and I have prevailed. This made me different from other, more standard aspirants to high office. Now, I grant you, such a ploy has its risks."

"I'm getting lost again, sir. What ploy?"

"Ignoring experts." The President leaned forward, extending his hands across the table, fists clenched, his eyes moist. Crockerman's expression was a rictus of pain. "I asked the Guest one thing, and received one important answer, from all of our questions . . . I asked it, 'Do you believe in God,' and it replied, 'I believe in punishment.' " He leaned back, looking at his fists and relaxing them, rubbing the palms, where fingernails had dug deep. "That must be significant. Perhaps the Guest is from another world, another place where transgressors have been dealt with severely. That thing out there in the 'Furnace,' Death Valley of all places . . . We have been told it will render the Earth down into slag. Total destruction. We have been told we cannot destroy it. I believe in fact we cannot."

Hicks was about to say something, but Crockerman continued, his voice low.

"God, a superior intelligence, sculpts us all, finds us wanting, and sends our material back into the forge to be reshaped. That thing out there. The Furnace. That's the forge of God. That's what we're up against. Might be up against."

"And the Australian artifact, the robots, the messages?"

"I don't know," Crockerman said. "It would clearly sound insane to claim the Australians were dealing with an adversary . . . But perhaps."

"Adversary . . . a kind of Satan?"

"Something opposed to the Creator. A force that hopes we will be allowed to continue our transgressions, to put all creation out of balance."

"I think there are better explanations, Mr. President," Hicks said quietly.

"Then please," Crockerman pleaded, "tell me what they are."

"I am not qualified," Hicks said. "I know almost nothing about what's happened. Only what you've told me."

"Then how can you be critical of my theory?"

The way Crockerman spoke, like a child though using grown-up words, chilled Hicks to the bone. A friend had once spoken to Hicks in a similar tone in London in 1959; she had died by her own hand a month later.

"It is not realistic," he said.

"Is anything about this situation realistic?" Crockerman asked. Neither had done much more than push the food around on his plate.

Hicks took a bite. The omelet was cold. He ate it anyway, and Crockerman began to eat his. Neither spoke again until the plates were empty, as if engaged in a contest of silence. The waitress took the plates away and poured more coffee into Hicks's cup.

"I apologize," the President said, wiping his lips with the napkin and folding it on the table. "I've been rude with you. That's unforgivable."

Hicks mumbled something about the strain they were all under, and how it was understandable.

"You give me a kind of perspective, however," Crockerman said. "I can see, just watching your reaction, how others would react. This is a very difficult time, in more ways than one. I've had to interrupt my campaign schedule. The election is less than a month away. Timing is very important. I see I need to trim the rough edges from my phrases . . ."

"Sir, it is not phrasing. It is perspective," Hicks said, his voice rising. "If you pursue these theories of cosmic recrimination, I can hardly imagine the damage you might cause."

"Yes. I see that."

Do you? Hicks asked himself. And then, examining Crockerman's suspicious, half-lidded expression, *Yes, perhaps you do . . . but that won't stop you.*

17——

October 9

Arthur unfolded a newspaper as the Learjet taxied across the runway. On a far apron, B-1 bombers lined up, their sleek tan, gray, and green shapes obscured by a layer of early morning sea haze. It took a few seconds for him to focus on the headlines. His thoughts were still on Harry Feinman, and on the autopsy.

The Guest had no discrete internal organ structure. Stuffed within the thoracic cage was shell-pink tissue continuous except for occasional cavities, more like a brain than anything else. The head consisted of the Lexan-like articulated bone material, arranged in large solid masses, with no discernible central nervous system. Small nodes the size of BBs interrupted the continuity of the bone; they appeared to be made of some sort of metal, perhaps silver.

Harry would soon be undergoing his own probing and examination in Los Angeles.

The plane completed its taxi and began to accelerate down the runway, small jets screaming thinly beyond the insulated walls.

Arthur focused on the newspaper. The front page headline read,

PRESIDENT ON SECRET
DEATH VALLEY VISIT
Details Unclear:
May Be Related to Australian Aliens

The same unscrambled transmission that had brought Trevor
Hicks to Furnace Creek had led other reporters, just hours later, to
reach similar conclusions. Hicks had struck a mother lode. The
others had had to make do with testimony from inhabitants of
Shoshone and one phone call to Furnace Creek Inn that had gotten through to the apartment of a maid who spoke only Spanish.
Bernice Morgan had not been interviewed. *Perhaps Crockerman
persuaded her,* Arthur thought, tracking the story several times to
see if he had missed any telling details.

General Paul Fulton, Commander in Chief of West Coast Shuttle
Operations, was on the flight with Arthur. He came forward as
soon as they were in the air and had finished their climb to 28,000
feet.

"Ah, the good old free press," he commented, taking the neigh-
boring seat. "Pardon me, Mr. Gordon. We haven't had time to just
sit and talk."

"You're going back to testify?"

"Before some key congressmen, before the Space Activities
Committee senators—God only knows what Proxmire is going to
make of this. How he got on that committee in the first place is
beyond me. The man's politically immortal."

Arthur nodded. He felt as if his brain were mush. He had hoped
to sleep through the entire flight, but Fulton seemed to have
something on his mind.

"A lot of us are worried about Crockerman's choice of Trevor
Hicks. He's a science fiction writer—"

"Only recently," Arthur said. "He's quite a decent science
writer, actually."

"Yes, and we actually don't fault the choice of Hicks, but we
wonder about the President's need to go beyond the . . . primary group. His staff and advisors and Cabinet. The assigned experts."

"He wanted a second opinion. He mentioned that a couple of
times."

Fulton shrugged. "The Guest shook him."

"The Guest shook me, too," Arthur said.

Fulton dropped the subject abruptly. "There will be two of our Australian counterparts in Washington when we arrive. Flown in fresh from Melbourne. They were spare parts down there, I suspect. The really important man—Quentin Bent—is staying behind. Do you know him?"

"No," Arthur said. "There's something of a gap between the Northern and Southern Hemispheres, science-wise, in all but astronomy. Bent's not an astronomer. He's a sociologist, I believe."

Fulton looked dubious. "Your colleague, Dr. Feinman . . . Is he going to be able to keep up?"

"I think so." Arthur recognized that he was taking a disliking to General Fulton, and wondered how reasonable that was. The man was only trying to gather information.

"What does he have?"

"Chronic leukemia."

"Terminal?"

"His doctors think it's treatable."

Fulton nodded. "I wonder if that's not a good diagnosis for the Earth."

Arthur didn't catch his meaning.

"Cancer," Fulton volunteered. "Cosmic cancer."

Arthur nodded reflectively and looked out the window, wondering when he would find time to call Francine, talk to Marty, touch base with the real world.

18———

Lieutenant Colonel Albert Rogers took the radio message in hand and climbed out of the rear door of the communications trailer, down the corrugated metal steps to the crunchy white sand. He didn't really want to think about the implications of his orders; thinking on such an esoteric level would do him no good whatsoever. The Guest was dead; Arthur Gordon had ordered his team to investigate the interior of the Furnace. Rogers would not allow anyone but himself to do it.

He had been planning for such a mission. He had drawn incomplete diagrams of the bogey's interior in a small notebook, little more than suppositions based on length, height, width, and the angle and length of the tube runnung through solid rock. Climbing the tube would present no problem—even where it angled straight up, he could take it like a rock climber in a chimney, back against one side, legs jackknifed and feet pressed against the other, inching his way up. He would carry a miniature digital video recorder, smaller than the palm of his hand, and a helmet-mounted finger-sized video camera. A Hasselblad for high-resolution pictures and a smaller, lighter automatic film-packed 35mm Leica completed his equipment. He doubted the investigation would take more than a day. There was, of course, the possibility that the bogey was honeycombed with interior spaces. Somehow, he doubted that.

As a sergeant and corporal brought the supplies he requested from the stores trailer, he drew up his itinerary and discussed emergency measures with his second-in-command, Major Peter Keller. Rogers then donned the chest pack and heavy climbing boots, coiled three lengths of rope neatly and hung them from his belt, and walked around the south side of the bogey.

He checked his watch and set its timer. It was six A.M. The desert was still wrapped in gray dawn, high cirrus stretching from horizon to horizon in a thin layer. The desert smelled of clean cold air, a hint of dry creosote bush.

"Give me a lift," Rogers instructed Keller. The major meshed the fingers of both hands to make a stirrup and Rogers stepped into the stirrup with his left foot. With a heave-ho, Keller lifted him into the tunnel. Rogers lay on his back in the angled shaft for a moment, staring at the first bend, about forty feet into the rock. "Okay," he said, punching the button on his watch for the timer to start. "I'm off."

They had decided against unwinding a telephone wire and communicating directly with him as he climbed. The video recorder was equipped with a small lapel mike, into which he would make oral observations; the video camera would make an adequate record of what he saw from moment to moment. If time and opportunity presented, he would take pictures with the other cameras.

"Good luck, sir," Keller called as he began his low-angle ascent up the tunnel.

"The hell with that," Rogers grunted under his breath. The first thirty feet were easy, a wriggling crawl. At the bend, he paused to shine a light up into the darkness. The tunnel angled straight up after the first thirty feet of incline. He noted this aloud for the record, then looked down over his stomach and legs at the cameo of Keller's face. Keller made an okay sign with circled thumb and index finger. Rogers blinked his light twice.

"I'm going into the belly of an alien spaceship," he told himself silently, grimacing fiercely to limber his tense jaw and face muscles. "I'm crawling up into an unknown. That's it. Don't be afraid." And he wasn't—a kind of energetic calm, almost a high, came over him.

He thought of his wife and four-year-old daughter living in Barstow, and a variety of scenarios stacked up behind their faces. Heroic dead father and lifetime benefits. Actually, he wasn't clear on the benefits. He should be. He vowed to check that out immediately when he got back. Much better thought: heroic live father and retirement at twenty years and going into some business, defense contract consultant maybe, though he had never thought of that before. First man inside an alien spaceship. Real estate was more likely. Not in Barstow, however. San Diego, maybe, though being ex-Navy or ex-Marine would be more help there.

He began to climb, rubber-soled boots grabbing the rock and hands bracing against the opposite wall. A foot at a time. No damaging the spacecraft; not even a scratch. He heaved himself up with a grunt, again locking his boots and hands against the rock. Smooth surface, nothing like lava. Featureless and gray, amorphous. Astronauts had been trained in geology when they landed on the moon. No need to train an Army colonel. Besides, this wasn't a natural place; what good would geology do?

At least it wasn't slippery.

He had climbed fifteen feet when he paused and shined his light forward. Another bend above him, beyond which they had not probed with the pole-mounted cameras. Truly unknown. Rogers conjured up the few science fiction movies he had seen. He had never been a big fan of science fiction movies. Most of his buddies had enjoyed *Aliens* when they watched it on a VCR just out of boot camp. He tried to forget about that one.

The Guest was dead. What if that made the others angry? What if they knew, somehow, and were waiting for him?

He was still calm, still slightly high, eyes wide, pupils dilated in the dark, face moist with exertion. Up, up, and then over the lip of the bend. He rested in the nearly level tunnel beyond the bend, shining his light into impenetrable darkness. Pulling out his notebook, he worked quickly to figure angles and distances. He was about fifteen or twenty feet from the outer surface. Shining his light on a notebook page with the chart of the interior, he drew in the level tunnel. His path resembled a dogleg tire iron, thirty feet into the mound at an upward angle, then straight up twenty feet or so, and now horizontally into the interior.

Silence. No sounds of machinery, no voices, no air moving. Just his own breathing. When he had rested a few minutes, he crawled, flashlight strapped to one wrist sweeping the tunnel with every motion.

Ninety feet ahead, the tunnel opened into a larger space. He did not hesitate. Eager to be out of the confinement, Rogers scrambled forward and grabbed the lip of the tunnel with both hands, pulling his head out. He played the light across the enclosed volume.

"I'm in a cylindrical chamber," he said aloud, "about thirty feet long and twenty across. I'm probably in the middle of the mound" —he referred to his sketch—"below the peak maybe sixty or eighty feet. The walls are shiny, like enamel or plastic or glass. Dark gray, with a bluish tint. The tunnel opens near the rear of the cylinder, and at the front"—he consulted his chart—"pointing northwest, there is another space, even larger. No sign of quarters or inhabitants. No activity."

He stood up in the cylinder, testing the surface with his boots. There was still enough traction to walk easily. "I'm going forward."

Rogers walked to the edge of the cylinder, keeping his light shined ahead. Then he opened his chest pack and pulled out two superbright torches. Holding them away from his eyes, he flicked the switches on both.

Mouth wide open, Rogers surveyed a cavern at least a hundred feet long and eighty feet high. The cylindrical chamber was squarely in the center of one end, placing him about twenty feet above the bottom. "It's full of shiny facets, like a gem," he said. "More like glass, not mirrors but shiny. Not just facets, either, but structures—beams, supports, braces. It's like a cathedral inside here, but made of blue-gray glass." He took several dozen pictures with the Hasselblad, then lowered the camera and just stared, trying to impress the memory and make sense out of what he was seeing.

From the end of the cylinder to the ornate gleaming surface below was a drop of at least thirty feet. No rappelling down; there was nothing to tie the rope onto, and he would not even try to hammer a piton into place.

"I can't go any farther," he said. "There's nothing moving. No place I'd call living quarters. No machinery visible, even. And no lights. I'm going to turn off the torches and see if anything glows afterward." He plunged himself into complete darkness. For a moment, his throat constricted and he coughed, the sound breaking into a chatter of echoes.

"I don't see anything," he said after a few minutes of darkness. "I'm going to turn the torches on to take more pictures." He reached for the switches and then paused, squinting. Directly ahead, burning dimly and steadily, was a tiny red light, no more than a star in the vastness. "Wait. I don't know if the video can pick that up. It's very weak. Just a single red light, like a pinprick."

He watched the gleam for several more minutes. All motions it made were easily explained by optical illusion; it changed neither in position nor brightness. "I don't think the ship is dead. It's just waiting." Then he shook his head. "But maybe I'm jumping to conclusions, just because of one little red light." Turning on his wrist flashlight, he mounted a telephoto lens on the Hasselblad and set the camera to a long exposure, then rested it on the lip of the cylinder, facing the red light. With a remote button, he opened the camera lens. When the exposure was complete, he reset for even longer and shot another. Then he turned on the torches and sat down to fill his memory with as much detail as he could. "It's still silent," he said.

After fifteen minutes, he got to his feet and instinctively brushed off his pants. "All right. I'm going back."

To his enormous relief, nothing interfered with his return journey.

19——

October 10

Edward Shaw learned of the Guest's death two days later, when they all received a visit from Colonel Phan. After a ten-minute warning, in which time Edward quickly dressed, the curtains were drawn and all four of them faced the small, muscular brown man in his pin-neat blue uniform, standing in the central laboratory.

"How long have we got, Doc?" Minelli asked. He had been getting more and more flippant, less predictable, as the days passed. He talked often of the President and how they would soon be "outta this dump." His speech more and more resembled a comic imitation of James Cagney. Minelli had never reacted well to overbearing authority. Edward had heard of a time, years before Minelli came to Austin, when he had been jailed on a minor dope charge, and had bloodied his face against a jailhouse door. Edward worried about him.

"You are all healthy, with no signs of contamination or illness," Phan said. "I plan no more tests for you. You have heard from your duty officer, I believe, that the Guest is dead. I have finished the first level of autopsy, and found no microbiologicals anywhere within its system. It appears to have been a completely sterile creature. This is good news for you."

"No bugs, m'lady," Minelli said. Edward winced.

"I have recommended that you be released," Phan said, staring levelly at each in turn. "Though I do not know when they will do so. As the President said, there are security concerns."

Edward saw Stella Morgan through her window and smiled at her. She did not return the smile; perhaps the light was wrong and she did not see him; perhaps she was feeling as depressed as Reslaw, who seldom said anything now.

The combination of free interaction through the intercom and separate confinement seemed to undermine the camaraderie Edward thought was typical of prison camp inmates. They were not being abused. They had nothing really solid to fight against. Their confinement, until now at least, had not been senseless. Consequently, they were not "drawing together" as Edward thought they might. Then again, he had never before been held in long-term detention. Maybe his expectations were simply naïve.

"We are preparing papers that you will sign, promising not to speak of these last few days—"

"I won't sign anything like that," Minelli said. "There aren't any best-sellers if I sign that. No agents, no Hollywood."

"Please," Phan said patiently.

"What about Australia?" Edward asked. "Are you talking with them?"

"Conferences begin today in Washington," Phan said.

"Why the wait? Why didn't everybody start talking weeks ago?"

Phan did not answer. "Personally, I hope all is made public soon," he said.

Edward tried to control a building anger. "Why can't we get together? Take us out of here and put us in a BOQ or something."

"Barbecue?" Minelli snorted.

"Bachelor officer's quarters," Edward explained, his lower lip trembling. He was beginning to cry. He checked that response immediately, putting on an air of indignant rationality. "Really. This is hell. We feel like we're in jail."

"Worse. We can't make zip guns or knives," Minelli said. "Bottom of the world, Ma!"

Phan regarded Minelli with an expression between irritation and concern. "That is all I have to tell you now. Please do not worry. I am sure you will be compensated. In the meantime, we have new infodisks."

"Goody," Minelli said. As Phan turned away, he shouted, "Wait! I'm not feeling well. Really. Something's wrong."

"What is it?" Phan asked, gesturing to a watch supervisor behind him.

"In my head. Tell them, Reslaw."

"Minelli's been disturbed recently," Reslaw said slowly. "I'm not doing too well, myself. He doesn't sound good. He's different."

"I'm different," Minelli concurred. Then he began to weep. "Goddammit, just put us back out where the rocks are. Let us go in our truck. I'll sign anything. Really. Please."

Phan glanced at them all, then turned and left abruptly. The curtains hummed back into place. Edward's drawer opened and he removed a newspaper and the new packet of infodisks. Hungrily, he read yesterday morning's headline.

"Christ," he muttered. "They know about the President. Stella!" He punched her number on the intercom. "Stella, they know the President came out here!"

"I'm reading," she said.

"Do you think your mother got through?"

"I don't know, really."

"We can hope," Edward said.

Minelli was still weeping.

20———

Hicks lay back against a pillow in the Lincoln Bedroom, a foot-high stack of reports on the round draped nightstand beside him, a small glass-globed lamp glowing softly above the reports. The late Empire-period pendulum clock on the marble mantelpiece ticked softly, steadily. The large, high-ceilinged room looked haunted, in a cozy sort of way; haunted by history, by association. This had been Abraham Lincoln's Cabinet room originally; here he had signed the Emancipation Proclamation.

He shook his head. "I'm crazy," he said. "I'm not here. I'm imagining all of it." For a moment, he hoped desperately that was true; that he was dreaming in the hotel room at the Inter-Continental, and that he would soon be promoting his novel for six minutes or less on another radio show, before another young announcer . . .

On the other hand, what was so undesirable about being in the White House in Washington, D.C., personally chosen by the President of the United States to advise him on the biggest event in human history? "The man doesn't listen," he murmured.

Hicks picked up the topmost report on the stack, a thick sheaf of photocopied papers on the Death Valley site, the Guest, and all that was known about the Great Victoria Desert site.

The Guest's interim autopsy report was third in the stack. Using a talent acquired across years of research, he skimmed the first two papers quickly, stopping only for essential details. The reports, not unexpectedly, were "safe"—hedged through and through with ambiguous language, craftily defused theories, prompt second-guessing. Only the autopsy report showed promise of being substantive.

Colonel Tuan Anh Phan, a man Hicks would like to meet, was clear and to the point. The Guest's physiology was unlike that of any living thing on Earth. Phan could not conceive of an environment that would evolve such a physiology. There were structures that reminded him, again and again, of "engineering shortcuts," totally unlike the more intricate, randomly evolved structures terrestrial biology exhibited. His conclusion was not hedged in the least:

"The Guest's body does not appear to be in the same biological category as Earth life forms. Some of its features are contrary to reasonable expectations. The only explanation I can offer for this is that the Guest is an artificial being, perhaps the product of centuries of genetic manipulation combined with complex bioelectronics. Since these abilities are far beyond us, any suppositions I might make as to the actual functions of the Guest's organs must be considered unreliable, perhaps misleading."

A chemical analysis of the Guest's tissues followed. There was no cell structure per se in any of the tissues; rather, each area or organ in the Guest's body appeared to have a separate metabolism, which cooperated with, but was not part of, other areas or organs. There was no central waste-disposal system. Wastes appeared to build up without relief in tissues. Phan thought this might have been the cause of death. "Perhaps nutrients unavailable in an Earth environment triggered processes below the level of detail our investigation can uncover. Perhaps the Guest, in its native environment, was attached to a complex life-support system that purged its body of waste products. Perhaps the Guest was ill and certain body functions were inactive."

Buried in a footnote: "The Guest does not appear to have been designed for a long life span." The footnote was signed by Harold Feinman, who had not attended the final parts of the autopsy. There was no further elaboration.

Despite the report's clarity, something was being left unsaid.

Feinman, at least, seemed to be hinting that the Guest was not what it appeared . . .

In the bottom report of the stack was an Australian booklet, prepared with obvious haste and considerable deletions. This booklet began with a synopsis of statements made by the mechanical visitors that had emerged from the Great Victoria Desert rock.

Hicks rubbed his eyes. The light was poor for reading. He had leafed through this booklet once already. Yet he needed to feel completely prepared for the next morning, when he accompanied the President into the Oval Office to meet with the Australian representatives.

"The comprehensibility of the mechanical beings' statements to our investigators is astonishing. Their command of English appears to be perfect. They answer questions promptly and without obfuscation."

Hicks studied the glossy color photographs inserted into the booklet. The Australian government had just two days before provided a set of these photographs along with video disks to every news organization in the world; the images of the three silvery, gourd-shaped robots hovering near a wood-posted razor-wire fence, of the great smooth water-worn red rock, of the exit hole, were in every civilized household in the world by now.

"The robots, by their every word, convey a sense of goodwill and benevolent concern. They wish to help the inhabitants of the Earth to 'fulfill your potential, to come together in harmony and exercise your rights as potential citizens of a galaxy-wide exchange.' "

Hicks frowned. How many years of fictional paranoia had conditioned him to be dubious of extraterrestrials bearing gifts? Of all the motion pictures made about first contact, only a bare handful had treated the epochal event as benign.

How often had Hicks's eyes misted over, watching these few films, even when he tried to keep a scientific perspective? That great moment, the exchange between humans and friendly non-human intelligences . . .

It had happened in Australia. The dream was alive.

And in California, nightmares.

The Guest does not appear to have been designed for a long life span.

He put the Australian booklet on the top of the stack and reached awkwardly over the stack to turn off the light. In the darkness, he disciplined himself to take regular, shallow breaths, to blank his mind and go to sleep. Even so, sleep came late and was not restful.

21——

October 11

Crockerman, wearing slacks and a white shirt but no coat or tie, a powdery patch of styptic pencil on his chin from a shaving cut, entered the office of his chief of staff, and nodded briefly at those assembled there: Gordon, Hicks, Rotterjack, Fulton, Lehrman, and the chief of staff himself, plump and balding Irwin Schwartz. It was seven-thirty in the morning, though in the windowless office time hardly mattered. Arthur thought he might never get out of little rooms and the company of bureaucrats and politicians.

"I've called you in here to go over our own material on the Great Victoria Desert bogey," Crockerman said. "You've read their booklet, I presume?" Crockerman asked. All nodded. "At my request, Mr. Hicks has been sworn in, and his security clearance has been processed . . ."

Rotterjack looked dyspeptic.

"He's one of us now. Where's Carl?"

"Still in traffic, I think," Schwartz said. "He called a half hour ago and said he'd be a few minutes late."

"All right. We don't have much time." Crockerman stood and paced before them. "I'll play his part. We have 'one or more' agents at the Australian rock. I need not tell you all how sensitive this fact is, but take this as a reminder . . ."

Rotterjack threw a very pointed glance at Hicks. Hicks received it calmly.

"Ironically, the information passed on to us only confirms what the Australians have been saying in public. Everything's Pollyanna as far as they're concerned. We're about to enter a new age of discovery. The robots have already begun to explain their technology. David?"

"The Australians have passed on some of the physics information the robots have given to them," Rotterjack said. "It's quite esoteric, having to do with cosmology. A couple of Australian physicists have said the equations are relevant to superstring theory."

"Whatever that is," Fulton said.

Rotterjack grinned almost maliciously. "It's very important, General. At your request, Arthur, I've passed the equations on to Mohammed Abante at Pepperdine University. He's arranging for a team of his colleagues to examine the equations and, we hope, file a report in a few days. The robots have not been confronted with the fact of our bogey. The Australians may want to leave it to us to tell them."

Carl McClennan entered the office, topcoat hung over his arm and briefcase half hidden in the folds. He looked around, saw there were no available seats besides the two reserved for the Australians, and stood by the rear wall. Hicks wondered if he should stand and give the national security advisor his seat, but decided it would win him no affection.

Crockerman gave McClennan a rundown of what had been discussed so far.

"I finished the first round of negotiations with their team leaders and intelligence experts last night. They've agreed to keep it secret," McClennan said. "The discussion today between the Aussies and ourselves can be open and aboveboard. No forbidden territory."

"Fine," Crockerman said. "What I'd like to work toward, gentlemen, is a way of presenting all the facts to the public within a month's time."

McClennan paled. "Mr. President, we haven't discussed this —" Both Rotterjack and McClennan cast unhappy glances at Hicks this time. Hicks kept his face impassive: *Not my show, gentlemen.*

"We haven't discussed it," Crockerman agreed, almost nonchalantly. "Still, this is what we should aim for. I am convinced the news will leak soon, and rather our citizens learn the facts of life from qualified personnel than from gutter gossip, don't you agree?"

Reluctantly, McClennan said yes, but his face remained tense.

"Fine. The Australians will be in the Oval Office in about fifteen minutes. Do we have any questions, disagreements, before we meet?"

Schwartz raised his hand and wriggled his fingers.

"Irwin?"

"Mr. President, is Tom Jacks or Rob Tishman on our list yet?" Schwartz asked. Jacks was in charge of public relations. Tishman was White House press secretary. "If we truly are going public in a month, or even if we're just thinking about it, Rob and Tom should be given some lead time."

"They aren't on the list yet; by tomorrow they will be. As for my esteemed Veep . . ." Crockerman frowned. Vice President Frederick Hale had had a falling-out with the President three months before; they hardly spoke now. Hale had involved himself in unsavory business dealings in Kansas; the resulting scandal had dominated newspapers for two weeks and nearly resulted in Hale's being "thrown to the wolves." Hale, as slippery and adept as any man in the Capital, had floundered ungracefully in the storm, but he had weathered it. "I see no reason to put him on the list now. Do you?"

Nobody indicated they did.

"Then let's adjourn to the Oval Office."

22——

Seated in chairs around the President's desk, the men listened intently as Arthur summed up the scientific findings. The Australians, both young and vigorous-looking, tanned in contrast to the pale features of the Americans around them, appeared serenely untroubled by what Arthur had just told them.

"In short, then," he concluded, "we have no reason to believe our Guest is being less than truthful. The contrast between our experiences is pretty sharp."

"That's true understatement," said Colin Forbes, the senior in age and rank of the two. Forbes was in his early forties, weathered and vigorous, with white-blond hair. He wore a pale blue sports coat and white slacks and smelled strongly of after-shave. "I can see what the fuss is about. Here we are, bringing a message of hope and glory, and your little green man tells you it's all a sham. I'm not sure how we can resolve the discrepancy."

"Isn't it obvious?" Rotterjack asked. "We confront your robots with what we've been told."

Forbes nodded and smiled. "And if they deny it all, if they say they don't know what the hell's going on?"

Rotterjack had no answer for that.

Gregory French, the junior Australian, with neatly combed and trimmed black hair and dressed in a standard gray suit, stood up and cleared his throat. He was obviously not comfortable in this high level of company. To Arthur, he looked like a bashful student. "Does anybody know if there have been other bogeys? The Russians, the Chinese?"

"No information yet," Lehrman said. "That's not a negative. Just a temporary 'we don't know.' "

"I think if we're the only ones blessed or cursed, we should get the issue resolved before any public release," French said. "This could tear people apart. Standing between devils and angels."

"I agree," Arthur said.

"There are problems with waiting," Crockerman said.

"Pardon me, sir," McClennan broke in, "but the possibility of unofficial release is much less disturbing than the impact of . . ." He waved his hands energetically through the air. "The confusion. The fear. We're sitting on a real time bomb. *Do you truly understand this, Mr. President?*" he practically shouted. McClennan's frustration with the President had come to a painful head. The room was silent. The national security advisor's tone had been far stronger than anyone would have expected, coming from the cautious Carl McClennan.

"Yes, Carl," Crockerman replied, eyes half lidded. "I believe I do."

"Sorry," McClennan said, slumping slightly in his seat. French, still standing, seemed acutely embarrassed.

"All right," Forbes said, gesturing with an elegant flip of his finger for French to be seated. "We confront our bogeys. We'd better get on with it. I invite as many of your people as you can spare to return with us. And I think I'll recommend to Quentin that we start shutting the doors again. Fewer press reports. Does this seem reasonable?"

"Eminently," Rotterjack said.

"I'm curious as to why Mr. Hicks is here," Forbes said. "I admire Trevor's work enormously, but . . ." He didn't finish his thought. Arthur looked at Hicks, and realized he genuinely liked and trusted the man. He could understand the President's choice. But that would cut no ice with McClennan and Rotterjack, who clearly wanted Hicks away from the center.

"He's here because he's as conversant on these subjects as anybody in the world," Crockerman said. "Even though we do not see eye to eye."

Rotterjack ineffectively masked his surprise, sitting up in his chair and then awkwardly leaning his elbow on the arm. Arthur watched him closely. *They thought Hicks might be behind the President's attitude.*

"I'm glad Trevor's here," Arthur said abruptly. "I welcome his insights."

"Fine with me," Forbes said, smiling broadly.

PERSPECTIVE

The New York Daily News, October 12, 1996: Sources in the State Department, on condition that they not be named, have confirmed that there is a connection between the disappearance and alleged government captivity of four people and the secret visit by President Crockerman to Death Valley earlier this week. Other informed sources have confirmed that both of these incidents are connected with the Australian extraterrestrials. In a related story, the Reverend Kyle McCabey of Edinburgh, Scotland, founder of the Satanic Invader's League, claims that his new religious sect now numbers its followers at a hundred thousand throughout the United Kingdom and the Irish Republic. The Satanic Invader's League believes that the Australian extra-terrestrials are representatives of Satan sent to the Earth to, in the Reverend's words, "soften us up for Satan's conquest."

23——

October 13

On the Hollywood Freeway, neck and back stiff from the early morning flight into LAX, Arthur Gordon grimly steered the rental Lincoln, listening to a babble about national lottery results on the radio.

His mind was far away, and visions of the river outside his Oregon home kept intruding into his planning. Smooth, clear green water, steady and unaware, working its natural way, eroding banks. How did each particle of dirt stripped from its place feel about the process? How did the gazelle, caught in the slash of a lion's paws, feel about becoming a simple dinner, all its existence reduced to a week or so of sustenance for another creature? "Waste," he said. "Goddamn waste." Yet he wasn't sure what he meant, or what all his thoughts were pointing to.

Cat's paws. Playing with the prey.

Suddenly, Arthur missed Francine and Marty terribly. He had spoken with them briefly from Washington before leaving; he had told them very little, not even where he was or where he was going.

Did a gazelle, caught in the meshing gears of a lion's paws, worry about doe and fawn?

Harry's home was a spacious split-level "stick-built" ranch house from the early 1960s, wandering over much of a eucalyptus-covered quarter-acre lot in Tarzana. He had purchased the home in

1975, before his marriage to Ithaca; it had seemed hollow then, with only one occupant, and was still a place of vast white walls and rug-dotted linoleum floors, a little chilly and severe for Arthur's taste.

Ithaca beyond any doubt ruled the roost. Tall, with dark red hair and features more suited to a Shakespearean actress than a Tarzana homemaker, her quiet presence balanced the broad rooms. Harry had once told Arthur, "Wherever she is, there's enough, and never too much." Arthur had known exactly what he meant.

She opened the door at Arthur's knock, smiled warmly, and extended her hand. Arthur took the fingers and kissed them solemnly. "Milady," he said ceremoniously. "Is the good doctor in?"

"Hello, Arthur. Good to see you. He's in and being insufferable."

"His treatments?"

"No. Something else, having to do with you, I presume." Ithaca would never inquire. "Can I get you coffee? It's been cold this winter. Today is especially dreary."

"Yes, please. The office?"

"Sanctum sanctorum. How's Francine? Marty?"

"They're fine." He stuck his hands in his pockets, obviously anxious to join Harry. Ithaca nodded.

"I'll bring the coffee into the office. Go."

"Thanks." He always felt like complimenting Ithaca on her appearance, which was, as usual, wonderful—but she did not take kindly to compliments. How she looked and dressed was as natural to her as breathing. He smiled awkwardly and headed down the hall to the office.

Harry sat in an overstuffed chair, fire crackling brightly in the grate. His office had originally been the master bedroom, and after his marriage, he had kept it there. There were three large bedrooms with fireplaces in the house, enough to go around. Stacks of books rose beside his chair, some of them huge, old, and well thumbed. An Olympia typewriter hung keyboard down over the fireplace like a hunting trophy, while from its return key dangled three carbon-encrusted test tubes looped together by a red ribbon. The story behind this had to do with Harry's doctoral thesis and was seldom told when Harry was sober.

In Harry's lap rested a copy of Brin and Kuiper's book on the search for extraterrestrial intelligence. McClennan and Rotterjack had kept copies of the same book on their office desks. Arthur also noticed Hicks's novel on the corner of a roll-around table, almost crowded off by stacks of infodisks.

"Finally, by God," Harry said. "I've been stuck here getting over nausea and waiting for the word. What's the word?"

"I'm to go to Australia with most of the task force. I'm leaving in three days, with a couple of hours stopover in Tahiti. We should just be able to put out a short report."

"The newshounds are on our trail," Harry said, raising his thick eyebrows.

"The President thinks we should release the story within a month. Rotterjack and the others aren't enthusiastic."

"And you?"

"Newshounds," Arthur concurred, shrugging. "We may not have much choice soon."

"They'll have to release those folks at Vandenberg. Can't hold them forever. They're physically clean and healthy."

Arthur closed the office door. "The Guest?"

Harry's face worked. "Bogus," he said. "I think it's as much a robot as the Australian shmoos."

"What does Phan think?"

"He's good, but this has stretched him. He thinks it's a product of a biologically advanced civilization, kind of a future citizen, sterile and largely artificial, but still *bona fide* an individual."

"Why do you disagree?"

"It was never meant to process wastes. Planned obsolescence. The Guest poisoned itself and broke down. There was no evidence of any way to void the wastes through any sort of external dialysis. No anus, no urinary tract. No valves, no exit points. No lungs. It breathed through its skin. Not very efficient for a creature its size. And no sweat glands. Unconvincing as hell. But—I'm not so convinced that I'm going to stand up and shout howdy before all the President's men. After all, that just complicates things, doesn't it?"

Arthur nodded. "You've read Colonel Rogers's report and seen his pictures?"

Harry held up a new infodisk, the security plastic sticker Day-Glo orange on its label. "An Air Force car brought it by yesterday. Impressive."

"Frightening."

"I thought you'd be spooked," Harry said. "We think alike, don't we?"

"We always have, within limits," Arthur said.

"Okay, I say the biology's a ringer. What about the rock?"

"Warren's brought in his report on the externals. He says it appears authentic, right down to mineral samples. However, he agrees with Edward Shaw about the suspicious lack of weathering. Abante can't make heads or tails of the interior. He says it looks like a set from a science fiction movie—pretty but nonspecific. And no sign of any other Guests."

"So what do we conclude?"

Arthur pulled a folding stool from behind the door, opened it, and squatted. "I think we see the outlines of our draft, don't you?"

Harry nodded. "We're being played with," he said.

Arthur held up an extended thumb.

"Now, why would they want to play with us?" Harry asked.

"To draw us out and discover our capabilities?" Arthur ventured.

"Are they afraid we can beat them if they aren't careful?"

"That might be an explanation," Arthur said.

"Lord. They must be thousands of years ahead of us."

"Not necessarily."

"How could it be otherwise?" Harry asked, his voice rising an octave.

"Captain Cook," Arthur offered. "The Hawaiians thought he was some sort of god. Two hundred years later, they drive cars just like the rest of us . . . and watch TV."

"They were subjugated," Harry said. "They didn't have a chance, not against cannon."

"They killed Cook, didn't they?"

"Are you suggesting some sort of resistance movement?" Harry asked.

"We're getting way ahead of ourselves."

"Damn right. Let's stick to basics." Harry folded the book on his lap. "You're wondering about my health."

Arthur nodded. "Can you travel?"

"Not far, not soon. Yesterday they pumped me full of magic bullets. Bullets to restructure my immune system, to strengthen my bone marrow . . . Thousands of little tame retroviruses doing their thing. I feel like hell most of the time. Still, I've got what's left of my hair. We're not doing radiation or heavy chemicals yet."

"Can you work? Travel around California?"

"Anywhere you want me, within a two-hour emergency hop to

UCLA Medical Center. I'm a wreck, Arthur. You shouldn't have chosen me. I shouldn't have agreed."

"You're still thinking clearly, aren't you?" Arthur asked.

"Yes."

"Then you're useful. Necessary."

Harry looked down at the folded book in his lap. "Ithaca's not taking this well."

"She seems cheerful."

"She's a good actress. At night, in her sleep, her face . . . she cries." Harry's own eyes were moist at the thought, and he seemed much younger, almost a boy, glancing up at Arthur. "Christ. I'm glad I'm the one who might die. If things were the other way around, and she was going through this, I'd be in worse shape than I am now."

"You're not going to die," Arthur said sternly. "We're almost into the twenty-first century. Leukemia isn't the killer it used to be."

"Not for children, Arthur. But for me . . ." He raised his hands.

"You leave us, and I'm going to be pretty damn inconsolable." Completely against his will, he felt his own eyes grow damp. "Remember that."

Harry said nothing for a moment. "The Forge of God," he finally commented, shaking his head. "If that ever gets into the papers . . ."

"One nightmare at a time," Arthur said. Harry called Ithaca to prepare a guest bedroom for Arthur. As she did that, Arthur placed a collect call to Oregon, the first he had had a chance to make in two days.

His conversation with Francine was brief. There was nothing he could tell her, except that he was well. She was polite enough, and knew him well enough, not to mention the news reports.

The call was not enough. When it was over, Arthur missed his family more than ever.

24——

October 20, Australia (October 19, USA)

A newsreel preceded the feature film on the Qantas flight to Melbourne, projected over the heads of passengers onto a tiny screen. Arthur looked up from his disk reader and open ring binder. Beside him, an elderly gentleman in a gray herringbone wool suit dozed lightly.

A computer-animated graphic of Australia Associated Press News Network filled the screen, backed by a jaunty jazz score. The rather plain, rugged middle-aged face of AAPN anchor Rachel Vance smiled across the darkened seats and inattentive heads. "Good day. Our lead story today is, of course, still the Centralian extraterrestrials. Yet another conference was held yesterday between Australian scientists and the robots, familiarly known as Shmoos, after comic artist Al Capp's remarkably generous characters, which they resemble in shape. While the information exchanged in the conference has not been released, a government spokesman acknowledged that scientists are still discussing theoretical physics and astronomy, and have not yet begun discussions on biology."

The spokesman appeared, a familiar face already. Arthur half listened. He had heard it all by now. "We have received no information about the density of living things in the galaxy; that is, we still do not know how many planets are inhabited, or what types of creatures inhabit them . . ."

His picture faded to a shot of the three Shmoos in motion down a dirt path to conference trailers set up in fields of dry spinifex grass near the huge false rock. The robots' floating propulsion was still eerie, deeply disturbing. In that motion could be signs of an immensely advanced technology . . . or of some sort of visual trick, a show for the primitive natives.

Vance returned, her smile warmly fixed in stone. "The Washington *Post* and *The New York Times* reported today that the remnant of an old volcano near Death Valley, California, has been closed off to the public. The *Post* makes a connection between this closing and the disappearance of three men and a woman, all allegedly held by military authorities in California."

Nothing new, but closer . . . perilously closer. Arthur leaned back in his seat and stared out of the window at the ocean and clouds passing in review tens of thousands of feet below. *Immense,* he thought. *It seems to be all there is. Ocean and clouds. I could spend my entire life traveling and not see all of it.* This did not necessarily demonstrate the size of the Earth, but it did put his life and brain in perspective.

He tried to nap. They would be in Melbourne in a few hours, and he was already exhausted.

The Rock, still unnamed, stretched for half a mile across the horizon in the early morning light, gloriously colored from the bottom up in layers of purple and red and orange. The sky overhead was a trembling dusty blue-gray, hinting at the heat to come. It was spring here, but there had been little rain. There was hardly a breath of wind. Arthur jumped down from the bulky, big-tired gray Royal Australian Army staff vehicle into red dust and stared across the golden plain at the Rock. The science advisor, David Rotterjack, stepped down behind him. Less than a dozen meters away, the first circle of razor-wire-topped hurricane fence began, curving in broad scallops through silver-gray mulga scrub and spiky spinifex.

Quentin Bent walked with a short-legged, almost eager waddle along the red dirt path to the edge of the road. Bent was in his mid-forties, of middle height, heavy and florid-faced, with a forward-swept bush of gray hair, an easy smile, and sharp, pessimistic blue eyes. He extended his hand to Rotterjack first. In another Army vehicle, Bent's assistants, Forbes and French, accompanied Charles Warren, the geologist from Kent State.

"Mr. Arthur Gordon," Bent said, shaking Arthur's hand. "I've just finished reading the draft American task force report. Your work, and Dr. Feinman's, largely, am I correct?"

"Yes," Arthur said. "I hope it was clear."

"All too clear," Bent said, lifting his chin as if smelling the air, but keeping his eyes on Arthur. "Very disturbing. Gentlemen, I've received a message from our Shmoos—we all call them that now, they can't really be offended, can they?—and we're scheduled to have a meeting with them at noon today in trailer three." Almost breathlessly, he said, "Each day . . . they travel from the Rock to our conference trailer. They never leave the vicinity of the Rock. Before then, we will have breakfast in the mess trailer, and then a tour of the site, if you're up to it. Did you get enough sleep, Dr. Gordon, Mr. Rotterjack, Dr. Warren?"

"Sufficient," Rotterjack said, his eyes dark.

Bent flashed a smile and waddled into place ahead of them. "Follow me," he said.

Arthur fell in step beside Warren, a man of middle height and build with wispy, thinning brown hair brushed across a bald spot and large eyes above a long nose. "What does it look like?" he asked.

"A lot like Ayers Rock, only smaller," Warren answered, shaking his head. "It's less convincing than the cinder cone in Death Valley. Frankly, I wouldn't have been surprised to find it at Disney World."

The breakfast went smoothly. They were introduced to several of the scientists measuring and analyzing the Rock, including the head of the materials team, Dr. Christine Carmichael. She explained that the minerals making up the Rock were all clearly earthbound—none of the surrounding "camouflage" material had arrived from space. Arthur tried to visualize the construction of the Rock, away from all human witnesses; he could not.

Other discussion was brief. Bent asked only three questions: how they planned to release the news (Rotterjack replied that at present there were no such plans), how they interpreted the Guest's story about planet-eating spacecraft (it seemed straightforward), and whether they believed there was a connection between the Death Valley cinder cone and the Rock. Rotterjack was unwilling to commit himself. Warren did not believe he had spent enough time on the project to render a useful opinion. Arthur nodded once; there was a definite connection.

"Can't have too many interstellar visitors in one year, eh?" Bent asked.

"It seems very unlikely," Arthur said.

"But not impossible?" Bent pursued.

"Not beyond possibility, but difficult to conceive."

"Still, we're all quite ignorant about what's out there, aren't we?" Forbes asked, smoothing back his white-blond hair with one hand.

"There could have been a wave of machine migrations, finally reaching this vicinity," French added. "Perhaps whole civilizations have grown up along an evolutionary timetable, and like rain precipitating out of a cloud, the time has come . . ."

Bent leaned over his now empty plates of steak, eggs, and fruit. "We're an optimistic bunch, Dr. Gordon. Our nation is younger than yours. Let me say, right out, that we have an interest in this being a good thing. The P.M. and the Cabinet—not to mention the Reverend Mr. Caldecott . . ." He glanced around, grinning broadly. Forbes and French mimicked his grin. "We *all* believe this could lift us into the forefront of all nations. We could be a center of immense activity, construction, education, research. If the Furnace is something horrible, which it seems to be, we might still cling to the notion that the Rock is different. Whether it serves us ill or not. Am I clear?"

"Perfectly clear," Rotterjack said. "We'd like to agree with you." He glanced at Arthur.

"We can't, however," Arthur said.

"For the moment, then, amicable disagreement and open minds. Gentlemen, we have a helicopter waiting."

In the late morning light, the Rock's colors had been subdued to a bright russet mixed with streaks of ocher. Arthur, looking through the concentric networks of tiny scratches in the helicopter's Plexiglas windows, shook his head. "The detail is astonishing," he shouted above the whine of the jets and the thumping roar of the blades. Warren nodded, squinting against a sudden glare of sun. "It's granite, all right, but there's no exfoliation. The banding is vertical, which is entirely wrong for this area—more appropriate to Ayers Rock than here. And where are the wind features, the hollows and caves? It's a reasonably convincing imitation—unless you're a geologist. But my question is, why go to all the trouble to disguise the Rock, when they knew they'd be coming out in the open?"

"They haven't explicitly answered several of our questions," Bent admitted. "Directly below us is the opening through which our Shmoos emerge to confer with us. There are two other openings we know of, both quite small—no more than a meter wide. Nothing has emerged from them. We haven't sent anybody in to investigate the openings. We think it best to trust them—not to look gift horses in the mouth, no?"

Arthur nodded dubiously.

"What would you have done?" Bent asked, showing a flash of irritation and perplexity.

"The same, probably," Arthur said.

The helicopter circled the Rock twice and then landed near the conference trailer. The engine noise declined to a rhythmic groaning whine and the blades slowed. Arthur, the Australians, and Rotterjack walked across the red dust and pea gravel to the gray and white trailer. It rose a meter above the ground on heavy iron jacks and concrete blocks, its eight rugged tires dangling sadly.

Bent pulled out a key ring and opened the white-painted aluminum door, ushering Gordon, Rotterjack, and Warren in, but going ahead of Forbes and French. Inside, an air conditioner hummed quietly. Arthur mopped his brow with a handkerchief and reveled in the cool air. Forbes and French pulled seats up to the spare conference table. French switched on a monitor and they sat to watch the opening in the Rock, waiting intently for the Shmoos to emerge.

"Have they ever asked to travel elsewhere?" Arthur asked.

"No," Bent said. "As I said, they don't leave the vicinity."

"And they haven't revealed whether they're going to land others soon?"

"No."

Arthur raised his eyebrows. Three gleaming gourd-shaped objects emerged from the two-meter-wide hole, descending to hover thirty or forty centimeters above the rugged ground. Bobbing and weaving gracefully, the Shmoos traversed the half kilometer between the trailer and the Rock, three abreast, reminding Arthur of gunslingers approaching a showdown.

His hands trembled. Rotterjack leaned toward Arthur and said matter-of-factly, "I'm scared. Are you?"

Bent looked at them both with a drawn, ambiguous expression. *We've brought him into our nightmare. He was innocent until we arrived. He was in a scientist's heaven.*

A wide hatch opened on the opposite side of the trailer, letting in a draft of hot air and the hot, dusty-sweet smell of the mulgas. In the sunlit glare outside, the Shmoos ascended a wide ramp and floated into the trailer, arraying themselves on the opposite side of the conference table. The hatch swung down again. The air-conditioner compressor rattled faintly on the roof.

Arthur surveyed the gleaming robots. Beyond their shape and the bluish-gunmetal gleam of their surfaces, they were featureless; no visible sensor apparatus, no sound-producing grilles or extruding arms. Blank.

Bent leaned forward. "Welcome. This is our fifteenth meeting, and I've invited three guests to attend this time. More will be attending later. Are you well? Is everything satisfactory?"

"Everything is satisfactory," the middle robot replied. Its voice was ambiguously tenor, neither masculine nor feminine. The inflections and assumed Australian accent were perfect. Arthur could easily picture a cultured and prosperous young man behind the voice.

"These gentlemen, David Rotterjack, Charles Warren, and Arthur Gordon, have traveled from our ally nation, the United States of America, to speak with you and ask important questions."

"Greetings to Mr. Rotterjack and Mr. Warren and Mr. Gordon. We welcome all inquiries."

Rotterjack appeared stunned. Since he was clearly unwilling to speak first, Arthur faced the middle Shmoo and said, "We have a problem."

"Yes."

"In our country, there is a device similar to your own, disguised as a volcanic cinder cone. A biological being has emerged from this device." He related the subsequent events concisely, marveling at his own apparent equanimity. "Clearly, this being's story contradicts your own. Would you please explain these contradictions to us?"

"They make no sense whatsoever," the middle robot said. Arthur controlled a sudden urge to flinch and run; the machine's tone was smooth, in complete control, somehow superior. "Are you certain of your facts?"

"As certain as we can be," Arthur said, his urge to flee replaced by irritation, then anger. *They're actually going to stonewall. God damn!*

"This is very puzzling. Do you have pictures of these events, or any recorded information we can examine?"

"Yes." Arthur lifted his briefcase onto the table and produced a folio of color prints. He spread the pictures before the Shmoos, who made no apparent move to examine them.

"We have recorded your evidence," the central robot said. "We are still puzzled. Is this perhaps attributable to some friction between your nations?"

"As Mr. Bent has said, our nations are allies. There is very little friction between us."

The room was quiet for several seconds. Then Rotterjack said, "We believe that both of these devices—yours and the cinder cone object in California—are controlled by the same—people, group. Can you prove to us that we are incorrect?"

"Group? You imply that the other, if it exists, is controlled by us?"

"Yes," Arthur said. Rotterjack nodded.

"This makes no sense. Our mission here is clear. We have told all of your investigators that we wish to gently and efficiently introduce humans to the cultures and technologies of other intelligences. We have made no threatening gestures."

"Indeed, you have not," Bent said placatingly. "Is it possible there are factions among your kind that oppose your actions? Someone perhaps trying to sabotage your work?"

"This is not likely."

"Can you offer any other explanation?" Bent asked, clearly frustrated.

"No explanations are apparent to us. Our craft is not equipped to dismantle worlds."

Arthur produced another packet of photos and spread them before the robots. "Half a year ago, a moon of the planet we call Jupiter—are you familiar with Jupiter?"

"Yes."

"The sixth moon, Europa, disappeared. We haven't been able to locate it since. Can you explain this to us?"

"No, we cannot. We are not responsible for any such large-scale phenomenon."

"Can you help us solve these mysteries?" Bent asked, a hint of desperation coming into his voice. He was clearly experiencing the same sense of dread that had long since come over all associated with the Furnace bogey. Things were not adding up. Lack of explanations at this stage could be tantamount to provocation . . .

"We have no explanations for any of these events." Then, in a conciliatory tone, "They are puzzling."

Bent glanced at Arthur: *We're getting nowhere.* "Perhaps we should begin with our regular schedule of discussions for the day."

The robot did not speak for several seconds. Visibly unnerved, Bent tensed his clasped hands on the desk.

"Possibly there is a problem of communication," it said. "Perhaps all of these difficulties can be overcome. Today's session is not important. We will cancel this meeting and meet again later."

With no further word, ignoring the polite objections of Quentin Bent, the Shmoos rose, backed away from the table, and passed through the hatchway. Desert heat once again beat in on the men in the trailer before the hatch closed.

Stunned by the sudden end of the interview, they simply stared at each other. Bent was on the edge of tears.

"All right," he said, standing. He glanced at the TV monitor perched high in one corner. Cameras conveyed the Shmoos' return to the Rock. "We'll see—"

A sharp crack and a roar rocked the trailer. Arthur fell from his chair in seeming slow motion, bumping into Rotterjack's chair, thinking on the way down, *It's begun.* He landed on hands and butt and quickly got to his feet, pulling on a table leg. Bent pointed to the monitor, still functioning though vibrating in its mount. The Shmoos were gone.

"They blew up," he said. "I saw it. Did anybody else see it—on the screen? They just exploded!"

"Jesus," Rotterjack said.

"Is somebody shelling them?" Forbes asked, looking sharply at Rotterjack and Arthur.

"God knows," Bent said. They scrambled outside the trailer and followed a raggedly organized team of scientists and soldiers down the path to where the Shmoos had last been seen. Fifty meters down the path to the Rock, three craters had been gouged in the dirt, each about two meters in diameter. The robots had left no sign—neither fragments nor burn marks.

Quentin Bent stood hunched over with hands on his knees, sobbing and cursing as he looked up across the blinding noonday plain at the Rock. "What happened? What in bloody hell happened?"

"There's nothing left," Forbes said. French nodded vigorously, his face beet red. Both kept glancing at the Americans: their fault.

"Do you know?" Bent asked loudly, turning on him. "Is this some goddamned American thing?"

"No," Arthur said.

"Airplanes, rockets . . ." Bent was almost incoherent.

"We didn't hear any aircraft . . ." French said.

"They destroyed themselves," Arthur said quietly, walking around the craters, careful not to disturb anything.

"That's bloody impossible!" Bent screamed.

"Not at all." Arthur felt deeply chilled, as if he had swallowed a lump of dry ice. "Have you read Liddell Hart?"

"What in God's name are you talking about?" Bent shouted, fists clenched, approaching Arthur and then backing away, without apparent aim. Rotterjack stayed clear of the men and the craters.

"Sir Basil Liddell Hart's *Strategy.*"

"I've read it," Rotterjack said.

"You're crazy," French said. "You're all bleeding crazy!"

"We have the incident on tape," Forbes said, holding up his hands to calm his colleagues. "We must review it. We can see if any projectile or weapon struck them."

Arthur knew very well he was not crazy. It was making sense to him now. "I'm sorry," he said. "I'll explain when everybody's in a better frame of mind."

"*Fuck* that!" Bent said, regaining some composure. "I want the physics group out here immediately. I want a message sent to the Rock now. If there's a war beginning here, let's not give the impression we started it."

"We've never sent or received transmissions from the Rock," Forbes said, shaking his head.

"I do not care. Send transmissions, as many frequencies as we can handle. *This* message: 'Not responsible for destruction of envoys.' Got that?"

Forbes nodded and returned to the trailer to relay the orders.

"Mr. Gordon, I'll try very hard to put myself in a suitable frame of mind. What the hell has strategy to do with this?" Bent asked, standing on the opposite side of the three craters.

"The indirect approach," Arthur said.

"Meaning?"

"Never come at your adversary from an expected direction, or with your goals clear."

Bent, whatever his state of mind, caught on quickly. "You're saying this has all been a ruse?"

"I think so."

"But then your Guest is a ruse, too. Why would they tell us they're going to destroy the planet, and then make that seem like a sham . . . tell us they're going to save us, and that's a sham, too?"

"I don't know," Arthur said. "To confuse us."

"Goddammit, man, they're powerful beyond our wildest dreams! They build mountains overnight, travel across space in huge ships, and if what you say is true, they dismantle whole worlds—why bother to deceive us? Do we send greetings to bleeding ants' nests before we trample them?"

Arthur could not answer this. He shook his head and held up his hands. The heat made him dizzy. Oddly—or not so oddly—what worried him most now was how the President would react when he learned what had happened here.

"We have to talk to Hicks first," he told Rotterjack as they climbed aboard a truck to be taken back to the outer perimeter.

"Why? Aren't we all in enough trouble already?"

"Hicks . . . might be able to explain things to the President. In a way he'll listen to."

Rotterjack lowered his voice to a whisper in the back of the vehicle. "All hell's going to break loose. McClennan and Schwartz and I will have a real fight . . . Whose side are you on?"

"I beg your pardon?"

"Are you voting for Armageddon, or do we have a chance?"

Arthur started to reply, then shut his mouth and shook his head.

"Crockerman's going to flip when he hears about this," Rotterjack said.

Arthur called Oregon from Adelaide's airport while waiting for the Army limo to pick up the United States group. He was exhausted from the day and the long flight back. It was early in the morning in Oregon and Francine answered with a voice full of sleep.

"Sorry to wake you," Arthur said. "I'm not going to be able to call for a couple of days."

"It's lovely to hear from you. I love you."

"Miss you both desperately. I feel like a man cut loose. Nothing is real anymore."

"What can you tell me?"

"Nothing," Arthur said, pinching his cheek lightly.

"Well, then, I've got something to tell you. Guess who called?"

"Oh, I don't know. Who? Not—"

"You guessed it. Chris Riley. He told me to write it down. 'Two new unusual objects the size of asteroids have been discovered, each about two hundred kilometers in diameter. They have the albedo of fresh ice—almost pure white. They are traveling in highly unusual orbits—both hyperbolic. They may or may not be huge, very young comets.' Does this make any sense to you? He said it might."

"Fragments of Europa?"

"Isn't this romantic?" Francine asked, still sleepy. "He said you might think that."

"Go on," Arthur said, his sensation of unreality increasing.

She continued to read the message. " 'If they are fragments of Europa, they are traveling along virtually impossible paths, widely separated. One of them will rendezvous with Venus next year, when Venus is at . . .' Just a second. Got another page here . . . 'at superior conjunction. The other will rendezvous with Mars in late 1997.' Got that?"

"I think so," Arthur said.

"Marty's asleep, but he told me to tell you that Gauge will now sit and heel at his command. He's very proud of that. Also, he's finished all the Tarzan books."

"Attaboy." His eyes closed for a moment and he experienced a small blackout. "Sweetheart, I'm dead on my feet. I'm going to fall over if I don't get to sleep shortly."

"We both hope you're home soon. I've gotten used to having you around the house. It seems empty now."

"I love you," Arthur said, eyes still closed, trying to visualize her face.

"Love you, too."

He climbed into the limo beside Warren and Rotterjack. "What have you heard about two ice asteroids?" he asked them.

They shook their heads.

"One will probably resurface Venus, and the other will wreak havoc on Mars, both next year."

Warren, despite his exhaustion, gaped. Rotterjack seemed puzzled. "What's that have to do with us?" he asked.

"I don't know," Arthur replied.

"Funny damned coincidence," Warren said, shaking his head.

"They're going to hit Venus and Mars?" Rotterjack asked, the implications sinking in slowly.

"Next year," Arthur said.

The presidential science advisor drew his lips together and nodded, staring out the window at passing traffic, light this late hour of the evening. "That can't be coincidence," he said. "What in the name of Christ is going on?"

25————

November 1, Eastern Pacific Time (November 2, USA)

Walt Samshow moved with a long-accustomed grace on the ladders of the Glomar *Discoverer*, sliding his hands along the rails as his feet pumped in a blur down the steps, stuffing his chin into his clavicle to remove his leather-brown, freckled, and sun-spotted bald pate from the path of passing bulkheads. Whatever effects of age dogged him on shore vanished; he was more spry at sea than on land. Samshow, a long-legged, narrow-faced bean pole of a man, had spent more than two thirds of his seventy-one years at sea, serving ten years in the Navy from 1942 to 1952, and then moving on to forty years of research in physical oceanography.

Deep in the ship's hold, spaced across an otherwise empty cargo bay, were his present crop of children: three upright, man-high, steel-gray cylindrical gravimeters measuring the gravity gradients of the trench ten thousand meters below. The *Discoverer* was on its sixth pass over the Ramapo Deep. The sea outside the hull was almost glassy, and the ship moved forward at a steady ten knots, as stable as bedrock, ideal for this kind of work. They could probably get accuracy to within plus or minus two milligals over the average of all six runs.

Samshow descended into the hold, his feet hitting the cork-covered steel deck lightly. His much younger partner, David Sand, smiled at him, face a corpselike green and purple in the glow of the color monitor. Samshow presented the covered aluminum plate he had carried down from the mess.

"What's the bill of fare?" Sand asked. He was half Samshow's age and almost half again his weight, strong and wide-faced, with eyes pale blue, a tiny Scots button of a nose, and a full head of wiry auburn hair. Samshow removed the plate's cover. Deep in the elder oceanographer's thoughts, Sand had become one of many sons; he treated younger assistants with the tough-minded affection he would have bestowed on his own child. Sand knew this, and appreciated it; in his entire career, he would probably have no better teacher, partner, or friend than Walt Samshow.

"Fried sole, spinach pie, and beets," Samshow said. The ship's Filipino cook took pride in his special Western meals, served twice a week.

Sand grimaced and shook his head. "That'll make me pretty heavy—might affect the results." Samshow set the plate down beside him and glanced at the gravimeters, spaced in a triangle in two corners and the middle of the opposite bulkhead.

"Wouldn't want to ruin an incredible evening," Sand murmured. He tapped a few keys intently, nodded at the display, and applied a fork to the beets.

"That good?"

"Damned near perfect," Sand said. "I'll eat and you can spell me in an hour."

"Your eyeballs are going to fall right out on the floor," Samshow warned.

"I'm young," Sand said. "I'll grow another pair."

Samshow grinned, returned to the ladder, and ascended through the maze of corridors and hatches to the deck. The Pacific lay around the ship as thick and slow as syrup, rippling iridescent silver and velvet black. The air was unusually dry and clear. From horizon to horizon the sky was filled with stars to within a few degrees of a fresh sliver of moon, a tiny thing lost in the yawn of night. Samshow rested his feet on the anchor chain near the bow and sighed in contentment. The week's work had been long and he was tired in a way he enjoyed, contented, deep in the mellowness brought on only by satisfactory results.

He glanced at his pocket navigator, tied in to a Navstar signal. The first approximation on the illuminated display read, >E142°32'10" N30°45'20"<, which put the *Discoverer* about 130 kilometers east of Toru Island. In four more hours, they would swing around again for a seventh pass.

He belched contentedly and began to whistle "String of Pearls."

Samshow had outlived one wife after thirty years of stormy, blissful marriage, the true love of his life, and now had two fine women who doted on him when he was ashore, about seven months out of the year. One was in La Jolla, a plump rich widow, and another was in Manila, a black-haired Filipina thirty years younger than he, distantly related to the long-gone and lamented President Magsaysay.

It was a warm, strange dry night, quiet and still, a night for deep thinking and old memories. He felt a sudden onslaught of laziness; the hell with science, the hell with perfect results and plus or minus two milligals. He'd rather be walking some beach watching breakers explode with phosphorescence. The feeling passed but left its mark; it was one of the few ways his body told him he was getting old. He turned and stepped over the chain, then froze, catching something odd in the upper half of his vision.

He jerked his head back. A tiny point of light arced rapidly from the north: a satellite, he thought—or a meteor. He could barely see it now. The point had almost lost itself among the stars when it suddenly brightened to blowtorch intensity, throwing two distinct flares southward at least three degrees. The flares lighted the entire sea in stark, eerie pewter, and then went out. The much dimmer object passed directly overhead. He made a mental note of the position—about four o'clock high—and was working on which constellation it had appeared in, when the object brightened again about twenty degrees farther south, much smaller, barely a pinprick. He had never seen a meteor like it—a real stunner, an on-again, off-again fireball.

"On the bridge! Heads up!" he yelled. "Hey! Everybody, look at this!"

The prick of light fell slowly enough to track easily. In a few minutes, it met the horizon and was gone, leaving tiny patches of green and red swimming in his vision.

Where it had struck, a column of water and steaming spray arose, barely visible in the moonlight, radiating a halo of cloud about ten degrees above the horizon.

"Jesus," Samshow said. He started for the bridge to ask if anyone else had seen it. Nobody had replied to his shout. He was halfway up the steps when a horrendous gonglike shudder rang through the ship. He paused, startled, and finished his climb to the bridge.

The first officer, an intense young Chinese named Chao, glanced at Samshow from the controls. The bridge and most instrumentation were illuminated in dull red, not to impair night vision. "Big storm coming," Chao said, pointing to the ship's status display screen. "Fast. Typhoon, waterspout. Don't know."

Four men leaped onto the bridge from three different hatches, and voices squawked on the intercom from around the ship.

"A meteor," Samshow explained. "Went down just like that, made a big spout about thirty kilometers due south."

Captain Reed, twenty years younger than Samshow but even more gray and grizzled, came onto the bridge from his cabin, nodded curtly, and gave him a dubious glance. "Mr. Chao, what is this coming?"

"Blow, Captain," Chao said. "Damn big storm. Coming fast." He pointed to the enhanced radar images. Clouds rushed at them in a blue and red scythe. The storm was already visible through the glass forward.

David Sand came from belowdecks huffing, red-faced, and swearing. "Walt, whatever that was, it's just screwed up everything. We have a—Jesus Christ!" He recovered from the sight of the approaching front and began swearing again. "It was going just fine, and now there's a jag on the graph."

"Jag?" Captain Reed asked.

"Extremely short wavelength anomaly. Deep decline, zero for an instant, then a slow increase—it's ruined! We'll have to recalibrate, maybe even send all three tubs back to Maryland."

The captain ordered the ship turned bow-on to face the storm. Warnings, whistles and shouts and electric bells, sounded all around the ship.

"What's happening?" Sand asked, concern finally replacing his anger.

"Meteor," Samshow said. "Big one."

The front hit seven minutes after Samshow saw the fireball strike the horizon.

The ship fell forward into canyonlike wave troughs, its bow knifing ten and fifteen meters into the black water, and then rode upward over the crests, the bow now pointing at the rain-lashed sky. Samshow and Sand tightly gripped rails mounted on the bridge bulkheads, grinning like fools, while the crew worked to control the ship and the Captain stared stonily forward.

"I've been through worse!" Samshow shouted at his partner over the roar.

"I haven't, I don't think," Sand shouted back.

"It's exhilarating. Something truly exotic—a real first. An observed large meteor fall in midocean, and its results. We'd better alert all coasts."

"Who's going to write the paper?"

"We'll do it together."

"I locked down the equipment after the anomaly. We'll have to make another run when this clears up."

The *Discoverer*, Samshow thought, would weather the storm easily enough. It was not going to be a long blow. When he was sure of this, as the violent rain and waves declined, he retired to his quarters to look up the facts and figures and equations he would need to understand what had just happened. Sand staggered down the stairs and corridors, stopping in Samshow's hatchway long enough to say he was going to check again on his blessed gravimeters.

The next day, when it was their turn to present the story by radio to the expedition's chiefs in La Jolla, they had still not sorted out their findings.

One thing puzzled them both immensely. All three gravimeters had registered the "jag" simultaneously. Shock had not caused the anomaly; the gravimeters had been designed to be carried aboard aircraft as well as ships, and could weather relatively rough treatment handily. Besides, the shock had occurred after the appearance of the spikes.

Sand put together a list of hypotheses, and revealed one candidly to Samshow when they were alone. "It's simple, really," he said in the galley over a late breakfast of corned-beef hash and butter-soaked wheat toast. "I made some calculations and compared the spikes on the three traces. The three tubs aren't really far enough apart to make the results authoritative, but I checked the digital record of each spike and found a very small time interval between them. I can explain the time interval in only one way. Doing a tidal analysis, and subtracting the ship's reaction as a gravitated object, the traces show an enormous mass, about a hundred million tons, traveling in an arc overhead."

"Coming from what direction?" Samshow asked casually.

"Due north, I think."

"How far away?"

"Anywhere from a hundred to two hundred kilometers."

Samshow considered that for a moment. Whatever the fireball had been, it had been far too small to mass at anything like a hundred tons, much less a hundred million. It would have spread the Pacific out like coffee in a cup if it had been a mountain-sized meteoroid. "All right," he said. "We ignore it. It's an official anomaly."

"On all three gravimeters?" Sand asked, grinning damnably.

PERSPECTIVE

NBC National News Commentator Agnes Linder, November 2, 1996:
The newest twist in a very twisted election year, the arrival of visitors from space, almost defies imagination. United States citizens, recent polls show, are in a state of rigid disbelief.

The Australian extraterrestrials have arrived on Earth too soon, some pundits have said; we aren't ready for them, and we cannot begin to comprehend what they might mean to us.

Presidential candidate Beryl Cooper and her running mate, Edgar Farb, have been on the offensive, charging that President Crockerman is hiding information provided by the Australians, and questioning whether in fact the United States is not behind the destruction-some say self-destruction-of the robot representatives in the Great Victoria Desert.

The American people are not impressed with these charges. How many of us, I wonder, have fixed any emotional or rational response at all? The scandal of the destruction of the extraterrestrials refuses to spread; the Australian government's accusations of American complicity have been practically ignored around the world.

We have lived our lives on a globe undisturbed by outside forces, and now we are forced to expand our scale of thinking enormously. Western liberal tradition has encouraged an inward-turning, self-critical kind of politics, conservative in the true sense of the word, and President Crockerman is the heir to this tradition. The more forward-looking, expansive politics of Cooper and Farb have not yet struck a chord with Americans, if we are to believe the recent NBC poll, which gives Crockerman a rock-steady 30 percent lead just three days before voters go to the polls. This, without the President issuing any statements or making any policy regarding the Great Victoria Desert incidents.

26———

November 3

Mrs. Sarah Crockerman wore a solemn, stylishly tailored gray suit. Her thick brown hair was carefully coiffed, and as she poured Hicks a cup of coffee, he saw her hands were immaculately manicured, the fingernails painted a metallic bronze, glinting softly in the gray winter light entering through French windows behind the dining table. The dining room was furnished in coffee-colored Danish teak, spare but comfortable. Beyond the second-story windows lay the broad green expanse of the U.S. National Arboretum.

Except for a Secret Service agent assigned to Hicks, a stolid-faced fellow named Butler, they were alone in the Summit Street apartment.

"The President kept this flat rented largely at my insistence," she said, replacing the glass pot on its knitted pad. She handed him the cup of coffee and sat in the chair catercorner from him, her nyloned knees pushing up against the table leg as she faced him. "Few people know it's here. He thinks we might be able to keep the secret another month or two. After that, it's less my private hideaway, but it's still here. I hope you appreciate how much this secret means to me."

Butler had gotten off the phone and now stood by the window, facing the doorway. Hicks thought he resembled a bulldog, and Mrs. Crockerman a moderately plump poodle.

"My husband has told me about his preoccupations, naturally," she said. "I can't say I understand everything that's happening, or . . . that I agree with all of his conclusions. I've read the reports, most of them, and I've read the paper you prepared for him. He is not listening to you, you know."

Hicks said nothing, watching her over the rim of his cup. The coffee was very good.

"My husband is peculiar that way. He keeps advisors on long after they've served their purpose or have his ear. He tries to maintain an appearance of fairness and keeping an open mind, having those about him who disagree. But he doesn't listen very often. He is not listening to you."

"I realize that," Hicks said. "I've been moved out of the White House. To a hotel."

"So my secretary informs me. You're still on call should the President need you?"

Hicks nodded.

"This election has been sheer hell for him, even though he hasn't been campaigning hard. Their 'strategy.' Let Beryl Cooper hang herself. He's sensitive, and he doesn't like not campaigning. He's still not used to being top dog."

"My sympathies," Hicks said, wondering what she was getting at.

"I wanted to warn you. He's spending a lot of time with a man whose presence at the White House, especially during the campaign, upsets many of us. Have you ever heard of Oliver Ormandy?"

Hicks shook his head.

"He's well known in American religious circles. He's fairly intelligent, as such men go. He's kept his face out of politics and out of the news the past few years. All the other *fools*"—she practically spat out the word—"have turned themselves into clowns before the media's cyclops eye, but not Oliver Ormandy. He first met my husband during the campaign, at a dinner held at Robert James University. Do you know of that place?"

"Is that where they asked for permission to arm their security guards with machine pistols?"

"Yes."

"Ormandy's in charge of that?"

"No. He leaves that to one of the bellowing clowns. He glad-hands politicians in the background. Ormandy is quite sincere, you know. More coffee?"

Hicks extended his cup and she poured more.

"Bill has seen Ormandy several times the past week. I've asked Nancy, the President's executive secretary, what they discussed. At first she was reluctant to tell me, but . . . She was concerned. She was only in the room for the second meeting, for a few minutes. She said they were talking about the end of the world." Mrs. Crockerman's face might have been plastered on, her anger stiffened it so. "They were discussing God's plan for this nation. Nancy said Mr. Ormandy appeared exuberant."

Hicks stared at the table. What was there to say? Crockerman was President. He could see whom he pleased.

"I do not like that, Mr. Hicks. Do you?"

"Not at all, Mrs. Crockerman."

"What do you suggest?"

"As you say, he doesn't listen to me anymore."

"He doesn't listen to Carl or David or Irwin . . . or me. He's obsessed. He has been reading the Bible. The *crazy* parts of the Bible, Mr. Hicks. The book of Revelation. My husband was not like this a few weeks ago. He's changed."

"I'm very sorry."

"He's called Cabinet meetings. They're discussing economic impact. Talking about making an announcement after the election. There's nothing you could tell him . . . . ?" she asked. "He seemed to place great trust in you at first. Maybe even now. How did he come to trust you? He talked about you often."

"It was a difficult time for him," Hicks said. "He saw me after he met with the Guest. He'd read my book. I never agreed with his assessment . . ."

"Punishment. In our bedroom, that's the key word now. He almost smiles when he talks about Ormandy's use of the word.

Punishment. How very trite that sounds. My husband was never trite, and never a sucker for religious fanatics, politically or otherwise."

"This has changed all of us," Hicks said softly.

"I do not want my husband undone. This Guest found his weakness, when nobody in three decades of politics—and I've been with him all that time—has ever gotten to him. The Guest opened him wide, and Ormandy crept into the wound. Ormandy could destroy the President."

"I understand." *He could do worse than that,* Hicks thought.

"Will you *please* do something? Try talking with my husband again? I'll get you an appointment. He'll do that much for me, I'm sure." Mrs. Crockerman stared longingly at the French windows, as if they might be an escape. "It's even strained our marriage. I'll be with him on election eve, smiling and waving. But I'm thinking about staying here now. I can only take so much, Mr. Hicks. I cannot watch my husband undo himself."

The air in the chief of staff's office was thick with gloom.

Irwin Schwartz, face long and forehead pale, startling in contrast to his florid cheeks, sat on the edge of his desk with one leg drawn up as far as his paunch would allow, raised cuff exposing a long black sock and a few square inches of hairy white calf. A small flat-screen television perched on his desk like a family portrait, sound turned down. Again and again, the screen replayed the single videotaped record of the explosion of the Australian robot emissaries. Schwartz finally leaned over and poked the screen off with a thick finger.

Around him, David Rotterjack and Arthur Gordon stood, Arthur with hands in pockets, Rotterjack rubbing his chin.

"Secretary Lehrman and Mr. McClennan are with the President now," Schwartz said. "There's nothing I can say anymore. I don't think I have his confidence."

"Nor I," Rotterjack said.

"What about Hicks?" Arthur asked.

Schwartz shrugged. "The President moved him out to a hotel a week ago and won't see him. Sarah called a few minutes ago. She spoke with Hicks this morning, and she's working on getting an appointment for him. Everything's tight now. Kermit and I have had it out several times." Kermit Ferman was the President's appointments secretary.

"And Ormandy?"

"Sees the President every day, for at least an hour. Off the calendar."

Arthur couldn't get Marty out of his wandering thoughts. The boy's grinning face was detailed and sharp in memory, though static. Heir apparent. He could not conjure an overall picture of Francine's face, just individual features, and that bothered him.

"Carl's got one last chance," Rotterjack said.

"You think he's giving him the good old 'presidential' speech?" Schwartz asked.

Rotterjack nodded.

Arthur glanced between them, puzzled.

"He's going to talk to the President about what it means to be presidential," Schwartz explained. "Taking coals to Newcastle, if you ask me. The Man knows everything there is to know about presidentiality."

"The election's day after tomorrow. Time to remind him," Rotterjack said.

"You and I both know he's got this election sewed up, as much as any election *can* be. You don't understand what's going on in his head," Schwartz said.

"You're supposed to be his cushion, his buffer, goddammit," Rotterjack shouted, one arm shooting out suddenly and almost hitting Arthur. Arthur backed away a few inches but did not react otherwise. "You're supposed to keep the crazy idiots away from him."

"We've done everything we can to save him from himself," Schwartz said. "McClennan tried ignoring his suggestions about national preparation. I pushed the meetings with the governors back in the schedule, lost the timetable the President drew up, changed the subject in Cabinet meetings. The President just smiled and tolerated us and kept hammering on the subject. At least everybody's agreed to hold off until after the election and the inauguration. But between now, and whenever, we have to put up with Ormandy."

"I'd like to talk with him," Arthur said.

"So would we all. Crockerman doesn't specifically forbid it . . . but Ormandy never lingers long enough for any of us to confront him. The man's a goddamn shadow in the White House."

Rotterjack shook his head and grinned. "You'd think Ormandy was one of *them.*"

"Who?" Schwartz asked.

"The invaders."

Schwartz frowned. "See what's going to happen if the President goes public? *We're* even beginning to think like gullible idiots."

"Have you thought what could be happening?" Rotterjack persisted. "If they 'manufactured' the Guest, couldn't they make robots that look human, human enough to pass?"

"I'm more frightened about what that idea can do to us than I am about it's being true," Arthur said.

"Yeah, well, there it is," Rotterjack said. "Take it for what it's worth. Somebody out there is going to think of it."

"It'll tear us apart," Schwartz said. "Just what *they* might want. Christ, now I'm talking like that."

"Maybe it's just as well we bring it out in the open," Arthur said. "We haven't accomplished anything keeping it quiet."

"Not the way *he'd* released it," Rotterjack said. "What'll you do if McClennan fails to get his point across—again?" he asked Schwartz.

"Eventually, after the election, I could resign," Schwartz said, his tone flat, neutral. "He might want to put together a wartime Cabinet anyway."

"Will you?"

Schwartz stared down at the sky-blue carpet. Arthur, following his gaze, thought of the myriad of privileges suggested by that luxurious color, so difficult to keep clean. A myriad of attractions to keep men like Schwartz and Rotterjack working.

"No," Schwartz said. "I'm just too goddamn loyal. If he does this to me—to us, to all of us—I'll resent him like hell. But he'll still be the President."

"There are quite a few congressmen and senators who'll work to change that, if he does go public," Rotterjack said.

"Don't I know."

"They'd be the real patriots, you know, not you and I."

Schwartz's face filled with pained resentment and frank acknowledgment. He half nodded, half shook his head and stood up from the desk. "All right, David. But we've got to keep the White House together somehow. What else is there? Who'll take his place? The Veep?"

Rotterjack chuckled ironically.

"Right," Schwartz said. "Arthur, if I make an appointment—if I ram it down the President's throat—can you get Feinman out

here, and can you and Hicks and he do your best to . . . you
know? Do what we can't?"

"If it can be in the next day or so, and if there are no delays."

"Feinman's that sick?" Rotterjack asked.

"He's in treatment. It's difficult."

"Why couldn't you have found . . . never mind," Rotterjack
said.

"Feinman's the best," Arthur replied to the half-stated query.
Rotterjack nodded glumly.

"We'll give it a try," Arthur said.

Arthur walked through the afternoon crowds at Dulles, suit
hanging on him, hands in pockets. He knew all too well that he
resembled a scarecrow. He had lost ten pounds in the last two
weeks, and could ill afford it, but he was seldom hungry now.

Glancing at the American Airlines screen of arrivals and depar-
tures, he saw he had half an hour until Harry's plane landed. He
had a choice between forcing down a sandwich or calling Francine
and Marty.

Arthur was still trying to remember his wife's face. He could
picture nose, eyes, lips, forehead, the shape of her hands, breasts,
genitals, smooth warm white stomach and breasts the color of late
morning fog, the texture of her thick black hair. He could recall
her smell, warm and rich and breadlike, and the sound of her
voice. But not her face.

That made her seem so far away, and him so isolated. He had
spent ages, it seemed, in offices and in meetings. There was no
reality in an office, no reality among a group of men talking about
the fate of the Earth. Certainly no reality surrounding the President.

Reality was back by the river, back in the bedroom and the
kitchen of their house, but most especially under the trees with
the smooth hiss of wind and the rushing music of water. There he
would always be in touch with them, could be isolated and yet not
alone, out of sight of wife and son yet able to get back to them. If
death should come, would Arthur be away from them, still performing his separate duties . . . ?

The airport, as always, was crowded. A large tight knot of Japanese passed by. He felt a special kinship with Japanese, more so
than with foreigners of his own race. Japanese were so intensely
interested, and desirous of smooth relations, one-on-one. He

walked around the knot, passed a German family, husband and wife and two daughters trying to riddle their boarding passes.

He could not remember Harry's face.

The open phone booth, with its ineffective plastic half bubble, accepted his credit card and thanked him in a warm middle-aged female voice, teacherlike and yet less stern, impersonally interested. Synthetic.

The phone rang six times before he remembered: Francine had told him the night before that Marty would have a dentist's appointment in the morning.

He hung up and crossed a central courtyard to a snack shop, ordering a turkey-pastrami sandwich and Coke. Twenty-five minutes. Sitting on a tall stool by a diminutive table, he forced himself to eat the entire sandwich.

Bread. Mayonnaise. Bird taste of turkey beneath an overlay of pastrami. Solid but not convincing. He made a face and took the last meatless dry double wedge of bread into his mouth.

For a moment, and no more, he felt himself slide into a spiritual ditch, a little quiet gutter of despair. To simply give up, give in, open his arms to the darkness, shed all responsibility to country, to wife and son, to himself. To end the game—that was all it was, no? Take his piece from the board, watch the board swept clean, a new game set up. Rest. Oddly, coming out of that gutter, he took encouragement and strength from the thought that if indeed they were going to be swept from the board, he could then rest, and there would be an end. *Funny how the mind works.*

At fifteen minutes after two, he stood at the gate, to one side of a crowd of waiting friends and families. The open double doors brought forth business men and women in trim suits gray and brown and that strange shade of iridescent blue that was so much in fashion, peacock's eyes Francine called it; three young children holding hands and followed by a woman in knee-length black skirt and austere white blouse, and then Harry, clutching a leather valise and looking thinner, older, tired.

"All right," Harry said after they hugged and shook hands. "You have me for forty-eight hours, max, and then the doctor wants me back to blunt more needles. Jesus. You look as bad as I do."

In the small government car, winding through the maze of a bare concrete parking garage, Arthur explained the circumstances of their meeting with the President. "Schwartz is putting aside half an hour in Crockerman's schedule. It's getting very tight. He's supposed to be in New Hampshire this evening for a final campaign rally. Hicks, you and I will be in the Oval Office with him, undisturbed, for that half hour. We'll do what we can to convince him he's wrong."

"And if we don't?" Harry asked. Had his eyes lightened in color? They seemed less brown than tan now, almost bleached.

Arthur could only shrug. "How are you feeling?"

"Not as bad as I look."

"That's good," Arthur said, trying to relax that anonymous something in his throat. He smiled thinly at Harry.

"Thanks," Harry said. "I have an excuse, at least. Is everybody else around here going to look like extras in a vampire movie?"

"What do you weigh now?" Arthur asked. The car moved out into watery sunlight. Snow threatened.

"I'm back to fighting trim. I weigh what I weighed in high school. Graduation day."

"What's the prognosis?"

Harry crossed his arms. "Still fighting."

Arthur glanced at him, did a frank double take, and asked, "Is that a wig?"

"You guessed it," Harry said. "Enough of that shit. Tell me about Ormandy."

The wide double doors to the Oval Office opened and three men stepped out. Schwartz nodded at them. Arthur recognized the chairman of the Securities and Exchange Commission and the Secretary of the Treasury.

"An emergency meeting," Schwartz murmured after they had passed. Hicks raised his eyebrow in query. "They're thinking of implementing Section 4 of the Emergency Banking Act, and Section 19a of the Securities and Exchange Act."

"What are those?" he asked.

"Temporarily close the banks and the stock exchanges," Schwartz said. "If the President makes his speech."

The President's secretary, Nancy Congdon, came to the doors and smiled at the four of them. "Just a few minutes, Irwin," she said, silently easing them shut.

"Do you need a chair?" Schwartz asked Harry. Harry shook his head calmly. He was already used to people being solicitous. *He takes it with something beyond dignity—with aplomb.*

The secretary opened the doors and invited them in.

Mrs. Hampton had redecorated the President's office, hanging the three windows behind the President's large, ornately decorated desk with white curtains and ordering a new oval green rug with the presidential seal. The room seemed filled with light, verdant and springlike despite the gray winter skies outside. Through the windows, Arthur caught a glimpse of the snow-patched Rose Garden. He had last been in the Oval Office a year and a half before.

Crockerman sat behind the Victorian-era desk, looking over a stack of briefs tucked into brown folders. Some of the folders, Arthur noticed, were marked DIRNSA—Director, National Security Agency. Others were from the offices of the Secretary of the Treasury and the Securities and Exchange Commission. *He's not going off half cocked. He's preparing, and he deeply believes in what he's doing. He hasn't stopped being presidential.*

"Hello, Irwin, Arthur . . ." Crockerman stood and reached across the desk to shake their hands. "Trevor, Harry." He pointed to the four leather-bottomed, cane-backed chairs arranged before the desk. Addressing Hicks in particular, he said, "Sarah mentioned I might be meeting with you."

"I think we've all joined forces, Mr. President," Schwartz said.

"Are you feeling up to this, Harry?" Crockerman asked, politely solicitous.

"Yes, Mr. President," Harry replied smoothly. "I'm not needed back with the mice and monkeys until the day after tomorrow."

"We need you here, Harry," the President said earnestly. "We can't afford to lose you now."

"That's not what I've been hearing, Mr. President," Harry said. Crockerman showed some puzzlement. "You haven't been listening to anybody I trust around here, much less myself."

"Gentlemen," Crockerman said, raising his eyebrows. "Time to speak openly. And I apologize for being inaccessible recently. Time has been precious."

Schwartz leaned forward on his chair, clasping his hands. As he spoke, he raised his eyes slowly from his feet to Crockerman's face. "Mr. President, we're not here to mince words. I've told Harry, and Trevor, and Arthur, that it's going to take some powerful persuasion to move you back onto a rational course. They've come loaded for bear."

Crockerman nodded and rested his hands lightly on the edge of the desk, as if he might push away at any moment. His expression remained pleasant, alert.

"Mr. President, the First Lady did indeed speak to me," Hicks said.

"She's not speaking to me, you know," Crockerman said levelly. "Or not often, at any rate. She doesn't share our convictions."

"Yes," Hicks said. "Or rather, no . . . Mr. President, my colleagues—" He cast a pleading look at Arthur.

"We assume you're still planning to tell the public about the Death Valley bogey," Arthur said, "and about the Guest."

"The story will break soon one way or the other," Crockerman said. "It must be kept quiet past the election and the inauguration, but after that . . ." He lifted three fingers from their grip on the edge of the desk and shrugged slightly.

"We're not at all sure about your emphasis, sir . . ." Arthur paused. "Surrender will not sit well with the country."

Crockerman hardly blinked. "Surrender. Accommodation. Nasty words, aren't they? But what choice have we against superhuman forces?"

"We do not know they are superhuman, sir," Harry said.

"It would take us thousands, perhaps millions of years to rival their technology—if indeed we can even call it technology. Think of the power to destroy an entire moon, and push its fragments into collisions with other worlds . . ."

"We don't know that these events are connected," Arthur said. "But I think we could equal them with a couple of hundred years of progress."

"What does it matter, two centuries or two millennia? They can still destroy our world."

"We don't know that," Schwartz said.

"We don't even know of whom we speak when we say 'they,' " Hicks said.

"Angels, powers, aliens. Whatever they might be."

"Mr. President," Hicks said, "we are not facing God's wrath."

"It seems we face something equivalent in force, whatever the ultimate source," Crockerman said. "Can something so catastrophic happen to the Earth without God's approval? We are His children. His punishments are not random, not when they're on such a huge scale."

Hicks noted that the President's pronoun for God had assumed traditional gender now. Was that Ormandy's doing?

"We have no evidence the Earth can be destroyed," Harry said. "What we need . . . we need a smoking gun, something that proves that the power they claim to have does indeed belong to them. We don't have a smoking gun."

"They reveal their intentions clearly enough," Crockerman said. "The self-destruction of the Australian robots shows them to be bringers of false testimony. When their lies are discovered, and pointed out to them, they vanish. Their message of hope is a deception. I believe I knew that, sensed it, before the news from Australia arrived. Ormandy certainly did."

"None of us puts any faith in Mr. Ormandy," Schwartz said.

Crockerman was obviously irritated by this, but kept his calm. "Ormandy does not expect the accolade of scientists. He—and I— believe affairs have passed out of the control of our particular witch doctors. Not to show disrespect for your hard work and expertise. He and I realized there was a job to do here, and that we are the only ones capable of doing it."

"What exactly will your job be, Mr. President?" Arthur asked.

"Not an easy one, I assure you. Our country doesn't believe in giving up without a fight. I acknowledge that much. But we cannot fight this. Nor can we go to our fate ignorant of what is happening. We have to face the music courageously. That's my job—to help my country face the end bravely."

Crockerman's face was pale and his hands, still pushing on the edge of the desk, trembled slightly. He might have been close to tears.

Nothing was said for several long seconds. Arthur felt a blanket of shock closing around him. *Microcosm of what the country will feel. The world. Not a message we want to hear.*

"There are alternatives, Mr. President. We can take action against the bogeys, both in Australia and Death Valley," Harry said.

"They're isolated," Schwartz said. "The political repercussions . . . almost nil. Even if we fail."

"We can't simply do nothing," Arthur said.

"We can do nothing effective, truly," Crockerman said. "I think it would be cruel to raise false hopes."

"More cruel to dash all hope, Mr. President," Schwartz said. "Are you going to close the banks and stock exchanges?"

"It's being seriously considered."

"Why? To preserve the economy? With the end of the world in sight?"

"To keep calm, to maintain dignity. To keep people at their jobs and in their homes."

Hicks's face was flushed now. "This is insanity, Mr. President," he said. "I am not a citizen of the United States, but I cannot imagine a man in your office . . . with your power and responsibility . . ." He waved his hands helplessly and stood. "I can assure you the British will not react so mildly."

Ganging up on him, Arthur thought. *Still can't see her face.*

Crockerman pulled open the folder marked DIRNSA. He pulled out a group of photographs in Mylar envelopes and spread them on the table. "I don't think you've seen the latest from the Puzzle Palace," he said. "Our NSA people have been very busy. The National Reconnaissance Office has compared Earth satellite photographs from the last eighteen months for almost all areas of the globe. I believe you initiated this search, Arthur."

"Yes, sir."

"They've found an anomaly in the Mongolian People's Republic. Something that wasn't there a year ago. It looks like a huge boulder." He gently pushed the photographs at Schwartz, who examined them and passed them on to Arthur. Arthur compared three key photographs, beautiful computer-enhanced abstractions of blue-gray, brown, red, and ivory. A white circle about an inch wide surrounded a bean-shaped black spot in one photograph. In two earlier, otherwise practically identical photos, the black spot was absent.

"That makes a triad," Crockerman said. "All in remote areas."

"Have the aliens talked with the Mongolians, the Russians?" Arthur asked. The Mongolian People's Republic, despite a fiction of autonomy, was controlled by the Russians.

"Nobody knows yet," the President said. "If there are three, there could easily be more."

"What sort of . . . mechanism do you envisage them using?" Harry asked. "You and Mr. Ormandy."

"We have no idea. We do not second-guess the agents of supreme power. Do you?"

"I'm willing to try," Harry said.

"Will you disband the task force?" Arthur asked.

"No. I'd like you to keep on studying, keep asking questions. I am still capable of admitting we might be wrong. Neither Mr.

Ormandy nor I are fanatics. We must talk with the Russians, and the Australians, and urge cooperation."

"Can we ask you to postpone your speech, Mr. President?" Schwartz asked. "Until we are more sure of our position?"

"You already have almost two months. I do not know to the day when the speech will be delivered, Irwin. But once it becomes clear to me when I must speak, it will not be postponed. I must go with my convictions. Ultimately, that's what this office is all about."

The four of them stood in the hallway outside, their half hour concluded, clutching copies of the NSA report.

"Fat lot of good my being here did," Harry said.

"I'm sorry, gentlemen," Schwartz said.

"He's going to be very effective on television," Hicks said. "He almost convinces me."

"You know the worst of it?" Arthur asked as they left through a rear door, Schwartz following them out to their cars. "He's not crazy."

"Neither are we," Schwartz said.

An hour after they left the White House, Hicks, Arthur, and Feinman ate lunch at Yugo's, a steak and rib restaurant favored by those in the know, despite its location in one of Washington's less decorative neighborhoods. They ate in silence, Hicks finishing his plate while Arthur and Harry barely picked at theirs. Harry had ordered a salad, a wilted and blue-cheese-overloaded mistake.

"We've done everything we can," Arthur said. Harry shrugged.

"What next, then?" Hicks asked. "Carry on scientists?"

"We haven't been shut down," Harry said.

"You've just been ignored by your Chief Executive," Hicks commented dryly.

"You've always been the odd man out here, haven't you?" Harry said. "Now you know how we feel. But at least we had a definite niche to fill."

"A role to play in the grand comedy," Hicks said.

Harry began to bristle but Arthur touched his arm. "He's right." Harry nodded reluctantly.

"So begins phase two," Arthur said. "I'd like for you to join us in a larger effort." He stared at Hicks.

"Outside the White House?"

"Yes."

"You've made plans."

"My plans take me back to Los Angeles, and nowhere else," Harry said.

"Harry will consult," Arthur said. "Presidents' minds can be changed any number of ways. If the direct approach doesn't work . . ." He smoothed his fingers across the granite-patterned Formica tabletop with a squeak. "We work at a grass-roots level."

"The President's a shoo-in, as you say . . ." Hicks reminded.

"There are ways of removing standing presidents. I think, once he makes his speech—"

Harry sighed. "Do you realize how long impeachment and a trial would take?"

"Once he makes his speech," Arthur continued, "all of us at this table are going to be in big demand on the media circuit. Trevor, your book is going to be the hottest thing in publishing . . . And we're all going to be on talk shows, news interviews, around the world. We can do our best . . ."

"Against the President? He's a very popular figure," Hicks said.

"Schwartz hit the nail on the head, though," Arthur said, picking up the tab from its plastic tray. "Americans hate the thought of surrender."

Hicks looked over the neatly folded clothes in his suitcase with some satisfaction. If he could pack his belongings with dignity and style, while all about him hung their laundry out to dry . . .

The number of stories about the self-destruction of the Australian aliens and the Death Valley mystery had declined in both newspapers and television. Election eve was gathering all the attention. The world seemed to be taking a deep breath, not yet consciously aware of what was happening, but suspecting, anticipating.

Hicks jumped as the desk phone beeped. He answered with a nervous jerk of the handset, fumbling it. "Hello."

"I have a phone call for Trevor Hicks from Mr. Oliver Ormandy," a woman stated in pleasant, well-modulated midwestern American.

"This is Hicks."

"Just a moment, please."

"I'm pleased to speak with you," Ormandy said. "I've admired your writings."

"Thank you." Hicks was too surprised to say much more.

"I believe you know who I am, and the people I represent. I've been discussing some things with the President, as a friend and advisor . . . sometimes, as a religious counselor. I think we should meet and talk sometime soon. Could you make a space in your schedule? I can have a car pick you up, bring you back, no difficulties there, I hope."

"Certainly," Hicks said. "Today?"

"Why not. I'll have a car pick you up at one."

Precisely at one, a white Chrysler limousine with a white landau roof drove up in the hotel loading zone and Hicks climbed in through the automatically opened door. The door closed with a quiet hiss and the driver, a pale, black-haired young man in a conservative dark blue business suit, smiled pleasantly through the glass partition.

Snow lay in white and brown ridges, rucked up at the street edges by plows. This was one of the coldest and wettest falls in memory. The air smelled unusually sharp and clean, intoxicating, pouring against his face through the window, opened a small crack by the driver at Hicks's request.

The car took him out of the concentric circles and confusing traffic loops of the Capital and into the suburbs, along expressways lined with young skeletal maples and out to country. An hour had passed when the Chrysler turned into the parking lot of a modest motel. The driver guided him through the lobby to the second floor and knocked on a room at the rear corner of the building. The door opened.

Ormandy, in his middle forties and balding, wore black pants and a gray dress shirt. His face was bland, almost childlike, but alert. His greeting was perfunctory. The driver closed the door and they were alone in the small, spare room.

Ormandy suggested he take an armchair by a circular table near the window. Hicks sat, watching the man closely. Ormandy seemed reluctant to get down to business, but since he could obviously manufacture no small talk, he turned abruptly and said, "Mr. Hicks, I have become very confused in the past few weeks. Do you know what is happening? Can you explain it to me?"

"Surely the President—"

"I'd like you to explain it to me. In clear language. The President is surrounded by experts, if you know what I mean."

Hicks drew his lips together and leaned his head to one side, organizing his words. "I assume you mean the spacecraft."

"Yes, yes, the invasion," Ormandy said.

"If it is an invasion." Now he was being overly cautious, reluctant to be pushed into conclusions.

"What is it?" Ormandy's eyes were childlike in their openness, willing to be taught.

"To put it bluntly, it seems that we've fallen in the path of automatons, robots, seeking to destroy our planet."

"Could mere machines do such a thing?" Ormandy asked.

"I do not know. Not human-made machines."

"These are Godlike powers you're discussing."

"Yes." Hicks started to rise. "I've been over all this with the President. I do not see the point in bringing me here, when you've advised the President to act contrary to—"

"Please sit. Be patient with me. I'm hardly the ogre you all think I am. I am way out of my depth, and just two nights ago, that really came home to me. I've talked with the President, and made my conclusions known to him . . . But I have not been at all sure of myself."

Hicks sat back slowly. "Then I presume you have specific questions."

"I do. What would it take to destroy the Earth? Would it be significantly harder than, say, destroying this place called Europa?"

"Yes," Hicks said. "It would take much more energy to destroy the Earth."

"Would it be done all at once, a cataclysm? Or could it begin in one place, spread out, like a war?"

"I don't really know."

"Could it begin first in the Holy Land?"

"There don't seem to be any bogeys in the Holy Land," Hicks said dryly.

Ormandy acknowledged that with a nod, his frown deepening. "Could there be a way of saying, scientifically, whether aliens can be considered angels?"

"No," Hicks said, smiling at the absurdity. But Ormandy did not see the absurdity.

"Could they be acting on behalf of a higher authority?"

"If they are indeed robots, as they seem to be, then I presume they are acting on the authority of biological beings somewhere. But we can't even be sure of that. Civilizations based on mechanical—"

"What about creatures that have gone beyond biology—creatures of light, eternal beings?"

Hicks shrugged. "Speculation," he said.

Ormandy's childlike face exhibited intense agitation. "I am way out of my depth here, Mr. Hicks. This is not clear-cut. We're certainly not dealing with angels with flaming swords. We're not dealing with anything predicted in apocalyptic literature."

"Not in *religious* literature," Hicks corrected.

"I don't read science fiction much," Ormandy said pointedly.

"More's the pity."

Ormandy smirked. "And I'm not in the mood to cross knives with you or anybody else. What I'm saying is, I'm not sure I can present this to my people in a way they'll understand. If I tell them it's God's will . . . How can *I* be sure of that?"

"As you said, there seem to be Godlike forces at work," Hicks offered. *Perverse, perverse!*

"My people still think in terms of angels and demons, Mr. Hicks. They dearly love halos of light and brilliancies, thrones and powers and dominations. They eat it up. They're like children. And no one can deny there is beauty and power in that kind of theology. But this . . . This is cold and political, deceptive, and I don't feel comfortable attributing such deception to God. If this is a work of Satan, or of Satan's forces, then . . . The President, with my help, I admit, is about to make a tremendous mistake."

"Can you get him to change his mind?" Hicks asked, less eagerly than he might have.

"I doubt it. Remember, he called me, not the other way around. That's why I say I'm out of my depth. I'm not so proud I can't admit that."

"Have you told him your misgivings?"

"No. We haven't met since I . . . became unsure."

"Are you fixed in a theological interpretation?"

"Emotionally, by all that my parents and teachers handed down to me, I must believe that God intervenes in all our affairs."

"What you're saying, Mr. Ormandy, is that when push comes to shove, and the end of the world comes on apace, you no longer yearn for apocalypse?"

Ormandy said nothing, but his frown intensified. He held out his beseeching hands, ambiguous, opinion fixed neither one way nor the other.

"Can you talk to the President again, at least *try* to get him to change his mind?" Hicks asked.

"I wish he'd never involved me," Ormandy said. He hung his head back and massaged his neck muscles with both hands. "But I'll try."

27——

November 5

Arthur was in a late night conference with astronomers in Washington, discussing the appearance of the ice objects and their possible connection with Europa, when word came that William D. Crockerman was projected to win election as President of the United States. Nobody was surprised. Beryl Cooper conceded the next morning, at one A.M., while the conference was still proceeding.

No conclusion was reached by the astronomers at the meeting. If the ice chunks had come from Europa, which seemed undeniable given their paths and composition, then their present almost straight-line orbits had to be artificial, and some connection with the extraterrestrials could be assumed. The facts were clear enough: both were fresh, almost pure water-ice; the smaller of the two, barely 180 kilometers in diameter, was traveling at a velocity of some 20 kilometers per second and would strike Mars on December 21, 1996; the larger, some 250 kilometers in diameter, was traveling at about 37 kilometers per second and would strike Venus on February 4, 1997. Whatever had caused Europa's destruction had not warmed the objects substantially, perhaps because ablation had carried away the heat. Both were quite cold and would lose little of their mass to vaporization by the sun's energy. Consequently, neither would show much of a cometary coma, and both would be visible only to sharp-eyed observers with telescopes or high-powered binoculars.

Arthur left Washington the next day, convinced that his team now had solid evidence for making a connection. He had sufficient time, he thought, to prepare a case and present it to Crockerman, that all of these events were linked, and that some grand strategy could now be worked out.

He could not convince himself the President-elect would listen, however.

November 10

Major Mary Rigby, the latest in their series of duty officers, buzzed them all at six-thirty in the morning to listen to the radio. Shaw bunched his pillows up and sat in his cot as "Hail to the Chief" played—a true Crockerman touch—and the Speaker of the House listened gravely to the announcement of the appearance of the President-elect of the United States.

"Maybe the old fart's going to write our ticket out of here," Minelli said, his voice raspy from a night of protests and shouting. Minelli was not doing well at all. This infuriated Edward. But cold, subdued fury had been his state of mind for the last two weeks. This experience was going to leave all of them warped in one way or another. Reslaw and Morgan said very little anymore.

"Mr. Speaker, honorable members of the House of Representatives, fellow citizens," the President began. "I have called this emergency conference after weeks of deep thought, and many hours of consultation with trusted advisors and experts. I have an extraordinary announcement to make, and a perhaps even more extraordinary request.

"You have no doubt been following with as much interest as I the events taking place in Australia. These events in the beginning seemed to bring hope to our stricken planet, the hope of Godlike intervention from outside, of those who would act to save us from ourselves. We began to feel that perhaps our difficulties were indeed only those of a young species, faltering in its early footsteps. Now these hopes have been dashed, and we find ourselves in even deeper confusion.

"My sympathies lie with Prime Minister Stanley Miller of Australia. The loss of the three messengers from outer space, and the mystery surrounding their destruction—perhaps self-destruction —is a deep shock to us all. But it is time to confess that it has been less of a shock to me and to a number of my advisors. For we have been following a similar series of events within our own country, kept secret until now for reasons which will soon become clear."

Disembarking from a shuttle bus at Los Angeles International Airport, on his way to Death Valley and then to Oregon for three days' rest, Arthur entered a lounge area to await his taxi and heard the President's voice. He sat before a color television with eleven other travelers, his face ashen. *He's jumping the gun.*

"Late last September, three young geologists discovered a hill in the desert not far from Death Valley, in California. The hill was not on their maps. Near this hill they found an extraterrestrial being, an individual in ill health. They brought this individual to a nearby desert town and notified authorities. The extraterrestrial being—"

Trevor Hicks listened from his Washington hotel room, the remains of breakfast spread on a serving tray at the foot of the bed. Just yesterday, he had learned that Mrs. Crockerman had moved to her flat permanently. Later that afternoon, he had heard the first rumors of David Rotterjack's resignation.

The President-elect's version of what happened in the Vandenberg laboratory was clear enough; he could find no fault so far.

". . . And as I spoke with this being, this visitor from another world, the story it told me was chilling. I have never been so deeply and emotionally affected in my life. It spoke of a journey across ages, of the death of its home world, and of the agency of this destruction—the very vehicle which had brought it to Earth, now landed in Death Valley and disguised as a volcanic cinder cone."

Ithaca called Harry in from the bathroom, where he had just finished taking his shower. She wrapped him in a thick terry robe as he stood before the television, feeling how warm his skin was. "Great fucking birds flapping in the air," he breathed.

"What?" Ithaca asked.

"He's making the announcement now. Listen to him. Just listen to him."

"When I asked the Guest if it believed in God, it replied in a steady, certain voice, 'I believe in punishment.'" The President paused, staring across the fully attended house. "My dilemma, and the dilemma of all my advisors, military and civilian, and of all our scientists, was simple. Could we believe that our extraterrestrial visitor and the visitors in Australia were linked? They told such different stories . . ."

There was a knock on Trevor's door. He closed his robe and hurried to open it, hardly even seeing who was outside, his attention still focused on the television.

"Hicks, I owe you an apology." It was Carl McClennan, dressed in a raincoat and clutching a bottle of something wrapped in a brown paper bag. "That's him, isn't it?"

"Yes, come in, come in." Hicks didn't bother to ask why McClennan was here.

"I've resigned," McClennan said. "I read his speech last night. The bastard wouldn't listen to any of us."

"Shhh," Hicks said, holding his finger to his lips.

"I wish that I brought news of some comforting solution to all who listen to me today. But I do not. I have never been a faithful churchgoer. Still, within myself I have held my own faith, and thought it wise, as the leader of this nation, not to impose this faith on others who might disagree. Now, however, through these extraordinary events, I have had my faith altered, and I can no longer keep silent. I believe we face incontrovertible evidence, proof if you will, that our days are numbered, and that our time on Earth—the time of the Earth itself—will soon be at an end. I have sought advice from those with more spiritual experience than I, and they have counseled me. I now believe that we are facing the Apocalypse predicted in the Revelation of John, and that on Earth, the forces of good and evil have made themselves known. Whether these forces be angels and demons, or extraterrestrials, seems to be of no importance whatsoever. I could say that I have spoken with an angel, but that does not seem literally true—"

* * *

"He's even departing from his text. *Damn* him," McClennan shouted, sitting with a bounce on the bed next to Hicks. "Doesn't he understand what he's unleashing? What social—"

"Please," Hicks admonished.

"I can only conclude that in some fashion, our history on Earth has been judged, and we have been found inadequate. Whether the flaw lies in our bodies, or in our minds, it is clear that the history of human existence does not satisfy the Creator, and that He is working to wipe the slate clean, and begin again. To do this, He has sent mighty machines, mighty forces which could begin, at any moment, to heat this Earth in God's forge, and beat it to pieces on a heavenly anvil."

The President paused again. Raised voices on the floor of Congress threatened to drown him out, and the Speaker had to rap his gavel many long minutes. The camera pulled back to show Crockerman surrounded by a phalanx of Secret Service men, their faces grim, trying to look in all directions at once.

"Please," the President pleaded. "I must conclude."

The noise finally subsided. Sporadic shouts of anger and disbelief rose from the representatives.

"I can only say to my people, and the inhabitants of Earth, that the time has come for us all to pray fervently for salvation, in whatever form it might come, whether we can expect it or not, or even whether we truly deserve salvation. The Forge of God cannot be appeased, but perhaps there is hope for each of us, in our private thoughts, to make peace with God, and find a way out from under the blows of His anger and disappointment."

Sitting in the airport lounge, a woman weeping softly beside him, several men loudly arguing with each other and the television screen, Arthur Gordon could only think of Francine and Martin.

"All hell's going to break loose," a bulky middle-aged black man shouted as he stalked out of the lounge.

"We'd better not fly now," a young man told the pregnant girl, hardly more than a teenager, sitting next to him. "They should ground all flights."

Trying to stay calm, angry at how deeply the speech had affected him, Arthur made his way through the morning crowds to an airline counter to again check his reservations to Las Vegas.

McClennan had stopped his tirade of swearing and now stood by the blank television, fumbling at a cigarette and lighter. He still wore his raincoat. Hicks had not moved from the edge of the bed.

"I'm sorry," McClennan said. "Christ, I haven't smoked in five years. I'm a goddamned disgrace."

"What will you do, now that you've resigned?" Hicks asked. *What an amazing situation. Straight inside line on this story.*

McClennan gave up on the cigarette in disgust. He flung it into the hotel ashtray, on top of an unused book of matches, and more gently lay his plastic lighter beside it. "I suppose the President will appoint replacements for David and myself. I imagine Schwartz will stay on. I imagine just about everybody will stay on." McClennan looked at Hicks with suspicion. "And you'll write about all of it, won't you?"

"I suppose I might, in the long run."

"Do you think he's crazy?" McClennan asked, pointing at the blank screen.

Hicks considered the question. "No."

"Do you think . . ." and here the rage returned, making McClennan's hands tremble, "he's violating his oath of office, to carry out the United States Constitution and promote the general welfare?"

"He's calling them as he sees them," Hicks said. "He thinks the end of the world is at hand."

"Christ, even if it is . . ." McClennan pulled out the desk chair and sat down slowly. "He's in trouble. He's showing his weakness. I wouldn't be surprised if there's a move now to block the inauguration, or to impeach him."

"On what grounds?" Hicks asked.

"Incompetence. Failure to promote the general welfare. Hell, I don't know . . ."

"Has he done anything illegal?"

"We've never had a President go nuts in office. Not since Nixon, anyway. But then, you think he isn't nuts. Listen, he disagreed with you, even after he brought you into the inner circle . . . What is he trying to do?"

Hicks had already answered that question, after a fashion, and saw no reason to do it again.

"All right," McClennan said. "What he's doing, what it all comes down to, is he's surrendering without a single shot being fired. We have no idea what these . . . bastards, these machines, these aliens, can do. We can't even be sure they're here to destroy the Earth. Is that even *possible?* Can you tear a world apart, or kill everything on its surface?"

"We ourselves can kill all life on Earth, if we so choose," Hicks reminded him.

"Yes, but the Guest talked about leaving nothing but rubble behind. Is that possible?"

"I suppose it is. You'd have to unleash enough energy to place most of the Earth's mass into orbit about itself, so to speak, or to give it escape velocity. That's an awful lot of energy."

"How much? Could we do it?"

"I don't think so. Not with all the nuclear weapons we have now. We couldn't even begin to."

"How advanced would a . . . Jesus, a civilization have to be to do that?"

Hicks shrugged. "If we posit a straight line of development from where we are now, with the rate of major breakthroughs increasing, perhaps a century, perhaps two."

"Could we fight them off? If they have that ability?"

Hicks shook his head, uncertain. McClennan took the answer for a negative. "So he calls them as he sees them. No way out. What if they aren't here to destroy the Earth, just to confuse us, set us back, keep us from competing . . . You know, like we might have done to the Japanese, if we'd known what they'd put us through, in the twentieth century . . . ?"

"The aliens are doing a good job of that, certainly."

"Right." McClennan stood again.

"What are *you* going to do?"

The ex–national security advisor stared blankly at the window. His look reminded Hicks of the expression on Mrs. Crockerman's face. Bleak, close to despair, beyond tears.

"I'll work in the background to save his ass," McClennan said. "So will Rotterjack. Damn us all, we're dedicated to that man." He raised his fist. "By the time we're done, that son of a bitch Ormandy won't know what happened. He is going to be one dead albatross."

28———

With three hours until his flight to Las Vegas, Arthur decided there would be time to take a taxi to Harry's house in the Cheviot Hills.

The cab took him up the San Diego Freeway and through a brightly decorated but impoverished Los Angeles barrio.

"D'ya hear what the President said, man?" the driver asked, glancing over the seat at Arthur.

"Yes," Arthur said.

"Isn't that something, what he said? Scared the piss out of me. Wonder how much of it is true, or whether, you know, he's gone off his nut."

"I don't know," Arthur replied. He felt strangely exhilarated. Everything was coming into focus now. He could actually see the problem laid out before him as if on a road map. His weariness and resignation had vanished. Now he was enriched by a deep, convicted fury, his distance and objectivity scorched away. The air through the cab window was sweet and intoxicating.

Lieutenant Colonel Albert Rogers finished listening to the recording of the broadcast and sat in the back of the trailer for several minutes, numb. He felt betrayed. What the President had said could not possibly be true. The men at the Furnace had not yet heard the speech, but there was no way he was going to keep it from them. How could he soften it for them?

"The bastard's surrendered," he murmured. "He's just left us here."

Rogers stood in the rear door of the trailer and looked at the cinder cone, dark and nondescript in the full morning light. "I can take a nuke right up inside that son of a bitch," he said quietly. "I can carry it in and stand over it until it goes off."

Not without the President's authority.

Actually, that wasn't entirely true.

But the President wouldn't actually stop them from making an attempt to defend themselves . . . would he? He hadn't said as much. He had simply stated that he thought it unlikely . . . what were his words? Rogers returned to the TV monitor and ran the tape back. ". . . The time has come for us all to pray fervently for salvation, in whatever form it might come, whether we can expect it or not . . ."

What did that mean?

And who would give Rogers his orders, the proper orders, now?

"He's feeling weak today. The trip to Washington didn't help him any," Ithaca said, leading Arthur to the bedroom. Harry lay back on thick white pillows, eyes closed. He looked worse than when they had parted a week ago. His facial flesh was sallow and blotchy. His breathing was regular, but when he opened his eyes, they seemed washed out, unenthusiastic. He smiled at Arthur and grasped his hand firmly.

"I'm going to resign," Harry said.

Arthur started to protest, but Harry waved it off. "Not because of that speech. I'm not going to be much use. I'm still fighting, but . . . It's getting worse very fast. I'm on a short rope. I can't leave town anymore, and I'm going to be in a hospital all the time by next week. You don't need that kind of grief now."

"I need *you*, Harry," Arthur said.

"Yeah. God knows I'm sorry. I'd much rather be up and about. You have a tough fight now, Arthur. What are you going to do?"

Arthur shook his head slowly. "McClennan and Rotterjack have resigned. The President hasn't given any orders to the task force."

"He wouldn't dare disband the group now."

"No, he'll keep us together, but I doubt he'll let us do anything. I talked to Hicks a few hours ago, and from what he says, Crockerman's even gone a step beyond Ormandy. Apocalypse. Get your papers in order. Here comes the auditor."

"He can't be all that . . ." Harry shook his head. "Can he?"

"I haven't talked to him since we went into the Oval Office together. Now comes the media sideshow. We are going to be roasted alive over a slow fire. Since I have no specific orders, I'm going to check into the Furnace, and then go back to Oregon for a few days. Hide out."

"What about the people in detention? Why are we holding them? They're healthy."

"They're certainly no security risk," Arthur agreed.

"We have the authority to let them go, don't we?"

"We're still ranked just below the President. I'll call Fulton." He still held Harry's hand. He hadn't let it go since sitting on the bed. "You've got to win this one, Harry."

"Feeling mortal yourself, huh?" Harry's face was serious. "You know, even Ithaca . . . She cries openly sometimes now. We cried together last night after she drove me back from the tests."

"Nobody's giving up on you," Arthur said with surprising vehemence. "If your damned doctors can't . . . we'll find other doctors. *I need you.*"

"I feel like a real shit, letting you down," Harry said.

"You know that's a—"

"I mean it. I am very sick now. I don't feel it yet, but in a week or two they'll start other treatments, and I'll be a wreck. I won't be able to think straight. So let me tell you now. We have to start fighting back."

"Fighting the Furnace, the Rock?"

"They've got us confused. They've accomplished that much . . . whoever they are. Blowing up their emissaries. Jesus! What a masterstroke. Giving us two stories, then making both seem like lies. And we've been a real good audience. It's time to do what we can."

"What is that?"

"You haven't been thinking about it?"

"All right," Arthur admitted. "I have."

"You have to reestablish your channels of communication with the President. Encourage McClennan and Rotterjack to stay on. If that's out of the question—"

"Too late now."

"—Then talk to Schwartz. He knows damn well what the public reaction is going to be. Americans won't accept this easily."

"I'd hate to see the polls as to how many people believe anything is happening."

"Leadership," Harry said, his voice husky. "He has to assert his leadership. And we have to fight back."

Arthur nodded abstractedly.

"Killing Cook. Remember?"

Arthur shook his head. "Only if they're not omnipotent."

"If they are, why would they try to confuse us?" Harry asked, his face darkening. He gripped Arthur's hand more tightly. There was a time when Harry's grip could have ground knuckles. Now it was a steady, insistent pressure; no more. "They have to believe we can hurt them somehow."

Arthur nodded. Another conclusion had occurred to him, however, and it frightened him. He could hardly put it into words, and he certainly would not reveal it to Harry now. *Poke a stick in the ants' nest,* he thought. *Watch them scurry around. Learn about them. Then stomp the nest.*

"Have you thought about what will happen to me if you don't pull through?" Arthur asked.

"You'll invite Ithaca up to Oregon, get her settled up there. Introduce her to friends. Find somebody promising who needs a good woman. Marry her off."

"Christ," Arthur said, crying now.

"See," Harry said, tears running down his own cheeks. "You really care."

"You bastard."

Harry rolled his head aside and pulled up a pillow cover to wipe his eyes. "I've never been jealous of you. I could go for years without seeing you, because I knew you'd be there. But Ithaca. He'd better be a damned good fellow, the one you introduce her to. If anybody's going to lie between her thighs but me, I'd better like him a hell of a lot."

"Stop this."

"All right. I'm tired. Can you stay around for dinner? I'm still able to eat. I won't be able to keep it down much after next week. The old-fashioned treatments."

Arthur told him he had to catch a plane shortly. Dinner was out of the question.

"Give me a call tomorrow, then," Harry said. "Keep me informed."

"You bet."

"And talk some more with Hicks. He could replace me."

Arthur shook his head at the whole idea.

"I don't want you to get the impression I've been pinned to the mat by this," Harry said. "I've been thinking crazy thoughts for days now. I'm going to write them down soon."

"Crazy thoughts?" Arthur asked.

"Putting it all in perspective. The aliens, my cancer, the Earth, everything."

"That's a tall order."

"You bet. Keeps my mind off the rest of this nonsense." He thumped his chest and abdomen with his hand. "Might even be useful, sometime . . ."

"I'd like to hear it," Arthur said.

Harry nodded. "You will. But not now. It still hasn't jelled."

29———

November 15

The blue and white taxi roared and jerked along the winding road up the slope of the hill with frightful speed and efficiency. Samshow sat rigid in the back, leaning this way and that against the curves, wondering if he should have accepted the invitation when there was so much work to be done. Outside, night jungle rushed by, relieved by lighted entrances to private roads and ghostly houses floating out above the hillside. Below, visible occasionally through the trees, lay the bright spilled jewel box of Honolulu.

Sand had told him there would be interesting people at the party. He had gone on ahead two hours before. The Glomar *Discoverer* had put in at Pearl Harbor that morning, and the invitation from Gina Fusetti had come by telephone at ten o'clock. Mrs. Fusetti, wife of University of Hawaii physics professor Nathan Fusetti, was known across the Pacific for her parties. "We can't turn this one down," Sand had said. "We need a few hours' rest, anyway."

Samshow had reluctantly agreed.

Fingers faltering through a palm full of dollar bills and change, he paid and tipped the driver and stepped back quickly to avoid a spray of gravel from the rear wheels. Then he turned and looked at a broad, split-level pseudo-Japanese house draped with hundreds of electric folding paper lanterns, its stone walkway flanked by carved lava tikis with candle-burning eyes.

Even from where he stood, he could hear people talking—but no loud music, for which he was profoundly grateful.

A tall young woman opened the door at his knock and smiled brightly. "Mom!" she called out. "Here's another. Who are you?"

"Walt Samshow," he said. "Who are you?"

"Tanya Fusetti. My parents . . . you know. I'm here with my boyfriend."

"You must be Doctor Samshow!" Gina Fusetti stalked intently through the archway leading to the sunken dining room, rubbing her hands and smiling gleefully. In her late sixties, hair gone completely white, she regarded Samshow with smiling, squint-eyed worship, ushering him inside, equipping him with a beer (Asahi) and a paper plate of hors d'oeuvres (teriyaki tuna and raw vegetables). "We're very pleased to have so distinguished an author and scientist with us," Mrs. Fusetti said, smiling her thousand-watt smile. "Mr. Sand is in a back room with some friends . . . He told us you'd be here."

Sand came through a side door. "Walt, glad you've finally come. Something extraordinary—"

"Ah, there he is!" She nodded at both of them, still smiling. "Such a pleasure to have men capable of saying something when they talk!" Another arriving guest drew her away. As she departed, she gave him an ushering wave of both hands—party, enjoy.

"She's pretty extraordinary," Samshow said.

"Acts like that with everybody. She's a charmer."

"You've been to her parties before?"

"I dated her older daughter once."

"You never told me that."

Sand shook his head and grinned. "Do you know Jeremy Kemp? He says he knows you."

"We shared a cabin years ago, I think—some expedition . . . no, it was during a seminar at Woods Hole. Kemp. Geophysicist, earthquakes, isn't he?"

"Right." Sand pushed him forward. "We all have to talk. This is a real coincidence, his being here, our being here. And I sort of broke our rules. I brought up our sighting."

"Oh?"

"We've already sent our data to La Jolla," Sand said, by way of an excuse.

Samshow was not completely mollified. Sand opened the door to a back bedroom. Kemp and two other men sat on chairs and on the bed's Polynesian print coverlet, beers and cocktails in hand. "Walt! Very good to see you again." Kemp stood, shifted his cocktail, and shook Samshow's hand firmly. Introductions were made and Samshow stood in a corner while Sand encouraged Kemp to explain his own scientific problem.

"I'm in resources discovery for Asian Thermal, an energy consortium in Taiwan and Korea. We're keeping track of Chinese oil, for Beijing—it's official—and we're trying to chart the whole southwestern Pacific all the way south to the Philippines. Partly we chart through seismic events and analysis of the wave propagation through the deep crust. Now this is at least as proprietary as what you've told me . . . Understood?" He glanced conspiratorially at the door. Sand closed it and latched it.

"My group has listening stations in the Philippines and the Aleutians. We're also tapped in to the U.S. Geological Survey Earthquake Information Center in Colorado and the Large-Aperture Seismic Array in Montana. We have an anomalous seismic event. We think it's a bad reading or a screwed interpretation. But maybe not. It's from the vicinity of the Ramapo Deep. We got it on the night of November first, Eastern Pacific Time."

"The night of our skyfall," Samshow said.

"Right. We place the time at about eight-twenty P.M. Right?"

"That's our time, within ten minutes," Sand acknowledged.

"Okay. Not an earthquake per se. Not a fault slide. More like a nuclear detonation—and yet, not. We get a PcP—reflection off the outer core—in Beijing and reflections from the P260P and P400P in Colorado, then we get P-prime-P-prime waves at the LASA in Montana. Not only that, but we get persistence inthe high-frequency P-waves. No Love or Rayleigh surface waves, just body waves. No immediate shear waves. Just compression waves and lots of really unusual microseisms, like something *burrowing*. Right in the Ramapo Deep. What could that be?"

Sand grinned like a small boy, mischievous. "Something that weighs perhaps a hundred million tons."

"Right," Kemp said, mirroring his grin. "So let's talk crazy. Anything that masses in at ten to the eighth metric tons, strikes the ocean like a mountain. But all you get is a minor squall. So it didn't transfer much of its energy. Very small profile. Just shot right through, lost a tiny, tiny percentage of its velocity to the water, maybe some heat as well. Something less than a meter wide."

"That's ridiculous," Samshow said.

"Not at all. A plug of superdense matter, probably a black hole. Hitting the ocean nearby, falling to the bottom of the Ramapo Deep, *voilà!* Burrowing."

"Incredible," Sand said, shaking his head, still grinning.

"All right. We both have anomalies. My people have a nuclear event profile that isn't, and you have a jag." Kemp lifted his drink. "Here's to shared mysteries."

Sand had his electronic notebook out and was busy entering figures. "A black hole that size would be a strong source of gamma rays, right?"

"I don't know," Kemp said.

Sand shrugged his shoulders. "But it's so dense and so small it falls directly to the center of the Earth. Actually, it bypasses the center because of Coriolis, and bounds up the other side. There's very little effective drag. It's just like passing through thin air."

Kemp nodded.

"When it reaches the core, it's traveling about ten kilometers per second. Can you imagine the shock wave coming off that thing? The whole Earth would ring like a bell—your microseisms. The heat released would be incredible. I don't know how to calculate that . . . We need somebody conversant in fluid dynamics. Its period—the time it takes to 'orbit' in its closed loop around the center of the Earth—would be about eighty, ninety minutes."

"Wouldn't whatever sound it makes get lost in background noise?" Samshow asked, feeling years out of date.

"Oh, we're hearing it, all right," Kemp said. "Chattering like an imp. Can I borrow your notebook?"

Somewhat reluctantly, Sand handed it to him. Kemp figured for a moment. "If we assume no frictional effects, it would come right up out of the antipodes of its entry point. But I don't know whether there would be drag—it's sucking in matter and releasing some of it as gamma rays, creating a plasma, or maybe it's . . . Hell, I don't know. Let's assume the core has very little drag effect on it. Maybe it doesn't break the surface . . ."

"But the shock wave does," Sand said.

"Right. So we'd have tremendous effects in . . ." Kemp's brow furrowed.

"South Atlantic Ocean," Samshow said. "Thirty south and forty west. About eleven hundred nautical miles east of Brazil, somewhere along the latitude of Pôrto Alegre."

"Very good," Kemp said, his smile fixed now. "Some seismic events there, and then, it swings back to Ramapo eighty or ninety minutes later. And again and again, until its motion is damped by whatever drag it feels and it rests right in the center of the Earth. Do you realize what a black hole could do at the center of the Earth?"

Samshow, suddenly troubled, stood and walked through an open sliding glass door to the veranda. He looked deep into the night jungle behind Mrs. Fusetti's house, quiet except for the noise of the party and the whirring of insects. "How in hell would something like this get to the Earth? Wouldn't our radar spot it, our satellites?"

"I don't know," Kemp said.

"There's definitely some correlation, Walt," Sand said. "Our gravimeters were working perfectly." He joined Samshow on the veranda.

"The party's full of talk about the President's announcement," Kemp said, standing in the open doorway. "What I've been thinking . . ."

Sand's eyes widened. "Oh, Jesus," he said. "I hadn't even . . ."

"So?" Samshow asked.

"Maybe it's not just a fantasy," Kemp said. "You have a jag we can't trace, a meteor strike you can't explain, and we have compression waves we can't explain. And the President has aliens."

"Now wait," Samshow interrupted. "We haven't got any information about the South Atlantic."

"Could this black hole, or whatever it is, cause substantial damage to the Earth?" Sand asked.

"It would eventually eat it up, swallow it completely," Kemp said.

"Then we'd better tell somebody," Samshow said.

Kemp and Sand looked at him like children chastised for being caught in a dirty game.

"Shouldn't we?" Samshow asked. "Who's going to San Francisco, to the American Geophysical Society convention?"

"I am," Kemp said.

"I'd like to," Samshow said, running on instincts now. Sand regarded him with some confusion. Perhaps he felt like backing down now, having carried things too far and seeing the Old Man take them all seriously. "Can we swing it, David?"

"I . . . want to try some calculations."

"We obviously don't have the expertise," Samshow said. "But somebody there will."

"Right," Kemp said. "I know just the fellow. Jonathan Post will be there."

The Furnace was now surrounded by three concentric wire fences, the innermost electrified. Troops patrolled the perimeter in Jeeps and helicopters. Beyond the barricades, hundreds of the curious sat idle in their cars, Jeeps, and trucks, binoculars trained on the black mound five miles or more distant. Still more hikers circled the forbidden area, none finding a way to get any closer.

A makeshift pressroom—little more than an unheated shack—stood at the main gate to the Furnace. Here, nine preselected reporters waited in abject boredom for news releases.

Except for the ubiquitous helicopters, the site itself was quiet. In the steady late morning sun, the cinder cone loomed black and purple, lava boulders and flows still in place, nothing changed, all silent and eternal.

As the blades and turbines on Arthur's helicopter ride from Las Vegas slowed, Arthur climbed down from a hatch and approached Lieutenant Colonel Rogers across the salty sand and gravel landing strip. Rogers greeted him with a handshake and Arthur handed him a folder.

"What's this?" Rogers asked as they walked alone toward the electronics trailer.

"These are orders telling you and your men to stay out of the bogey and do nothing to disturb the site," Arthur said. "I received them in Las Vegas. They're from the office of the President."

"I already have orders to that effect," Rogers said. "Why send more?"

"The President wants to make sure you understand," Arthur said.

"Yes, sir. Tell him—"

"We aren't communicating regularly," Arthur said. He glanced around the area and put his hand on Rogers's shoulder. "We're going to have senators and congressmen all over this place in a few days. Senate subcommittees are inevitable. Congressional oversight committees. Anything you can imagine."

"I heard that senator from Louisiana, what's his name—Mac something."

"MacHenry."

"Yeah," the colonel said, shaking his head. "On the radio. Calling for impeachment."

"That's the President's problem," Arthur said coldly. "MacHenry's not alone." They stopped twenty yards from the trailer. A path had been cleared between the landing strip and the complex of Army equipment. Bored soldiers had bordered the path with uniformly sized, whitewashed lava boulders. "I have something important to ask you. In private. This seems to be as good a place as any."

"Yes, sir."

"Is there any way to destroy the bogey?" Arthur asked.

Rogers stiffened. "That option hasn't been mentioned, sir."

"Could you do it?"

The colonel's face was a battleground of conflicting emotions. "My team can do damn near anything, sir, but it would take specific orders to even discuss such an option."

"This is off the record," Arthur said.

"Even off the record, sir."

Arthur nodded and looked away. "I'm only going to be here for a few hours," he said. "You have your orders—but frankly, I don't have any specific orders. And I believe my authority supersedes yours here, am I correct?"

"Yes, sir, except where you might contradict direct orders from the President."

"You have no orders to prevent *me* from entering the bogey, do you?"

Rogers thought that over. "No, sir."

"I'd like to do that."

"It's not difficult, sir," Rogers said.

"Only difficult if you're the first one in, right?"

Rogers smiled faintly.

"I'll have your lead to follow. Tell me what I need to know, and what sort of equipment will be necessary."

PERSPECTIVE

AP News Network in Brief, November 17, 1996, Washington, D.C.:
Representative Dale Berkshire, R-V., recommended before the full Congress today that the House Judiciary Committee begin hearings on President-elect Crockerman's actions with regard to the Death Valley spacecraft. "There is strong sentiment among my people for impeachment," Berkshire said. "Let the process begin here and now." Berkshire and numerous other congressmen have reportedly asked the House and Senate to delay the President-elect's inauguration ceremonies. No action on a delay has been taken at present.

30——

November 17

Mary, the duty officer, greeted them over the intercom with a smile in her voice. "Rise and shine," she said. "You're getting out today. I just heard it from Colonel Phan."

Edward had been awake for hours. He had not been able to sleep much the last couple of days. The cool clean plastic smell of cubicle air filled his entire body; he could not remember what real air tasted like. Minelli had been worse than usual, babbling sometimes, weeping, and Edward's anger had curled up inside him, helpless, hot, yet anesthetic, slowing him down rather than pushing him to action. Action resulted in nothing.

"You're a liar, Mary, Mary," Minelli said. "We're prisoners for life." An Air Force psychologist had spoken with Minelli and concluded the man was suffering from "extreme cabin fever." So were they all.

"We're not security risks anymore?" Reslaw asked.

"I guess not. You're healthy and the President's announcement makes the rest pretty unnecessary, don't you think?"

"I've been thinking that for days," Reslaw said.

At ten A.M. Colonel Phan appeared with General Fulton. The isolation chamber window covers were withdrawn and Fulton greeted them all solemnly, apologizing for the inconvenience. Minelli said nothing.

"We've announced your release," Fulton said, "and made arrangements for a press conference at two this afternoon. We have new clothes for you and all your confiscated personal effects."

"A cheap suit and ten bucks in pocket," Minelli said.

Fulton smiled grimly. "You're free to say whatever you want. There's no sense our stonewalling; we've had perfectly good reasons for everything we did. I hope, even now, that you can see those reasons. I don't expect sympathy."

Edward bit his lip gently, eyes focused on Fulton's cap. Then he looked in the direction of Stella's window and saw her standing in the white fluorescent light, gaunt, almost ghostly. She had lost a lot of weight. So had Reslaw. Minelli, strangely, had become almost plump.

"I've taken the liberty of having Mr. Shaw's Land Cruiser given a thorough check-over at our motor pool garage. The oil's been changed, engine tuned, and a new set of tires put on. Think of it as the least we can do. We've also arranged for monetary compensation for your time here. Should you need any medical attention in the next few years, that's on us, too. I assume one or more of you will sue us." Fulton shrugged. "All right. Your hall doors will be opened in five minutes. If you're up to it, I'd like to thank each of you personally and shake your hand. My gratitude is sincere, but I won't require you to acknowledge."

"Shake the fucking President's hand," Minelli roared. "Ah, Christ, let me out."

Fulton walked with the watch supervisor down the connecting corridor between the cells, his face ashen. "This whole thing . . . has become the worst screwup . . . of my entire career," he said, eyes half closed.

Within half an hour, the four stood in sunshine outside the smooth concrete walls of the Experimental Receiving Laboratory, blinking. Edward made a point of keeping close to Stella. She seemed frail, excessively quiet, her face drawn and haunted like that of a starved child.

"You going to make it?" Edward asked.

"I want to go home. I'm clean, but I want to take a shower at home. Does that make sense?"

"Perfect sense," Edward said. "Wash off all the prison cooties."

She smiled broadly, then opened her arms wide and held them out to the sky, making an ecstatic feline wriggle. "God. The sun."

Minelli covered his eyes with one hand against the sun, stretching the other hand out palm-up to catch the rays. "Beautiful," he said.

"What do you want to do, Edward?" Stella asked.

"Take a hike," Edward said without hesitating. "Get back out to the desert."

"If any of you wants to spend some time in Shoshone . . ." Stella paused. "It might be silly, you probably want to get as far away from here as possible, but you can stay at our house. I realize you must have other things to do."

"We're at loose ends," Reslaw said. "I am, anyway."

They passed General Fulton and Colonel Phan as the watch supervisor escorted them into a small auditorium near the base public information office. An Air Force lawyer talked to them about their immediate future and offered legal assistance, including the agenting of book and movie offers, without fee. "I think I'm pretty good, and so does the Air Force," he said. "Nothing mandatory, of course. If you don't like me, the service will pay for any lawyer you choose, within reason."

The press conference, though an ordeal, was mercifully brief—only half an hour. They sat alone at a long table while approximately three hundred reporters competed to ask questions, one at a time, through remote microphones. For Edward, the questions blurred into one another: How did you find the alien? Were you actually looking for spaceships and aliens? Are you going to sue the Air Force or the United States government? ("I don't know," Edward replied.) What do you think of the Australian spaceship? Of the President's address to the nation? ("If we are being invaded," Minelli said, "I think his message sucks.") Bernice Morgan, Stella's mother, sat in a roped-off section. She wore a belted print dress and carried a broad white sun hat. Her face was calm. Beside her sat the Morgan family lawyer, older and much more grizzled than the military counsel, in a dark blue suit, clutching a briefcase.

By three, they were back in the auditorium. Stella stood beside her mother while their lawyer discussed the circumstances of their release. He then offered to represent all four of the detainees, as he referred to them.

A staff sergeant handed Edward a bag containing the keys to his Jeep, and they were all given their packets of personal effects. "I can drive you all right out of here," Edward said. "If we can avoid the reporters . . ."

"That's going to be difficult. If you'd like an escort . . ." the military counsel offered.

"No thanks. We'll manage."

Reslaw and Minelli went with Edward. Stella accompanied her mother to the lawyer's limousine. "Where are we going?" she asked Edward.

"I'll take up your offer if it's still open," Edward said. Minelli and Reslaw agreed.

"Open to all."

The Jeep and the limousine pulled away from Vandenberg's main eastern gate, away from the crush of reporters. A few valiant camera trucks and press cars followed them, but Edward managed to shake them off by taking a devious route through Lompoc.

The climb up the shaft was not difficult; Rogers had indicated it was a much more impressive journey mentally than physically. Yet Arthur was not entirely certain why he was making the trip. What could the hollow interior tell him, that he hadn't already seen in Rogers's photographs and video?

Still, he had to do it. His inner confusion had to be resolved. He half hoped for some intuitive breakthrough. And perhaps something would have changed—a change that might indicate where the truth actually lay.

Arthur clambered around the second bend and crawled on all fours along the last stretch of tunnel. In a few minutes, he emerged into the broad cylindrical antechamber, switching on the video camera mounted over his ear.

His lamps played off the complex faceting of the opposite side of the main chamber. Walking to the lip of the antechamber, circling the beam of his torch over the faceted cathedral vastness, he tried to make out the red light Rogers had photographed. He couldn't see it. Taking a deep breath—as he imagined Rogers had done before—he turned off all his lights and settled into a squat a couple of meters from the edge.

Circular. Designed for weightless conditions? How could all this crystalline structure survive planetfall? What in hell is the function? After five minutes, he still couldn't make out a red light in the vastness. "One change, at least," he noted aloud for the recorder.

He switched on the torch again and scrutinized the faceting intently, moving his eyes a few degrees, then again, trying to discern some pattern or evident function. It was beautiful, which implied a pattern, but beyond that . . .

Could all the facets be used to focus some sort of radiation drive? If so, then was the throat of the drive where he was now standing, in the (presently) closed antechamber? Would the tunnel into the mound then represent a kind of relief valve, left open to evacuate the contents of the chamber after landing? There were no traces of hot exhaust blast outside. Perhaps all that had been obscured after the landing, during the time the craft was camouflaged.

If he stood on tiptoes, he still could not hold the torch high enough to put it in the focal center of the antechamber cylinder, which was about two meters above the greatest stretch of his arms. A simple stepladder . . . and he could see if the facets reflected the beam directly back at him.

Even from where he stood, that didn't seem likely.

What would Marty think, knowing his daddy was even now standing inside an alien spacecraft? What would Francine think?

If it is a spacecraft. Everybody seems to assume that. Perhaps the spacecraft left machines to construct this, and it was never in space at all. If so, why?

The cool dark quiet was profound, almost comforting. *Reminds me of an anechoic chamber. Maybe the facets are dampers of some sort.* He whistled sharply. The whistle returned, muted but clear. His voice, however, did not return. He shut off the microphone and shouted several times to make that point. The first two shouts were wordless, mere yells, apelike, and somehow he felt better after them. The third shout came out of him so rapidly he had no time to think.

"What the hell are you doing here? What are you doing to us, goddammit?"

Embarrassed, his face hot, Arthur approached the lip again and pointed his torch at the facets directly below. He thought of the Guest's triple sherry-colored eyes, protruding from the surrounding dusty gray-green flesh. *What a nightmare. All of it. Day by day we learn and it means nothing, has no pattern. We are befuddled being befuddled. Deliberate.*

He tried to subdue his unreasoning rage. Surely there were ways to bring a nuclear weapon into this chamber. Backpack nukes hadn't been manufactured for twenty years, and had never been field-tested. What else was in the arsenal that could be hauled into the chamber by one or at most two men?

Lieutenant Colonel Rogers knew. He had thought of just such a contingency before Arthur had broached the subject. His reaction —immediate, brusque—made that clear. If two were thinking of it, then others were, as well. How could they circumvent Crockerman's authority over all nuclear weapons?

What good would it do?

"I'd like to ask you a few more questions," he said, leaving the mike off. "Just between one human individual and whatever, whoever you are. Are we no more to you than a nest of ants? You go to the trouble to create an artificial being . . ." He was convinced of that, though the proof was not absolute. "You feed us two stories, maybe more. What are you telling the Russians in Mongolia? Are you telling them the universe is run on socialist principles? We thought, years past . . . we thought the arrival of something like you would change us all. You've taken advantage of that. You seem to know us better than we know ourselves. Or are we just so simple you can predict our behavior? If you're superior, then why are you torturing us? *How many civilizations have you destroyed?"*

He did not expect an answer. The circular gray-faceted cathedral interior gloomed around him, silent and implacable, unreal despite his intense scrutiny.

"You're going to eat the Earth, and spit it out, and move on," he continued, his voice trembling. His rage was almost overwhelming; he wanted to smash things. With some haste, he retreated to the tunnel, to reach the outside before his decorum vanished completely and he wept in frustration.

Once through the twisted tunnel and standing in the desert sun, he immediately faced Rogers and two sergeants and weeping was again out of the question.

"Your red light has gone out," he said, doffing his gear. "Nothing else has changed."

"How did it feel, sir?" Rogers asked softly.

"Like I was of no consequence whatsoever," Arthur said.

The officer smiled grim agreement and helped him remove the camera.

PERSPECTIVE

New York Times editorial, November 20, 1996:
The election of President William D. Crockerman may have been a colossal blunder. Had
the nation been given the complete facts about
the present situation-facts concerning the
existence of yet another alien device in Death
Valley, California-and had we been informed
about the President's attitude to these alien
devices, how many Americans would have voted
for a President who seems to accept impending
destruction with open arms?

Perhaps there is no hope. Perhaps the Earth
is doomed. But for the President of the United
States to admit defeat and urge us all to say
our prayers is-and we do not hesitate to use
the word-treasonous.

The *Times* Editorial Board is unanimous in
recommending that the House Judiciary Com-

mittee investigate the President-elect's actions, and vote on whether or not to recommend impeachment.

31———

It took Reuben Bordes three weeks to come to grips with his mother's death, and it happened in a bizarre and darkly comic way.

His father, as tall as Reuben but getting plump about the middle, had for the time being given up on life, his rough bearded face dark grayish olive from grief and stress, sitting in the ragged lounger in the living room, napping before a dark TV.

It was up to Reuben to keep the house clean and make sure all the chores were done as his mother would have wished. He took that upon himself as a duty to the both of them. His father would recover. Life would go on. Reuben was sure of that.

On a Wednesday, three weeks exactly after the funeral, Reuben pulled out the old upright vacuum cleaner and plugged it into a herniated wall socket. The plug threatened to fall out, but held long enough for Reuben to kick the button with his naked toe and switch the machine on. He then methodically ran the vacuum over the patchy Oriental-design carpet and the wood floors, swooping down on dust kittens and moving chairs and coffee table when necessary. He vacuumed around his father, who smiled up at him and tried to say something, but could not be heard over the racket. Reuben patted his shoulder in passing.

In the bathroom, as he passed the machine carefully over the almost-new throw rug, the vacuum started laboring. He thought he smelled hot metal and electricity. Punching the button with his toe, he tipped the machine over, flipped two latches, and removed the bottom metal cover. In some amazement, he stared at the roller brush and belt.

Thick strands of his mother's fine, long crinkly black hair had wrapped around the entire length of the roller, filling the groove of the rubber belt and impeding its progress.

Reuben picked the hair off delicately with long, spatulate fingers, examining broken pieces of it in his palms. He pulled loose a thick tangle and made a motion to drop it into the wastebasket. He couldn't follow through.

He sat back against the kitchen door, holding the tangle to his cheek. For a moment, his thoughts were filled with a velvet nothingness.

Then it came. His head thumped against the door and he wept quietly, not wanting his father to hear, finally covering up by switching the vacuum on again. With his mother's hair removed, it ran smoothly and loudly.

Warren, Ohio, lay acquiescent under an old blanket of snow, some of it still clean, some pushed up in dirty brown and black-spotted ridges by the roadways. Skeletal trees stood out against the yellowing dusk, and gusts of sharp cold wind leaped around him like invisible dogs, glad to see you, happy to have you here. Reuben clutched the two library books under his arm, one on how to pass the civil service exam for the Postal Service, another containing the short stories of Paul Bowles. Reuben, who had fancied himself a Muslim in his early teens—to his mother's horror—had steeped himself in the lore of Africa and the Middle East. Bowles intrigued him even more than Doughty or T. E. Lawrence.

Reuben had quit high school the year before to work. His formal education had been fitful, but his intelligence, when focused, was a devouring and almost frightening thing. When Reuben Bordes latched on to a question or a book or a subject that interested him, his short, broad face tightened with an intent, fixed expression and his eyes enlarged until it seemed they might fall out of his head.

He was tall and strong and feared nobody. His route through the darkening streets, between the dirty brick buildings and along narrow service alleys behind businesses, was not chosen for its shortness or logic. Reuben needed to delay. Getting back to his father was necessary, but he did not relish the intensity of pain he felt at home.

Halfway there, pacing through slush puddles behind a liquor store, he saw a silvery glint in the shadows beside a dumpster. He walked on, turning his head, thinking it was nothing more than a broken bottle. But the glint persisted. He returned to the dumpster and peered into the shadows. A glittering toylike thing, perhaps a kid's broken robot, rested on a dark brown and nondescript lump. He peered closer.

The toy sat on a dead mouse or a small rat. Very slowly, the toy lifted one of six jointed shiny legs, and then brought it down again. The leg pierced the rodent's skin.

Reuben stood up and backed away. Night was almost on him.

The way the spider or whatever it was had raised its leg—with a clockwork precision, an oily smoothness—scared him. It was not a toy. It was not an insect. It was something spider-shaped and made of metal and it had caught and killed a mouse.

With slow grace, the spider stepped off the mouse and turned to face Reuben, two front legs held high as if to defend itself. Reuben backed up against a rough board fence, eight or nine feet away, twenty feet from the street. He glanced to his left, ready to run.

Silver flashed on the fence boards behind him. Reuben screamed and pushed off with his arms and shoulders but the flash followed, sitting on his shoulder where he couldn't see it clearly. He brushed it away and felt its heavy, resisting sharp legs let go of his shirt. The spider fell into the slush with a splash and leaden clunk.

"Oh, Jesus, help!" Reuben screamed. The street beyond the alley was empty of pedestrians. A car drove by but the driver didn't hear him. "Help!"

He ran. Two spiders ambled into his path and he tried to stop, feet sliding out from under him in a patch of wet ice. He fell on his back in the dirt and slush. Moaning, he rolled over, the wind knocked out of him, and lifted his head. A spider waited with front legs raised not a foot from his face, a small line of green luminosity drawn between the legs where its eyes might have been. Its body was smooth, a single elongated egg shape. Its legs were jewel-fine.

No joke.

Nobody makes things like that.

He faced the thing, breath coming back in sharp jerks, his arms tingling from the fall. Something moved along his back, gently pinching, and he could not reach up to grab it or brush it off. He could not scream again; there wasn't enough air in his lungs. Then the weight and the legs were in his hair. Something sharp brushed his scalp. Pricked.

Reuben moaned and lay his head down in the slush, his eyes closed, his face masked with a rictus of fear. After a few minutes, he felt himself getting up and lying back against the fence, his movements poorly coordinated. Nobody came by, or if they did, they did not stop. He was still behind the liquor store. He was dirty and wet and he looked like a filthy drunk. A cop might come along to investigate, but nobody else.

He was very cold but not frightened anymore. There was a high vibration in his skull that reassured him. Reuben suddenly decided to fight the reassurance and his whole body stiffened, slamming his head against the fence so hard the wood cracked.

That sobered him. What parts of his head could still think, urged caution. He could taste blood in his mouth. *This is how an animal feels in the wild when the zoo people come,* he thought.

The vibration continued, waxing and waning, lulling him even through the bone-chilling cold and damp. He tried several times to get up, but he had no control over his limbs; they tingled as if asleep.

He felt a crawling behind his head. A spider delicately climbed down the front of his coat, legs prodding and lifting the edge of his hip pocket where it lay rucked up in his lap. The thing disappeared into the pocket, legs folding as it entered. The bulge it made was barely noticeable.

His legs stopped tingling. With some effort, Reuben stood, wobbling back and forth uncertainly. He checked himself over and found no injuries, no blood or evidence of abrasions, and only a few tender bruises. When his hand went toward his pocket, he thought better of it—or rather, something else urged caution—and slowly withdrew his arm. Hand held idly out, shivering and puzzled, Reuben looked around the alley for more of the spiders. They were gone.

The mouse lay still beside the dumpster. Reuben was allowed to kneel and examine the tiny carcass.

It had been neatly dissected, its purple, brown, and pink shiny organs laid out to one side, incisions made here and there, as if samples had been taken.

"I have to go home," Reuben said to nobody or nothing in particular.

He was allowed to finish his walk home.

32———

Arthur was delayed three days unexpectedly in Las Vegas to speak informally with three congressmen from the House Judiciary Committee. His first evening back home, back with his family and the river and the forest, he sat on the living room throw rug, legs curled into a lotus. Francine and Marty sat on the couch behind him. Marty had laid the fire in the grate all by himself, lighting the carefully placed tinder with a long match.

"Here's what's happening, really, as much as I know," he said, raising himself on his arms and sweeping his locked legs around to face them. And he told them.

The heater came on at midnight and blew warm air over Arthur and Francine as they lay in bed in each other's arms. Francine's head rested on his shoulder. He could feel her eye movements as she stared into darkness. They had just made love and it had been very good, and against all his intellectual persuasions, he *felt* good, at home, at rest. Not a word had been said between them for fifteen minutes.

She lifted her head. "Marty—"

The phone rang.

"Oh, Christ." She rolled out of his way. He reached across her to pick up the phone.

"Arthur, Chris Riley here. I'm sorry I woke you up—"

"We're awake," Arthur said.

"Yes. This is a bit of an emergency, I think. There are some guys in Hawaii who'd like to talk with you. They heard I knew your home number. You can call them now or I—"

"I'd like to be incommunicado, Chris, at least for a couple of days."

"I think this could be very important, Arthur."

"All right, what is it."

"From the little they've told me, they might have found the—

you know, what the press is talking about, the weapon the aliens might use against us."

"Who are they?"

"One is Jeremy Kemp. He's a conceited son of a bitch and hell to deal with, but he's an excellent geologist. The other two are oceanographers. Ever hear of Walt Samshow?"

"I think so. Wrote a textbook I read in college. He's pretty old, isn't he?"

"He and another fellow named Sand are with Kemp in Hawaii. They say they saw something pretty unusual."

"All right. Give me a phone number." He switched on the light over the nightstand.

"Samshow and Sand are on board a ship in Pearl Harbor." Riley enunciated the number and name of the ship for him. "Ask for Walt or David."

"Thanks, Chris," Arthur said, hanging up.

"No rest?" Francine asked.

"Some people think they might have found the smoking gun."

"Jesus," Francine said softly.

"I'd better call them now." He got out of bed and went into the den to use the extension there. Francine followed a few minutes later, wrapped in her robe.

When he had finished with the call, he turned and saw Marty standing beside her, rubbing his eyes.

"I'm going to San Francisco this weekend," he said. "But I've still got a couple of days with you guys."

"Show me how to use the telescope, Dad?" Marty asked sleepily. "I want to see what's going on."

Arthur picked the boy up and carried him back to his bedroom.

"Were you and Mom making love?" Marty asked as Arthur lay him down in the bed and pulled the covers over him.

"You got it, Big Ears," Arthur said.

"That means you love Mom. And she loves you."

"Mm-hm."

"And you'll go away but you'll come back again?"

"As soon as I can."

"If we're all going to die, I want you both here, with me, all of us together," Marty said.

Arthur held his son's hand for a long moment, eyes moist, throat gnarled with love and a deep, inexpressible anguish. "We'll start with the telescope tomorrow, and you can look tomorrow night," he finally said in a harsh whisper.

"So I can see them come," Marty said.

Arthur could not lie. He hugged his son firmly and stood by the bed until Marty's eyes were closed and he was breathing evenly.

"It's one o'clock," Francine said as he slipped under the covers beside her.

They made love again, and it was even better.

November 22

"Gauge! Bad dog! Dammit, Gauge, that's a *frozen* chicken. You can't eat that. All you can do is ruin it." Francine stomped her foot in fury and Gauge slunk from the kitchen, berry-colored tongue lolling, ashamed but pleased with himself.

"Wash it off," Arthur suggested, sliding past Gauge to stand in the kitchen door, grinning.

Francine held the thoroughly toothed but whole bird in two hands, shaking her head. "He's mangled it. Every bite will have his mark."

"Bites within bites," Arthur said. "How recursive."

"Oh, shut up. Two days home and *this.*"

"Blame it on me, go ahead," Arthur said. "I need a little domestic guilt."

Francine put the bird back on the countertop and opened the sliding glass door. "Martin! Where are you? Come chastise your dog for me."

"He's outside with the telescope." Arthur examined the chicken sadly. "If we don't eat it, that's one bird's life wasted," he said.

"Dog germs," Francine argued.

"Hell, Gauge licks us all the time. He's just a puppy. He's still a virgin."

Dinner—the same bird, skinned and carefully trimmed—was served at seven. Marty seemed dubious about his portion of leg and thigh, but Arthur warned him his mother would not take kindly to their being overfastidious.

"You made me cook it," she said.

"Anything interesting?" Arthur asked his son, pointing up.

"It's all twinkly out there," Marty said.

"Clear night tonight?" Arthur asked.

"It's slushy and cold," Francine said.

"Lots of stars, but I mean . . . you know. Twinkly like faraway firecrackers."

Arthur stopped chewing. "Stars?"

"You told me only supernovas would get bright and go out," Marty said seriously. "Is that what they are?"

"I don't think so. Let's go look."

Francine dropped her wing in disgust. "Go ahead. Abandon dinner. Arthur—"

"Just for a minute," he said. Marty followed. After hanging back by the service porch door for a minute in protest, Francine joined them in the backyard.

"Up there," Marty said, pointing. "It's not doing anything now," he protested.

"It's awful cold out here." Francine looked at Arthur with an unexpressed question on her face. Arthur examined the sky intently.

"There," Marty said.

For the merest instant, a new star joined the panoply. A few seconds later, Arthur spotted another, much brighter, a couple of degrees away. The sparkles were all within a few degrees of the plane of the ecliptic. "Oh, Christ," he muttered. "What now?"

"Is this something important?" Francine asked.

"Dad*dy,*" Marty said nervously, glancing at his parents, alarmed by the tone of their voices.

"I don't know. I don't think so. Maybe it's a meteor shower." But the sparkles were not meteors. He was sure of that much. There was one person he could call who might know—Chris Riley. Always Riley, a still point in the moving world.

In the darkened den, he dialed Riley's home phone. On the first attempt, it was busy. A few moments later, Riley answered, breathless.

"Chris, hello. This is Gordon, Arthur Gordon."

"My man. Just the man." Riley paused to catch his breath. "I hear you set up a meeting with Kemp and Samshow. I'd like to be there, but it's getting real busy here. I've been running out to the telescope and back. I should get a phone out there."

"What's happening?"

"Have you seen it? All through the plane of the ecliptic—asteroids. They're blowing up like firecrackers! Since dusk, apparently. I just got confirmation from Mount Laguna and somebody left a message a few minutes ago from Pic du Midi in France. The asteroid belt looks like a battlefield."

"Damn," Arthur said. He glanced over his shoulder and saw Marty and Francine standing in the doorway, Marty with his arms wrapped tight around his mother's waist.

"When is this task force going to come clean?" Riley asked. "Lots of people are really angry, Arthur. The President shoots his mouth off, and nobody else is talking."

"We can't be sure this is connected."

"Arthur! For God's sake! Asteroids are blowing up! How the hell could it not be connected?"

"You're right," Arthur said. "I'm flying to San Francisco tomorrow. How many sparkles so far?"

"Since I've been watching, at least a hundred. Got to run now."

Arthur said good-bye and hung up. Marty was owl-eyed, Francine only slightly more restrained. "It's all right," he said.

"Is it starting?" she asked. Marty began to whimper. Arthur had not heard his son whimper in recent memory—months, a year.

"No. I don't think so. This is far away, in the asteroids."

"Are they sure it's not shooting stars?" Marty asked, a very adult rationalization.

"No. Asteroids. They're out beyond Mars, most of them between Mars and Jupiter."

"Why out there?" Francine asked.

Arthur could only shake his head.

33——

November 23

Minelli had spent the night lying in a lounger by the broad picture windows. He was there now, head lolling, snoring softly. Edward tightened the knot on the bathrobe he had borrowed from Stella and walked past the lounger to stand by the glass. Beyond a concrete patio and a dried-up L-shaped ornamental fishpond, frost whitened several acres of winter-yellow grass.

Coming here had been a good idea. Shoshone was peaceful, isolated without being cut off. For a few days at least, they could rest, until the crowds of reporters found them again. The few townspeople aware of their return were making sure nobody knew where they were. They spent most of the day indoors, and only Bernice answered the phone.

He heard Minelli stir behind him.

"You missed the show," Minelli said.

"Show?"

"All night long. Like a parade of lightning bugs."

Edward raised an eyebrow.

"No joking, and I'm not crazy. Out over the mountains, all night long. Clear as a bell. The sky twinkled."

"Meteors?"

"I've seen meteors, and *these* wasn't *them.*"

"End of the world, no doubt," Edward said.

"No doubt," Minelli echoed.

"How are you feeling?"

"Rested. Better. I must have given everybody a bad time back there."

"They gave *us* a bad time," Edward corrected. "I was feeling a little nuts myself."

"Nuts." Minelli shook his head and cocked a dubious glance at Edward. "Where's Reslaw?"

"Still sleeping." He and Reslaw had shared a middle bedroom. "These folks are real nice. I wish I'd had a mother like Bernice."

Edward nodded. "Are we going to stay here," he asked, "and keep imposing, or are we going back to Texas?"

"We're going to have to face the music eventually," Minelli said philosophically. "The press awaits. I watched television a little last night. The whole country's gone nuts. Quietly, mind you, but nuts all the same."

"I don't blame them."

The phone rang.

"What time is it?" Minelli asked. Edward glanced at his watch. "Seven-thirty."

On the second ring, the phone was silent.

They stared at it apprehensively. "Bernice must have answered it in the back bedroom," Minelli said.

A few minutes later, Stella came out, followed by her mother, both unselfconsciously attired in flannel pajamas and flower-print robes. Bernice smiled at them. "Breakfast, gentlemen? It's going to be a long day."

"That was CBS," Stella said. "They keep sniffing."

"We can only fool them so long," Bernice said.

Edward looked across the quiet, frosty field. A pickup truck parked just off the highway held two men in brown coats and cowboy hats—locals sworn to keep "snoops" from setting up cameras and interfering with the Morgan family's privacy. Even at a hundred yards' distance, they looked formidable.

Stella shook her head. "I don't know what to say. We didn't do anything important. I didn't, anyway. You found the rock."

Edward shrugged. "What's to say about that?"

Reslaw, dressed in jeans and a blue-and-white-striped long-sleeved shirt, walked out of the hallway, past the entrance alcove and the baby grand piano in an adjacent corner. "Somebody ask about breakfast?"

"Coming up," Mrs. Morgan said.

"You know," Edward said, "it was probably a bad idea to come here. For you two. We all need our rest, but your mother has been through a lot."

Bernice Morgan walked stiffly into the kitchen. "It was exhilarating, really," she said. "I haven't had a fight like that in years."

"Besides, she got to talk to the President," Stella said, grinning.

"Makes me ashamed to be a Democrat," she said. "Mike and the boys are keeping a watch. I just have to make sure they don't get too zealous. You stay as long as you want."

"Please stay," Stella said, looking at Edward. "I have to talk. To all of you. I'm still confused. We should help each other out."

"What about the fireworks?" Minelli asked. "Maybe there's something on the news now."

He stretched and swung his legs off the lounger, then stood and walked across the linoleum floor and wide Navajo rugs to the living room, a few steps from the marble-top pedestal table in the open dining area. He sat in front of the television. Slowly, as if it might be hot, he turned it on, then backed up, licking his lips. Edward watched him with concern.

"Just cartoons," Minelli said quietly. Without changing channels, he lay back to watch, as if he had forgotten his original purpose. Edward walked over and changed channels for him, looking for news. On the twenty-four-hour News Network, an announcer was finishing a story on conflict between the Dominican Republic and Haiti.

"Nothing," Minelli said pessimistically. "Maybe I was seeing things."

Then, "Astronomers in France and California have offered varied explanations for last night's unprecedented meteor activity in the solar system's asteroid belt. Seen throughout the Western Hemisphere, clearly visible to the naked eye in areas with clear skies, bright explosions flashed throughout the ecliptic, the plane occupied by the Earth's orbit and the orbits of most of the sun's planets. Speaking from his phone in Los Angeles, presidential task force advisor Harold Feinman said it might take days to analyze data and learn what had actually happened deep in space, beyond the orbit of Mars. When asked if there was any connection between the meteor activity and the alleged spacecraft and aliens on Earth, Feinman declined to comment."

"Smart man to admit he's an idiot," Minelli said. "Asteroids. Jesus."

Edward flipped past other channels, but found nothing more.

"What do you think, Ed?" Minelli asked, slouching back in the corner of the broad L-shaped couch. "What the hell did I see? More end-of-the-world shit?"

"I don't know any more than they do," Edward said. He entered the kitchen. "Do you have a doctor in town? A psychiatrist?" he asked Bernice.

"Nobody worth the name," she answered, her voice as low as his. "Your friend's still not doing too well, is he?"

"The government got rid of us in a real hurry. He should be in a hospital somewhere, resting, cooling down."

"That can be arranged," she said. "Did he actually see something?"

"I guess so," Edward said. "I wish I'd seen it."

"Day of the Triffids, that's what it was," Minelli said enthusiastically. "Remember? We'll all go blind any minute now. Break out the pruning shears!"

Stella stood by the stove, methodically cracking eggs into a pan one by one. "Momma," she said, "where's the pepper mill?" She brushed past Edward, tears in her eyes.

34——

Walt Samshow stepped from the cab on Powell Street under the shadow of the St. Francis Hotel awning and turned around briefly to look across at long, silent lines of hundreds of marchers parading around Union Square, a cable car grumbling by covered with swaying tourists, spastic traffic of cars and more cabs, civilized mayhem: San Francisco, other than the marchers, not terribly different from his memories of it in 1984, the last time he had been downtown.

In the spacious, elegant lobby of the St. Francis, with its polished black stone and dark lustrous woods, Samshow began hearing the rumors practically the moment he set his luggage down by the front desk.

The convention of the American Geophysical Society was in full swing. Kemp and Sand had gone ahead, and apparently big things had happened since their arrival Thursday. Now it was Saturday and he had a lot to catch up on.

As he checked in, two professorial young men passed by, engaged in earnest conversation. He caught only three words: "The Kemp object—"

The bellhop carted his luggage over thick carpet to the elevator. Samshow followed, unwinding his arms and stretching his fingers. Two other conventioneers—an older man and a young woman— stood near the elevators, discussing supersonic shock waves and how they might be transmitted through mantle and crust.

Reporters and camera crews from three local television stations and as many national news networks were in the lobby when Samshow returned from his room to check in at the convention desk. He avoided them deftly by walking around several pillars.

With his badge and bag of pamphlets and program guides came a note from Sand:

> Kemp and I will meet you in Oz at 5:30. Drinks
> on Kemp.
>
>   D.S.

Oz, Samshow learned from a desk clerk, was the bar and disco at the top of the "new" tower of the St. Francis. He looked at his frayed sports coat and his worn-out running shoes, decided he was easily ten years behind the times and thousands of dollars short in refurbishing his wardrobe, and sighed as he entered the elevator.

The trip from Honolulu to La Jolla had been arranged by the Scripps Institution of Oceanography. He had paid for that by lecturing the night before at UCSD. It never ceased to dismay him, after twenty-five years, how popular he was. His huge, expensive book on oceanography had become a standard text, and hundreds of students were only too pleased to listen to, and shake hands with, the modern Sverdrup.

On his own tab, he had taken a flight out of Lindbergh Field to San Francisco. Not yet did he have a clear idea what they were all doing here; there was still much work to be done on the Glomar *Discoverer*, beginning with the collation of billions of bits of data from their passages over the Ramapo Deep.

He suspected much of that data would be pushed aside indefinitely now. Sand's gravimeter anomaly would be the key element. Somehow, that saddened him.

Braced against the ascent of the high-speed elevator, he realized he had been feeling his age for the past week. Psychologically, he had been caught up in the national malaise that had followed Crockerman's announcement. He felt no different from the young people carrying their blank signs just across the street. What was there to protest? Apocalypse could not be repealed by the democratic process. Even now, the instrument of that destruction—or *an* instrument—might be lancing through the Earth's core.

The Kemp object. *That* attribution, he assured himself, would change shortly. Sand-Samshow object . . . Not a catchy name, but it would have to do. Yet . . . why? Why lay claim to the discovery of the bullet that might have *everyone's* name on it?

The elevator door opened and Samshow stepped out into a blare of noise. Oz glittered, silver and gray, glass-walled and high-ceilinged. Young people in elegant dress danced across the central floor, while drinkers and talkers sat and stood on the surrounding raised carpeted areas. The sweet smells of wine and Bourbon wafted from a passing waitress's tray.

Samshow winced at the noise and glanced around, looking for Sand or Kemp. Sand stood in a corner waving to catch his eye.

Their round table was barely a foot across, and five people were crowded around it: Kemp, Sand, two others he did not recognize, smiling as if they were old friends, and now himself. He shook hands as Sand introduced Jonathan V. Post, an acquaintance of Kemp's, dark and Levantine with a gray-shot curly beard, and Oscar Eglinton from the Nevada School of Mines. Post declaimed a brief and embarrassing poem on meeting the legendary Old Man of the Sea. When he was finished, he smiled broadly.

"Thank you," Samshow said, not very impressed. The waitress came and Post sacrificed his own Corona that Samshow might have a drink sooner.

He had once downed a case of Corona in two days while whale-watching at Scammon's Lagoon. That had been in 1952. Now more than one beer gave him heartburn.

"We have to fill you in, Walt," Sand said. "Kemp talked with seismologists in Brazil and Morocco. One of them is here—Jesús Ochoa. We have the nodal traces. October thirty-first. The disruptions and shock waves. There's been high surf in some very suspicious places, and seismic events like nobody's ever seen . . ."

"Thirty-five south, forty-two west," Kemp said, with the same smug grin he had worn a week ago in Hawaii.

"He convinced me that was good enough evidence to talk to Washington. They referred me to Arthur Gordon—"

"The President isn't interested, apparently," Kemp said, his grin vanishing. "We couldn't even talk to the new national security advisor, what's his name . . ."

"Patterson," said the muscular, dark-tanned Eglinton.

"But Gordon says he'll be here tonight to talk with us. There's going to be a lot to discuss. Post here has spoken to some physicists and space scientists. Chris Riley, Fred Hardin. Others. Asteroids are on their mind."

"You're all convinced we've got something appropriate, a true extraterrestrial bullet?"

"We have more than that," Kemp said, leaning forward. Sand put a hand on his arm, and Kemp nodded, falling back into his seat. Sand leaned over to Samshow as if to explain something delicate.

"There was a central Atlantic fireball sighted by a cargo ship four days ago. Like the previous object, as far as we can discover, *nobody* picked it up on radar coming in. Similar phenomenon—deep-ocean splash, small storm, and peculiar seismic traces. This fireball was much brighter, though—blinding, huge, leaving a glowing tail behind it. Captain and crew were treated for retinal burns. The doctors treating them noticed hair loss and strange bruises and questioned them, and they admitted to having bloody stools. Everyone on deck is suffering from severe radiation exposure."

"Meteors don't do that," Kemp said. "And then . . . we have records of another seismic event in the same area as the cargo ship. Burrowing," he added triumphantly. "Trace like a bomb explosion. And then . . . microseisms and deep P-waves."

Samshow raised his eyebrows. "And?"

"More nodal traces," Sand said, "and even stronger microseismic activity . . . This was either a bigger object, more massive, or . . ."

"It's different," Kemp said. "Don't ask me how."

"They're talking about a Kemp object downstairs," Samshow said. "Far be it from me to worry about attribution—"

"We'll straighten that out at the symposium tomorrow morning," Kemp said. "Gordon will attend, and everything we know will be laid before the convention."

"And the public?"

"Nobody's told us to keep it secret," Sand said.

"There are camera crews downstairs."

"We can't hold this back," Kemp said.

"Can't we wait until it's confirmed?"

"That could be months," Sand said. "We may not have the time."

Samshow frowned deeply. "Two things bother me," he said. "Besides this god-awful noise. One." He held up a single finger. "How in hell can any of this theorizing do us any good? And two." A second finger. "Everybody here seems to be having such a *fine* time."

Sand glanced at the others. Post appeared suddenly crestfallen.

"The gods are dancing on our grave," Samshow said, "and here we are, like kids in a toy store."

35——

Reuben Bordes stood by the screen door, staring out at the cold rain washing the streets of Warren, half smiling and half frowning. His lips moved slowly to some inner song, and his eyes longed for something far away.

"Close the door, boy," his father demanded, standing in the hallway, dressed in ragged pajamas. "It's *cold* outside."

"All right, Pop." He swung the door closed and turned to watch his father settle into his easy chair. "Can I bring you anything?"

"I've eaten lunch, and I've had my nap, and I've been a lazy s.o.b. all day. Why should you bring me anything?" His father looked at him through rheumy, exhausted eyes. He was still crying at night, still sleeping with his arms wrapped around a pillow. Reuben had seen him in the morning, fast asleep, his face wreathed in empty bliss, his dead wife's thick feather pillow clutched firmly to him under the scattered blankets.

"Just asking," Reuben said.

"I'd invite them to meet my mum. My mother."

But she's dead.

"You could turn on the tube."

"What channel?" Reuben asked, kneeling before the television.

"Find me that show where everybody argues about the news. Take my mind away."

Reuben found the WorldWide News Network and waddled back, still crouched, hands dangling between his knees.

"You know, you don't have to hang around to keep me happy," his father said. "I'm working out Bea's death. I'm getting it straight in my head. I'll live."

Reuben smiled over his shoulder. "Where would I go?" he asked. But he knew he'd be leaving soon. There were necessary things to do. He had to carry what was in his coat pocket; he had to find the person that something was for. He had been given memories of a voice, a distinct English accent, but little more.

He leaned back against his father's knees and listened as the hosts of *Freefire* squared off against each other, bristling even as they announced their guest. The young liberal's stiffly formal visage seemed to soften.

"He's acted as advisor to the President on the Death Valley spaceship, and he's well known in scientific and journalistic circles. He's had over forty books published, including his recent prophetic novel, *Starhome,* a scientific romance about first contact. His name is Trevor Hicks, and he's a native of Great Britain."

"Citizen of the world, anymore, actually," Hicks said.

Reuben stiffened.

Voice.

I'd take them home to meet my mum. My mother.

"That's him," he said.

"Who?"

Reuben shook his head. "Where is he?"

"They're in Washington, like always," his father said.

"—Mr. Hicks, are we to understand that it was you who first advised President Crockerman to reason with these invaders?" the eager-faced conservative asked.

"Not at all," Hicks said.

Reuben's brow furrowed with the intensity of his concentration. *That's the one. He's Trevor Hicks. His name, his voice.*

"Then what did you tell the President?"

"Gentlemen, the President would not have listened to me no matter what I said. He hoped for a sympathetic ear, and I tried to provide that, but I am as adamantly opposed to his policy regarding the spacecraft as I imagine you are, Mr. . . . Mr. . . ."

"What *do* you recommend we do with the spacecraft? Should we destroy it?"

"I doubt that we could, actually."

"So you *do* hold defeatist views—"

Reuben trembled with excitement. *Washington, D.C.* He had

enough money saved to go there. Big town, though. Where would Trevor Hicks be in Washington, D.C.?

He listened closely, hoping to pick up clues. By the end of the show, he had a fair idea where to begin.

The next morning, at dawn, Reuben stood in the door to his parents', his father's, bedroom. His father stared at him from the bed, blinking at the orange hall light behind his son's silhouette.

"I've got to leave now, Pop."

"So sudden?"

Reuben nodded. "It's important."

"Got a job?"

Reuben hesitated, then nodded again.

"You'll call?"

"Of course I'll call," Reuben said.

"You're my son, your momma's son, always. You remember that. Make us proud."

"Yes, sir." Reuben went to the bed and hugged his father and was surprised again at how light and frail he seemed. Years past, his father had loomed a muscled giant in Reuben's eyes.

"Good luck," his father said.

Reuben pulled the overcoat around him and stepped out into the early morning frost, his boots crunching and slipping on the glazed steps. In one deep side pocket, the metal spider lay curled tight as an untried puzzle. In the other jingled two hundred dollars in change and bills.

"Good-bye, Momma," he whispered at the locked door.

36——

The afternoon had been tiring and the early evening showed signs of being even more strenuous. Samshow had already attended the public presentation of two papers in rooms filled half with geologists and half with TV correspondents and camera crews, ever hopeful of finding new revelations. What they got for the most part were technical presentations on resources discovery, migration of metallic ores in deep crust, and discussions of pinpointing Middle Eastern underground nuclear tests.

Samshow had left the last presentation and wandered into the spacious white-tiled men's rest room of the St. Francis.

He glanced up at his image in the mirror. Two young men in business suits, hair trimmed short, faces shaved so clean they might have been beardless adolescents, took positions at the urinals.

"This oxygen reading bothers the hell out of me," said one.

"Not just you," said the other.

"There's no place for it to come from. Increase by one percent." He shook his head as he zipped up. "More of that, and we'll all be drunk."

He rejoined Kemp and Post and they walked to the elevator, squeezing in beside four bewildered elderly tourists and two middle-aged geologists dressed in jeans and old sweaters. Arthur Gordon had arrived too late on Saturday to attend their first scheduled meeting. He had invited them to come to his room at seven, to talk and perhaps join him for late dinner after.

The hotel room was small. Post and Kemp sat on the bed, leaving the two guest chairs for Samshow and Gordon. Arthur shook Samshow's hand firmly and offered ice water. As he poured the glass in the bathroom, he asked, "Is there any consensus on this object supposed to be burrowing through the crust?"

He returned and handed Samshow the glass.

"None," Post said. Samshow agreed with a small nod.

"Maybe there's no consensus, but nobody doubts that something's there," Kemp said.

"Are you convinced your meteor sighting and the seismic traces are connected?" Arthur asked Samshow.

"I suppose I am," Samshow replied. "The South American traces we predicted did occur."

"And the object is still making noise."

"I talked with my company stations in Manila and Adak this morning," Kemp said. "Still grumbling like an old bear."

"Are the sounds weakening at all?"

"We think so. Our measurements aren't so precise we can be sure at the moment."

Post removed an electronic notepad from his pocket. "That's probably deceleration because of drag."

"And the second object . . . ?" Arthur prodded.

Somebody knocked at the door. "That's Sand, probably," Samshow said. Post got up to open the door.

Sand came in clutching a thick bunch of computer printouts. "Naval Ocean Systems just came through. I pulled these off the conference printer after setting up a data link." He spread the sheets out on the table. "There's half a dozen folks downstairs who can't wait to look these over, but since Mr. Gordon made the arrangements, I thought he should be the first. I've also got more on the oxygen figures, and Coomaraswami in Sri Lanka has distributed a paper on . . ." He pulled a stack of copies from his briefcase and handed them around the room. "On reduction of mean sea levels."

"Jesus," Samshow said. He took a copy and scanned it quickly. "Jesus H. Christ."

Arthur hefted the printout and pursed his lips. "What about the second object?" he asked again.

"Actually, that's shown . . ." Sand stood beside his chair and riffled through the sheets. "Right here. Wave analysis of the microseisms. There are two objects, orbiting around the center of the Earth—within the mantle and the inner and outer cores. They are slowing down at the rate of about one percent a day . . . *and,*" Sand said, almost triumphantly, "the supercomputers at UCSD have duplicated the effects using several different models. The best model requires an object less than a few centimeters wide, very long—hundreds of meters long—traveling at between two and three kilometers a second."

"What in *hell* would do that?" Samshow asked.

Nobody answered.

"Eventually, because of drag the objects will settle down at the center, right next to each other, right?" Arthur asked.

"Inevitably," Sand said.

Samshow finished his glass of water and set it on the table. He held a cube of ice in his mouth, bouncing it back and forth from the hollow of one cheek to the other with his tongue. "Would the President understand this, Mr. Gordon?" he asked.

"I don't understand it," Arthur replied.

"Two objects," Samshow said, "orbiting inside the Earth, missing each other, I presume, their harmonic motions being damped until they meet at the center. What does that remind you fellows of?"

Kemp didn't answer. Sand shrugged. Post's expression was one of extreme puzzlement, then slow enlightenment. "A fuse," he said. "It's like a timer. Is that what you're thinking?"

"I don't know what I'm thinking. We're all running around so fast, we're bound to fall flat on our butts . . . But yes, I suppose, a fuse or a bomb comes to mind."

"A timer powered by gravity," Post mused. "That's elegant."

"So what happens when they meet?" Kemp asked. "You might get one black hole. Nothing more exciting about one black hole, compared with two . . ."

"If they are black holes. The computer analysis says they can't be. They're drawn out now, elongated like worms, and the second one is different," Sand said. "Look at its traces. High radiation in the atmosphere. It's making more noise than the first. And remember the sighting—it sparked like a sonofabitch when it came through the air. Walt? How did you describe the first?"

"Two long, bright flares at first. Then small, much less bright."

Post's hand worked restlessly with his shirt collar. "Hell, it could be a plain old meteor, too," Arthur said. "Meteors spark. Would an amateur know the difference?"

"But what about the radiation? Every guess we make, we go out on a limb," Sand said.

"No kidding," Post chuckled.

Samshow leaned forward. "But let's assume the second one was a more spectacular fall. Bigger object?"

"The traces could indicate a slightly bigger object. Or . . . explosive disturbances along its path?" Sand suggested.

Arthur listened, amused by the creative confusion. "What would release radiation?"

"Small black holes might," Post said. "But they'd be considerably smaller in cross section than a few centimeters, if they massed in at only a hundred million tons. I don't think they'd make much of a show at all. And if they're putting out gamma rays at a high enough level to irradiate sailors dozens of kilometers away . . ." His face fell. "They're not going to last very long. Besides, they can't be black holes, remember?"

"What do you mean, about them not lasting very long?" Samshow asked.

Post made a frustrated face. "They're not black holes. We can be pretty sure of that. But, all right, black holes put out radiation all the time. When they're big, they're colder than the universe around them, but they're not at absolute zero . . . Still, the effect is a net intake of energy. But after tens of billions of years, or if they were created small to begin with, they become much hotter, and lose their mass much more rapidly, percentage-wise. When they drop down to about ten thousand tons of mass, they explode all at once—ten thousand tons of pure energy." He worked quickly on his calculator. "Not enough to cause much damage if they're deep inside the Earth, actually."

"But what we have is a hundred *million* tons," Sand said. "Or maybe twice that, if we count the second object."

"I was getting to that," Post said, holding up a hand. "The worst case is that the black hole, or holes, could suck up mass inside the Earth, grow, and eventually suck up all of the Earth."

The group looked at each other, wondering how much they were willing to believe, how far out they might be willing to go.

"That wouldn't make sense if the aliens had any intention of using the Earth's raw material to make more spaceships," Post said.

"What about something else, something we know nothing about?" Arthur persisted.

Samshow laughed. "You're saying we know anything about black holes?"

More silence.

"Maybe it's trivial," Samshow finally said. "But I'd like to discuss this oxygen increase and decrease in mean sea level . . . what are the figures?"

"Oxygen level up one percent, mean sea level decreased by one centimeter. What if they're related?"

"I'm sure we've all been thinking about that," Arthur said. "Something might be dissociating seawater into hydrogen and oxygen, on a huge scale."

"So?" Sand prompted. "Where's the hydrogen?"

"I haven't the slightest idea," Samshow said. "Just thought I'd mention it."

Post's frown intensified. "Very interesting," he said.

"Has anybody got any *good* news?" Arthur asked. "Something to cheer us up before we go to dinner?"

Nobody did.

37——

November 24

On a rare, dangerous but necessary outing to the town, Edward sat in the café, a plate with the remnants of a large hamburger and fries pushed to one side, and looked over the papers sent by his department head in Austin. Chits for release of back pay, amended W-2 forms, suggested teaching schedules for the next semester. A liability waiver from the school's attorneys, asking that the school be released from whatever slight responsibility it might have had for their being in Death Valley. The implication was, of course, that signing all these papers—especially the last—would mean his reinstatement and the resumption of his career.

Minelli entered the café and sat down quietly beside him. "You going to sign?"

"I don't see why not," Edward said. "You?"

"Sure. Back to normal." He grinned wanly and lifted a thumb, then looked at the thumb intently. "Hitchhiking back into life. The old school's acting as if they're afraid of us."

The waitress, young and plump and bright-faced, came out of the kitchen with a keypad. "You want to order something?" she asked.

"How's the meat loaf?" Minelli asked.

The waitress lifted her eyes heavenward. "Not recommended," she said. "We don't have any, actually."

"Nah, nothing for me."

"Anything else?" she asked Shaw. He declined. She issued a printed bill from the front of the keypad and he handed her his charge card.

"We should cut our book deals soon," Minelli said.

"There haven't been any offers," Edward reminded him.

"They're . . ." Minelli seemed to lose his train of thought.

"Reslaw thinks we're just lying too low to get any offers. We should talk to that Air Force attorney, or maybe to Mrs. Morgan's lawyer."

"You really want to write a book now?" Edward asked softly. "Go back over all we've been through, when *nobody* really knows what's going on yet?"

"You mean, why try anything until it's all over . . ."

Edward nodded. "We can stay here for another couple of days, spend some time out in the desert—"

"Away from Death Valley."

"Right. And then get back to Austin and hope the reporters have forgotten about us."

"Fat chance," Minelli said.

Reslaw came into the café and slid into the seat beside Minelli. He withdrew a folded New York *Times* from under his arm and spread it in a clear space on the table. The headline read:

MYSTERY OBJECT MOVING WITHIN EARTH

"That's where we should be," Reslaw said, pointing to the picture of a meeting room in the St. Francis Hotel. "Talking to these people." There were pictures of Kemp, Sand, and Samshow on the next page.

"What could we tell them?" Edward asked. "What do we know that they don't?"

Reslaw shrugged. "At least we'd be doing something useful."

"If they wanted to talk to us, they'd let us know."

"The President came to talk to us," Minelli said. "Look what he's done. We're a jinx. Did you ever think perhaps the alien put something in all of our minds . . . ?" He made a vague gesture toward his temple, eyes wide. "Something that makes us stupid and weak? Maybe it's making the President say things he doesn't mean."

Edward looked at Reslaw. "Anything in your head?"

"Not that I can feel."

"It's not impossible," Minelli said.

"No," Edward admitted, "but it's paranoid as hell, and that's the last thing we need, more fear."

Minelli turned the paper around to face him and read the article quietly.

"Stella says there have been more people on the highway, stopping at the motel, the trailer park," Reslaw said. "Most are going out to the cinder cone." He bit off an ironic laugh and shook his head. "I remember an old 'Peanuts' cartoon with Snoopy. The end of the world is coming, so let's hide under a sheet. With eyeholes cut out." He made circles around his eyes with his fingers and peered at Edward.

"Stop it," Minelli said pleasantly. "You're acting like me. Only one crazy fellow allowed in this group."

"What gives you privileges?" Reslaw asked, equally pleasant.

"Weak character. It's on my résumé." Minelli handed the paper to Edward. "This is really going to send them into a tailspin. They call it the smoking gun, whatever the hell it is. We've already been shot in the head, maybe, and we just haven't died yet."

"You do have a way with words," Reslaw said, staring at the palm of one hand. The waitress approached and he ordered a milkshake and a hamburger.

Edward finished the article and stood, dropping his tip on the table. "If everybody's going to be camping on the desert, there's no sense our looking for solitude. We should clear out of here and get back to Austin and leave these good people alone."

"Makes sense to me," Minelli said.

"What about your book deals?" Reslaw asked.

"Fuck fame and fortune. Who'd have time to spend the money?"

Stella had invited Edward to join her on a horseback ride that afternoon. They loaded four bales of alfalfa into the Morgan Company jeep and drove to a run-down corral a mile outside town. Three horses—a roan, a chestnut quarter horse, and a small, energetic pinto—stood with ears attentive in the middle of a broad pasture.

"I haven't had time to ride for months," Stella said, lifting a bale from the back of the Jeep and hefting it to a half-demolished feed pen within the fence. All three horses approached warily, tails swishing. "They're half wild by now." She smiled at him, flicking straw from the sleeves of her Pendleton. "Up to a challenge?"

"I'm an amateur. I haven't ridden in years."

The horses gathered to snuffle at the alfalfa, then settled in to feed. Stella hugged the pinto's neck and it regarded her with a wild pale eye, though not resisting her caress. "This is Star. Used to be my horse all the time. When I came back from school, I'd ride her all over the desert, out to the opal beds and down to the Indian digs, across the dry creek beds. We had a good old time, didn't we?"

Star munched.

"You should ride the chestnut gelding, that's Midge," she suggested. "Midge is even-tempered. Get acquainted."

Edward approached the chestnut and stroked its neck and mane, murmuring "Good horse, nice friendly horse."

After a few minutes of reacquainting the horses with human company, Stella brought two blankets and saddles from the Jeep. Star accepted the blanket skittishly, Midge with resignation.

"I'll get on them both first," Stella said. "Try them out and get them used to riders." She adjusted the cinch on Star and mounted easily. The pinto backed away from the alfalfa and paced around the feed pen nervously, then stood still and hoofed the soft dirt and old straw in a corner. Stella dismounted and approached Midge. Edward backed away.

She mounted Midge just as gracefully. Midge bucked from the feed and reared, throwing Stella on her back in the dirt. Edward yelled and grabbed the reins and kept his feet clear of the prancing hooves. When he had guided the horse away, he sidled it into a corner and went to help Stella to her feet.

"I'm fine. Just embarrassed." She brushed her jeans with quick, disgusted strokes.

"Gentle, hm?" Edward asked.

"He's your horse, obviously."

"I'll try to convince him of that."

A few minutes later, Midge accepted Edward's weight without protest, and Stella rode the pinto beside them. They walked to the far end of the corral and she dismounted to lift the wire loop on a sun-bleached gate.

Shoshone, like most of the desert resorts in the area, sat on a thermal hot spring that poured hundreds of gallons of water a minute out across the desert, and had done so, without letup, for decades. The runoff formed a creek that meandered under California 127, borax pans covered with grass and scrub, throwing up thick fringes of cattails along its banks.

They rode across the creek and into the dry desert beyond, coming finally to a borax-topped decline. With some prodding, the horses slid down the decline. They rode in shadow through the Death Valley sage of a quiet gully, glancing at each other and smiling but saying nothing.

The gully spread out onto a broad plain and the sage gave way to hummocky yellow salt grass. Part of an old narrow-gauge mining railway ran to their left, rails rusting on a long embankment of cinders and gray dirt. Birds called out in the stillness and a thick rat snake slid its meter length through the scrub.

"All right," Stella said, reining her horse up short and facing him. "I'm just about cured. How about you?"

Edward nodded. "This sure helps."

She sidled the pinto closer to him and patted its shoulder. "I've lived here all my life, with a few years at school and traveling. Europe. Africa. Peace Corps. My mother and sister and I have done everything we could to keep the town together after my father died. It's become my life. Sometimes it's an awful responsibility—you wouldn't think that, would you, since it's so small? But it weighs on me. Mother takes it in her stride."

"She's a wonder," Edward said.

Stella leaned her head to one side, looking sadly at the gravel. "You know, I said I was a radical. It was my sister who was the real radical. She went to Cuba. She has a complete set of Lenin and Marx on her bookshelves. She loves Shoshone as much as I do, but she had to leave. We think she's in Angola. Lord, what a place to be now. Me, I'm just a capitalist like all the rest."

"Hard on your mother, I guess."

"Who, me or my sister?" Stella smiled.

"I meant your sister. I suppose both of you."

"What about your family?"

"None to speak of. My father vanished more than twenty years ago, and my mother lives in Austin. We don't see much of each other."

"And your connections at the university?"

"I'm not sure I'll stay there, now."

"No long-term plans?"

Edward brushed at a buzzing horsefly and watched it veer across the hummocks until it vanished. "I don't see why."

"Mother and I have been making plans for selling mineral rights. We'll redo the town's sewage line with a government loan, but this extra money—that could keep the town going for years, even if the tourists keep flocking over to Tecopa."

"The big resort."

She nodded. "What a disaster for us all. Tecopa used to be a bunch of shacks built over hot springs. Rowdy. Now it's plush. The desert is like that."

"It's beautiful here. Something big could happen to Shoshone."

"Yes, but would we want it to?" She shook her head dubiously. "I'd like to keep it the way it was when I was a girl, but I know that's not practical. The way it was when Father was alive. It seemed so permanent then. I could always come back." She shook her head slowly, looking out across the grass to a lava-covered hill beyond. "What I'm getting around to saying is, we could use a geologist here. In Shoshone. To help us work out the mineral rights and figure out what we have, exactly."

"That would be nice," Edward agreed.

"You'll think it over?"

"Your tourist business should be real good for the next few months," he said.

Stella made a face. "We're just getting the freaks now. Religious nuts. All going out to the cinder cone. Who needs them? Everybody else is going to stay at home and wait it out. Do you think it's all going to go away?"

"I don't know." But he did know, in his gut. "That's not true, actually. I think it's all over."

"The things inside the Earth?"

"Maybe. Maybe something we don't even know about."

"It makes me so goddamned mad," Stella said, her voice breaking. "Helpless."

"Yeah."

"But I'm going to keep on planning. Maybe the whole deal will fall through. The commodities markets are going crazy. Maybe nobody will want to buy mineral rights now. But we have to keep working."

"I don't think I can stay," he said. "It sounds wonderful, but . . ."

Her eyes narrowed. "Restless?"

"I don't think I can really have a home now. Not even here, nice as this is."

"Where will you go?"

"I'll travel. Probably break away from Reslaw and Minelli. Go out on my own."

"Sometimes I wish I could do that," she said wistfully. "But my roots are too deep here. I'm not enough like my sister. And I have to stay with Mother."

"There was a place," Edward said, "where my father took my mother and me before he ran away. My last summer with him, and the best summer I've ever had. I haven't been back since. I didn't want to be disappointed. I wondered if it would have changed . . . For the worse."

"Where was that?"

"Yosemite," he said.

"It's beautiful there."

"You've been there recently?"

"Last summer, driving through on the way to the wine country. It was really lovely, even with all the people. Without crowds, it would be wonderful."

"Maybe I'll go there. Live on my back salary. I've dreamed about it, you know. Those peculiar dreams where I go back and it's completely different, but still something special. I think to myself, after all those years of just dreaming about being there, I'm finally back. And then I wake up . . . and it's a dream."

Stella reached out to touch his arm. "If . . . it works out, you can come back here after."

"Thank you," Edward said. "That would be nice. My teaching position will certainly be closed by that time. I can't expect them to wait forever."

"Let's strike a deal," Stella said. "Next summer, you come back here and help Mother and me. After you go to Yosemite, and after the world gets its act together."

"All right," Edward said, smiling. He reached out and touched her arm, and then leaned forward to kiss her on the cheek. "It's a deal."

PERSPECTIVE

Compunews Network, November 29, 1996, Frederick Hart reporting:
Here in the winter desert, only a few miles

from Death Valley proper, it gets bitterly
cold at night, and thousands of campfires
light up the grass and sand around the govern-
ment-declared National Security Site. In the
middle of the site, rising against the clouds
of stars like a great black hump, is the so-
called Bogey, the imitation extinct volcano
that has burrowed into the national imagination as the Kemp objects have burrowed into
the Earth's core, and into our nightmares.
People have come here from around the world,
kept back a mile from the site by barbed wire
and razor-wire barricades. They seem to have
come to worship, or to just sit quietly under
the warm desert sun and stare. What does it
mean to them, to us? Should they wish to storm
the site, will the Army be able to keep them
back?

Among their numbers are approximately ten
thousand Forge of Godders, with their various
prophets and religious guides. The American
branch of this cult has arisen in just three
weeks, sown in the fertile religious ground of
the American South and West by the President's
blunt, uncompromising words. I have spoken
with these people, and they share the President's convictions. Most are fundamentalist
Christians, seeing this as the Apocalypse
predicted in the Bible. But many come from
other faiths, other religions, around the
world. They say they will stay here until the
end. As one cultist told me, "This is the center. This is where it's at. Forget Australia.
The End of the World begins right here, in
Death Valley."

38———

December 1

Lieutenant Colonel Rogers, in mufti of hunter's cap and bush jacket and denims, hands in jacket pockets, stood at the edge of the Furnace Creek airstrip. A sleek eight-passenger private LearFan Special coasted to a stop twenty yards beyond, its two in-line props swishing the air with a diminishing chop-chop-chop. The plane's landing lights were extinguished and its side door opened. Two passengers—a man and a woman—stepped down almost immediately, peering around in the darkness, then approached Rogers.

"The President refuses to see any of us," said the man. Dressed in a recently donned and still disarrayed overcoat, black suit, and a silk shirt, he was very portly, late middle-aged, and completely bald. The woman was slender, in her forties, with large attractive eyes, a narrow jaw, and full lips. She, too, wore an overcoat and beneath that a dark pants suit.

"What does your group plan now?" the woman asked.

Rogers rubbed his jaw reflectively. "My group . . . hasn't fixed its plans yet," he said. "We're not used to this kind of activity."

"Congress and the committees are really on Crockerman's tail. They may bring him down," the man said. "We still haven't gotten McClennan and Rotterjack to join us. Loyalists to the last." The bulky bald man curled his lip. Loyalty beyond pragmatism was not something he understood. "Even so, it may be too late. Have you talked to the task force?"

"We're going to keep them out of this, as much as possible," Rogers said. "I talked to Gordon, and he even broached this sort of plan to me, but we don't know which of them might have supported his decision covertly."

"Do you have the sleeping bag?" the woman asked.

"No, ma'am."

"Do you know where you'll get it, if the time comes? Oak Ridge is in my district . . ."

"We will not get it from civilian sources," Rogers said.

"What about the codes, the complications, the authorization you'll need . . . the chain of command?" the woman persisted.

"That's on our end. We'll take care of it. If the time comes."

"They have the smoking gun, goddammit," the man said. "We've already been shot."

"Yes, sir. I read the papers."

"The admiral should know," the man said, with the air of drawing their conversation to a conclusion, "that our group can do no more in a reasonable period of time. If we do bring the President to ground, it will take months. We can't stop or delay the swearing in. The recommendation from the House Judiciary Committee will take weeks. The trial could drag on for half a year beyond that. He's going to hold out for at least that long. That puts the ball in your court."

Rogers nodded.

"Do you know when you'll act?" the woman asked.

"We don't even know if we can, or whether we will if we can. It's all up in the air."

"Decisions have to be made soon," she reiterated. "Everybody's too upset . . . this is too extraordinary a conclave for it to stay secret long."

Rogers agreed. The two returned to their LearFan Special and the plane's counterrotating props began to spin again, with eerie softness. Rogers returned to his truck and drove away from the airport as the plane whined into the blackness and silence of the overcast night.

Around the bogus cinder cone, for a distance of several hundred yards, soldiers patrolled well-lighted squares of the desert in Jeeps and on foot. Beyond the patrols and the fences, a mile from the object of their interest, the civilians gathered in trucks and vans and motor homes. Even this late, almost into the morning, campfires burned in the middle of wide circles of mesmerized watchers. Raucous laughter in one area was countered by gospel singing in another. Rogers, maneuvering his truck down the fenced approach corridor to the site, wondered if they would ever sleep.

39———

December 15

Two o'clock in the morning, the phone beside their bed rang, and Arthur came awake immediately, leaning forward to pick up the receiver. It was Ithaca Feinman. She was calling from a hospital in Los Angeles.

"He's going fast," she said softly.

"So soon?"

"I know. He says he's fighting, but . . ."

"I'll leave . . ." He looked at his watch. "This morning. I can be down there by eight or nine, maybe earlier."

"He says he's sorry, but he wants you here," Ithaca said.

"I'm on my way."

He hung up and wandered into the living room to look for Francine, who said she had not been asleep, but had been sitting on the living room couch with Gauge's head in her lap, worrying about something, she wasn't sure what.

"Harry's going, or at least Ithaca thinks so."

"Oh, God," Francine said. "You're flying down there?"

"Yes."

She swallowed hard. "Go see him. Say . . . Say good-bye for me if he's really . . . Oh, Arthur." Her voice was a trembling whisper. "This is an awful time, isn't it?"

He was nearly in tears. "We'll make it through," he said.

As Francine folded some shirts and pants for him, he slipped his toiletries into a suitcase and called the airport to book a flight for six-thirty. For a few seconds, dithering in the yellow light of the bedside lamp, he tried to gather his wits, remember if he had left anything behind, if there was anybody else he should notify.

Francine drove him to the airport. "Come back soon," she said, then, realizing the double implication, she shook her head. "Our love to Ithaca and Harry. I'll miss you."

They hugged, and she drove off to get Marty ready for school.

At this hour, the airport was almost deserted. Arthur sat in the sterile black and gray waiting area near his gate, reading a discarded newspaper. He glanced at his watch, and then looked up to see a thin, nervous-looking woman, hardly more than a girl, standing a few feet away, staring at him. "I hope you don't mind," she said.

"Beg pardon?"

"I followed you from your house. You're Arthur Gordon, aren't you?"

Arthur narrowed his eyes, puzzled. He didn't answer.

"I know you are. I've been watching your house. I know that sounds terrible, but I have. There's something I have to give you. It's very important." She opened the shopping bag and took out a cardboard box large enough to hold a baseball. "Please don't be alarmed. It's not a bomb or anything. I showed it to the airport security people. They think it's a toy, a Japanese toy for my cousin. But it's for you." She held out the box.

Arthur looked her over carefully, then said,

"Open it for me, please." He seemed to be operating on some automatic program, cautious and calm at once. He hadn't given much thought to assassination attempts before, but he could be a likely target for Forge of Godders or anybody tipped over the edge by the news of the last few weeks.

"All right." She opened the box and removed an ovoid object, steel or silver, brightly polished. She held it out to him. "Please. It's important."

With some reluctance—it *did* resemble a toy more than anything sinister—he took the object. Quickly, it unfolded its legs, gripped his palm, and before he could react, nipped him on the fleshy part of the thumb. He stood up and tried to fling it away, swearing, but it would not let go. Warmth spread quickly up his arm and he sat down again, face pale, lips drawn back. The young woman retreated, shaking her head and crying. "It's important," she said. "It really is."

"All right," Arthur said, more calm on the exterior than deep in his mind. The spider crawled into his suit coat, cut through the fabric of his shirt, and nipped him again on the abdomen.

The woman walked off quickly. He paid her little attention.

By boarding time, he was beginning to receive information, slowly at first. On the aircraft, as he pretended to nap, the information became more detailed, and his fear subsided.

40———

Hicks had stayed in Washington, hoping with a kind of desperate hope that there was still something he could do. The White House did not summon him. Beyond the occasional television interviews, fewer and fewer since the fiasco on *Freefire*, he was woefully unoccupied. His book had sold in a fresh spurt the past few weeks, but he had refused to discuss it with anybody. His publishers had given up on him.

He took long, cold walks in the snow, ranging a mile or more from the hotel in the gray midafternoons. The government was still paying his expenses; he was still ostensibly part of the task force, although nobody on the task force had talked with him since the President's speech. Even after the extensive reports of explosions in the asteroids, he had been approached only by the press.

When he was not out walking, he sat in his room, dressed in an oatmeal-colored suit, his overcoat and rubbers laid out on the bed and the floor, staring at his image in the mirror above the desk. His eye tracked down slowly to the computer on the desktop, then to the blank television screen. He had never felt so useless, so *between*, in his life.

The phone rang. He stood and picked up the receiver. "Hello."

"Is this Mr. Trevor Hicks?" a young male voice asked.

"Yes."

"My name is Reuben Bordes. You don't know me, but I've got a reason to see you."

"Why? Who are you, Mr. Bordes?"

"I'm just a kid, actually, but my reason is good. I mean, I'm not dumb or crazy. I'm in the bus station right now." The youth chuckled. "I went to a lot of trouble to find you. I went to the library and learned your publisher, and I called them, but they couldn't give your address . . . you know."

"Yes."

"So I called them back a couple of days later, I couldn't think of anything else to do, and said I was with the local television station, and we wanted to interview you. They wouldn't give me your address even then. So I figured you might be staying in hotels, and I started calling hotels. I've been doing that all day. I think I got lucky."

"Why do you need to talk to me?"

"I'm not a nut, Mr. Hicks. But I've had some odd things happen to me in the last week. I've got some information. I know somebody . . . well, who wants to get in touch with you."

The lines in Hicks's face deepened. "I don't think it's worth the bother, do you?" He started to put the phone down.

"Mr. Hicks, wait. Please listen and don't hang up just yet. This is important. I'd have to come out to the hotel and find you if you hung up."

Oh, Christ, Hicks thought.

"I'm being told something now, something important." The youth didn't speak for a few seconds. "All right. I got it now. The asteroids. There's a battle, there was a battle going on out there. There's this place called Europa, it's a moon but not our own, isn't it? That wasn't a battle. We have friends coming. They needed the . . . what was it, water under the ice in Europa? For power. And the rock way under the water and ice. To make more . . . things. Not like the machines in Australia and Death Valley. Do you understand?"

"No," Hicks said. A spark went off in his head. Something intuited. The boy's accent was urban, middle-western bland. His voice was resonant and he sounded convinced and rational, words crisp. "You could be a complete nut, whoever you are," Hicks said.

"You said you'd take them home to meet your mom. Your mother. They heard you out around Europa. When they were building. Now they're here. I found one dissecting a mouse, Mr. Hicks. Learning all about it. I think they want to help, but I'm very confused. They haven't hurt me."

Hicks remembered: he had made that statement in California, on a local radio show. It would have been very difficult for a midwestern teenager to have heard it.

There was something earnest and truly awed and frightened in the young man's voice. Hicks glanced at the ceiling, licking his lips, realizing he had already made his decision.

He had always been something of a romantic. To stay in journalism so long, one had to secretly believe in events full of drama and significance, key moments, points of turnaround in history. He was beginning to shake with excitement. *Instincts conflicting—reporter's instincts, survival instincts.*

"Can you come out to the hotel?" he asked.

"Yeah, I can take a cab."

"I'll meet you in the lobby. I'd rather be careful, you know. I'll be in the middle of lots of people." He hoped the lobby was crowded. "How will I know you?"

"I'm tall, like a basketball player. I'm black. I'll be in an old green army coat."

"All right," Hicks said. "In an hour?"

"I'll be there."

PERSPECTIVE

KNBC man-in-the-street interview, December 15, 1996, conducted at the gate to the Universal Studios tour "Earthbase 2500" attraction:

Anchor: We're asking people what they think about the President's proclamation.

Middle-aged Man *(Laughs)*: I don't know . . . I can't make heads or tails, can you? *(Cut away)*

Anchor: Excuse me, we're asking people what they think about the President's statement that the Earth is going to be destroyed.

Young Woman: He's crazy, and they should get him out of office. There aren't any such things as what he's talking about.

Anchor: Standing here, in the shadow of a gi-

ant invading spacecraft, its weapons aimed at
the crowd, how can you be so sure?
Young Woman: Because I'm educated, dammit.
He's crazy and he shouldn't be in office.
Anchor (*Moving on to an adolescent boy*): Ex-
cuse me. What do you think of the President's
statement that aliens have landed and are in-
tent on destroying the Earth?
Adolescent Boy: It scares me.
Anchor: Is that all?
Adolescent Boy: Isn't that enough?

41——

What Arthur saw, in the bed, was already a ghost: thin wrinkled
arms pale on the counterpane, face blotched, pale translucent
green oxygen tube going to his nose, drugs seeping into his arm
controlled by a small blue box with a flat-screen readout.

His oldest and dearest friend had become ancient, shrunken.
Even Harry's eyes were dull, and the grip of his hot hand was
weak.

A curtain had been stretched between Harry's bed and the
room's other occupant, a heart patient who slept all during Arthur's visit.

Ithaca sat in a chair at Harry's right, face tightly controlled but
eyes rimmed in sleepless red, hair drawn into a bun. She wore a
white blouse and skirt with a reddish-brown sweater. She would
never wear black, Arthur knew; not even to Harry's funeral.

"Glad you could come," Harry said hoarsely, his voice barely a
whisper.

"I didn't think it would be so soon," Arthur said.

"Magic bullets missed their target." He gave a tiny shrug of his
shoulders. "Status report: I'd cash in, but who stole my bag of
chips?"

Simply talking tired Harry now. He closed his eyes and let go of

Arthur's hand, withdrawing his slowly until it dropped to the sheet. "Tell me what's going on in the real world. Any hope?"

Arthur spoke of the conference and the objects within the Earth.

Harry listened intently. "Ithaca reads from the newspapers . . . I've been watching TV," he said when Arthur finished. "I finished my essay . . . about two days ago. Dictating. It's on tape." He pointed to a portable recorder on the nightstand. "Good thing, too. I can't concentrate now. Too many . . . ups and downs. Sons of bitches. Can no more will them away . . . than I can make myself healthy, huh?"

"I guess not," Arthur said.

"All the king's men." He drummed his fingers softly on the bed. "Anybody willing . . . to kill Captain Cook?"

Arthur smiled, his cheek twitching.

"Hope. Let's hope." Harry rolled his head to one side, facing a framed poster of sequoias to the left of the window. "The essay is for you alone. I don't want it published. It's not my best work. Use it . . . as you see fit." He closed his eyes. "Sometimes I don't know whether I'm dreaming or not. I wish I was dreaming now."

Arthur turned to Ithaca. "Harry and I have to speak alone for just a few minutes."

"All right," Ithaca said, with barely concealed resentment. She stood up and went into the corridor.

"Something juicy?" Harry asked, opening his eyes again.

"Do you remember when we were eleven, and I played that trick on you?"

"Which one?" Harry asked.

"I said I had been inhabited by a spaceman. That my body was being used to help investigate the Earth."

"Jesus," Harry said, shaking his head, smiling. "I'd forgotten about that one. You really took it to extremes."

"I was a kid. Life was dull."

"You spent three weeks acting like an alien whenever you were around me. Asking all sorts of weird questions, telling me about life on your planet."

"I never apologized for pulling that on you."

Harry held up one hand.

"You told me you had prayed to God to tell you whether I was a spaceman or not, and God had said—"

"God had told me you were a fraud." Harry's face seemed almost healthy now, with the memories coming back. "I was a pretty rampant little theologian then. So you ducked out."

Arthur nodded. "I said I'd be going away, and never coming back—the alien inside me, rather. And it did."

"You refused to acknowledge you had ever acted like an alien. Total memory blank. What a scam."

"Our friendship survived. That surprised me a little, years later, thinking about it . . ."

"I wouldn't have believed you if I hadn't wanted to. As you say, life was dull."

Arthur looked down at Harry's shriveled arms. "It wasn't right. I deeply regretted it. It might be the only thing between us I do regret . . ."

"Besides stealing Alma Henderson from me."

"That was a favor. No. I mean it. I especially regret doing that to you now, because . . . I'm about to do it again."

Harry's grin took an edge of puzzlement. Arthur's expression was deadly serious, but enthused; his arms fairly twitched with holding something in, and he reached up to pinch his cheek, as he always did when thinking.

"All right," Harry said.

That brought the tears to Arthur's eyes. The way Harry accepted whatever was coming from him, without hesitation, forthrightly. *You could be married a million years and such instant rapport would be impossible.* Arthur loved Harry fiercely then. The tears slid down his cheek and he took a deep breath, then leaned over and whispered in his friend's ear.

"Christ," Harry said when he had finished. He stared earnestly at Arthur. One finger slowly tapped the blanket. "Now I know I'm dreaming." He blinked at the cloud-filtered sunshine coming through the window curtains. "You wouldn't . . ." Abandoning that question, he said, "When did this happen to you?"

"This morning."

Harry looked at the curtain. "Ithaca. She can tell me. I've been confused. She left . . ."

Arthur took the metal spider from his pocket and held it before Harry's face, resting it in his palm. It moved its legs in a slow, restless dance. Harry's eyes widened and he made an effort to back up against the pillows. "Christ," he repeated. "What is it? What is it doing here?"

"It's a miniature von Neumann probe," Arthur said. "It explores, recruits. Does research. Gathers samples. It makes copies of itself." He returned the spider to his pocket. "Captain Cook has his own enemies," he said.

"So what are you, a slave?"

Arthur didn't respond for a moment. "I don't know," he said. "Who else . . . ?"

Arthur shook his head. "There are others."

"What if it's another . . . layer of deception?" Harry asked, closing his eyes again.

"I don't think it is."

"You're saying there's hope."

Arthur's expression changed to puzzlement. "That's not the word I'd use. But there's a new factor, yes."

"And this is all you know."

"All I know," Arthur said. He touched Harry's arm. They sat quietly for a few moments, Harry thinking this over. The effort tired him.

"All right," he said. "I've known you long enough. You told me so I could die with some good news, maybe, right?"

Arthur nodded.

"They let you tell me."

"Yes."

Harry closed his eyes. "I love you, old buddy," he said. "You've always managed to come up with the craziest things to keep me amused."

"I love you, too, Harry." Arthur stepped outside the room to call Ithaca in. She resumed her seat, saying nothing.

"I think you must . . . have a lot of work to do," Harry said. "I can't think straight and . . . I'm too tired to talk much now." He waved his finger: time to go.

"Thanks for coming by," Ithaca said, handing him the tape from the small recorder. Arthur hugged her tightly, then bent over the bed and took Harry's head gently between his hands.

Thirty years. I can still recognize him behind the mask of sickness. He's still my beloved Harry.

Arthur squinted, trying to hold back the flooding warmth in his eyes, trying to *will* another world where his friend would not be dying—ignoring for the moment the Earth's own illness, ignoring the general for the particular, a more human scale of magic—and knowing he would fail. Also trying to memorize something already passing: the shape of Harry's face, the set of his eyes, slightly athwart one another, even more elfin in his illness, though glazed; unable to imagine this fevered face with rounded nose and high forehead and strawlike patchy hair, even this ill frame, decaying in a grave.

"I'll carry you around with me wherever I go," he said, and kissed Harry on the forehead. Harry reached up slowly and hooked his hand around Arthur's wrist, touching his heated lips to Arthur's right palm.

"Same here."

Arthur left the room quickly, eyes forward. In the parking lot, he sat behind the wheel of the rental car, stunned, his head seeming stuffed with sharp twigs. "Thank you for letting me do that. I'd like to go back to my family, if there's time."

As the sun rose high over Los Angeles, nothing constrained him from returning to the airport and taking the next available flight back to Oregon.

42——

Hicks leaned against a massive marble-covered pillar, watching dozens of people enter and leave the hotel lobby. Most were dressed in business suits and overcoats; the weather outside was brisk and there had been cold rain just an hour before. Many others, however, seemed ill equipped for the weather; they were out-of-towners, gawkers.

Much of official Washington had seemed to come to a standstill. With the Senate, the House of Representatives, and the White House in open conflict now, such petty considerations as budgets had to wait. The tourist trade, oddly, had momentarily increased, and hotels through much of the city were jammed. *Come see your Capital in an uproar.*

After an hour, he still had not spotted Bordes, so he checked for messages at the desk. There were none. Feeling more isolated than ever, his stomach sour and his neck tense, he returned to the pillar.

It was remarkable how life went on without apparent change. By now, most of the people on Earth were aware the planet might be under sentence of death. Many had neither the education nor the mental capacity to understand the details, or judge for themselves; they relied on experts, who knew so very little more than they. Yet even for those with more education and imagination, life went on—conducting business (he imagined the events being discussed over expense-account lunches), politics almost as usual (House investigations notwithstanding), and then back at the end of the day to family and home. Eating. Visits to the bathroom. Sleeping. Lovemaking. Giving birth. The whole cyclic round.

A tall, gangly black youth in a green army overcoat passed through the rotating front door, paused, then walked ahead, looking right and left suspiciously. Hicks clung to the security of not moving, not making himself conspicuous, but the boy's head turned his way and their eyes met and held. Bordes raised one hand tentatively in greeting and Hicks nodded, pushing away from the pillar with his shoulder.

The youth approached him quickly, coat swishing around his ankles. An embarrassed grin crossed his face. He stopped two yards from Hicks and offered his hand, but Hicks shook his head angrily, refusing to touch him.

"What do you want from me?" he asked the boy.

Reuben tried to ignore Hicks's discomfiture. "I'm pleased to meet you. You're an author, and all, and I read . . . Well, forget that. I have to say some things to you, and then get back to work." He shook his head ruefully. "They're going to work all of us pretty hard. There's not much time."

"All of who?"

"I'd feel better talking where nobody will pay attention," Reuben said, staring steadily at Hicks. "Please."

"The coffee shop?"

"Fine. I'm hungry, too. Can I buy you lunch? I don't have a lot of money, but I can get something cheap for both of us."

Hicks shook his head. "If you convince me you're on to something," he said, "I'll spot *you* lunch."

Reuben led the way to the hotel cafeteria, emptying now as the lunch hour ended. They were led to a corner booth, and this seemed to satisfy the boy's need for privacy.

"First," Hicks said, "I have to ask: Are you armed?"

Reuben smiled and shook his head. "I had to come here as soon as I could, and I'm almost broke now as it is."

"Have you ever been in a mental institution, or . . . associated with religious cults, flying-saucer cults?"

Again, no.

"Are you a Forge of Godder?"

"No."

"Then tell me what you have to say."

Reuben's eyes crinkled and he leaned his head to one side, his mouth working. "I'm being given instructions by, I think they're little machines. They were dropped all over the Earth a month ago. You know, like an invasion, but not to invade."

Hicks rubbed his temple with a knuckle. "Go on. I'm listening."

"They're not the same . . . whatever you'd call the things that are going to destroy the Earth. It's hard to put in words all the pictures they show me. They don't show me everything, anyway. They asked me to just come to you and give you something, but I didn't think that was fair. The way they came on to me wasn't fair. I didn't have any choice. So they say, in my head"—he pointed to his forehead with a long, powerful forefinger—"they say, all right, try it your way."

"How do they oppose these enemies?"

"They seek them out wherever they go. They spread out between the . . . stars, I guess. Ships with nothing alive, not like you and me, inside them. Robots. They visit all the planets they can, around stars, and . . . They learn about these things that eat planets. And whenever they can, they destroy them." Reuben's face was dreamy now, his eyes focused on the water glass before him.

"So why haven't they come forward sooner? It may be too late."

"Right," Reuben said, glancing up at Hicks. "That's what they tell me. It's too late to save the Earth. Almost everybody and everything is going to die."

Despite his skepticism, these words hit Hicks hard, slowing his blood, making his shoulders slump.

"It's awful. They came too late. They had to stop off at this moon, this place with water and ice—Europa. They converted it into hundreds of thousands, millions, of themselves, of ships to spread out. They use hydrogen in the water for energy. Fusion.

"It's not just the Earth that's being eaten. The asteroids, too. And really, there was more danger, I guess, of these planet-eaters getting away from the asteroids. Easier to move away from the sun. Something . . . Damn, I wish I knew more about what they're showing me. They fought them in the asteroids. Now they can focus on Earth . . . The trouble is, they can't explain all of it to me in words I understand! Why they chose me, I don't know."

"Go on."

"They can't save the Earth, but they can save some of it. Important animals and plants, germs, some people . . . They tell me maybe one or two thousand. Maybe more, depending on the odds."

The waitress took their order, and Hicks leaned forward. "How?"

"Ships. Arks, like Noah's," Reuben said. "They're being made right now, I guess."

"All right. So far, so good," Hicks said. *Damn . . . he's actually convincing me!* "How do they speak to you?"

"I'm going to put my hand in my pocket and show you something," Reuben said. "It's not a gun. Don't be afraid. Is that okay?"

Hicks hesitated, then nodded.

Reuben drew out the spider and put it on the table. It unfolded its legs and stood with the glowing green line on its "face" pointed at Hicks. "People are meeting up with these things all over, I guess," Reuben said. "One of them got me. Scared the shit out of me, too. But now I can't say I'm doing anything against my will. I almost feel like a hero."

"What is it?" Hicks asked softly.

"No name," Reuben said. He picked it up and secured it in his pocket again as the waitress approached. She laid their food on the table. Hicks paid no attention to his baked fish. Reuben brought the spider out again and laid it down between them. "Don't touch it unless you agree, you know, to be part of all this. It sort of stings you, to talk." The boy bit into his hamburger voraciously.

Stings? Hicks pulled back a scant inch farther from the table. "You're from Ohio?" he finally managed to ask.

"Mm." Reuben rocked his head back and forth in satisfaction. "God, it's good to eat again. I haven't eaten in two days."

"They're in Ohio?"

"They're all over. Recruiting."

"And now they want to recruit me. Why? Because . . . they heard me on the radio?"

"You'd have to talk to it, them," Reuben said. "Like I said, they don't tell me everything."

The spider did not move. *Doesn't look like a toy. It's so perfect, a jeweler's fantasy.*

"Why are they doing this?"

The boy shook his head, mouth full.

"Let me . . . well, at the risk of putting words into your mouth, let me see if I understand what you're saying. There are two different kinds of machines in our solar system. Correct?"

Reuben nodded, mouth full again.

"One type wants to convert planets into more machines. We've been told that much. Now there's an opposing type that is designed to destroy these machines?"

"Exactly," Reuben said after swallowing. "Boy, they were right to pick you."

"So we're dealing with von Neumann probes, and probe killers." He pointed to the spider. "How can these pretty toys destroy planet-eating machines?"

"They're just a small part of the action," Reuben said.

Hicks picked up his fork and flaked away a bite of fish. "Incredible," he said.

"You got it. At least you're learning about it the slow and easy way. Me, this thing nearly blew my mind."

"What else do you know?"

"Well, I see things, pretty clear sometimes, really muddy sometimes. Some things have already happened, like the arrival of the machines that want to save us. They destroyed Jupiter's moon, to, like, make more of themselves, and for energy. But the cavalry arrived a little late—just after the Indians occupied the fort." He shrugged his shoulders. "After the bogeys came down on Earth. I suppose it's stupid to make jokes, but it's all crazy in my head, and I don't want it to make *me* crazy. Some things I see haven't happened yet, like, I see the Earth being blown into little rocks, more asteroids. And then these spaceships mining the rocks, eating them, making more machines."

"What do the machines look like?"

"That's not too clear," Reuben said.

"How is the Earth going to be destroyed?"

Reuben paused and lifted a finger. "At least two ways. This is pretty clear, actually. I hope I can find the right words. There are things, bombs, whizzing around inside the Earth. I think we know about these, right?"

"Maybe," Hicks said.

"And there are machines crawling deep in the ocean. Are there ditches in the ocean?"

"Trenches?"

"Yeah, that's it. Crawling along ocean trenches. They turn water into gases, hydrogen and oxygen, I think . . . H_2O. The oxygen bubbles off. These machines put the hydrogen into more H-bombs. And then they lay these bombs along the trenches, thousands of them. All over the Earth. I think they make the bombs go off all at once."

Hicks stared at the boy. "I'd like to have you talk to some other people," Hicks said.

The boy looked uneasy. "All I'm supposed to do is give you this." He pointed to the spider. "Am I making sense so far?"

Hicks stared at the silvery machine. "You're scaring the hell out of me."

"Is that good?"

"You've earned your lunch. If I make a phone call, will you be here when I come back?"

"Order me another hamburger, I'll stay here all day."

"You've got it," Hicks said. He flagged down the waitress. Again, Reuben pocketed the spider.

Outside the cafeteria, near the entrance to the men's rest room, Hicks found a phone booth. He had inserted his card into the slot and picked up the mouthpiece when he realized he hadn't the slightest idea whom to call. He had some vague notion to talk to Harry Feinman or Arthur Gordon, but he didn't know where they were, and it would probably take hours to track them down. Besides, Feinman was reputed to be very ill, perhaps dying. The task force had been scattered to the four winds after the President's speech.

Dithering, he replaced the mouthpiece and stared at a potted palm, biting the corner of a fingernail. *I am excited, and I am absolutely terrified.* He lifted one eyebrow and glanced across the lobby. *Hidden dramas.*

He could take the boy's spider and open himself—make himself vulnerable—to whatever the boy was experiencing. But he wasn't at all clear on what that meant. Would he give up his free will, become an agent of whoever controlled the spiders? Perhaps the spiders controlled themselves—more examples of machine intelligence.

There was no way of knowing whether or not they were controlled by the machines threatening the Earth. Another layer of deception.

Hicks sought the safety of the men's room and locked himself in a stall. Even after he had urinated, he stood behind the door, trying to control his shivers. *Why a spider? Not the most reassuring shape to choose.*

A battle in the asteroids. But perhaps it's not a battle at all; just part of the demolition and making of more planet-killer probes.

He closed his eyes and saw a shower of huge starships radiating outward, leaving behind the rubble of a ruined solar system. Would even the sun become part of this interstellar disease?

He fumbled at the stall latch and stepped out, brushing past a well-dressed, elderly gentleman with a cane. "Windy day out," the gentleman said, nodding and half turning to track Hicks with his gentle eyes.

"Yes indeed," Hicks returned, pausing at the door, glancing back.

The gentleman nodded at him again, and their gazes held. *God. Is he one? Possessed by a spider?*

The old man smiled and proceeded into the stall Hicks had vacated.

Hicks returned to the cafeteria and resumed his seat in the booth. "How many people have been recruited, so far?"

Reuben had eaten nearly all of his second hamburger. "They haven't told me," he said.

Hicks clasped his hands in front of him. "Do you feel that you've been possessed?"

Reuben squinted. "I honestly don't know. If they're not lying to me, they're helping all of us, and I'd rather be doing this than something else. Wouldn't you?"

Hicks swallowed hard. "Do you still have free will?"

"Enough to argue. It takes my advice, sometimes. Sometimes, it doesn't listen, and then it moves me around, so I suppose then I don't have control. But it seems to know what it's doing, and as it says, there isn't time enough to explain to everybody."

"You are extraordinarily persuasive," Hicks said.

"Thank you. And thanks again for the food." Reuben dabbled a french fry through a smear of catsup and lifted it in salute before biting into it.

"Where's the spider?"

"Back in my pocket."

"Can I take it with me, make up my mind later, after I've talked to people?"

"No, man, you touch that spider, it's going to . . . you know. Have you. I'm obliged to tell you that much."

"I can't really agree under those circumstances," Hicks said. *Fear and caution win out.*

Reuben stared at him, disappointed. "It really needs you."

Hicks shook his head, adamant. "Tell them, it, that I cannot be coerced."

"Looks like I made a mistake, then," Reuben said.

Something brushed Hicks's hand where it lay on the seat's vinyl. He had hardly turned his head to glance down when he felt a slight prick. With a scream, he leaped up out of the booth, banging one knee on the underside of the table. He fell over on the carpet and a tumbler of water spilled on his legs and feet. Pain shot up his leg and he held his knee with both hands, grimacing.

Three other patrons and two waitresses gathered around him as his vision cleared. Sharp warmth moved rapidly up his arm, into his neck, his face, his scalp. The pain subsided. He pulled his lips back and shook his head: so stupid.

"Are you all right?" a man asked, bending over him.

"I'm fine," Hicks said. He searched rapidly for an explanation. "Bit my tongue. Very painful. I'm fine."

He got up on an elbow and examined his hand. There was a tiny red spot on his thumb. *It stung me.*

Reuben was not in the booth. The man helped Hicks to his feet and he brushed himself off, thanking the others and apologizing profusely for creating a fuss. His hand touched an egg-sized lump in his coat pocket. "There was a young man with me. Did you see where he went?" He glanced nervously at the floor and the booth seat, looking for the spider. *But it's in my pocket,* he reminded himself.

"There's somebody leaving now," a waitress said. She pointed.

In the archway to the cafeteria, Reuben glanced over his shoulder at Hicks and smiled.

The boy walked briskly into the lobby, turned, and vanished. There was no need to follow him, so Hicks picked up the check and paid the waitress. He was shaking all over and wanted to cry, but didn't know whether it was British reserve or the instructions flowing through him that helped him maintain.

Doesn't feel bad, actually. Of course, I'm not in control . . .

He returned to his room, lay back in the bed, and closed his eyes. His shaking subsided and his breathing became steady. He rolled over on his side. The spider climbed out of his pocket and attached itself to the base of his neck.

What Reuben had tried to explain, then, unfolded before him in much more detail. An hour later, he wondered why he had even thought of resisting.

Sometime in the evening, the spider released his neck and crawled across the bed, dropping to the floor. He watched with less than half his attention; information was still flowing into him, and while some of it was incomprehensible, within a few minutes the flow would change, and he could understand more.

The spider climbed the television stand and quickly, with surprisingly little noise, drilled into the base. For an hour, sounds of cutting, stray beams of light, and puffs of smoke and dust issued from the television. All was quiet and still for another hour. Then two spiders dropped through the hole. Both crawled into Hicks's pocket.

"Bloody hell," Hicks said.

PERSPECTIVE

The Andrew Kearney Show (Syndicated Home Info Systems Net), December 19, 1996; guest appearance by science fiction writer Lawrence Van Cott:
Kearney: Mr. Van Cott, you've written sixty-one novels and seven works of nonfiction, or

rather, it says here, speculative nonfiction. What is that?

Van Cott: Science fiction without characters. Non-fact articles.

Kearney: We've been hearing for the last couple of months about the means by which the President's aliens will destroy the Earth. We've heard about things falling from the sky near the Philippines and in the Atlantic, passing into the Earth's interior. Two such objects have been sighted so far. Last night I interviewed Jeremy Kemp himself. He says that we have evidence the objects are causing a ruckus inside the Earth, below the crust.

Van Cott: From what I've heard, you should be interviewing Walter Samshow and David Sand. They saw one of the objects first.

Kearney: They're not available, apparently. (Van Cott shrugs)

Kearney (Leaning forward): What could these objects be? You're a science fiction writer; perhaps you can speculate in ways scientists won't, or can't.

Van Cott: It's a serious subject. I don't think speculation is what we need right now. I'd prefer to wait and see what the experts think.

Kearney: Yes, but you have degrees in physics, mathematics . . . (Glances at his notes) I'd say you're as much an expert as anyone, if we assume you've kept up on the reports. Have you?

Van Cott: I've read or listened to all that's been made public.

Kearney: Out of professional interest?

Van Cott: I'm always interested when reality catches up with me.

Kearney: Surely you have some theories.

Van Cott (Silent for a moment, tamps his pipe with his finger, looks up at the overhead lights): All right. (Leans back, holding out *the bowl of his pipe)* If these objects are as heavy as we think, they should be very big. But when they hit the ocean, they didn't make much of a splash. So they can't be both heavy . . . *(Clasps his hands together around the bowl of the pipe and shakes them, then withdraws them to arm's length)* and big. Heavy and small, that's something else. Not much energy transfer to the ocean or the sea bottom. Not much of an impact area. So we can draw some logical deductions. One, each object is very dense. Say they're made of neutronium. That fits the bill. We may not need black holes. Neutronium is matter squeezed down to push electrons and protons together to make neutrons. Nothing but neutrons. Never mind where the aliens would get this neutronium. Don't ask me. I don't know for sure. I also don't know how they keep a lump of neutronium squeezed together. The second one throws off a lot of sparks and causes radiation poisoning. Some people say the second one is making most of the noise, inside. *(Pokes the pipe down at the floor)* That speaks to me. That tells me something. Two objects, let's assume one is neutronium, then the other might be made of antineutrons, antineutronium.

Kearney: Neutrons are neutral particles, as I understand it. How can there be antineutrons if they're neutral?

(Music rises)

Van Cott *(Sighing):* That takes a while to explain. Why not break for a commercial, and then I'll tell you.

(Break)

Van Cott: Neutrons are electrically neutral, but that doesn't mean they can't have antiparticles. When two antiparticles meet, they annihilate each other completely. So now we have two objects, falling through the Earth. Neutronium is very dense compared with rock. The objects-let's call them bullets-would orbit within the Earth, passing through the core as if it were very thin air. They would be very cold-neutronium, being dense, would absorb lots of heat. They would not slow much at all during each orbit.

The antineutronium bullet would interact with the Earth's matter and create what's called an amti-plasma, which would prevent the antineutronium from blowing up all at once. This bullet would slow down much more rapidly. So finally it comes to rest at the center of the Earth, spitting and sparking, making lots of noise. When the other bullet slows down enough to also come to rest, the two meet . . . and I'm not sure what would happen after that.

Kearney: Maybe this anti-or whatever-plasma would keep them separated.

Van Cott *(Nodding):* Smart thinking. Maybe, and then again-maybe not. Maybe the pressure at the Earth's core would hold them together long enough for them to fuse.

Kearney: What would happen then?

Van Cott: Complete or almost complete annihilation of a hundred or two hundred million tons of matter. *(Holds his hands clenched in a double fist, spreads his fingers, and moves the hands slowly apart)* Think of it as a kind of time-delay bomb with a fuse controlled by gravity.

Kearney *(Considerably sobered):* That . . . Mr. Van Cott, that is a very disturbing thought. Have you spoken about this to anybody else?

Van Cott: No, and I'll probably be sorry I mentioned it here. It's my private speculation. I don't suppose it's private anymore.

43———

December 23

Walt Samshow and David Sand had been aboard the Glomar *Discoverer* for only an hour when they received an urgent phone call from Jeremy Kemp. Otto Lehrman, the Secretary of Defense, had released pictures from three Navy Kingfisher subtracker satellites just that morning. Why the pictures had been released was not explained; Kemp surmised it was part of a power struggle in Washington between the President and his decimated Cabinet and the military. Sand quickly hooked up a computer slate to the phone and Kemp transmitted the photos from California. There were more than a hundred.

An hour later, Samshow scrolled through the pictures on the slate screen while Sand asked Kemp about the details.

All of the pictures were of deep-ocean regions, taken from low-Earth-orbit submarine-tracking satellites. The satellites were equipped with laser spectrometers to detect oil and other detritus from submarine operations and ocean weapons testing.

The first fifteen pictures tracked the atmosphere and ocean surface above the deep trenches from south of the Philippines to the Kamchatka Peninsula, at approximately five-hundred-kilometer intervals, with little magnification. All were in false color to show concentrations of free oxygen in the near-ocean atmosphere. Within each picture were dozens of red dots against the general blue and green background.

The next group of ten showed waters off the western coast of Central America, with similar dots. In groups of two or three pictures, the ocean surfaces above all the world's deep trenches were shown to be regions of high free-oxygen concentration. Several unenhanced color photographs of very high magnification focused on an area three hundred kilometers east of Christmas Island in the Indian Ocean. They showed several square kilometers of ocean turned white with what appeared to be froth or spume. Then Samshow reminded himself of the scale: each tiny bubbling speck would have to be tens of meters across.

Here was the source of the atmosphere's increase in oxygen. No natural phenomenon could be blamed for such a display.

"So much for that," Kemp said. "Did you catch the *Andrew Kearney Show* last night?"

"No," Sand said. "We're not watching much TV here."

"Have you ever met Lawrence Van Cott?"

Sand hadn't.

"I have. He's sharp. He said something on the *Kearney Show* that's got Jonathan Post very excited. I haven't heard the tape yet, but Post says Van Cott may be on to something. Not black holes. Neutronium pellets?"

"Still out of my league," Sand said. He wanted to get back to the satellite data. Kemp passed on a few more items of information and then hung up. Sand reexamined the photographs on the slate as Samshow scrolled through them again.

"Why oxygen?" he asked. "Volcanic activity?"

"I don't think so," Samshow said. "Not in my experience. Something is definitely dissociating seawater into hydrogen and oxygen. But only the oxygen is showing up . . ."

"Some*thing?*" Sand asked softly. "What, machines? Where?"

"There don't appear to be bubbles above the ocean plains. Only in the trenches, and here and here, in known fracture zones." He scrolled back. "Wherever there are deep cracks in the crust, something is storing up hydrogen and releasing oxygen."

Sand made a clench-jawed *tsk-tsk*. "Kemp says oxygen is up by another percentage point in the Pacific region, and half a percent in central Eurasia."

"Approaching dangerous concentrations," Samshow said. "We're going to see conflagrations . . . forests, cities."

"I've already given up smoking, thank God," Sand said.

44———

Edward Shaw sat in a comfortable antique chair in the bar of the Stephen Austin Hotel—alone, with a whiskey sour in one hand and a fistful of Smokehouse almonds in the other. He had returned to Austin to straighten out his affairs, as might a man condemned to death by lingering illness. He found himself unable to cope with ordinary life any longer.

Austin and environs had been his final effort to get in touch with the past and attempt at least a symbolic reconciliation. His last girlfriend—almost a fiancée—had married a bank vice-president and wanted nothing to do with him. The university had taken his departure philosophically.

He had even broken free of Reslaw and Minelli in Arizona, though Minelli had promised to meet him in Yosemite in late March, weather allowing. He did not want his malaise to burden them. Reslaw, lightly bearded, hair cut to a thin shag, told them he was going to Maine to live with his half brother.

Edward had come back to his hometown to discover that his two-bedroom apartment had been emptied and rented to another tenant the month before—having been forgotten by the government agents looking after his affairs during his quarantine. That seemed a rather major oversight. At least the landlady had been kind enough to store his belongings in the event of his return. He had sold the furniture, but—to his own amusement—learned he still had a few things he couldn't bear to part with. These he had stored in a rental shed at the exorbitant rate of one hundred dollars a month, paid in advance for five months.

These things done, Edward became what he wanted to be, footloose and fancy free.

He had few doubts that the Earth would soon come to an end. He had bought a small-caliber pistol in case that end might prove too painful. (Pistols were at a premium now.) He had apportioned his savings and the government money to allow him a full five months of travel.

He had no urge to step outside the boundaries of the United States. Purchasing a small motor home (trading in his Land Cruiser) had depleted his assets by about a third. Now, for his final day in Austin, he was spending the night in the hotel, wrapped in a peculiarly enervated melancholy.

He was anxious to get moving.

He would travel around the country, and in late March or April he would end up in Yosemite, where he would settle in. The first part of his journey would give him a great overview of North America, as much as he could cover—something he had always wanted to do. He would spend a few weeks in the White River Badlands of South Dakota, a few days in Zion National Park, and so on, hitting the geological highlights until by full circle he came back to his childhood and the high rocky walls of Yosemite. Having surveyed some of what he wanted to see of the Earth, he would then begin to catalog his interior country.

Good plans.

Then why did he feel so miserable?

He could not shake free of the notion that one spent one's life with a treasured friend or loved one. Edward had always been essentially a loner. He felt no need to see his mother; she had kicked him out of the house at sixteen, and he had lost touch with her years ago. But there was still the myth, the image of the dyadic cyclone, as John Lilly had called it . . . the pair, facing life together.

He finished the whiskey sour and left the bar, brushing salt dust from his hand with the screwing motion of a bunched-up napkin. The doorman nodded cordially at him and he nodded back. Then he went for a two-hour walk around downtown Austin, something he had never done since he had been a student.

It was Sunday and the town was quiet. He wandered past white picket fences and black iron fences surrounding old well-kept historic houses. He studied bronze historical plaques mounted on pillars. Leaving the older neighborhoods, he finally stood in the center of concrete and stone and steel and glass pillars, the balmy midwinter Texas breeze rippling his short-sleeved shirt.

A human city, yet very solid and substantial-looking.

How could it just go away?

Not even geology encompassed the instant demise of worlds.

The next morning, having slept soundly enough and with no memorable dreams, Edward Shaw began his new life.

45——

December 24

Lieutenant Colonel Rogers sat in his trailer, waiting for word from the civilian liaison, a small, dapper saintly faced NSA man named Tucker. Tucker had but one role in this conspiracy—there was no other word for it—and that was to convey whether or not the weapon had been acquired.

The Sunday New York *Times* lay spread across a desk below three blank television monitors. On the front page, three headlines of almost equal size vied for attention:

PRESIDENTIAL CRONY ASSASSINATED
Reverend Ormandy Shot by Lone Gunman in
New Orleans

CROCKERMAN VETOES ALIEN DEFENSE ACT

FORGE OF GODDERS GATHER TO "PROTECT"
ALIEN CRAFT
Gathering of England-Based Cultists in
California

The whole world was going mad, and taking him along. In the past week, he had three times violated his oath as an officer. He was participating in a conspiracy that would ultimately subvert the expressed orders of the Commander in Chief of the United States Armed Forces. Within two weeks, sooner if all went as planned, he would attempt to destroy the very object the cultists surrounding the site wished to protect.

What disturbed him most of all was that he was not more disturbed. He hated to think of himself as a hardened radical, but he had indeed been radicalized, and he was no longer able to see and think of opposite courses of action. All he could see was a threat to his nation and a government in complete disarray. Extraordinary times, extraordinary measures.

The trailer phone rang. He answered and the command center operator told him he had an outside call from CINCPACFLEET— Commander in Chief, Pacific Fleet.

Tucker's voice came on the line. He was, more than likely, calling from the aircraft carrier *Saratoga* operating a hundred miles due west of San Clemente Island. He had, more than likely, just finished speaking with Admiral Louis Cameron.

"Colonel Rogers, we have an arrow and all the feathers we need."

"Yes."

"Do you understand?"

"I understand."

"Your next contact will be Green."

"Thank you."

He hung up the phone. Green was Senator Julio Gilmonn, Democrat, California. Gilmonn was chairman of the Senate Alien Defense Subcommittee. He would ride in a big limousine through the cordon of cultists and onto the site in approximately ten days. He would be heavily guarded.

In the trunk of the limousine would be the "arrow," a three-kiloton warhead originally designed for an antisubmarine missile aboard the *Saratoga*.

Carrying this warhead in a custom sling, Rogers would enter the bogey.

He folded the newspaper neatly and stood to make his afternoon rounds.

PERSPECTIVE

*CBS Daylight News, January 1, 1997, hosts
Tricia Revere and Alan Hack:*
Revere: Were you in Times Square or watching
it on TV?
Hack: TV. I value my life.
Revere: I've never seen anything like it. An
absolute frenzy.
Hack: They think it's our last year on Earth.
(Shakes his head at comment off camera) The
hell with that. Let's be real. They do. So
they're going to party.

46——

January 3, 1997

The wonder of it was that Arthur still felt like a private individual. He had driven Marty through drizzling rain to school, in a fit of parental solicitude—the school bus was perfectly adequate and stopped less than fifty yards from the front door. Returning, while parking in the carport, he had heard distant voices, some speaking English, most not. He had sat in the car with eyes closed, listening as if he were on some ham radio or satellite dish connection, but the voices had stopped, replaced only by a humming expectancy.

He had walked into the house, removing his overcoat. Francine had met him with a cup of hot cocoa. His eyes misting, he had sipped the cocoa, put it down on the kitchen counter, and hugged her. She had moved against him with more and more enthusiasm, verging on desperation, and he had led her into the bedroom, where they had made love.

He had not been "watched."

When not carrying out specific tasks, he was as free—within rational limits—as anybody he knew. He would not even contemplate leaving his zone of activity, the northwestern area of the United States. And if he tried to do so, he would be prevented. But there was plenty of work to do here, and more would be coming later on . . .

He lay with his head on his wife's ample tummy, hand around one breast, dozing lightly. She curled a lock of his hair in one finger and watched him with that womanly calmness he had so often marveled at. There had been passion, even obsession, in their bed that morning, yet now she was as placid as a crockery madonna.

He could tell her about the spider. Nothing would prevent him. He lifted his head and was about to speak, but then stopped. *So who's in charge? Is it me, hesitating, or something else?* It was him. She had enough to think about without learning her husband was possessed. That word amused and irritated him. It did not describe what was happening . . .

Why don't they take her, too? Possess her?

Because they didn't need her, and their resources were limited. Suddenly his spine tingled and his neck tightened. Only one or two thousand . . . What if nobody in his family was among that chosen group? None of his friends, colleagues, acquaintances? What if *he* was not?

"Something wrong, Art?" she asked, stroking his forehead.

He shook his head and caressed her nipple.

"You make me feel like something other than a mother and PTA member," she said. "You should be ashamed of yourself."

"Oh, I am," he said. "Thoroughly."

The rain gusted against the windows and a cold wind howled under the eaves. Ominous, patently ominous, yet it made him feel safe and warm. He could lie nude beside his woman in an enclosed warm bedroom and feel himself a master of infinite space. His body did not yet understand.

A network was being formed. Abruptly, he knew that libraries were being raided in New York, Washington, D.C., and elsewhere.

What was their scheme? Would they literally pluck up the Sistine Chapel and disks of Bach and the entirety of the Parthenon or Angkor Wat and lift them into space, along with the geniuses of Earth? Somehow, that seemed obvious and very naïve.

He had listened many times to Harry's "essay" on the tape. Ever since, he had been mulling it over, comparing Harry's ideas with what the nascent network was relaying to him.

In his head, a concept more than a word: *grammars.*

Hooked to that concept was a maze of connotations: grammar of a planet's ecosystem, from genetic material on up, how the species fit together as "words" in a "book," the structure of evolving plots and the implications for a denouement . . .

Grammar of society, how human groups interact as part of the overall ecosystem . . .

Fruit, gonads, a planet's reproductive system, a fertile pseudopod reaching up into space away from the surface and having to learn *Jesus Jesus.*

To learn about deep vacuum and gravitation and the wind between worlds, the ecosystem of Earth must evolve an "organ" or arm equipped with perception and logic, just as life had once adapted to the land by developing certain kinds of eyes and limbs and neurological structures. Sentences in Earth's book using the syntax of land-walking, space-walking, all implied by the original ecosystem grammar, all inherent. As on a thousand other worlds with similar living grammars. Humans were the Earth's organ for crossing between worlds and stars.

They speak Life. They know what to take to keep the essence, the basic meaning, of the planet intact.

That was what he was being told. Harry had said, on the tape,

"I've spent twenty years of my life as a biologist. You, Arthur, kept me up to date in other disciplines; you got my mind working fifteen years ago when you gave me Lovelock's book on 'Gaia.' Recent events have made me dig out some of my own old theories and speculations, made after reading Lovelock and Margulis. We've talked about them, off and on, but I was never so sure of myself that I put them down on paper. Now I'm pretty sure, but I'm too weak to put them on paper, so . . . this.

"Gaia is the entire Earth, and she's come alive, she's been an organic whole, a single creature, for over two billion years now. We can't make complete analogies between Gaia and human beings, or dogs or cats or birds, because until recently we've never studied

actual independent organisms. Dogs and cats and birds—and humans—are not independent. We are bits and pieces of Gaia. So is every other living thing on the Earth. Imagine a single cell trying to make analogies between its cytoplasm and organelles, and the role it plays in a human body; it's going to be misled if it compares too rigidly.

"So Gaia, the Earth, is the first independent organism we've studied. I'll call her a 'planetism.' A planetism is made up of plants and animals and microorganisms, and these are made up of cells, or are themselves cells. Cells are made up of cytoplasm and organelles and so on. An organism regulates itself with hormones, neurotransmitters, and it does its work and gets its nutrition with enzymes and other substances . . . all organized, on schedule, synergistic. Self-controlled.

"Gaia does her work with ecosystems. Like any organism, a planetism has a schedule and certain goals to meet. She grows and develops and goes through different stages in her life. Sometimes she undergoes radical shifts, destroying whole ecosystems. Maybe she's experimenting in ways that smaller organisms cannot; she reaches a dead end, clears some of the slate, and starts over. I don't know. But ultimately she has to do what all living things do— mature and reproduce.

"How can a planetism make others like herself? She came into being—probably—without outside interference, though maybe she's the offspring of another planetism. Maybe life was seeded here a long, long time ago. I don't think so, frankly. I think most planetisms have no parents, at least not right now, and so they're free to develop on their own schedule. This takes a long, long time, but eventually she finds a way to reproduce. She develops a reproductive strategy.

"The planetism has found ways to use more and more of her raw materials and surface area. She dominated the oceans, then spread plants and animals out to conquer the barren continents. These plants and animals had somehow become specially suited to life on land. I suspect more than random chance was at work, but I'm too weak to argue about that now. It's irrelevant to my scheme.

"Now, after ages, humans are here, and we're not doing too badly. We've got an organ as important as the legs on an amphibian—a highly developed brain. Suddenly, Gaia is becoming self-aware, and looking outward. She's developing eyes that can look

far into space and begin to understand the environment she has to conquer. She's reaching puberty. Soon she's going to reproduce.

"I know you're way ahead of me now. You're saying, 'That means human beings are the Earth's gonads.' And I am saying that, but the analogy is weak at best. In time, Gaia would probably have sacrificed everything on Earth—all her ecosystems—to promote human beings. Because we're more than gonads. We are the makers of spores and seeds, we are the ones who understand what Gaia is, and we will soon know how to make other worlds come alive. We will carry Gaia's biological information out into space, on spaceships.

"You know, this idea puts a lot of problems in perspective. Gaia has nurtured us, but she has also goaded us, and sometimes tormented us. She's used all of her resources to make sure we don't feel too comfortable. Diseases that used to help regulate ecosystems have suddenly become stimulants. We're working hard to control all the diseases that harm us, and in doing so, we're understanding life itself, and coming to understand Gaia. So Gaia uses diseases to stimulate and instruct. Is it any real coincidence, you think, that in the twentieth century, we've been hit by so many retrovirus and immune system epidemics? We can't solve these epidemics without understanding life to the nth degree. Gaia is regulating us, regulating herself, making herself ready for puberty.

"Because that's what would have happened. Gaia would have sent us out, and we would have carried her within our spaceships. Maybe we would have made Earth unlivable, and that would be one more reason to leave the seed pod, because it's all dead and shriveled. But that would only be natural. Maybe we would have preserved Earth and gone outward. It's like the dilemma for parents who either make life a hell for their kids to get them out, or the kids have enough gumption to get out on their own, to break loose. Not that I know these problems firsthand, as a parent . . . but I remember being a kid.

"Of course, Gaia isn't the only planetism. There are probably billions of others, some of them part of seeding networks—planetisms with parents. Some are independent. And when they get out into the galaxy, they find they are in competition. Suddenly they're part of an even larger, much more complex system—a galactic ecology. Planetisms and their extensions—intelligences, *technological civilizations—then develop strategies to compete, and to eliminate competition.*

"Some planetisms take the obvious route. They exploit and try to spread rapidly. They're like parasites, or young diseases that haven't learned how to live harmlessly within a host. Other planetisms react by seeking and destroying the extensions of these parasites. Eventually, I suppose, if the galaxy itself is to come alive —become a 'galactism'—it's going to have to knit together the extensions of all its planetisms, put them in order. So the parasites either fit in and contribute or they are eliminated. But in the meantime, it's a jungle out there.

"You talked to me a long while back about Frank Drinkwater. Drinkwater, and others like him, have maintained for years that there is no other intelligent life in our galaxy. He claims that the lack of radio signals from distant stars provides the proof. He also thought the lack of von Neumann machines confirmed that we are alone. He was too impatient. Now, obviously, he's wrong.

"We've been sitting in our tree chirping like foolish birds for over a century now, wondering why no other birds answered. The galactic skies are full of hawks, that's why. Planetisms that don't know enough to keep quiet, get eaten.

"I'm just about done now. Too tired to elaborate. Maybe you've already thought this through. Maybe you can find it useful, anyway.

"You've been my own goad and barb sometimes, Art. Thank you for that. You are my very dear friend, and I love you.

"Take care of Ithaca, as much as she needs it.

"My love to Francine and Marty, too.

"I hope and pray you all make it, though for the life of me, I can't figure out how."

Harry had known, almost by instinct. He was still alive, hanging on in Los Angeles, too weak to do much besides sleep. Arthur suddenly felt a panic at the thought of a world without him. What would he do? Now, more than ever, Harry was necessary . . .

"Art," Francine said. He tried to relax and brought his gaze down from the ceiling, to her face. "Are you thinking about Harry?"

He nodded. "But that's not all." Without considering the consequences, moving ahead on an instinct he hoped was as good as Harry's, he had made up his mind. "There's something big going on," he said. "I've been afraid to tell you."

"Can you tell me?" she asked, squinting as if reluctant to hear. Enough change, enough shock in the news without it coming into her house any more than it already had.

"It's not a government secret," he said, smiling. He told her about the encounter in the airport, the information in his head, the formation of the network. It spilled from him in a confessional torrent, and he interrupted only to let Gauge in when the pup howled miserably in the garage.

Francine watched her husband's shining eyes and his beatific face and bit her lip.

When he was finished, he shivered and shrugged all at once. "I sound completely nuts, don't I?"

She nodded, a tear falling down her cheek.

"All right. I'll show you something very strange."

He went to the locked upper-hall cupboard and drew down a cardboard box. In the bedroom, he drew off the lid. Within the box, to his surprise, lay not one but two identical spiders, motionless, their green linear eyes glowing. Francine backed away from the open box.

"I didn't know there was another," he said.

"What are they?"

"Our saviors, I think," Arthur answered.

Will she be saved? he asked the humming expectancy in his head. She reached out to touch the spiders, and he was about to stop her, warn her, when he realized it didn't matter. If they had wanted her to be "possessed," the new spider—wherever it came from—would have already taken her. Hesitantly, she reached out to touch one. It did not react. She stroked the chromium body thoughtfully. The spiders moved their legs in unison, and she withdrew her hand hastily. The motion stopped.

"It's like they're alive," she said.

"I think they're just very complicated machines."

"They take samples, store information . . . and they . . ." She swallowed hard and wrapped her arms around herself. She began to shiver, her teeth clacking. "Ooo-o-h, Ar-rthur . . ."

He reached out to hug her tightly, laying his cheek on the top of her head, nuzzling her.

"I'm still here," he said.

"Everything is so unreal."

"I know."

"What . . . what do we do now?"

"We wait," he said. "I do what I must do."

Her expression as she craned her head back to face him was a mix of fascination and repulsion. "I don't even know that you are who you say you are."

He nodded. "I can't prove that."

"Yes, you can," she said. "Please, maybe you can. Maybe I know already." She folded herself more compactly into his arms and hid her face against his chest. "I don't want to think . . . I've lost you already. Oh, God." She pulled away again, mouth open. "Don't tell Marty. You haven't told Marty?"

"No."

"He couldn't take it. He has nightmares already about fire and earthquakes."

"I won't tell him."

"Not until later," she said firmly. "When we know for sure. What's going to happen, I mean."

"All right."

Then it was time to dress and pick up Marty from the school. They drove together through the drizzle.

That evening, after Marty had gone to bed and while they sat together on the couch in the living room reading, legs entangled, the phone rang. Arthur answered.

"I have a call for Arthur Gordon from President Crockerman."

Arthur recognized the voice. It was Nancy Congdon, the White House secretary.

"Speaking."

"Hold on, please."

A few seconds later, Crockerman came on the line. "Arthur, I need to speak with you or Feinman, or with Senator Gilmonn . . . I assume you're in touch with him, or with the Puzzle Palace?"

"I'm sorry, Mr. President . . . I haven't spoken with the senator or the NSA. Harry Feinman is very ill now. He's dying."

"That's what I was told." The President said nothing for a long moment. "I'm under siege here, Arthur. They still can't get a vote through in the House, but they're maybe two votes down . . . I'm not sure I know everybody who's laying siege, but I thought you might be able to speak to them. You don't need to admit complicity . . . or whatever you would call it."

"I may not be the right man, Mr. President," Arthur said.

"In the past few hours, I have been denied access to the war room. I've fired Otto Lehrman but that hasn't stopped a thing. Jesus, they've actually threatened to withdraw the troops around the White House! All they've done is clearly illegal, but these people . . . They can afford to wait me out. Something's going on. And I *need to know what it is*, for Christ's sake. I'm the *President of the United States*, Arthur!"

"I don't know anything about this, Mr. President."

"Right. Hold to the party line. For whatever it's worth, I'm not a stubborn idiot. I've spent the last few weeks agonizing over this. I've spoken with Party Secretary Nalivkin. Do you know what they're doing? They're negotiating with the bogey in Mongolia. He says the world is on the brink of a socialist millennium. That's what the spacecraft in Mongolia is telling him! Arthur, give it to me straight . . . Is there anybody I can talk to who can put me back in the chain of command? I am not an unreasonable man. I can be reasoned with. God knows I've been thinking this all over. I'm willing to rethink my position. Have you heard about Reverend Ormandy?"

"No, sir."

"He's dead, for Christ's sake! They shot him. Somebody shot him."

Arthur, face pale, said nothing.

"If they aren't talking to you, then who would they be talking to?"

"Have you called McClennan, or Rotterjack?" Arthur asked. Both of them had sworn allegiance to Crockerman even after their resignations.

"Yes. I can't get through to them. I think they've been arrested or kidnaped. Is this a revolution, a mutiny, Arthur?"

"I don't know, sir. I honestly don't know."

Crockerman muttered something Arthur didn't hear clearly and hung up.

47——

January 4

Reuben Bordes met the Money Man near the Greyhound bus terminal on Twelfth Street. The white-haired, paunchy stranger wore a dark blue wool suit, pin-striped golden silk shirt, and alligator-skin shoes. He seemed perfectly happy to pass Reuben a plump gray vinyl zippered bag filled with hundred- and thousand-dollar bills. Reuben shook his hand firmly, smiled, and they parted without a word said between them. Reuben stuck the envelope into the pocket of his olive-green army coat and hailed a cab.

Instructions given, he sat back in the seat, happier than he had ever been in his life. With this money, he could be traveling in style now: taxicabs, airplanes, fine hotels wherever he went. But more than likely the money would be spent on other things. Still, the thought . . .

There was an extensive shopping list in his head. His first stop would be the Government Printing Office Data Center. There he would purchase four sets of data disks containing the entire public-domain nonfiction records of the Library of Congress. Each set, on five hundred disks, occupied the space of a good-sized filing cabinet, and he did not know why four copies were necessary, but he would pay for them all in cash with about half of the money in the envelope.

He stood in line at the service counter of the Data Center for ten minutes, and then stepped up to the clerk, a young, balding man with a full red beard and a sharply appraising stare.

"Can I help you?" the clerk asked.

"I'd like four sets of number 15-692-421-3-A-G."

The clerk wrote the number down and consulted a terminal. "That's nonfiction, complete, L.C.," he said. "Including all reference guides and indices?"

Reuben nodded.

The clerk's stare became more intense. "That's fifteen thousand dollars a set," he said.

Reuben calmly unfolded a roll of money and counted out sixty thousand-dollar bills.

The clerk examined the bills carefully, rubbing them, holding them up close. "I'll have to call my supervisor," he said.

"Fine," Reuben said.

A half hour later, all the formalities cleared away, Reuben wrote down where he wanted the sets sent—a mailing address in West Virginia.

"What will you *do* with them all?" the clerk asked as he handed Reuben the receipt.

"Read them," Reuben said. "Four times."

He regretted that flippancy as he walked south on Seventh Street toward the National Archives, but only for a moment. Instructions were pouring in rapidly, and he had little time to think for himself.

48——

January 5

Lieutenant Colonel Rogers came out of a sound sleep at four A.M., just minutes before his wristwatch alarm was set to go off. He deactivated the alarm and switched on the small lamp at the head of his narrow bunk. For a luxurious minute, he lay still in the bunk, listening. All was quiet. All calm. It was Sunday; most of the Forge of Godders had moved to Furnace Creek the night before for a huge rally planned this morning by the Reverend Edwina Ashberry.

He dressed quickly, putting on climbing boots and pulling two hundred-foot lengths of nylon rope from a knapsack in the trailer's corner. Rope in hand, he looked down, brows knitted, at the small desk and telephone. Then he dropped the ropes on the bunk and sat in the chair to write a letter to his wife and son, in case he did not make it back. That took five minutes. He was still ahead of schedule, so he spent five more minutes carefully shaving, making sure every long bristle on his neck was scraped off: military clean. He brushed his teeth and combed his hair meticulously, glancing at the letter. Unhappy with the wording, he quickly recopied the message onto a fresh piece of paper, signed it, folded it into an envelope, and posted the envelope on his message board with address and instructions.

At four-thirty he descended the trailer steps and stood in the bitterly cold desert darkness, a steady wind dragging at his coat and pants legs. At the east end of the camp was Senator Julio Gilmonn's car, in a fenced-off square reserved for the munitions locker. Gilmonn himself stood with two aides, a handsome, stern-looking middle-aged black woman and a young white male, bulky and clean-cut, near the inner gate leading to the rock.

"Good morning," Rogers said as he approached. Gilmonn extinguished a cigarette after taking one last frowning, concentrated drag and shook Rogers's hand.

"There are still a few Forgers out there," the senator said, pointing to the outer-perimeter fence. "Have you made any plans for clearing them?"

Rogers nodded. "In fifteen minutes we'll set off a siren and announce an emergency situation. Nothing specific. Then we'll evacuate the camp through the corridor. If the Forgers haven't cleared out by then . . ." He shrugged. "The hell with them."

"That could alert the . . . bogey," the young aide said.

Rogers acknowledged that possibility. "It hasn't done anything for months that we know of," he said. "We'll just take the risk. There are about a thousand people out there now."

The woman regarded Rogers with an expression between severe doubt and motherly concern, but said nothing.

"Who else is involved?" Gilmonn asked.

"I'm having two of my staff officers help me carry the weapon to the entry. They'll evacuate at that point. And there's your expert, of course. Where is he?"

Gilmonn pointed to a figure walking through a spotlighted area a few dozen yards away. "He's coming now."

The "expert" was a young naval lieutenant, lean and of middle height, with thin, precise eyebrows and short-cut tight brown hair, dressed in civvies and carrying a large bag and a briefcase. He greeted the others quietly and asked to be taken to the weapon.

Gilmonn opened the gate with the key Rogers had entrusted to him, and then lifted the trunk lid. Within was an orange-striped silver cylinder about a foot and a half wide and two feet long, lying in an aluminum cradle. The radiation-warning trefoil was prominently featured at three points on the cylinder.

"We don't have a presidential authorization code," the lieutenant explained matter-of-factly. "So I've had to take an unarmed, stockpiled missile warhead and remove the PAL—the permissive action link, the code box. This causes a fatal mechanical failure in the detonator and proximity fuse—fatal to the mechanism, not to me. So I've had to engineer my own time fuse and detonator and match them with the warhead. With higher authorization, I've taken a Navy plane wave generator and klystron and the necessary black boxes and cobbled them together. I can guarantee that it will work." He smiled almost apologetically and turned to Rogers. "Sir, you will be able to deactivate this weapon, should you encounter something unexpected, right up to the last second before it goes off. So pay close attention."

Rogers listened carefully as the lieutenant removed a cover plate from one end of the cylinder and explained the procedure. He then explained it all over again, checking Rogers's face at each crucial point to make sure he understood. "Got that, sir?" the lieutenant asked.

"Yes," Rogers said.

"I apologize we couldn't find a backpack nuke—a SADM—for you, sir," the lieutenant said. "But they've been out of stock for about twenty years. They've all been scrapped or dumped. This only weighs about a third again as much as a SADM—special atomics demolition munition," he explained for the benefit of the senator's aides. "But you should be able to haul it up with no difficulty if the shaft is as smooth as you've said. Then push and pull it for the next leg, and when you can stand, haul it into position using your backpack. You seem to be in good shape, sir, and you should be able to complete the mission . . ." The lieutenant shook his head. "Sorry. I don't mean to tell you your business, sir."

"No problem," Rogers said.

"Just one question. Nobody back home was able to answer something for me. How strong is this bogey, internally?"

"We don't know," Rogers said.

"Strong enough, possibly, to have survived a descent from orbit," Gilmonn said.

"If it offers even token resistance to the weapon, then I can't estimate the effect on the surrounding countryside," the lieutenant said. "Unless it stays integral, which I really doubt, there's going to be hot rock and shrapnel all over this valley. I don't know how far away you'll have to be, sir."

"I'll have a Jeep," Rogers said.

"Drive like hell," the lieutenant recommended. "And another thing. What sort of drive mechanism might it have?"

Rogers shook his head. "There's no outlets, no nozzles or . . . Nothing we've seen."

"If there is a drive mechanism—which seems logical, if we think of it as a spaceship—then the explosion could set it off."

Rogers took a deep breath. "I've thought about that," he said.

"We've detected no radiation in or around the bogey," Gilmonn said. "If there's any drive mechanism, I doubt very much they use rocket fuel."

"Yeah, but what *do* they use?" the lieutenant asked.

"Everything we do here involves some risk," Gilmonn said. "And if they think we can be bamboozled by our own imaginations . . . How much stronger does that make them? What has that kind of thinking done to us already?"

The sirens began to wail, echoing back from the mountains, painful and terrifying. Loudspeakers around the perimeter announced:

"This is an emergency. This is an emergency. Evacuate all personnel immediately." The message repeated, louder than the sirens, until Rogers felt he might jump out of his skin. Around the site, car horns began to honk. Headlights flashed like the eyes of wary animals. Gilmonn held his hands to his ears. "Are we going ahead, or are we going to stand here and waffle?"

Rogers nodded. "We're on."

The lieutenant reached into the bag and pulled out a white jacket with a crotch strap. "Residual radiation protection, sir. Put this on now," he shouted over the din. He pulled out another and donned it himself, connecting the crotch flap to a loop on the back.

The jacket weighed perhaps twenty pounds and seemed reasonably flexible, with overlapping sheets of leaded plastic sewn into its fabric.

"You do me, and I'll do you." Rogers helped secure the straps and the lieutenant reciprocated.

"Let's go, sir," the lieutenant said. Together, they lifted the weapon from its cradle in the car's trunk onto a hand truck. It weighed at least sixty-five pounds, perhaps seventy. "No need to be delicate, sir. It's made to withstand missile launch and ocean impact. We'd have to take a sledgehammer to it to do any damage."

Rogers opened the inner perimeter gate and they pulled the hand truck a hundred yards across the pounded sand and gravel trail to the entry hole.

The lieutenant lifted the cylinder from its cradle by himself and lowered it on one end into the sand. The sirens continued to scream and the loudspeakers repeated the evacuation order, over and over, painfully monotonous.

The first suffusion of dawn outlined the Greenwater Range in ghostly purple. Bouncing headlight beams still cut through the air around the site, but fewer in number now.

"Looks like they're moving out," Gilmonn said.

"Time for the camp to evacuate," Rogers said. "I'll need the lieutenant and one other, that's it."

"I'm staying until you're in the tunnel and the arrow's up there with you," Gilmonn said.

"We call it a 'monkey' now, sir, not an arrow," the lieutenant corrected him.

"Whatever the hell," Gilmonn said.

"Monkey on my back," Rogers said.

The lieutenant pulled an inch-thick Teflon sheet from the weapon's accessory kit and wrapped it tightly around the cylinder, belting it with three straps and a clasp. The top and bottom of the sheet projected over the ends of the cylinder, blunting any sharp edges that might hang up inside the tunnel. He then attached two ropes to sunken eyebolts in the upper end, on each side of the cover plate. "All set, sir?"

Rogers nodded. "Let's go."

The lieutenant removed the cover plate and set the timer. "You have forty minutes, sir, from the time I flip this switch. We'll stay down here for fifteen minutes. You'll have your Jeep to drive clear after we leave."

"Understood," Rogers said.

He climbed into the hole, paying out the ropes from loops in his belt, and scrambled to the first bend, then braced himself there. "Bring it up," he said. The lieutenant flipped the switch, closed the plate, and hefted the weapon up into the hole. Rogers pulled it up the length of the first segment of the tube, hand over hand on the rope.

He then called down to the lieutenant and Gilmonn. "Around the first bend," he said. "I'm climbing the vertical shaft."

"Thirty-five minutes, Colonel," the lieutenant replied.

Rogers glanced up the shaft and held his rasping breath momentarily, trying to hear something. Surely the bogey wouldn't just let him haul the weapon in, without some resistance?

He coiled the ropes and secured them to his belt, then suspended the monkey on a rope secured to a stake he hammered into the lava. He climbed the chimney as he had before, bracing back against one side and feet against the other, inching his way. That took an additional five minutes. Twelve minutes had passed and he was tiring, but not yet winded.

Crouching in the low, almost horizontal tunnel, he jerked free the slipknot attaching the monkey to the stake, and began to haul it up the chimney as fast as he could. The cylinder weighed at least seventy pounds and the effort made his arm muscles knot.

With the cylinder almost over the edge, he heard Gilmonn's voice echoing from below.

"How are you doing, Colonel?"

"Almost there," he answered. His arms were twin agonies. The radiation jacket chafed and was becoming a major irritation.

"We're going now."

"You have twenty-five minutes," the lieutenant added.

"Gotcha."

He switched on the electric torch, placed the warhead perpendicular to the tunnel, and rolled it ninety feet to the lip of the antechamber. Resting his arms for only a moment, he scrambled over the weapon, detached the ropes, then lifted it and waddled ducklike to deposit it in the center of the cylindrical space. He placed it on its end and opened the cover plate to see that the timer was still working. It was. He closed the cover plate.

As he shined the torch at the larger chamber beyond, a grin flickered on his lips. The impassive gray faceting reflected the beam back in a myriad of dull gleams. "Here's thanks for you," he murmured.

Twenty minutes. He could be down the tunnel and two miles away. He pulled a knife from his trouser pocket and sliced away the crotch strap on the jacket, then shrugged it off and flung it aside. He slid along the horizontal tunnel, ignoring the heat of the friction on his elbows and butt, and stopped long enough to take a deep breath and prepare to shinny down the chimney. Instinctively wary of heading into even the most familiar darkness, he played his torch beam down.

Three yards below, the beam met a dead end.

Rogers stared at the blockage in disbelief.

It might have been there through all eternity, a flat plug as dark and featureless as the walls of the chimney itself.

"Holy Christ," he said.

Eighteen minutes.

He was out of the horizontal tunnel and beside the bomb before he could even think. With amazing dexterity, he had the cover plate open and his finger on the cutoff switch. And then he froze, his face wet with sweat, salty drops stinging his eyes.

No way out. Even if he stopped the timer on the monkey, he could not think of any way he could escape. A dozen unlikely possibilities lined themselves up in panicky parade. Perhaps another opening had been made elsewhere. Perhaps the bogey was coming alive, finally, even preparing to lift off.

Perhaps a bargain was being struck.

Deactivate the bomb, and we'll let you go.

He backed away from the cylinder, his torch swinging back and forth on the floor nearby. *Why did it close up? Has it been active all along, watching us, guessing everything we'd do?*

He propped himself against the curve of the antechamber near the horizontal tunnel. Sixteen minutes.

In five or six minutes, it probably wouldn't matter whether he got out or not. He wouldn't be far enough away from the bogey to survive the hail of shrapnel. He could not conceive of any vessel, even the size of a small mountain, withstanding an internal blast of three kilotons.

Rogers shook his head slowly, trying to concentrate, keep his mind from wandering. He could turn off the weapon and see if the way was opened again. *Tit for tat. Scratch my back, I'll scratch yours. Sorry, it was all a big misunderstanding.*

Kneeling beside the monkey, he again reached out for the switch.

You know, this is the first time we've actually gotten a reaction.

He thought that over, biting his lower lip, fingers tensing and relaxing over the switch.

"Maybe you feel threatened," he said aloud. "Maybe for the first time we're getting through to you."

Somehow, that wasn't convincing.

He could not bring himself to flip the switch. He would not be able to reset the timer if he shut the weapon off; the lieutenant had not shown him how to do that.

Fourteen minutes.

The first blow for our side. I'm in charge.

He sat down beside the monkey, reaching out to bring up the radiation jacket and drape it over his knees. *Quandary.*

The silence within the chamber was absolute.

"If you're listening, damn you, then talk to me," he said. "Tell me about yourself." He chuckled and that sound scared him worst of all, for it told him how close he really was to flipping the switch. He might see his wife and kid again if he flipped the switch; they might not have to receive and read the letter he had posted on his bulletin board. He could see Clare's face, mourning, and his chest hurt.

William's face, sweet five-year-old deviltry pure.

What would he think of himself if he deactivated?

His career might as well be over. He would have fallen back in the face of enemy action and jeopardized their entire defense effort. Others had risked their careers, perhaps even their lives. Rogers did not, right now, want to contemplate how many people up the line had helped to procure this weapon, and how they felt at this moment: possible traitors, lawbreakers, risk-takers. Acting in defiance of the President. Mutineers, rebels.

"God damn, you know us so well," he said to the darkness. "You've twisted us every which way, so casual, and now you think you've got us again." No reply.

The silence of deep space. Eternities.

Twelve minutes.

How many times would his hand reach out, the body pleading, and how many times would something undefined pull it back?

"I won't touch it. Come on out and deactivate it yourself. Maybe I won't put up a fight. Maybe we have something in common now!"

He was hyperventilating. Clasping his hands before his mouth, he tried to rebreathe each gulp of air and slow his frantic lungs. Did judgment of one's courage, valor, require the appearance of nobility, or was an act alone sufficient? If by the end of the—he checked—eleven minutes, he was on the floor, a screaming, weeping madman capable only of keeping his finger away from the switch, would he still get to the Army Valhalla and toss off a few with all the dead heroes? Or would he be turned away, sent to the showers? *Wash off that stink of fear, soldier.*

He didn't want Valhalla. He wanted Clare and William. He wanted to say good-bye in more words than he had put in the letter. In person.

"Please God, let me be calm," he said hoarsely. He flattened his cupped hands into a gesture of prayer, pinching the tip of his nose between his index fingers, closing his eyes. It might have been easier if he had brought a pistol along. "Jesus Jesus Jesus Christ."

Don't let me fuck this one up. Dear God keep my hand from that switch. Hit them back hit them back in the face. God I know you don't take sides but I'm a soldier God and this is what I have to do. Take care of them please Lord of all of us and help us save our home our world. Let this mean something please God.

Nine minutes. He crawled down the horizontal tunnel again and saw the plug was still in place. To make sure it was solid, and not just an illusion, he jumped the three yards and landed his feet squarely on the flat grayness, flexing his knees to break the shock, slamming his elbows and lower arms against the chimney wall. Solid. He stomped on it several times. Nothing. Grimacing from his bruised heels, he braced himself and climbed out of the well, returning to the antechamber.

He refused to allow himself to get closer than six feet from the monkey.

Another way out.

Not likely.

Tit for tat.

"What are you doing, learning more about us, setting up another experiment? Will I or won't I?" He stood on the edge of the antechamber, waving his torch beam across the semiglossy cathedral facets. "I can't make sense out of any of this. Why did you come here? Why can't you just go away, leave me with my wife and family?"

That was enough talking, and a fine sentiment to end all the words he had ever spoken. *No more words,* he vowed. He broke the vow immediately. Breaking small vows helped him keep to the big one.

"So why don't we talk? I'm not going to push that switch. I won't be around to tell anybody. Talk to me, show me what you're all about."

Five minutes.

"I hear you might have gone clear across this galaxy, gone from star to star. You're part of a planet-eating machine. That's what the newspapers are saying. Lots of people speculating. Aren't you curious what we'd think, what I'd think if I knew the truth? So talk to me." *Give me something to hang on to. Some reason.* "I'm not touching that switch! That bomb is going to go off."

What if it didn't?

What if he had to spend the next few weeks in here, dying of thirst, all for nothing, because the aliens had found some way to deactivate the weapon? What if they kept him there to starve just as punishment for trying?

Three minutes.

"I'm a dead man," he said, and realized the truth of that. He was a dead soldier already. There was no escape, no way out between his convictions and his duty. That thought calmed him considerably, and he sat on the lip of the antechamber, as he had sat once before, legs dangling out over the darkness. "So where's your light?" he asked. "Show me your little red light."

He wouldn't even know when it had happened. He wouldn't hear anything, see anything.

One minute.

Frozen men become warm again
And rabbits drug themselves in the wolf's jaws
God gives us ways out
I'm still thinking
But it doesn't hurt now.
I know how very small and inconsequential
I

From six miles away, Senator Gilmonn put on the smoky gray glasses the lieutenant gave to him and looked across the desert at the distant black hump that was the bogey. The cultists had scattered all across the desert floor, most out of the area, farther away than his small group, but some hiding behind piles of rock and other cinder cones. He had no idea how many of the diehards would survive.

"He's not out of there," the lieutenant said, removing a pair of radio headphones. Observers in the mountains had not seen Rogers leave the bogey.

"I wonder what happened?" Gilmonn asked. "Did he plant the . . . it?"

Beams of brilliant red light shot up from the false cinder cone, and the desert floor was illuminated by a small sun. Huge black fragments twisted upward in silhouette against the fireball, disintegrating, the smaller fragments falling back in smoking arcs. The sound was a palpable wall, more solid and painful than loud, and a violent blast of dusty wind progressed visibly over the scrub and sand and rock. When it hit, they had a hard time staying on their feet.

The dust cleared momentarily and they saw a tall, lean pillar of cloud rising, a fascinating ugly yellow-green, shot through with pastel pinks and purples and reds.

The lieutenant was weeping. "My god, he didn't get out. Dear Jesus. What a blast! Like a goddamned pipe bomb."

Senator Gilmonn, too stunned to react, decided he simply did not understand. The lieutenant understood, and his face was shiny with tears.

Fragments of rock and glass and metal fell for ten miles around for the next ten minutes. At six miles, none of the fragments exceeded half an inch in diameter.

They took refuge in the trucks and waited out the shower, and then drove away from the site to the decontamination center in Shoshone.

49———

January 6

The network between the Possessed was beginning to knit and connect. Arthur could feel its progress. This both excited and saddened him; the time he was spending with Francine and Marty might be coming to a close.

If she could not accept what had happened, he would have to continue without them.

Arthur did not know quite how she was taking his revelation, until, in the morning, he overheard her talking to Marty in the kitchen. He had just finished a thorough check of the family station wagon and was wiping his hands on a paper towel before passing through the swinging door.

"Dad's going to have a lot of work to do soon," Francine said. Arthur paused behind the door, crumpled towel in one hand, his jaw working.

"Can he stay with us?" Marty asked.

He could not see them, but he could tell that Francine was by the sink, facing the center of the kitchen, where the boy stood. "What he's doing is important," she said, not answering Marty's question. She didn't know the answer.

"He's not working for the President now. He told me."

"Right," Francine said.

"I wish he could stay home."

"So do I."

"Is he going someplace without us?"

"I don't understand what you're asking, Marty."

"Is he going to leave us here when the Earth blows up?"

Arthur closed his eyes. The towel was a tight ball in his fist.

"He's not leaving us anywhere. He's just . . . working."

"Why work when everything's going to stop?"

"Everybody has to work. We don't know everything's going to stop. Besides, he's working so that maybe it won't . . . stop." The catch in her voice made him raise his head to keep the tears from dropping down his cheek.

"Mr. Perkins says there isn't much we can do."

"Mr. Perkins should stick to arithmetic," Francine said sharply.

"Is Dad ascared?"

"Afraid."

"Yeah, but is he?"

"No more than I am," she said.

"What can he do to stop things?"

"Time for us to take you to school now. Where's your father?"

Mo-ommm! Can he?"

"He's working with . . . some people. They think maybe they can do something."

"I'll tell Mr. Perkins."

"Don't tell Mr. Perkins *anything*, Marty. Please."

Arthur stepped back a few feet to make a noise, came through the door, and dropped the thoroughly wadded towel into the trash bag under the sink. Marty stared at him with wide eyes, lips pressed together and sucked inward.

"Everybody ready?"

They nodded.

"Have you been crying, Daddy?" Marty asked.

Arthur said nothing, simply staring between them.

"We're a team, aren't we, honey?" Francine said, hugging him and gesturing for Marty to come. The boy was not of an age to be enthusiastic about physical affection, but he came and Arthur knelt, one arm around Francine's waist, one arm wrapped around his son.

"We sure are," he said.

What he received, in the way of messages, was a peculiar shorthand unlike anything he had ever experienced before. The flow of information came as truncated visuals, bits of spoken conversations (sometimes delivered by separate and identifiable voices, sometimes monotoned or not auditory at all), and as often as not, simply as memories. He could not remember receiving the memories, but they were there, and they informed his planning and action.

By that evening, as he lay in bed again beside his wife, as yet more rain pattered gently on the roof and windows, he knew that:

Lehrman, McClennan, and Rotterjack had formed a delegation to inform the President of the destruction of the Furnace bogey. (Lehrman was one of the Possessed.)

The President had listened to the information, delivered largely by Rotterjack, and had said nothing, simply shaking his head and gesturing for them to leave.

He saw:

A Soviet vacationer from Samarkand (Arthur did not know whether male or female) watching a conifer forest burn in the Zerafshan Mountains, sending thick white walls of smoke over the craggy alpine ridges.

Large sections of New York (Queens and the Bronx), Chicago, and New Orleans on fire, with no sign of the blazes being brought under control. Much of Tokyo had been leveled by four major fires in the past week. Half of Beijing had been consumed by fire following an apparently natural earthquake.

Lying awake, not knowing whether Francine was asleep or simply lying still, Arthur received these memories that were not his, and made decisions about his family's immediate future.

Wherever he went, they would go with him; their unity was far more important than any home or security. In approximately a month, they would remove Marty from school and travel together.

He would soon be called to Seattle. From there, he would work his way down the Pacific coast to San Francisco, performing his duties along the way. Apparently, most of his work would consist of gathering records of culture—documents, music, films, whatever was on a list that would be fed to him a section at a time. The decisions as to what should go on this list were being made by others on the network. *And who does the choosing?*

He had again the nightmare thought:

The Possessed are simply being used. There are no saviors. There are only plunderers, and they use us as slaves to loot the Earth of all they can carry away.

How many were Possessed now?

Ten thousand.

A round number, growing larger each day.

And room on the arks for as few as *two thousand.*

If he was chosen, he decided, and Marty and Francine were not, he would stay. He would refuse. *Won't I?* And that was the worst nightmare thought of all. Arthur could not be sure that when the time came, given the opportunity denied to his wife and son, he would not leave them.

I can stay. I will stay.

"Are they talking to you?" Francine rolled over in the dark and faced him. He smiled at her and pulled her close.

"No," he said. "Not right now."

"Where are the spiders?"

"In their box." He had taken a wooden box and given the spiders a home on the upper shelf of the office closet. Neither of the spiders had moved for days.

"What kind of people do they need?"

"I have no idea," Arthur answered.

"Do you remember that night, when Grant and Danielle and Becky were visiting, and Chris Riley called . . . To tell you about Europa?"

He nodded.

"I was really afraid then. I don't know why. I knew it was far away."

Arthur saw Europa boiling, great chunks of ice flashing into linear rays of steam, other chunks lifting away, and beneath it all, a spreading, perfectly smooth sphere of light, as white and pearly as parachute silk and bright as the sun, *pushing* the ice and steam out into space . . .

"What really happened to Europa?" she asked.

"I think our friends . . . our . . . friends, ate it," he said. "Turned it into more of their own spacecraft." *And the huge chunks of ice, sent inward to Mars and Venus?* No images or memories explained them.

"Then I shouldn't have been afraid."

"Oh, yes," Arthur said. "You were right to be afraid. You knew before I did."

She nodded in agreement. "I did, didn't I? What does that make me? Psychic?"

She was talking just to be talking. He knew that, and he didn't mind; her words soothed him.

"A woman," he said.

"How quaint."

He grinned against her hair and kissed her.

"It's funny, but in all of this, I've been thinking of you and Marty, and . . . my book. The Huns and Mongols and Scythians and Indo-Europeans . . . All those people and my book. I'll never get it finished."

"Don't be so sure," he said, but it hurt him to say it.

"Do you think these probes are like the hordes? Migrating, ravaging, pushed on by famine or overpopulation?"

"No," he said. "It's a big galaxy. We've seen nothing like that." *But would we know where and how to look?*

"Why are they doing it, then?" she asked.

"You listened to Harry's tape."

"I'm not sure I understood it."

"You understand it as well as I do," Arthur said, squeezing her shoulders.

Long dark shape, a single needle, pointing at Europa's heart, the rocky core, wrapping long collecting fields around the ice and steam, gathering it in, paring away the hydrogen atoms from the oxygen, fusing them. Piercing the core . . .

And again, no more.

"Have you decided yet?" Francine asked softly.

"Decided what?"

"Marty asked this morning . . ."

"I thought I'd made that clear."

"I just need to be told again."

"Yes. We're staying together. I'm taking you both with me, wherever I go."

"Good," she said.

Francine finally slept, but Arthur did not. He was haunted by his "memory"—Lehrman's, actually—of the expression on the President's face.

Do you believe in God?

I believe in punishment.

PERSPECTIVE

The Los Angeles Electronic Times, unsigned editorial in the Opinion Track, January 10, 1997:

The news of the Death Valley anomaly's destruction has spread around the world like a shock wave. At first, we have exulted–a blow struck against the enemy. But the bullets still rumble through the Earth's interior. The anomaly in Australia is still intact. Rumors of a Russian anomaly are rampant. The Earth is still besieged. The opinion of a well-known science fiction writer, expressed on a late night talk show, has rapidly become public dogma; that these "bullets" are superdense capsules of neutron matter and antimatter, destined to meet at the Earth's center and destroy us all. We have no way of

knowing the truth of this. It seems clear,
however, that there is little we can do, and
however irrationally, our hope fades fast.

50——

January 15

Walt Samshow took his sandwich out on the starboard wing of
the bridge of the Glomar *Discoverer* and stared down at the bow
wave and the sullen blue-black ocean as he ate. They had left Pearl
Harbor the morning of the day before, zigzagging across the ocean
in search of atmospheric oxygen concentrations above the Molokai
Fracture.

Occasionally an insignificant crumb of white bread would drift
down from his meal into wet oblivion. He imagined some wandering zooplankton would soon know where it was, and partake of it.
Nothing was ever truly lost, if you only had access to all the eyes
and senses in the universe, as he sometimes imagined God did.
God himself had no eyes; He made eyes and put living things in
charge of them, that He might witness the majesty of creation
from an objective viewpoint.

David Sand came up the stairs and leaned on the railing beside
Samshow, eyes red from lack of sleep. "We're twelve hours from
the fracture," he said. "Captain's turned in and Chao's going to
stand deck watch from here on."

Samshow nodded and chewed.

"Not much enthusiasm, is there?" Sand asked.

"We're working, at least," Samshow said after swallowing.

"Fanning in the radio room says the Navy has three ships out
here, just cruising back and forth . . ." He made two doubled-
back sweeps with his hand. "Back and forth. Looking."

"Has the House voted for impeachment yet?" Samshow asked,
straightening, legs expertly compensating for the gentle sway. He

crumpled his sandwich wrapper and stuffed it into his shirt pocket, behind pens and pencils.

"Not that I know of," Sand said.

"I sometimes think we deserve to die, we're all so goddamned stupid." Samshow's tone was unperturbed, mild. He might have been making an observation about a seabird.

Sand smiled uncomfortably and shook his head. "Voice of experience," was all he managed to say.

"Yeah. I've kept up with the news and I've read books and I've worked with all sorts of people for sixty-odd years, and I've seen one kind of stupid, and another. We all bump into each other every day of our lives, by guess and by golly, and we render our opinions whether we know anything or not, and if anybody catches us out we lie . . . Ah, shit on it." He shook his head. "I'm just feeling uncommonly sour today."

"Right." Sand brushed his sun-dried hair from his eyes.

"They've got us, you know that? We're down and we're weak and there's not a goddamn thing we can do now except go out and look . . ."—he raised his eyebrows and pursed his lips—"and say, 'yep, by golly, there it is. We're bleeding to death.' They knew exactly what to do. They used their decoys, and we fell for them. It's like they know stupidity from generations back, thousands of years back. Maybe they've found stupid hayseed worlds all across the galaxy. So now they have us confused and on our backs kicking and they've got the knife at our throats, like slaughtering a goddamned pig." He gripped the railing and rocked on his heels gently. "I have never in my life felt so useless."

Sand cocked his head to one side. "It still seems theoretical to me," he said. "I can't believe anything's really happening."

"It's been raining for two days in Montana, and they still can't put out the fires," Samshow said. "Now there's a grass fire in central Asia that's burned half a million acres. They can't control it, needless to say. And the fire in Tokyo. We're not only stupid, all our crazy folks are going to burn us out before the world goes kablooey. All our sins hang around our necks."

Fanning, barely twenty, a graduate student from the University of California at Berkeley, came onto the bridge and stuffed his hands in his pockets, hunching his shoulders in excitement. "I've just figured it out. Some of the Navy's coded messages," he said. "They're not working real hard to hide anything. They have a deep submersible somewhere out there." He removed a hand from one pocket and swept the horizon. "I think it's one of their biggies, a nuclear. With treads. They say it's crawling along the bottom."

"Anything else?" Sand asked facetiously. "Or is it a secret?"

Fanning shrugged. "Maybe we're going to do something," he said. "Maybe we're going to try again. Knock out something important, not just a rock. Up the President, man," he said, and lifted an expressive finger.

January 30

Edward stood in the parking lot of the Little America Restaurant and Motel, motor home idling nearby, and scanned the smoky northern horizon. The fire had been burning for five days now and was completely out of control. The orange and brown cloud stretched to the limits of east and west, turning the sun an apocalyptic flame red. Tendrils of gray smoke had passed over the highway and motel, dropping ghostly flakes of fine white ash. From what he had heard on the radio, there was no way he could go any farther north; two hundred thousand acres of Montana were ablaze, and yesterday the flames had stretched hungrily into Canada.

Seated at the RV's dining table, he charted a southwesterly route on an auto club map with a yellow marker, then climbed into the driver's seat and strapped himself in.

The cold northern air was delicious, even thickened by the smell of burning timber. He had never known air so invigorating.

Edward pulled out of the parking lot and headed west.

He hoped Yosemite would still be there when he arrived.

PERSPECTIVE

Sky and Telescope On-line, February 4, 1997:
Today, Venus is at superior conjunction, behind the sun and out of sight. Today is also the
projected date of the impact of a huge chunk of
ice, allegedly from Europa. What this will do
to Venus is a fascinating question. The impact
will cause enormous seismic disruption, perhaps even deep-mantle cracking and a rear-
rangement of the planet's internal structure. Venus has virtually no water; with the
trillions of tons of water provided by the ice
ball, and the renewed geologic activity, the
planet could, in a few tens of thousands of
years, become a garden of Eden . . .

51——

February 19

"About a third of the kids have been taken out of school,"
Francine said, putting the phone down. She had just phoned to tell
the attendance office that Marty would be vacationing with them.
Arthur carried a box of camping gear and—for no particular reason—the Astroscan through the living room to the station wagon
in the garage.

"Not surprising," he said.

"Jim and Hilary called to say Gauge is doing fine."

"Why can't we take Gauge with us?" Marty called from the garage.

"We talked about that last night," Arthur said.

"He could sit on my lap," Marty offered, squatting beside the station wagon and sorting toys.

"Not for long," Arthur predicted. "He's got kids to play with, good people to look after him."

"Yeah. But *I* don't have *him.*"

There was nothing Arthur could say to that.

"I called the auto club," Francine said, "and asked what traffic was like between here and Seattle, and down the coast. They say it's really light. That's surprising. You'd think everybody would be off playing hooky, off to Disneyland or the parks."

"Lucky for us," Arthur said from the garage. He rearranged the crammed boxes in the back of the wagon. Marty sat on the concrete, continuing to pick halfheartedly through his toys.

"This is hard," he said.

"You think you have problems, fellah," Arthur said. "What about my books?"

"Are we just going to lock up?" Francine asked, standing in the door from the garage to the house. She carried a box filled with disks and papers—the notes she had made for her book.

"Just like we're going on vacation," Arthur said. "So we're atypical."

"It is strange, isn't it, that everybody's staying home, now of all times?" She crammed the box into a spare corner of the station wagon.

"How many people really understand what's happening?" he asked.

"That's a point."

"The kids at school understand," Marty said. "They know the world's going to end."

"Maybe," Arthur said. Again, trying to reassure them hurt him. *The world is going to end. You know it, and* they *know it.*

"Maybe everybody wants to be together," Francine said, returning to the kitchen. She brought out a box of canned and dried food. "They want to be someplace familiar."

"We don't need that, do we?" Marty asked, shoving aside a pile of unwanted metal and plastic robots and spacecraft.

"All we need is each other," Arthur agreed.

In the office, he reached into the back of the closet's upper shelf and took out the wooden box containing the spiders. It felt peculiarly light. He opened the box. It was empty. For a moment, he stood with the box in his hand, and for some reason he could not understand he smiled. They had more work to do. He glanced at his watch. Wednesday. Ten A.M.

Time to be on the road.

"All packed?" he asked.

Marty surveyed the pile of rejected toys and clutched a single White Owl cigar box filled with the chosen. The cigar box had come down from Arthur's father, who had had it from *his* father. It was tattered and reinforced with tape and represented continuity. Marty treasured the box in and of itself.

"Ready," the boy said, climbing into the back seat. "Are we going to sleep in a lot of motels?"

"You got it," Arthur said.

"Can I buy some toys where we go?"

"I don't see why not."

"And some pretty rocks? If I find them, I mean."

"Nothing over a ton," Francine said.

"The boulder that broke the Buick's back," Arthur said, going into the house for a final check.

Good-bye, bedroom, good-bye, office, good-bye, kitchen. Refrigerator still full of food. Good-bye, knotty-pine paneling, elevated porch, backyard, and wild plum tree. Good-bye, smooth and singing river. He passed Gauge's wicker bed in the service porch and felt a lump in his throat.

"Good-bye, books," he whispered, looking at the shelves in the living room. He locked the front door, but did not turn the dead bolt.

52——

February 24

Trevor Hicks, his work finished in Washington, D.C., had taken a train to Boston, single suitcase and computer in hand. At the station, he had been met by a middle-aged, brown-haired scattered-looking woman dressed in a black wool skirt and old flower-print blouse. She had taken him to her home in Quincy in a battered Toyota sedan.

There he had rested for two days, watched owlishly by the woman's five-year-old son and seven-year-old daughter. The woman had been husbandless for three years, and the old wood-frame house was in severe disrepair—leaky pipes, decrepit wallboard, broken stairs. The children seemed surprised that he did not share her bedroom, which led him to believe she had not lacked for male company. None of this mattered much to Hicks, who had never been judgmental even before his possession. He spent much of his time sitting on the broken-down living room couch, thinking or interacting with the network, helping a dozen other people in the Northeast compile lists of people to be contacted, and/or prepared for removal from the Earth.

All of his life, Hicks had worked with high-powered personalities—bright, knowledgeable, contentious, and often cantankerous men and women. Most of the people he now communicated with in the network fit this description. To his surprise, whatever maintained and governed the network did not discourage high-powered behavior among the network's members. There was considerable debate, even acrimony, as first the categories of contactees and "saved" were decided, then specific communities, and finally specific individuals.

The Bosses (or Overlords or Secret Masters, all titles applied at one time or another to the anonymous organizers) had apparently decided that humans, with broad supervision, knew best how to choose and plan for their own rescue. Hicks sometimes had his doubts.

Over a dinner of macaroni and cheese served on a bare oak table, as the children listened, Hicks asked his hostess about her role in the rescue.

"I'm not sure," she said. "They got to me about six weeks ago. I took in three people about a week after that, and they stayed here for a few days and then left. Some more people after that, and now you. Maybe I'm a den mother."

The daughter giggled.

They could have chosen more hospitable lodgings. But he kept that thought to himself.

"What about you?" she asked. "What are you doing?"

"Making up a list," he said.

"Who's going, who's not?"

He hesitated, then nodded. "Actually, we're concentrating more on a list of others to recruit. There's a lot of work left to be done, and not nearly enough people to do it."

"I don't think my kids and I are going," the woman said. She stared at the table, her face slack, then slowly lifted her eyebrows and stood. "Jenny," she said, "let's clear the table."

"Where ain't we going, Mama?" the boy asked.

"Hush up, Jason," the daughter ordered.

"Mama?" Jason persisted.

"Nowhere, and you pay attention to your sister, what she says."

They had to start somewhere, Hicks thought. *She was one of the first. They didn't know where to begin.* The suspicion of her inadequacy—if that was the right word—of her inability to qualify for the migration, did not prevent her from seeing the good they were doing, or the necessity of their work.

If we have any free will at all now.

That question was still unanswerable. Hicks preferred to think they did have free will, which implied that this woman demonstrated a truly admirable human quality: selfless courage.

Two days later, she drove him to the airport, and he boarded an airliner for San Francisco. Only on board the aircraft did he realize that he had heard the names of the woman's children, but not her own.

High above the Earth, over the deck of obscuring clouds, Hicks napped and typed notes into his computer and realized he was not, for the moment, on call. The network had released him for these few hours and he was not privy to the ordered flow of voices and information. He had time to think, and to ask questions. *How did the spiders get through airport security?* That seemed easy enough. They had departed his luggage in the scanners, crawled through the mechanisms, and reentered the luggage beyond the sensors' range. Or they had means of altering their X-ray shadows. Human sensory apparatus had failed completely from the beginning; if the bogeys could land on Earth without being detected, what was so amazing about a spider passing through airport security?

He mused about these things behind his closed eyes, relishing the temporary privacy. Then, on impulse, he inserted a CD carrying the texts of his complete works into the computer and called up *Starhome*. Scrolling through page after page, he skimmed the long sections of characterization (reasonably adept and no more) and intrigue and politics and read in more detail the passages of speculations and extrapolations. *It's not a bad book,* he thought. *Even now, two years after I finished it, it engages my interest, at least.*

But the pride was largely masked by a sadness. The book dealt with a future. What future was there? Certainly not the one he had envisaged—a future of humans and extraterrestrials interacting on a vast mission of adventure and discovery. In some respects, that now seemed pitifully naïve.

Life on Earth is hard. Competition for the necessities of life is fierce. How ridiculous to believe that the law of harsh survival would not be true elsewhere, or that it would be negated by the progress of technology in an advanced civilization . . .

And yet . . .

Somebody out there was thinking altruistically.

Or perhaps not.

Altruism is masked self-interest. Aggressive self-interest is a masked urge to self-destruction.

He had written that once in an unpublished article on third-world development. The developed nations could serve their interests best by fostering the growth and development of less privileged, weaker nations . . .

And perhaps that was what was happening here.

But many experts on strategy had read his article and criticized it severely, citing many historical examples to prove him wrong.

"Whose interests does the Soviet Union serve?" one reader had asked him. The Soviet Union, he had acknowledged, was stronger than ever—apparently—but faced enormous problems coordinating the nations and peoples it had absorbed, problems that others thought might prove fatal in the long run. "But not yet—and how many nations last for more than centuries?" the critic had responded.

Now apply the theory of necessary altruism to groups of intelligent beings that have survived tens of thousands of years. If only one of them launches planet-eating, civilization-destroying probes, and none of them respond by launching probe-killers—

Who wins?

Probe-killers, then, were definitely launched in self-interest. But why attempt to preserve possibly competing civilizations? Why not just destroy the planet-eaters and be done with it?

The network was not available to him; all he had were implanted memories, information he was not always able to access without the help of the network.

He often spurred thought by letting his fingers speak. Now he opened a file and began to type. The first few sentences came out as gibberish and he erased them. *There is an answer here, inside me. I know it.*

But try as he would, he could not bring it all together.

I don't know why they're trying to preserve us.

When he was outside of the soothing and persuasive direction of the network, that lack of an answer worried him.

Harry Feinman could not make a connection with his past. That time, when he had been mobile and free of pain, was fiction, something concocted by his imagination. He could not conceive of ever having made love or of having eaten a full meal. In the few moments of lucidity left to him each day, he searched his body for any sign of that past and found nothing. All was failing. He was a different person; Harry Feinman had already died.

Most of the time he spent sleeping or nearly asleep, heavily doped. He thought or dreamed vaguely of life after death and decided the question didn't really matter; anything, even complete oblivion, was better than this half-and-half existence.

Ithaca drifted in and out of the room like a cloud. When he was in pain, between medications, she sat by him sharp as a razor, saying nothing as he lay rigid, teeth clamped.

You pays your money coming in, going out. Ticket price for this ride: pain.

The difference between day and night was not clear to him anymore. Sometimes the lights were down when he was awake, sometimes not.

There was a miraculous hour when somehow his medication was perfectly balanced, and he felt almost normal, and in this time he cherished Ithaca's presence. He told her he wanted her to marry again and she accepted this unintentional but necessary torture with the calmness he had come to expect and rely on; then he remembered having told her several times before.

"Why worry about it?" she asked quietly. "We'll probably all be gone soon anyway."

Harry shook his head as if disagreeing, but she looked at him with her "Oh, come on" look, one eyebrow arched, and he said, "I'd like to see that. What a show that'll be, if it comes."

"If?" Ithaca smiled ironically. "You're my favorite pessimist. Now you sound hopeful."

"Just barely hopeful," Harry said.

"What did Arthur tell you?"

"Never try to hide anything from my woman." Harry took a moment to remember. "He said the planet is covered by little spiders now."

Ithaca leaned forward. "What?"

"The cavalry is here, but it's probably come too late."

She shook her head, not understanding.

"He showed one to me. A little robot. They're harvesting the Earth before it goes. Trying to save a little breeding population, I'd guess. Like a zoo expedition. And they're destroying the machines that are doing this to us."

"Arthur told you all this?"

He nodded. "I thought he was nuts, then he showed me one of the spiders. He seemed . . . not happy, but he seemed to know he was doing something useful. He thought maybe they were controlling his thoughts, but he said he didn't mind, and he couldn't be . . ." Harry's weakness came on him and he closed his eyes for several minutes. "He said they knew what was best, probably."

Ithaca studied his face closely, leaning forward. "I saw one," she said softly. "I think I did. In the garden."

"One what? Spider?"

"Silver." She held up her open hand. "Big as this. It ran away before I could see it clearly, but when I looked—it had been on the trunk of the old live oak—there were cuts through the bark, knife cuts. I thought I was seeing things, or just mistaken. Harry, should we tell people?"

"What good?" he asked. His thoughts were blurring again, so he said no more and only held her hand lightly in his.

Ithaca called the Gordon house the next evening and received no answer. The last part of Harry had died, finally, at eleven in the morning.

53——

March 10

The Glomar *Discoverer*, its engines in reverse against a steady surface current and a constant twelve-knot southwesterly wind, drifted at the edge of a vast sea of lime-green and gray and white foam. The air was filled with a constant churning roar. High overhead, peculiar clouds were forming—swirling bands, curving upward as if along the inside of a funnel.

Walt Samshow scanned the foaming sea to the distant horizon and could see no end to it. He hardly needed to breathe at all now. Most of the men held wet rags over their noses and mouths. Nosebleeds were common; the delicate nasal tissues were deteriorating under the drying, burning effect of too much of a good thing: oxygen.

"We can't stay here long," Sand said, standing beside him on the bridge.

"Do we have our samples and readings?" Samshow asked. Sand nodded.

"Any word from the Navy ships?"

"They've left the area already. We've been listening for the deep submersible, but all we hear is the roar of bubbles."

"Tell the captain we should pull back ourselves," Samshow said. "Can anybody fight this?" He had directed his question out over the bridge railing, but Sand shook his head.

"I doubt it."

"It's like watching the whole ocean being dismantled," Samshow said. He pulled a bottle of eyedrops from his peacoat pocket and leaned his head back to administer them.

Sand refused the bottle when Samshow offered it. "It's scary."

Samshow grimaced. "It's goddamned *exhilarating,* and I don't mean the oxygen. You can see the end of things, you can see a plan —or at least some outline of a plan—and it's horrifying, it's grand."

Sand stared at him, not comprehending.

"Forget it," Samshow said, waving the almost empty bottle of eyedrops. "Tell the captain to get us the hell away from here."

Sand bumped into Chao, the first mate, in the bridge hatchway. Apologizing, he stood back and Chao held out a scribbled note.

"From Pearl Harbor, and from San Francisco!" he said.

"What?" Sand asked.

"Report of a seismic disturbance in Mongolia. Not an earthquake, a bomb. Perhaps ten megatons. Not an air burst, an underground or something like it."

Samshow looked at the figures on the scrap of paper. "They're no fools," he said.

"You think they blew up the Russian bogey?" Sand asked.

"What else?" Chao grinned broadly. "Maybe we can get them all! Maybe the Australians, too, eh?"

"Where will they get a bomb?" Sand asked.

"If they even want to," Samshow said.

"Only a fool would hesitate now," Chao said. "Put the bastards out of action, cut their lines of communication!"

"Hear that freight train down there?" Samshow pointed figuratively and emphatically down through the deck and the ocean, and jabbed his finger to deepen the thrust to the mantle and core below. "As long as that's running, we've accomplished nothing."

"If the theories are correct," Sand said.

"Still, we got them!" Chao refused to have a wet blanket thrown over his enthusiasm. He stared defiantly at Samshow then dipped his head and raised one leg over the bottom of the hatchway to return to the bridge.

54———

Edward Shaw drove the Itasca into Fresno and stopped for gas. The sky to the north was free of smoke but deeper blue than he had ever seen it at this latitude. There was a lot of fine ash in the air from the fires in the Soviet Union and China.

Winter was coming to an end prematurely; across the Sierras, snow was receding rapidly.

California—with the exception of San Diego, where fires had spread north from Tijuana—seemed to have escaped the worst of the conflagrations. Yosemite was intact. That might be explained by the lack of tourists; the roads were unnaturally empty. A few radio stations had gone off the air, abandoned by their personnel. The news broadcasts he had heard driving into Fresno were far from encouraging.

The Kemp–Van Cott objects within the Earth were slowing more rapidly than before. It seemed both scientific and public perception that the harmonic swings of these two (or more, some said) "bullets" were ticking away the Earth's final days. The current estimate was thirty days before they met at the Earth's core. Sentence of death.

He bought basic groceries and several six-packs of beer in the convenience store, then drove through the city, stopping on impulse at a sprawling three-level shopping mall just off the highway in Pinedale.

"What in *hell* am I doing?" he asked himself after he had parked the RV. He sat in the driver's seat, looking across the half-filled parking lot. "I *hate* shopping centers." He got out and carefully locked up. In faded blue jeans, Pendleton jacket, and running shoes, he could have passed for any of the locals who wandered on the lowest level of the mall, going from window to window, alone or with girlfriends or family. Still unsure why he was where he was, Edward sat on a bench near a flower-shop kiosk and watched the people passing, concentrating on the men.

Life as usual? Not quite.

The expressions on the men's faces, young or old, seemed fixed, dazed. There was no joy in their shopping. The children still showed enthusiasm, and the women for the most part appeared either calm or blank. *Why? Women are supposed to feel things more than the men. Why the difference?*

After an hour of watching and puzzling, he stood and approached a bookstore, the only conceivable place in the mall he might find something of interest. Looking through the travel section and picking out books about Yosemite, he heard a commotion near the front counter. A florid, stocky man in white shirt and gray slacks came in shouting, "Hey, hey! Hear this? Hear about this yet?"

He flashed a newspaper around, his face wreathed with a smile. "The Russians blew up theirs, too. That's two down! Just the Aussies now, and we'll have them!"

No one showed much enthusiasm.

We're down and nearly out, Edward thought. *The whole planet feels like the four of us did at Vandenberg. What does it matter if we take a small chunk out of them?*

He bought the books and quickly left the mall.

On California state highway 41, driving north, passing a car perhaps every five minutes, he nodded his head and clenched his jaw, suddenly realizing why he had made the Pinedale stop. The books were of course superfluous; he had gone there to say good-bye to part of his culture.

If this is going to be an extended wake, he thought, *might as well say my farewells to everybody.*

Edward followed 41 into the park and took the long, winding drive along a nearly empty Wawona Road, the shadow of Jeffrey and Ponderosa pines crossing his windshield. It was four o'clock and the cool, sweet, green-scented air came through his half-opened side window with strobing warm bursts of sun between stands of trees. Large patches of snow dripped by the roadside, edges round and glittering.

The Wawona tunnel opened onto Inspiration Point and a view of the length of the valley. He parked the RV in the small paved lot, three spaces over from a lone unoccupied car. Climbing down, savoring the moment, he walked to the edge and stood by the railing, hands in pockets, a silly grin on his face.

I'm a kid again.

This is what he remembered most clearly—the valley floor, green with thick pine growth, and in western shadow, the Merced River reflecting snake curves of clear blue sky. Bridal Veil Falls cut its famous brilliant white arc and died in foggy spray against the rocks below. Above the falls, the Cathedral Rocks framed granite monstrosities beyond. On the left, the face of El Capitan glowered gray and pure, dominating the valley from this perspective.

Over twenty years ago, I wondered what it would be like to wander through a mass made of that much granite. There are places inside no one has seen ever, a vast space of solid rock, silent and still, frozen.

Beyond and behind El Capitan rose the Three Brothers and North Dome, from this angle a simple superfluity of rock capped with snow, sure to assume their proper characters when seen from below. Almost on a par with the white peak of Clouds Rest, and above the lower of the Cathedral Rocks, was the calm, bright-faced assertion of Half Dome.

The cold wind drove up the valley and whipped Edward's hair. *I'm not dreaming. By God, I'm finally here, and this isn't a dream.* He felt compelled to make sure and kicked his boot lightly against a post rail.

For more than twenty years, in his dreams, this had been the place of his greatest happiness, his peace. Nowhere else had he ever felt quite so much at ease, he thought; and his almost monthly returns in sleep to this valley, these monoliths, kept reminding him of what he had lost.

His father, whom he had lost—who had lost him, as well—and his mother, who ignored him. The peace and self-assurance of childish ignorance, or perhaps it was enlightenment; he didn't care.

By five-thirty, Edward had carried the last of his equipment from the Curry Village parking lot to the tent cabin he had reserved (needlessly) three weeks before. He checked out the cabin, a raised wooden platform covered with oft-patched white canvas, placed in isolation in the middle of trees close to the talus slope of Glacier Point. The cabin's single light bulb gave sufficient if not bright light, and the two army-blanketed metal-frame beds were in good repair and comfortable.

He followed the road past the Curry Village shops and over a stone bridge and then crossed the meadow. A red-winged blackbird in a nearby bush took exception to his presence. He grinned and tried to chirp back in a friendly manner, but the bird would have none of his overtures. That didn't matter; he knew he belonged there as much as the bird.

From the middle of a meadow, surrounded by tussocks of grass, he rotated to survey his new world. The valley was dark and quiet; the rich, deep blue evening sky hovered on motionless air. He heard the distant echoes of people laughing and talking, their voices bouncing from the granite walls of Glacier Point, Sentinel Rock, and the Royal Arches aross the valley. At the base of the Royal Arches he could make out the lights of the Ahwanee resort hotel. To the west a few hundred yards, a few campfires and electric lights revealed the extent of Yosemite Village.

He and his parents had lodged the last night of their journey in the Ahwanee, after spending a week in the tent cabins. He was still debating whether he would do that when the end approached.

Sublime peace.

How would the people of the world fare if all could spend their lives in this kind of beauty? If humans were rare enough that almost any meeting was precious?

He turned on his flashlight and shone it ahead as he returned to the tent cabins. On a flat-topped granite boulder just down the slope from his cabin, he laid out the Coleman stove and a pot of water and fixed a quick supper of ramen soup, throwing an onion and a hot dog in with the noodles.

He walked in darkness to the showers, wearing only an off-white knee-length terry-cloth robe, shaving kit in hand. A Steller's jay hopped along behind him, watching closely for dropped crumbs. "It's dark," he told the bird. "Go to sleep. I've eaten already. Where were you? No food now." The bird persisted, however; it knew humans were liars.

The communal showers—a large wood-paneled building, women to the left, men to the right—were practically empty. An attendant at the towel and soap station lounged back on his stool and only leaned forward when Edward approached. "Step right up," the young man said, flourishing a small bar of soap and a towel. "No waiting."

Edward smiled. "Must be dull."

"It's *wonderful,*" the attendant said.

"How many people here?"

"In the entire valley? Maybe two, three hundred. At Camp Curry, no more than thirty. Perfectly peaceful."

Edward showered in a clean, virtually unused stall, then shaved himself with a disposable razor in a mirror long enough to accommodate fifteen or twenty men. One other came in to shower, smiling cheerfully. Edward nodded cordially, feeling like privileged nobility, packed up his kit, and returned to the tent cabin.

By eight, he had had enough of reading the books he had bought in the shopping mall bookstore. He turned out the overhead light and plumped up the pillows, and then lay sleepless for an hour, thinking, listening.

Somewhere in the valley, a group of kids sang folk songs, their young voices rising high in the starry darkness. They sounded like cheerful ghosts.

I'm home.

55——

Reuben turned nineteen on March 15, in Alexandria, Virginia. He celebrated by buying himself a doughnut and a carton of milk in a small bakery, and then stood on the street, drawing suspicious glances. He had bought a new overcoat and a fedora, but tall, muscular young blacks, standing idle, dressed even in inconspicuous nonconformity, were not a favored attraction in the tourist district. He did not care. He knew what he was doing.

With a flourish, he tossed the carton and the waxed-paper doughnut wrapper into a public trash can, wiped his lips delicately with the knuckle of his index finger, and unlocked the door of a faded silver 1985 Chrysler LeBaron. He had purchased the car with cash in Richmond and had already, in just three days, put four hundred miles on it. It was the first car he had ever bought, and he didn't care whether he owned it or not. He had sole use of it, and that was what counted.

The remainder of the bag full of cash—about ten thousand dollars—he had stashed in the trunk under the spare tire.

"Okay," he said, listening to the engine smoothly idling. "Where to?"

He squinted a moment. Now, the orders usually came from people, and not from the indefinite nonvoice of what those on the network called the Boss. Reuben had even come to recognize the "signatures" of certain human personalities he communicated with, but this time, they were not familiar to him.

"Cleveland it is," he said. He pulled several maps from the glove compartment and used a yellow marker to draw his course along the highways. He had spent the last few days stealing hundreds of books and optical disks from libraries in Washington and Richmond, and buying hundreds of others from bookstores. He had passed all of these on to three middle-aged men in Richmond, and he had no clear idea what they were going to do with them; he hadn't asked. Clearly, the Boss was interested in literature.

With some relief—he did not enjoy thievery, even in a good cause—he took to the open road.

Spring was coming fast. The hills surrounding the Pennsylvania Turnpike were already rich green, and trees were bringing forth leaves that they would not have time to shed. There would be no summer or autumn.

Reuben shook his head, thinking about that, hands on the wheel. When he was on the road, the network rarely spoke to him, and that gave him plenty of time—perhaps too much time—to wonder about things.

He refilled the LeBaron's tank in New Stanton and parked in front of a diner. After a quick meal of a hamburger and a small green salad, he paid his tab and looked over a rack of postcards, choosing one showing a big white barn covered with Pennsylvania Dutch hex symbols. Purchasing a few stamps from a machine, he scribbled on the back of the card,

> Dad,
>   Still working steady here and elsewhere.
> Thinking about you.
>   Take care of yourself.
>
> Reuben

and dropped it into the box outside the diner.

He made it to Cleveland by eight. A quiet rain fell as he checked into an old hotel near the bus depot. He parked the LeBaron in a public parking garage, uncomfortably aware that he would not be driving it to the final destination. Somebody would pick him up and take him there.

He was no more than a couple of miles from Lake Erie, and that —so the network had told him—was where he would have to be in the early morning.

Reuben regarded himself in the bathroom's spotty mirror. He saw a big kid with a patchy beard and strong, regular features. He saluted the big kid—and the network—and went to bed, but didn't sleep much.

He was scared. Tomorrow, he would meet other people in the network—some of the people behind the voices. That didn't frighten him. But . . .

Something in the lake waited for them.

How much did he trust the Secret Masters?

What did it matter?

He'd be on the lake shore, at the Toland Brothers Excursion Terminal, at six A.M., clean-shaven and freshly showered and dressed in the new suit he had purchased in Richmond for just such an occasion.

56——

Trevor Hicks stepped out of the rental car under a big iron trestle and screened his eyes against the sun. He saw Arthur Gordon crossing the street. Gordon waved. Hicks, exhausted from the drive and still nervous, made a feeble gesture of acknowledgment. He had never become used to driving in the United States. Unable to find a quick route by surface streets, he had taken the freeway to get to the Seattle waterfront, then had driven in circles beneath the bridge for ten minutes, twice barely missing other cars in the narrow aisles. Finally he had managed to park just down the long concrete steps from the Pike Place Market. Across the street, warehouses converted into restaurants and shops vied with new buildings for views of the bay. Sea gulls wheeled and squeaked over a half-eaten hamburger in the street, lifting on spread wings to dodge passing cars.

Gordon approached and they shook hands awkwardly. Despite having communicated recently on the network, they hadn't seen each other since their first meeting in the Furnace Creek Inn. "My wife and son are in the aquarium," Gordon said, pointing down the street. "That'll keep them busy for a couple of hours."

"Do they know?" Hicks asked.

"I told them," Arthur said. "We're staying together, wherever I go. We're driving to San Francisco next week."

Hicks nodded. "I'm staying here. I hear there's going to be activity in the sound soon." He made a face. "If you can call it 'hearing.' "

"Any idea what sort of activity?" Arthur asked.

Hicks shook his head. "Something important. In San Francisco, too."

"I've had that impression."

"I'm sorry about your friend," Hicks said.

Arthur stared at him, puzzled. "Sorry?"

"Mr. Feinman. It was in the papers yesterday morning."

Arthur hadn't thought of Harry much since leaving Oregon. "I haven't been reading the papers. He . . ."

"Monday," Hicks said.

"Christ. I . . . Ithaca probably called, and we were gone." He lifted his head. "I told him about the network, too."

"Did he believe you?"

"I think he probably did."

"Then maybe it helped . . . No, I suppose that's silly."

Arthur stood with hands in pockets, shaken despite the months of preparation. He felt vaguely guilty for not thinking of Harry; he had called several times before leaving Oregon, and had been unable to speak to his friend. He took a deep breath and indicated they should climb the stairs to the market. "I wanted him to know that not everything was lost. I hope it helped. It's so difficult sorting everything out."

They passed in silence through the mostly empty aisles, stopping at a bakery to buy coffee and sitting at a white wrought-iron table placed between shops.

"How have they kept you busy?" Arthur asked.

"I've been visiting libraries, universities. Locating people . . .

That's how I'm most useful, apparently. I help find people the network is looking for, scientists, candidates."

"I haven't been doing much of anything yet," Hicks said. "Do you know . . . who the candidates are?"

"Not really. There are so many more names than places. I don't think any of *us* are making the final choices."

"Terrifying, isn't it?" Arthur said.

"In a way."

"Have you heard anything about the bogeys? On the network, I mean."

"Nothing," Hicks said.

"Do you think we've slowed them down, done any good by blowing them up?"

Hicks smiled grimly. "No. Just about as effective as Crockerman."

"But he didn't . . . at least, I presume he had nothing to do with the action in Death Valley."

"That's right," Hicks said. "He's done nothing. So have the hotheads. Certainly, they've boosted our morale a little . . . but nobody believes they've fixed anything. The bullets still spin."

"Then what purpose did the bogeys serve?" Arthur asked.

"You stated it once. They were a distraction, a misdirection. We've concentrated almost all our attention on them."

Arthur blinked. "I didn't think they were just decoys."

Hicks shook his head. "Neither did I."

Arthur pushed aside his sweet roll, all appetite gone. "They dropped them here, to deceive us, *test* us, as if we were laboratory mice?"

"I would say so, now, wouldn't you?"

Arthur shook his head. "That *burns.*"

"Insult before injury," Hicks said.

"Have you discussed this with others on the network?"

"No. We've been far too busy with other things. But the network has been given no instructions whatsoever by the Boss regarding the bogeys. We have not been instructed to recruit the President. You know that Lehrman is Possessed?"

Arthur nodded.

"The Boss has written off our entire military and government effort. Obviously." Hicks held out his hands and stood, gathering his foam-plastic cup and waxed-paper wrapper. "So I stay here, help with whatever effort is made in Seattle. And you move south."

Arthur remained seated, stunned. He should have assembled all the facts. He was disappointed in himself to find he had still harbored some illusions.

"Sorry to be the one to tell you about Mr. Feinman," Hicks said. Arthur nodded.

"Tonight I'm joining a group staying on Queen Anne Hill," Hicks said. "We'll reconnoiter from there." He held out his hand. "Best of luck to you and your family."

Arthur stood and shook it firmly. "Good-bye," he said.

They looked at each other, not voicing the single question too obvious to ask. *Is he chosen? Am I?*

Hicks returned to his car. A few moments later, after surveying the fresh fish stalls and vegetable markets and purchasing a pound of smoked salmon and several bags of fruit, Arthur descended the stairs and crossed the parking lot and street to join Francine and Marty at the aquarium.

57——

March 20

An ancient Chevy Vega with Texas license plates crossed the stone bridge in the opposite direction and honked at Edward. Edward turned and saw a collage of bumper stickers covering the back of the car, including the trunk and lower corners of the rear window. One glaring Day-Glo pink sticker immediately caught his eye: REGISTER PUSSY NOT FIREARMS. A faded yellow plastic square hung in the window's upper corner: CAUTION! CHILD DRIVING.

"Hey, Edward!"

"Minelli!" He walked to the window and leaned down to wrap his hand around the back of Minelli's neck. "You madman. You own this?" He spread his palm at the Vega.

"Bought it three weeks ago, complete with decoration. A beauty, isn't it?"

"I am genuinely glad to see you."

"I am glad to be *seen*. I was rough for a while after we parted. You went back to Texas?"

"That's right," Edward said. "How about you?"

"I made a scene in the institute office. They pulled my papers and kicked me out and said go ahead, sue us. I was going nuts. I bought this and I've been driving around ever since. I went to Shoshone again and dropped by the grocery store. Said hi to everybody. Stella wasn't there. She was off in Las Vegas talking to lawyers about mineral deals. Bernice was there. She asked about you. I said you were fine. Are you?"

"I'm great," Edward said. "Park and take a walk with me."

"Where to?"

"I hear there are rock climbers on El Capitan."

"Hot damn. Just like Disneyland."

Minelli parked the car under a cloud of blue exhaust. He patted the trunk before opening it. "Why spend lots of money on something that doesn't have to last more than a month or two?"

"Looks like it could break down in the middle of nowhere," Edward commented.

"Hey, I've always relied on the kindness of strangers."

"With your sense of humor, that could be dangerous."

Minelli shrugged and spread his arms out to the sun. "Ultraviolet rays, do your worst. I don't give a fuck anymore."

They followed the asphalt road for two miles, past the Three Brothers, then took a trail for another mile and stood in the El Capitan meadow, looking up at the massive ancient wall of gray granite. A pale streak showed where a sheet of rock had broken off in 1990, revealing unweathered surface.

"It is magnificent. I haven't been here in ten, twelve years," Minelli said. "Why'd you come?"

"Childhood memories. Best place on Earth."

Minelli nodded emphatically. "Wherever I am right now is the best place on Earth, but this is better than most. I don't see anybody up there. Where are they?"

Edward held up a small pair of field binoculars. "Look for ants trailing ropes and bags," he said. "There's five or six up there today, I hear."

"Christ," Minelli said, shading his eyes. "I see a black spot. No. It's a blue spot. Color of my sleeping bag. Is that one?"

Edward drew a line with his finger from the tiny speck of blue. "Look above that a couple of degrees. Here." He handed Minelli the binoculars. Minelli swept them back and forth in decreasing arcs and stopped, brows rising above the eyepieces. "Got him. Or her. Just hanging there."

"There's another above that one," Edward said. "They must be a team. You can barely see the ropes between them."

"How long does it take to get to the top?"

"A day, someone told me. Maybe longer. Sometimes they overnight up there, hanging in a bag, or on a ledge if they're lucky."

Minelli returned the binoculars. "Makes me queasy just thinking about it."

Edward shook his head. "I don't know. I could get into it. Think of the accomplishment. Standing up on top, looking out over everything. Be like building a skyscraper and knowing it was yours."

Minelli made a dubious face. "What else is happening here? The place is deserted."

"Practically. There's a group meeting in the amphitheater at Curry Village this evening. A band is holding a concert tomorrow evening. The rangers are really loose. Some of them are giving tours on the weekend."

"Everybody's staying home. Mr. and Mrs. Momanddad huddling next to their TVs, huh?"

Edward nodded, then raised the binoculars, spotting another climber. "Do you blame them?"

"No," Minelli said quietly. "If I had a home or anybody I cared about—a woman, I mean—that's where I'd be. I said good-bye to my sister and mom. They don't know what the hell's happening. They're too ignorant to be scared. Mom says, 'God will take care of us. We're his children.' Maybe He will. But if He doesn't, I'm with you. I don't hold grudges. I can still admire the Old Dude's masterworks."

"It might be nice to be ignorant," Edward said, lowering the binoculars.

Minelli shook his head adamantly. "At the end, I want to know what's happening. I don't want that . . . panic, when it comes. I want to know and sit and watch as much of it as I can. Maybe that's the best seat in the house." He pointed to the mottled rock face. "Up on top somewhere."

* * *

Since Edward's tent cabin had two bunks, he offered one to Minelli, but he turned it down. "Look," he said, "they're not even charging for them now. I asked down at the village and the fellows there say go ahead, sleep in one, just keep it clean yourself. Me, I'm going to want someone of the opposite sex with me when it happens. How about you?"

"That would be nice," Edward agreed.

"All right, then. We party together, find women—some smart women, I mean, who know what's going on as much as we do—and we party some more. I brought some food in with me, and the village store is stocked to the rafters with beer and wine and frozen food. We're going to have a good time."

At dusk, they showered and put on clean clothes and walked to the amphitheater, passing the wood-frame cabins. A middle-aged couple sat in folding chairs before the open door of a cabin, listening to a portable radio turned down low. They nodded greetings to each other.

"Going to the meeting?" Edward asked.

The man shook his head. "Not tonight," he said. "It's too peaceful tonight."

"You'll hear it from here, anyway," Minelli warned.

The man and woman smiled and shooed them away. "Tell us if there's anything interesting."

"Casual," Minelli commented to Edward as they passed the Curry Village administration building and general store.

The valley was wrapped in cool shadow. Straying clouds obscured the tops of Half Dome and the Royal Arches. Edward zipped up his suede jacket. The amphitheater—benches arranged in curves before an elevated log and wood-beam stage—was full, people of all ages milling while engineers worked on the sound system. The loudspeakers popped and hummed; echoes of the crowd and the electronic noises bounced back at varying intervals from several directions. They found a bench halfway out from the stage and sat, watching the others, being watched in turn. A scruffy gray-bearded man of about sixty-five in a khaki bush jacket offered them unopened cans from a half-empty case of Coors and they accepted, popping and sipping as the gathering came to order.

A tall middle-aged park ranger climbed onto the stage and stood before the microphone, raising the stand to her level. "Hello," she said, smiling.

The audience replied in kind, a low, warm murmur.

"My name—some of you know me already—is Elizabeth Rowell. There are about three hundred and fifty of us in the Yosemite now, and a few more coming in each day. I think we all know why we're here. We're all kind of surprised there aren't more here, but some of us understand that, too. This is my home, and I plan on staying *home.*" She thrust out her jaw and looked around the audience. "So do others, and not many people live here year-around, as I do. Those of you who have left your homes to come here, you're welcome to stay.

"We're awfully lucky. Looks like the weather is going to be warm. It may drizzle off and on, but there's not going to be much rain and no snow at all for a week or so, and all the passes are open. I just wanted to say that the park rules still apply, and we're all behaving as if things are normal. If you need help, we're fully staffed with rangers. Park police are on duty. We haven't had any trouble, and we don't expect any. You're good folks."

The man with the Coors box smiled and raised his can to that.

"Now, I am here basically to introduce folks. First, there's Jackie Sandoval. Some of you know her already. She's volunteered to be our spokesperson, sort of, tonight and for the rest of our stay. Jackie?"

A small, slender woman with long black hair and doll-like features came on stage. Rowell lowered the microphone for her.

"Hello," she said, and again the warm sound emanated from the crowd in the amphitheater. "We're here to celebrate, aren't we?" Silence. "I think we are. We're here to celebrate how far we've come, and to count our blessings. If what the experts tell us is true, we have three to four weeks to live in this wilderness, to appreciate the beauty and to think back on our lives. How many have had a chance for that kind of retrospective?

"We are a community—not just all of us here, but people everywhere. Some of us have stayed at home, and others have come here, perhaps because we recognize that all of Earth is our home. Each night, if we wish, if we all agree, we'll gather in the amphitheater and share our dinner, perhaps have people sing for us; we'll be a family. As Elizabeth said, all are welcome. I notice some bikers camped at Sunnyside. They haven't caused any trouble, I've been told, and they are welcome. Maybe for once in our history we can all be together, and appreciate what we can share. Tonight, I've asked Mary and Tony Lampedusa to sing for us, and then there's going to be a dance at the Yosemite Village visitor center. I hope you'll come.

"First, there's a couple of announcements. We're pooling our books and videotapes and such at the Ahwanee to make a kind of library. Anybody who wants to contribute is welcome. The park service has chipped in a lot of books about Yosemite and the Sierras. I'm the librarian, so to speak, so talk to me if you want to read anything, or donate anything.

"Oh. We're also arranging for a music library. We have fifty portable optical disk players used for recorded park tours and about three hundred music disks. If you want to donate more, anything is appreciated. Now, here's Tony and Mary Lampedusa."

Edward sat with the half-full beer can between his knees and listened to the high, sweet folksinging. Minelli shook his head and wandered off before they were done. "See you at the dance," he whispered to Edward in passing.

The dance began slowly on the open-air wooden deck of the visitors' center. A ranger's powerful stereo system provided the music, mostly rock tunes from the eighties.

About half the people in the park were single. Some who weren't single acted as if they were, and a few arguments broke out among couples. Edward heard one man telling his wife, "Christ, you know I love you, but doesn't this make anything different? Aren't we all supposed to be together here?" The woman, shaking her head tearfully, was having none of that.

Minelli had no luck finding a partner. His appearance—short, on the edge of unkempt, his grin a little too manic—did not attract the fit, well-groomed single females. He glanced at Edward across the open-air pavilion and shrugged expressively, then pointed at him and held a hand out, thumbs up. Edward shook his head.

Everybody was on edge that night, which was only to be expected. Edward stood to one side, unwilling to approach a woman just yet, willing only to watch and evaluate.

The dance ended early. "Not a great dance," Minelli commented as they walked in the dark back to Camp Curry. They separated near the public showers to go to their separate tent cabins.

Edward was not ready for sleep, however. Flashlight in hand, he walked west along a trail and came to the Happy Isles, where he stood on a wood bridge and listened to the Merced. In the distance, he could hear Vernal and Nevada falls roaring with snowmelt. The river ran high on the bridge pilings, black as pitch in the deeps, dark blue-gray in turbulence.

He glanced up at the stars. Through the trees, just above Half Dome, the sky was twinkling again, tiny intense flashes of blue-green and red. Fascinated, he watched for several minutes, thinking, "It's not over out there. Looks like somebody's fighting." He tried to imagine the kind of war that might be fought in space, through the asteroids, but he couldn't. "I wish I could understand," he said. "I wish somebody would tell me what this is all about."

Suddenly, his whole body ached. He clenched his jaw and slammed his fist on the wooden railing, screaming wordlessly, kicking at a post until he collapsed on the wooden deck and clutched his throbbing foot. For a quarter of an hour, back against the rail, legs spread limp, he cried like a child, opening and closing his fists.

A half hour later, walking slowly back to the camp, flashlight beam showing the way, he realized what he had to lose.

He climbed the steps to his tent cabin and collapsed on the bed without undressing. Tomorrow night, he would not hesitate to ask a woman to dance, or to return with him and stay with him. He would not be shy or principled or stand on his dignity.

There was simply no time for such scruples.

He did not understand what was happening, but he could feel the end coming.

Like everybody else, he knew it in his bones.

58———

Reuben came awake at five o'clock. Eyes wide, he oriented himself: spread-eagled on a short single bed in a small, shabby hotel room. His nighttime thrashings had pulled the upper sheet and blankets loose and he was only half covered.

Sitting on the side of the bed, he put on his ballpackers (that's what his father always called jockey briefs) and a T-shirt and his pants. Then he pulled the curtains on the narrow window and stood in front of it, looking out at the predawn light coming up over the city. Gray buildings, old brick and stone darkened by last night's sleet and snow; orange streetlights casting lonely spots on wet pavement; a single ancient Toyota truck driving through slush below the window and slowly cornering past an abandoned and boarded-up storefront.

Reuben showered, put on his new suit, and was out of the hotel by five-thirty. He had paid his room tab the night before. He stood shivering for a moment by the abandoned storefront, listening to the network, getting his final directions. The old Toyota came down the street again and pulled to the curb in front of him. A man just a few years older than Reuben, dressed in overalls and a baseball cap, sat behind the wheel. "Need a lift?" he asked, reaching over to open the opposite door. Heat poured from the cab. "You're heading down to the Toland Brothers Excursion Terminal. You're the second I've picked up this morning."

Reuben slid into the passenger side and smiled at the driver. "Awful early to be out driving," he said. "I appreciate this."

"Hey, it's in a good cause," the man said. His gaze lingered on Reuben's face. He did not appear happy that his passenger was black. "That's what I'm being told, anyway."

They took East Ninth Street to the Municipal Pier. The driver let Reuben out and drove away without saying another word.

Dawn was something more than a promise as he walked along the pier and approached the heavy iron bars and gate beneath the giant painted TOLAND BROS. sign. A plump, grizzled man of something less than seventy years and more than sixty stood behind the gate with a flashlight in hand, waggling a cigar between his teeth. He saw Reuben but did not move until the young man was less than two yards away. Then he pushed off from the bars next to the closed gate and shined his flashlight on Reuben's face.

"What can I do for you?" he asked sharply. The cigar was soggy and unlighted.

"I'm here for the morning excursion," Reuben said.

"Excursion? To where?"

Reuben stretched out an arm and pointed vaguely at Lake Erie. The man scrutinized him for several long moments in the flashlight beam, then lowered the lens and called out, "Donovan!"

Donovan, a short, clean-cut fellow in a cream-colored suit, about as old as the plump man but far better preserved, came out of a shed near the office.

Donovan glanced quickly at Reuben. "Network?" he asked.

"Yes, sir."

"Let him in, Mickey."

"Goddamn fools," Mickey muttered. "There's still ice on the lake. Making us go out before the season." He leaned his head to one side and concentrated on keying the padlock and releasing a chain from the gate latch. He tugged the chain out of the eye with a conspicuous machine-gun *snick-tink,* pulled the gate inward, and bade Reuben enter by swinging a large, callused red hand.

Halfway down the pier, past an old, boarded-up seafood restaurant, a two-decked excursion boat named the *Gerald FitzEdmund* belched diesel from twin motors through stern pipes just above the waterline. The boat was easily capable of carrying two or three hundred passengers, but at this hour it was practically deserted. Donovan walked ahead of Reuben and gestured for him to cross the roped boarding ramp.

"We'll cruise the lake for an hour or two," Donovan said. "We've been told to leave the three of you out there. Wherever 'there' is. It's mighty damned cold to be sailing today, let me tell you."

"What are we going to do out there?" Reuben asked.

Donovan stared at him. "You don't know?" he said.

"No."

"Christ. I *presume*"—he used the word as if it had an official flavor, yet was not at all familiar to his lips—"I *presume* that you'll find something out there before we drop you off. Or maybe you'll just freeze to death."

"I hope to God we do," Reuben said, shaking his head dubiously. "Find something out there, I mean." *They haven't done me wrong yet.*

He walked toward the bow and joined a white boy some four or five years younger than he, and a well-dressed black woman about thirty. A stiff, icy breeze cut across the deck, blowing the woman's hair past her face. She glanced at him, then faced forward, but said nothing. The boy held out his hand and they shook firmly.

"My name's Ian," the boy said, teeth chattering.

"Reuben Bordes. Are both of you network?"

The boy nodded. The woman gave the ghost of a grin but did not turn away from her view of the lake.

"I'm possessed," Ian said. "You must be, too."

"Sure am," Reuben said.

"They make you do things?" Ian asked.

"They're making me do this."

"Me, too. I'm a little afraid. Nobody knows what we're doing."

"They'll take care of us," the woman said.

"What's your name, ma'am?" Reuben asked.

"None of your damned business. I don't have to like any of this; I just have to do it."

Ian gave Reuben a screw-faced glance and cocked an eyebrow at her. Reuben nodded.

Donovan and Mickey were climbing to the pilot house on the upper deck. A man in a dark blue uniform was already at the wheel. With only the six of them aboard, the excursion boat pulled away from the dock and headed out onto the smooth, lazy morning waters of the lake. Chunks of ice slid spinning past the bow. "We'd better go inside or we'll freeze, ma'am," Reuben suggested. The woman nodded and followed him into the enclosed passenger area.

Fifteen minutes into the cruise, Mickey descended to the lower deck with a cardboard box and a Thermos. "The galley ain't open," he said, "but we brought these things aboard with us." He peeled the top of the carton back to reveal doughnuts and three foam cups.

"Bless you," the woman said, sitting on a fiberglass bench. Ian picked two doughnuts and Reuben followed his example. Mickey poured steaming coffee as each held a cup. "Donovan tells me nobody knows what's out there," he said, capping the Thermos.

Reuben shook his head and dropped sprinkles of powdered sugar from his doughnut into the coffee.

"So what do we do if there's just water? Let you drown?"

"Something's out there," the woman said.

"I'm not doubting it. I just wish I didn't feel so damned creepy. Everything's gone to hell the last few months. Thank God it's not the season. No tourists. The President's going nuts. Whole world."

"Are you part of the network?" Ian asked.

Mickey shook his head. "Not me, thank God. Donovan is. He's told me about it, and he showed me the spider. Damned thing wouldn't bite me. Shows you what the hell I'm worth. I've thought about calling up the newspapers, but who would believe me? Who would care? Me and Donovan, we've worked the lakes for thirty

302 • Greg Bear

years, first fishing smelt, then running geehawks—that's tourists—all around. I named this boat. It's a joke."

Nobody understood, so he cleared his throat. "I tell people, 'Wreck of the Edmund Fitzgerald.' Remember that song? Ore tanker went down. Big wave or something broke its keel and it sank without a trace. But what the hell—geehawks don't know nothing about the lakes. They think lakes are puddles. These lakes are goddamned oceans, landlocked oceans. You could hide anything at the bottom, whole cities . . ." He glared at them for emphasis, one pencil-thin eyebrow raised. "So I've been thinking. No need to talk about what I've been thinking. I'll just let that sit with you, and with Donovan. If the goddamned spider doesn't bite me, sure I'll cooperate—he's my partner—but I say the hell with it, and with everything else."

He walked aft with the box and Thermos, shoulders twitching. The woman ate her single doughnut delicately, leaning her elbow against the back of the bench, watching him leave. "So what have you two been doing?" she asked, suddenly familiar and friendly.

Ian sat beside her, holding his coffee cup against the boat's gentle sway in the crook of one folded leg. "I've been looting the libraries at Cleveland State," he said. "And you?"

"Case Western," she said. "I and about six others. Two of them are hackers. They brought a truck into the data storage center at the main library and ran cables into the building and took everything they could get their hands on."

"I sent records from the Library of Congress to this fellow in Virginia," Reuben said. "And other stuff. I recruited Trevor Hicks." Neither Ian nor the woman knew who Hicks was. "Have you met any of the ones below the bosses—the humans I've heard on the network, giving orders?"

"I have," the woman said. "One of them's my husband. We were separated, filing for divorce, when we were both possessed. I've had to work with him, and take orders from him, the last two months. He works for the State Department."

Cleveland was no longer visible to the south. There was nothing but blue ice-dotted lake and a fast-disappearing mist from horizon to horizon. They had been on the water for over an hour.

"Do you think there's anybody who's got the whole picture?" Ian asked. "Any human, I mean."

"I haven't met one if there is," Reuben said.

"My husband gives orders, but he doesn't know everything."

Ian licked crumbs and sugar from his fingers. "I hope they have a bathroom on this tub," he said, walking aft.

The boat's motors cut back to a throaty gurgling rumble. The water had taken on a slight chop and as they circled, Reuben felt queasy. *I'm going to regret that doughnut.*

"All right," Donovan called on the loudspeaker from the pilot house, "this is where we're supposed to be. Anybody getting messages?"

"Not me," the woman said, standing and brushing doughnut crumbs from her coat.

"Christ," Donovan commented dryly.

They had circled for ten minutes when Ian sang out, "Thar she blows!" He had ascended to the upper deck and now leaned over the railing beside the pilot house, pointing east. Reuben and the woman returned to the bow and followed his point and saw a dead gray block rising from the water, about the size and shape of a moving van's trailer. The pilot gunned the motors and moved them closer to the protuberance.

"What is it?" Ian shouted. "A submarine?"

"I don't know," Reuben said, half laughing. He was excited and more frightened than ever. The woman's face was a stiff mask, but her wide-eyed, glassy stare gave her away.

The boat came to within a few yards of the gray block. The bow wash slapped against it.

A square hatch about as tall as Reuben opened in the smooth dull surface at the level of the boat's bulwarks.

"It's an elevator," the woman said. "No, it's a stairway. We're supposed to go inside. You, me, and him." She pointed at herself, Reuben, and Ian on the upper deck. "Nobody else."

"I know," Reuben said. *At least it's not rocking.*

Donovan stood by the port gangway and pulled it aside as the pilot brought the boat as close to the block as he dared. Mickey wheeled a shorter gangplank to the gangway and pushed it out to the block's entrance. It was safe enough and no more. The woman crossed first, impatient, buffeted by the wind, gripping the single raised handrail tightly; then Reuben, and finally Ian.

She was already descending a spiral staircase within the block when Reuben stopped at the rear of the alcove. He peered down after her. Ian came up behind him.

"That's it?"

"That's it," Reuben affirmed.

"Better go, then."

They descended. Above them, the hatch shut with a gentle hum.

59——

There was a wildly canted floor, smoke coming up through the boards and tile, a gout of steam and rock, and the walls falling away. He felt himself lifted and screamed.

Sitting upright in the bed, Arthur blinked at the unfamiliar room. Marty was on his hands and knees crying hysterically in the next bed.

Francine put her arms around Arthur.

"There's nothing," she said. "There's nothing." She let him go and crawled out from under the covers to embrace Marty. "Dad was having a nightmare," she said. "He's all right."

"It was *here*," Arthur said. "I felt it. Ahh, *God*."

Marty was quiet now. Francine came back to their bed and lay next to him. "You'd think they'd help you with your dreams or something," she said, somewhat bitterly.

"I wish they'd blocked that one," he said. "I could—"

"Shhh," Francine said, wrapping her arms around him now. She was shivering. "Bad enough if we have to live through it. Why do we have to dream about it, too?"

"Have you dreamed about it?"

She shook her head. "I will, though. I know I will. Everybody will, the closer it gets." Her shivers turned into something more. Her teeth clicked together as she held him. Arthur stroked her face with his fingers and tightened his grip on her, but she was not to be consoled. Without tears, she shook violently, silently, her neck muscles locked with the effort of not making a sound, not scaring Marty.

"We-we-we wou-would *die*," she whispered harshly.

"Shh," he said. "Shh. I'm the one who had the nightmare."

"We would d-die," she repeated. "I w-want to scream. I

n-n-need to scream, Art." She glanced at Marty, still awake, listening, watching from where he lay.

"Is Mommy all right?" Marty asked.

Arthur didn't answer.

"Mommy!" Marty barked.

"I-I'm fine, honey." Her shaking hadn't diminished.

"Your mother's scared," Arthur said.

"Stop it," Francine demanded, glaring at him.

"We're all very scared," Arthur said.

"Is it happening now?" Marty asked.

"No, but we're worried about it, and that gives me nightmares, and makes your mommy shiver."

Francine closed her eyes in an agony of maternal empathy.

"Everybody's ascared," Marty declared. "Not just me. Everybody."

"That's right," Arthur said. He rocked Francine gently. She relaxed her wrinkled brows but kept her eyes closed. Her shaking had slowed to an occasional shudder. Marty came from his bed to theirs and wrapped his arms around Francine, placing his cheek against her shoulder.

"It's all right, Mom," he said.

"It's all right to be afraid," Arthur said to nobody in particular, staring at the flowered wallpaper illuminated by a small nightlight pointing the way to the bathroom.

They were in a bed-and-breakfast inn a few miles south of Portland.

The network was not active.

He had been set on his course, given his instructions.

I could use a little sympathy, too.

But none was offered.

PERSPECTIVE

Excerpt from New Scientist, March 25, 1997:
The emergence of a new and radically altered Venus from behind the sun has given planetary geologists many things to ponder. It was supposed that the impact of a block of ice two hundred kilometers in diameter would cause enormous seismic disruption, but there is no sign of that. Some, in fact-connecting the impact with events on Earth-have theorized that the block was artificially "calved" into many smaller chunks, distributing the impact more evenly around the solar system's second planet.

What we now see is a naked Venus, her atmosphere transformed into a cloak of transparent, superheated steam. Surface features thus revealed are little different from what we had expected from the evidence of past planetary probe radar scans.

Planetologist Ure Heisinck of Göttingen University believes that the atmosphere may now have a built-in heat-transfer mechanism that will allow it to cool; that eventually the steam will condense and the resulting opaque white clouds will reflect more of the sun's heat into space than they will absorb. More cooling will occur, and eventually rain will fall, which will turn again into steam on the planet's surface. The steam will condense in the upper atmosphere, conveying heat back into space. In a few centuries, Earthlike conditions may prevail . . .

LACRIMOSA DIES ILLA!

60——

Smoky haze hung high over the valley from fires in the east: Idaho, Arizona, Utah. The morning sun glowered bright orange through the pall, casting all Yosemite in a dreamy shadow-light the color of Apocalypse.

Edward walked past the general store and saw Minelli sitting in the open doorway of his car in the parking lot, listening to the radio with one leg drawn up on the other knee, picking mud out of his boot tread with a twig.

"What's the word?" Edward asked, leaning his walking stick on the car's bumper.

"Nothing close to us yet," Minelli answered. "Fires to the south, spreading south but not north, and fires to the east about three, four hundred miles."

"Anything else?"

"The bullets have dropped below microseismic background. Nobody can hear them now." He smirked and flipped the mud-tipped twig onto the asphalt. "Makes you wish we were out there at work, doesn't it? Feeling the patient's pulse."

"Not really," Edward said. "Walking today?"

"Been," Minelli said, gesturing to the west. "Since about five. It's nice getting up in the dark. The sunrise was spectacular. Lots of my habits are changing. I'm feeling very calm now. Does that make any sense?"

"Denial, anger, withdrawal . . . acceptance," Edward said. "The four stages."

"I don't *accept* at all," Minelli said. "I'm just calm about what's going to happen. Where are you going?"

"I'm taking the Mist Trail up to Vernal and Nevada falls. Never been there."

Minelli nodded. "You know, I've specked out where I want to be when the crunch comes." He raised a finger to Glacier Point. "You can see everything up there, and it's going to be spectacular. I'll hike up and camp out for a week or however long it takes, just to be ready."

"What if you meet some kind female?"

"I expect she'll go with me," Minelli said. "But I'm not holding out much hope." He rubbed his beard and grinned fiendishly. "I'm not grade-A Choice."

Edward glanced at a sticker in the side window: BORN TO RAISE HECK. "*Mazel,*" he called back over his shoulder, walking east.

"I'm a Catholic boy. I don't know that stuff."

"I'm Episcopalian," Edward said.

"When are you coming back?"

"In time for the meeting at five."

Edward followed the switchbacks of the first leg of the Muir Trail, pausing on rock-masonry vantage points to gaze out over gorges filled with roaring white water. He was halfway up the steep Mist Trail by eleven. The smell of moss and spray and damp humus filled his nose. Vernal Fall bellowed constantly on his left, ghostly clouds of moisture soaking his clothes and beading on his face and hands. He grimaced against the chill but refused to wear a parka or anything else that would isolate him.

The wet dark gray trail rocks reflected the sky and became a somber orange-brown. When the breeze blew thick fingers of mist in his direction, he seemed suspended in a warm amber fog, the fall and weathered, moss-covered granite walls lost in a general vaporous void.

I Saw Eternity the other night, he quoted, and not remembering the rest, concluded aloud with, "And it gave me quite a fright . . ."

At the top of Vernal Fall, he walked across a broad, almost level expanse of dry white granite, one hand on an iron railing, and stood near the wide, sleek green lip of plummeting water. Here was the noise and the power, but little of the wetness; observation and immediacy and yet isolation. The true experience, Edward thought, would be sweeping down the falls in the middle of the water, suspended in cold green and white, curtains of bubbles and long translucent vertical surfaces distorting all sky and earth. What would it be like to live as a water sprite, able to magically suspend oneself in the middle of certain death?

He looked across at Liberty Cap and thought again of the vast granite spaces within the domes, unseen. *Why an obsession with places out of view?*

He frowned in concentration, trying to bring up the monstrous big thought he had so loosely hooked. *Living things see only the surface, can't exist in the depths. Life is painted on the surface of the real. Death is the great unexplored volume. Death rises from the inaccessible,* depth *and* death *sounding so much alike . . .*

There had been only three other people on the trail that morning, one descending, two climbing behind Edward. Another he had not seen, a blond-haired woman in a tan parka and dark blue shorts lugging a big expensive blue backpack. She stood on the opposite side of the granite block, looking over Emerald Lake, the pool where water from 600-foot Nevada Fall rested before slipping over the shorter Vernal Fall. She must have camped overnight, or was perhaps on the morning leg of a long trek around the rim of the valley.

The woman turned and Edward saw she was strikingly beautiful, tall and Nordic, a long face with perfectly cut nose, clear blue eyes, and lips both sensual and faintly disapproving. He looked away quickly, all too intensely aware she was outside his range. He had long since learned that women this beautiful paid little attention to men of his mild appearance and social standing.

Still, she seemed to be alone.

Came that high, painful interior singing he had always known when in the presence of the desirable and inaccessible woman, not lust, but an almost religious longing. It was not a sensation he wanted now; he did not wish to be seduced away from worshiping the land, the Earth, to focus on a single woman, let alone one he could not possibly have. The woman or women he had imagined the night before would not evoke this kind of response; they would be safe, undemanding, undistressing. Quickly, with nothing more than a polite smile and nod, he passed the woman where she stood by the bridge and continued along the trail.

In the rocky tree-spotted upland meadow beyond Emerald Lake, he found a natural granite bench and laid out his lunch of two processed-American-cheese sandwiches and dried fruit, very much like what he had eaten on hikes in the valley as a boy. Facing the white plume of Nevada Fall, still a few hundred yards distant, he chewed crescents from a leathery apricot and brewed hot tea on a tiny portable stove.

Someone came up behind him, tread so light as to be almost undetected. "Excuse me."

He twisted his torso and stared at the blond woman. She smiled down on him. She was at least six feet tall. "Yes?" he asked, swallowing most of a mouthful of half-chewed apricot.

"Did you see a man here, a little taller than I, with a very black full beard and wearing a red parka?" She indicated the man's height with a hand held level above her head.

Edward hadn't, but the woman's worried expression suggested that it would be best if he paused to consider before answering. "No, I don't think so," he said. "There aren't many people here today."

"I've been waiting two days," she said, sighing. "We were supposed to meet here, at the Emerald Lake, actually."

"I'm sorry."

"Did you see anybody like him down on the valley floor? You came up from there, didn't you?"

"Yes, but I don't remember any men with black beards and red parkas. Or any with just black beards, for that matter—unless he's a biker."

"Oh, no." She shook her head and turned away, then turned back. "Thank you."

"You're welcome. May I offer some tea, fruit?"

"No thank you. I've eaten. I carried food for both of us."

Edward watched her with an embarrassed smile. She seemed unsure what to do next. He half wished she would go away; his attraction to her was almost painful.

"He's my husband," she said, staring up at Liberty Cap, shading her eyes against the hazy glare. "We're separated. We met in Yosemite, and we thought if we came back here, before . . ." Her voice trailed off and she made a negligible shrug of her shoulders and arms. "We might be able to stay together. We agreed to meet at Emerald Lake."

"I'm sure he must be here someplace." He gestured at the lake and trail and the Nevada Fall.

"Thank you," she said. This time, she did not smile, simply turned and walked back toward the head of Vernal Fall and the descending Mist Trail. He watched her go and took a deep breath, biting into his second sandwich. He stared at the sandwich ruefully as he chewed. "Must be the white bread," he told himself. "Can't catch a beauty like that with anything less than whole wheat."

At three, the meadow and the perimeter of the lake, the falls and the trail below, were empty. He was the only human for miles, or so it seemed; might even be true, he thought. He crossed the bridge and lingered in the trees on the other side, with only the roar of the falls above and below and snatches of birdsong. He knew rocks of any description but little about birds. Red-winged blackbirds and robins and jays were obvious; he thought about buying a book in the general store to learn the others, but then, what use applying names? If his memories were soon to be scattered fine-ground over space, education was a waste.

What was important was finding his center, or pinning down some locus of being, establishing a moment of purity and concentrated awareness. He did not think that was possible with people all around; now was a chance to try.

Prayer perhaps. God had not been on his mind much recently, a telltale void; he did not wish to be inconsistent when all the world was a foxhole. But consistency was as useless now as nature studies, and not nearly so tempting.

The valley was still in sun, Liberty Cap half shadowed. The smoke had cleared some and the sky was bluer, green at the edges of the haze, more real than it had been.

"I am going to die," he said out loud, in a normal tone of voice, experimenting. "What I am will come to an end. My thoughts will end. I will experience nothing, not even the final end." *Rising rocks and smoke and lava. No; probably not like that. Will it hurt? Will there be time for pain?*

Mass death; God was probably busy also with mass prayer.

God.

Not a protector, unless there be miracles.

He shuffled his booted feet in the dry trail dirt. "What in hell am I looking for? Revelation?" He shook his head and forced a laugh. "Naïve sonofabitch. You're out of training; your prayer muscles, your enlightenment biceps, they're all out of shape. Can't lift you any higher than your goddamned head." The bitterness in his voice shook him. Did he really want revelation, confirmation, assurance of existence or meaning beyond the end?

"God is what you love." He said this softly; it was embarrassing to realize how much he believed it. Yet he had never been particularly good at love, neither the love of people in all its forms nor the other kinds, except perhaps love of his work. "I love the Earth."

But that was rather vague and broad. The Earth offered only unthinking obstacles to love: storms, rock slides, volcanoes, quakes. Accidents. Earth could not help being incontinent. Easy to love the great mother.

The wind picked up and carried droplets of mist above the Vernal Fall and over the forest, landing cool and lightly stinging-tickling on his cheek. He thought of down on his cheek and not whiskers, and of wanting his father to stay with them, even then knowing (truly did he realize it then?) that the unknit would soon separate.

That time, in Yosemite, had not been altogether blissful. The memories he now recovered were of a young boy's ignorant but sharp eye, observing a man and a woman, shakily acting the roles of mother and father, husband and wife, not connecting anymore.

The boy had been unable to foresee what would happen after the separation so obviously but so deniably coming.

He squinted.

Earth = mother. God = father. No God = no father = inability to connect with the after.

"That," he said, "cuts the fucking cake." He swatted at a gnat and hefted his pack higher on his back, descending along the wet dark gray rock steps carved out beside Vernal Fall, and then following the path above the foaming, violently full Merced.

Pausing with a slight smile, he left the path and stood on a granite boulder at the very edge of the tumult, contemplating the lost green volumes of water beneath and between the white bubbles. The roar seemed to recede; he felt almost hypnotized. He could just lean forward, shift one foot beyond the edge, and all would end very quickly. No suspense. His choice.

Somehow, the option was not attractive. He shook his head slowly and glanced up at the trees on the opposite side of the spill. Glints of silver shined through the boughs and moved along the trunks. It took him a moment to resolve what he was seeing. The trees were crawling with fist-sized silvery spiders. Two of them scuttled along a branch, carrying what appeared to be a dead jay. Another had stripped away a slice of bark from a pine trunk, revealing a wedge of white wood.

He thought of the Guest, and did not doubt his eyes.

Who controls them? he asked himself. *What do they mean?* He watched them for several minutes, vaguely bothered by their indifference, and then shrugged—yet another inexplicable marvel —and returned to the path.

Edward was back in the valley, freshly showered and in clean jeans and white shirt, by five o'clock, as he had promised. The amphitheater was more crowded than it had been for yesterday's meeting. No music was scheduled; instead, they had a minister, a psychologist, and a second ranger arrayed before the podium, waiting their turn after Elizabeth's introduction. Minelli grumbled at the New Age lineup, but he stayed. There was a bond growing between all of them, even those who had not spoken; they were in this together, and it was better to *be* together than otherwise, even if it meant sitting through a handful of puerile speakers.

Edward looked for but did not see the jilted blonde in the audience.

61——

After three days of interrogation by the FBI and agents from the National Security Agency, as well as six hours of intense grilling by the Secretary of the Navy, Senator Gilmonn had been set free from his office and apartment in Long Beach, California. He had ordered his chauffeur to drive east.

Nobody had been able, or particularly willing, to hang anything on him, though the trail of the arrow or monkey or whatever from the U.S.S. *Saratoga* to his car was reasonably well defined. Given more than a mere two and a half months of investigation and second-guessing, he might have been in some trouble, and the captain of the *Saratoga* relieved of his command, but things had changed markedly now in these United States. It was a different nation, a different government—functioning to all intents and purposes without a head. The President, under impeachment, was still in office but with most of his strings of influence and therefore power severed.

Gilmonn's incarceration, which might have been *pro forma* half a year ago, was now simply out of the question.

For all that, what had they accomplished? They had killed Lieutenant Colonel Rogers and perhaps thirty Forgers who had refused to vacate the desert around the bogey. They had blown the bogey into scattered pieces. Yet few involved in the conspiracy believed, now, that they had done anything to even postpone, much less remove, the sentence of death placed on the Earth.

He stood on the sand near the gravel road that passed within two miles of the site of the disintegrated bogey, binoculars hanging on a leather strap from his neck, face streaming with sweat under the brim of his hat. The white limousine that he had hired with his own money waited a few yards away, the chauffeur impassive behind his dark glasses and blue-black uniform.

Army and government trucks passed along the road every few minutes, some bearing radiation stickers; many of those outward bound, he knew, carried fragments of the bogey. He was not privy to what they were finding. Basically, his presence was tolerated, but now that the conspiracy had accomplished what virtually everybody wanted, those directly involved, while not charged, were being shunned. Scapegoats might be too strong a word . . . and it might not be.

Gilmonn unabashedly cursed Crockerman for having forced them all into an untenable and illegal no-man's-land of circumventions and conspiracies.

And still, deep in the Earth, what some—mostly geologists—had called "the freight trains" and others "bullets" rumbled toward their rendezvous. They could not be traced anymore, but few doubted they were there. The end might be a matter of days or weeks away.

Gilmonn entered the limousine's rear door and poured himself a Scotch and soda from the dispenser. "Tony," he said, slowly twirling the glass between the fingers of his right hand, "where do you want to be when it happens?"

The chauffeur did not hesitate. "In bed," he said. "Screwing my brains out, sir."

They had talked a great deal during the drive from Long Beach. Tony had been married only six months. Gilmonn thought of Madeline, his wife for twenty-three years, and while he wanted to be with her, he did not think they would be screwing their brains out. They would have their kids together, and their two grandchildren, perhaps in the ranch house in Arizona. A huge family gathering. The whole clan hadn't been together in five or six years.

"All that, and we didn't accomplish a *God*damned thing, Tony," he said with a sudden deep flood of bitterness. For the first time since the death of his son, he felt like cursing God.

"We don't know that for sure, Senator."

"I do," Gilmonn said. "If any man has a right to know he's failed, I do."

HOSTIAS ET PRECES TIBI, LAUDIS OFFERIMUS

62——

March 27

During his last hours, Trevor Hicks sat at his computer skimming and organizing genetic records sent from Mormon sources in Salt Lake City. He was staying at the home of an aerospace contractor named Jenkins, working in a broad living room with uncurtained windows overlooking Seattle and the bay. The work was not exciting but it was useful, and he felt at peace, whatever might happen. Despite his reputation for equanimity, Trevor Hicks had never been a particularly peaceful, self-possessed fellow. Bearing and presentation, by English tradition, masked his true self, which he had always visualized as frozen—with extra memory and peripheral accomplishments—somewhere around twenty-two years of age, enthusiastic, impressionable, quick-hearted.

He rolled his chair back from the table and greeted Mrs. Jenkins —Abigail—as she came through the front door, carrying two plastic bags full of groceries. Abigail was not possessed. All she knew was that her husband and Trevor were involved in something important, and secret. They had been working straight through the day and night, with very little sleep, and she brought in supplies to keep them reasonably comfortable and well fed.

She was not a bad cook.

They ate dinner at seven—steaks, salad, and a fine bottle of chianti. At seven-thirty, Jenkins and Hicks were back at work.

Being at peace, Hicks thought, worried him somewhat . . . He did not trust such flat, smooth emotions. He preferred a little undercurrent of turbulence; it kept him sharp.

The alarm went through Trevor Hicks's brain like a hot steel lance. He glanced at his watch—the battery had run down without his noticing, but it was late—and dropped the disk he had been examining. He pushed the chair back and stood before the living room window. Behind him, Jenkins looked up from a stack of requisition forms for medical supplies, surprised at Hicks's behavior. "What's up?"

"You don't feel it?" Hicks asked, pulling on a rope to open the curtains.

"Feel what?"

"There's something wrong. I'm hearing from . . ." He tried to place the source of the alarm, but it was no longer on the network. "I think it was Shanghai."

Jenkins stood up from the couch and called for his wife. "Is it starting?" he asked Hicks.

"Oh, Lord, I don't know," Hicks shouted, feeling another lance. The network was being *damaged*, links were being severed—that was all he could tell.

The window afforded a fine nighttime view of the myriad lights of downtown Seattle from Queen Anne Hill. The sky was overcast, but there had been no reports of thunderstorms. Still . . . The cloud deck was illuminated by brilliant flashes from above. One, two . . . a long pause, and by the time Mrs. Jenkins was in the living room, a third milky pulse of light.

Mrs. Jenkins looked on Hicks with some alarm. "It's just lightning, isn't it, Jenks?" she asked her husband.

"It's not lightning," Hicks said. The network was sending contradictory pulses of information. If a Boss was on-line, Hicks could not pick its voice out through the welter.

Then, clear and compelling, the messages came through to Hicks and Jenkins simultaneously.

Your site and the vessel in the sound are under attack.

"Attack?" Jenkins asked out loud. "Are they starting it now?"

"Shanghai Harbor was an ark site," Hicks said, his voice full of wonder. "It's been cut from the network. Nobody can reach Shanghai."

"What . . . What . . ." Jenkins was not used to thinking about these things, whatever his value to the network as a local organizer and procurer.

"I believe—"

His own inner thoughts, not the Boss's, said before the words could come out, *They're defending us but they can't stop everything from getting through. They've never told us this before, but they must have put ships or platforms or something in orbits to watch over the Earth—*

"—we're being bombarded—"

Light fell through the clouds and expanded.

this is a war after all but we haven't quite thought of it that way didn't suspect they would do this to us

"Jenks . . ."

Jenkins hugged his wife. Hicks saw the flash of red and white, the lifting of a wall of water and rock, and the rush of a darkening shock wave across the lights of the city and houses on the hill. The window exploded and he closed his eyes, experienced a brief instant of pain and blindness—

On the last leg of the marathon drive into San Francisco, speeding down an almost-deserted 101 at well over the speed limit, Arthur felt a severe pain in the back of his head. He gripped the wheel tightly and pulled to a halt at the side of the highway, his body rigid.

"What's wrong?" Francine asked.

He twisted around, threw his arms up on the back of the seat, and looked through the rear window of the station wagon. A hellish blue and purple glow was spreading to the north, above and beyond Santa Rosa and the wine country.

"What's wrong?" Francine repeated.

He twisted around to face forward again, and leaned over the wheel to peer up at the skies above San Francisco and the Bay Area.

"More asteroids, Dad!" Marty cried out. "More explosions!"

These were a lot closer and a lot brighter, however, as sharp as blowtorches, leaving red spots in his vision. The Bay Area was still over twenty miles away, and these flashes were high in the night sky. Some kind of action, another battle, was taking place perhaps no more than a hundred miles above San Francisco.

Francine started to get out of the car but he stopped her. She stared at him, face twisted with fear and anger, but said nothing.

Four more high flares, and then the night returned.

Arthur was almost surprised to find himself weeping. His anger was a frightening thing. "Those bastards," he said, pounding the wheel. "Those goddamn bloody fucking bastards."

"Daddy," Marty whimpered.

"Shut up, goddammit," Arthur shrieked, and then he grabbed his wife's arm with his left hand and reached for Marty in the rear seat with his right. He shook them firmly, repeating over and over again, "Don't ever forget this. If we survive, don't you ever, ever forget this."

"What happened, Art?" Francine asked, trying to keep calm. Marty was screaming now, and Arthur closed his eyes in grief and sorrow, the anger turned inward because he had lost control. He listened to a few of the voices on the network, trying to piece things together.

"Seattle's gone," he said. *Trevor Hicks, all the others.*

"Where's Gauge, Dad?" Marty asked through his tears. "Is Gauge alive?"

"I think so," Arthur said, shaking violently. The enormity. "They're trying to destroy our escape ships, the arks. They want to make sure there are no humans left."

"What? Why?" Francine asked.

"Remember," he repeated. "Just remember this, if we make it."

It took him almost twenty minutes to become calm enough to pull back into the slow lane. San Francisco and the Bay Area had been adequately protected. Suddenly, and without reservation—without any persuasion whatsoever—he loved the Bosses and the network and all the forces arrayed to protect and save them. His love was fierce and primal. *This is what a partisan feels like, watching his countryside get pillaged.*

"They bombed Seattle?" she asked. "The . . . aliens, or the Russians?"

"Not the Russians. The planet-eaters. They tried to bomb San Francisco, too." *And Cleveland, which had survived, and Shanghai, which had not, and who knows how many other ark sites?* A fresh shiver worked down from his shoulders to his sacrum. "Christ. What will the Russians do? What will *we* do?"

The car's steering wheel vibrated. Above the engine noise, they heard and felt a shuddering groan. The rock-borne vibrations of Seattle's death passed under them.

63————

At two in the morning, Washington, D.C., time, Irwin Schwartz reached out for the urgently beeping phone from his office cot and punched the speaker button. "Yes?" Only then did he hear the powerful whuff-whuff of helicopter blades and the screaming roar of jet turbines.

It was the late night White House military staff duty officer. "Mr. Schwartz, Mr. Crockerman is being evacuated. He wishes you to join him on the helicopter."

Schwartz had duly noted the officer's reluctance to call Crockerman "President." He was now strictly "Mr. Crockerman." If you don't act the office, you don't get the title. "What sort of emergency?"

"There have been strikes on Seattle and some kind of action over Cleveland, Charleston, and San Francisco."

"Jesus. Russian?"

"Don't know, sir. Sir, you should get out on the lawn as soon as possible."

"Right." Schwartz did not even grab his coat.

On the White House lawn, dressed in the undershirt and pants he had worn as he slept, Schwartz ducked instinctively under the high, massive rotor blades and ran up the ladder, his bald head unprotected against the chill downdraft of spring night air. A Secret Service agent stood by until the hatch was closed, and then watched the helicopter lift away to take them all to Grissom Air Force Base in Indiana.

The staff officer and a Marine guard hugged Crockerman's sides, the Marine carrying the "football" and the staff officer carrying a mobile data and command center—MODACC for short—hooked up to the helicopter's communications system.

There were three Secret Service agents aboard the craft, as well as Nancy Congdon, the President's personal secretary. Had Mrs.

Crockerman been in the White House, she would have been evacuated as well.

"Mr. President," the staff officer began, "the Secretary of Defense is in Colorado. State is in Miami at a governors' meeting. The Vice President is in Chicago. I believe the Speaker of the House is being airlifted from his home. I have some information regarding what our satellites and other sensors have already told us." He spoke louder than he needed to over the engine noise; the cabin was well insulated.

The President and all the others aboard listened closely.

"Seattle is gone, and Charleston is a ruin—the strike appeared to be centered at twenty klicks out in the ocean there. But our satellites show no missile launches from the Soviet Union or any fish at sea. No missiles at all were detected coming from the Earth. And apparently some sort of defensive system came into play over San Francisco and Cleveland, perhaps elsewhere as well . . ."

"We don't have that kind of defense," Crockerman said hoarsely, barely audible. He fixed his eyes on Schwartz. Schwartz thought he looked two days dead at least, eyes pale and lifeless. The vote to impeach had taken the last bit of starch from him. Tomorrow would be—*would have been*—the beginning of the Senate trial on whether he would stay in office or be removed.

"Correct, sir."

"It's not the Russians," observed one of the Secret Service agents, a tall black Kentuckian of middle years.

"Not the Russians," Crockerman repeated, his face taking on some color now. "Who, then?"

"The planet-eaters," Schwartz said.

"It's begun?" the young Marine lieutenant asked, gripping the briefcase as if to keep it from flying away.

"God only knows," Schwartz said, shaking his head.

The MODACC beeped and the staff officer listened intently over his sound-insulated headphones. "Mr. President, it's Premier Arbatov in Moscow."

Crockerman stared once again at Schwartz for a long moment before reaching for the mike and headphones. Schwartz knew what the stare meant. *He's still the Man, damn us all to hell.*

64——

Arthur drove the car into the driveway of Grant and Danielle's hillside home in Richmond just before midnight. He was still shaken; the memory of the network's pain and loss lingered like a bizarre, bitter-sharp taste on the tongue. He sat with hands on the wheel, staring straight ahead at the rough wood garage door, and then turned to Francine.

"Are you all right?" she asked.

"I think so." He glanced over the seat at Marty. The boy sprawled on the back seat, eyes closed, his head lolling slightly over the edge, mouth open.

"Thank God he's asleep," Francine said. "You gave us both a scare."

"I gave you a scare?" Arthur asked, his weariness breaking down before a sudden upwelling of anger. "Jesus, if you could have felt what I felt—"

"Please," Francine said, face deadly grim. "We're here. There's Grant now."

She opened the car door and stepped out. Arthur stayed in the seat, confused, then closed his eyes for a moment, tentatively searching for the network, trying to learn what had happened. There had been little on the radio beyond repeated reports of some unknown disaster in Seattle; it had been less than an hour.

He half expected the superpowers to stumble into nuclear war; perhaps members of the network were preventing that even now. But he had to go on faith. For the moment, he was cut loose from the circuit of network communications.

Arthur took a murmuring Marty into his arms. Grant showed them to a bedroom with a queen-sized bed and a folding cot. Danielle—now asleep, Grant said—had made up the beds and laid out towels for them, as well as putting a late night snack of fruit and soup on the kitchen counter. Francine tucked Marty into the cot and joined Grant and Arthur in the kitchen.

"Have you heard what happened?" she asked Grant.

"No . . ." Grant's shirt and slacks were wrinkled and his silver-gray hair was tousled; he had apparently nodded off on the couch, getting up as he heard their car approach.

"We saw a flash to the north," Arthur said.

"Arthur thinks it was Seattle," Francine said. Her look was almost a challenge: *Go ahead, tell us you know. Tell us how you know.*

Arthur stared at her, dismayed. Then it came to him: she was suddenly amidst family. She did not have to rely completely on him. She could vent a few of her own doubts and tensions; Marty was asleep and wouldn't hear. He understood this well enough, but it still hurt. On top of the pain he had felt earlier, this small betrayal was almost more than he could stand.

"We heard on the radio," Arthur said, taking the easy way out. "Something happened in Seattle."

Francine nodded, her face bloodless, teeth clenched. "Radio," she said.

"What, for God's sake? I have a brother in Seattle," Grant said.

The airborne sound of Seattle's death rattled the house windows. Grant glanced warily at the ceiling. Arthur checked his watch and nodded.

"It's gone," Arthur told him. "The entire metropolitan area."

"Jesus Christ!" Grant cried, jumping from his stool. He went to the wall phone at the end of the counter and fumbled at the keypad.

"We didn't hear that on the radio," Francine said softly, her shoulders slumping. She stared past her folded hands at the carpet.

"It's busy. Everything's tied up," Grant said. He loped into the den to switch on the television. "When did you hear this?"

"We saw the flash about fifty minutes ago," Francine said, glancing up guiltily at Arthur. He held out his hand, wriggling his fingers, and she grasped it, covering her face with her other hand. She shuddered, but no tears would come.

The commentator's voice came to them through Grant's expensive sound system, resonant and authoritative, but with more than a hint of fear. "—reports now from Seattle and Charleston, that the two cities have been destroyed by what appear to be nuclear explosions, but there are contradictory reports of no accompanying radiation. We still have no idea what actually happened although it is now clear that at least these two seaboard cities, on the

East and West Coasts, have been leveled by unprecedented disaster. The government has issued statements that our nation is not yet in a state of war, which leads some sources to state that the explosions were not caused by nuclear missiles, at least not those of the Soviet Union. Indeed, flashes over the cities of San Francisco and Cleveland have led some to speculate that the destruction of the Earth has begun, and that we are witnessing—"

"Tell him," Francine said, keeping her voice low. "Tell him. I believe you. Really I do. They need to know."

Arthur shook his head. She brought her hands over her face again, but her trembling had stopped. "I can't tell them, and you must not," Arthur said. "It would only hurt them."

Danielle appeared in the hallway door, wearing a long silk gown with a chenille robe thrown over it. "What's happened?" she asked.

Francine embraced her and led her into the den. Arthur regarded the untouched bowls of soup, thinking, *Not yet . . . But it can't be much longer.*

65———

A knock on his tent-cabin door awakened Edward at eight o'clock. He glanced at his watch and scrambled into his pants, then opened the door to see Minelli and a plump black-haired woman in black T-shirt and black jeans. Minelli reached out a hand. "Congratulate me," he said. "I've found Inez."

"Congratulations," Edward said.

"Inez Espinoza, this is my friend Edward Shaw. He's into rocks, too. Edward, Inez."

"Pleased to meet you," Inez said.

"We met at the dance last night. Pity you weren't there."

"I was depressed," Edward said. "I couldn't handle company."

"There's a story going around about robot insects. Inez says she saw a bunch of them up behind Yosemite Village. What do you think they are?"

"I saw some, too," Edward said. "Wait a minute. I'll get dressed and we'll fix breakfast."

Over Coleman-stove toast and hard-boiled eggs, Edward told them what he had seen below the Mist Trail. Inez nodded and regarded him with her large brown eyes, obviously content to say little.

"What do you think they are?"

"Hell, if the bastards can make fake aliens, they can turn out robot spiders. They're surveying the Earth. Conducting a general assay before they blow it up."

Inez spontaneously began to weep.

"Hey, let's not talk about that shit," Minelli said. "She's sensitive. Her old man was killed on a Harley on the highway a couple of days ago. She was thrown clear." Inez sobbed and dabbed at her eyes, revealing a nasty scrape and bruise on her forearm. "She hitched a ride here. She's a sweetheart." Minelli hugged her and she hugged him back.

A small, skeletally thin man with a high, square forehead walked past the rock where they breakfasted. He carried a baseball bat almost as big as himself and seemed bemused.

"What's up, man?" Minelli asked.

"Just heard it on the radio. The aliens nuked Seattle and Charleston and Shanghai last night. I was born in Charleston." He continued down the path, bat dangling from an unenthused wrist.

Inez hiccuped spasmodically.

"What're you going to do?" Minelli called after him.

"Going to catch some of those fucking chrome bugs out in the woods and smash them," the man answered, not stopping. "I want to get my licks in."

Minelli set down his tin cup of tea and slid down from the rock. Inez took his offered hand and did likewise with surprising grace. "I think it's time we hiked up to Glacier Point," Minelli said quietly. "Want to come?"

Edward nodded, then shook his head. "Not yet. I'll be up there soon."

"All right. Inez is coming with me. We'll tent out. Welcome to join us."

"Thanks."

The pair walked down the path under the pines to Curry Village.

Edward climbed the stairs into his tent cabin and pulled a topographical map of the valley and regions south from his map folder. Lying on his stomach across the beds, he fingered the Four Mile Trail up to Union Point, and then on to Glacier Point, and compared other vantages.

There were none better and so accessible. Glacier Point offered some facilities. *But if things get rocking, won't it just split off and fall, and take us with it?*

Did it matter? What was an hour or so, one way or another?

Edward entered his card number into the pay phone keypad and dialed Stella's home number in Shoshone. After three rings, Bernice Morgan answered, and told him Stella was at the store, taking inventory. "Life goes on," she said. "I can transfer you from here."

After a few clicks and hums, the store phone rang and Stella answered.

"This is Edward," he said. "I've been wondering what you're up to."

"The usual," Stella answered. "Where are you now?"

"Oh, I'm in Yosemite. Settled in. Waiting."

"Is it what you thought it would be?"

"Better, actually. It's beautiful. There aren't very many people."

"What did I tell you?"

"You've heard about Seattle and Charleston?"

"Of course."

Edward detected a hint of resolve in her voice. "Still planning on staying in Shoshone?"

"I'm a homebody," Stella said. "We heard from my sister, though. She's coming home from Zimbabwe. We're picking her up in Las Vegas the day after tomorrow. You're welcome to join us . . ."

He surveyed the riverbanks and trees and meadows beyond the clutch of pay phones. *This feels right. This is where I belong.* "I was hoping I could convince you to come here. With your mother."

"I'm glad you asked, but . . ."

"I know. You're home. So am I."

"We're a stubborn pair, aren't we?"

"Minelli is here. I don't know where Reslaw is. Minelli's found a girlfriend."

"Good for him. How about you?"

Edward chuckled. "I'm just too damned choosy," he said.

"Don't be. You know . . ." Stella stopped, and there was silence over the line for several seconds. "Well, maybe you know."

"If we could have more time," Edward said.

"Is the deal still on?" she asked.

"Deal?"

"If this all turns out to be a false alarm."

"We still have a deal."

"I'll be thinking about you," Stella said. "Don't forget."

What would life with Stella be like? She was tough-minded, intelligent, and more than a touch willful; they might not get along, and then again they might.

Both of them knew they would not have the time to find out. "I won't forget," he said.

In the Curry Village general store, he stocked up on dried soups and various pouches of gourmet camp food. The supplies were running out. "Trucks haven't come in here for two days," the young woman clerk said. "We keep calling, they keep saying they're coming. But nobody's doing much now. Just sitting back and waiting. Damned morbid, if you ask me."

He added a pair of dark sunglasses and paid for the supplies with the last of his cash. All he had now were credit cards and a few traveler's checks. No matter.

He had hoisted the plastic bag and was about to leave when he saw the blond woman at the back of the store, picking through a bin of half-rotten apples. Taking a concealed deep breath, Edward replaced his bag on the counter, motioned with his finger to the clerk that he would be back, and walked to the rear.

"Find your husband?" he asked. The woman glanced at him, smiled sadly, and shook her head.

"No such bad luck," she said. She held up a particularly bruised apple and inspected it ruefully. "I'm a fruitophile, and look what they offer."

"I have some pretty good apples in my . . . Back at the cabin. I'll be leaving for Glacier Point soon. You're welcome to them. Too heavy to carry more than one or two on a hike."

"That's very kind," she said. She dropped the apple into the bin and held out her hand. Slender, cool, strong fingers; he shook the hand with moderate firmness. "My name is Betsy," she said, "and my maiden name is Sothern."

"I'm Edward Shaw." He decided to go for broke. "I'm not with anybody."

"Oh?"

"For the duration," he said.

"How long is that?" she asked.

"Somebody said less than a week. Nobody knows for sure."

"Where's your cabin?"

"Not far from here."

"If you feed me a nice, crisp, juicy apple," she said, "I'm liable to follow you anywhere."

Edward's smile was spontaneous and broad. "Thank you," he said. "This way."

"Thank *you*," Betsy said.

In the tent, he found her the best red apple and polished it with a clean dishcloth. She bit into it, wiped away a dribble of juice running down her chin, and watched him arrange the supplies in his backpack.

"I hope you're not one of those ignorant people," she said abruptly. "I don't mean to sound ungrateful, but if you think everything's rosy, and God's going to save us, or something like that . . ."

Edward shook his head.

"Good. I thought you looked smart. Sweet and smart. We don't have much time left, do we?"

"No." He flipped the pack over and buckled it, glancing at her.

"You know, if I had it all to do over again," she said, "I'd choose men like you."

This pricked Edward a little. "That's what all the beautiful women say. There aren't any maidens in foxholes, or something to that effect."

"Jesus." She smiled. "I like that. Do you . . . pardon me for asking . . . do you have any devastating, immediately fatal communicable diseases?"

"No," Edward said. "Hardly any."

"Neither do I. Are you expecting anyone?"

"No."

"Neither am I. Pleased to make your acquaintance." She held out her hand, and Edward shook it delicately by the fingertips, then grinned and pulled her toward him.

66

The network came alive in Arthur's head at eight in the morning. He opened his eyes, wide awake but feeling as if he had been stunned, and rolled over to shake Francine's shoulder. "We have to be going," he said. He got out of bed and slipped into his pants. "Get Marty dressed."

Francine moaned. "Yes, sir," she said. "What now?"

"I'm not sure," he said. "We've been told to be a certain place in an hour. In San Francisco."

Marty sat up on the cot, rubbing his eyes. "Come on, sport," Francine said. "Marching orders."

"I'm sleepy," Marty said.

Francine grabbed Arthur's arm and pulled him close to her, staring up into his face with a stern expression. "I'm only going to say this once. If you're crazy and this is all for nothing, I'll . . ." She grabbed his nose, and not in play; the tweak she gave it was exquisitely painful. Eyes watering, Arthur took her hand in both of his and rubbed it. "Do you understand me?"

He nodded. "We have to hurry." Despite his throbbing nose, he was almost ecstatic. *Why hustle all of us somewhere this early in the morning? They have plans . . .*

His ecstasy faded when he met Grant, wrapped in a robe, in the hallway, with his daughter following close behind. "You came in awful late to be getting everybody up so early," Grant said. "We've had quite a night. I don't think I slept more than an hour . . . Danielle may not have slept at all."

Danielle sat at the kitchen counter, drinking a cup of coffee, when they trooped through the swinging door. Her face was pale and she had been smoking; the brimming ashtray told a plain tale of a full night of cigarettes. "Such early birds," she said unenthusiastically.

"We have to be going," Arthur said.

Danielle raised an eyebrow. "We thought you'd stay awhile."

"We thought so, too. But I spent last night thinking, and we should be . . . out of here as soon as possible. There's a lot to be done."

Danielle leaned her head to one side in query as Francine and Marty came into the kitchen. Marty smiled shyly at Becky; Becky ignored him, glancing between her mother and father.

"What in hell is going on with this family?" Danielle asked, her voice sharp. "Goddammit, Francine, where are you going?"

"I don't know," Francine answered bluntly. "Arthur's in charge."

"Are you all crazy?" Danielle asked.

"Now, Danny," Grant said.

"I've been up all night trying to figure this out. Why are you leaving now? Why?" She was on the edge of hysteria. "Something's going on. Something with the government. Is that why you're here? You're going to leave us all, let us die!"

Arthur's heart sank. She might be close enough to the truth. All his excitement seemed to drain.

"We're going into the city today," he said. "I have business there, and Marty and Francine have to come with me."

"Can we come along?" Danielle asked. "All of us. We're family. I would feel a lot better if we all came along."

Francine looked at him, eyes filled with tears. Marty's lower lip was quivering, and Becky stood beside her mother, one arm around her, confused into silence.

"No," Grant said. Danielle jerked her head around.

"What?"

"No. We will not panic. Arthur has work to do. If it's work for the government, fine. But we will not panic in this house if I have anything to say about it."

"They're *going someplace,*" Danielle said softly.

Grant agreed to that with a brief nod. "Maybe so. But we have no business horning in."

"That's goddamned reasonable of you," Danielle said. "We're your goddamned family. What are you doing for *us?*"

Grant searched Arthur's face, and Arthur sensed his confusion and fear and determination not to let things get out of control. "I'm keeping us in our house," he said, "and I'm keeping us civil, and dignified."

"Dignity," Danielle said. She upended her cup of coffee on the floor and rushed out of the kitchen. Becky stood by the spill and sobbed silently, painfully.

"Daddy," she said between tight spasms.

"We're just arguing," Grant told her. He kneeled beside her and wrapped an arm around her shoulder. "We'll be okay."

Arthur, feeling like an automaton, gathered their things from the bathroom and spare bedroom. Francine sought her sister in the master bedroom and tried to soothe her.

Grant confronted Arthur in the driveway. Morning fog was thick over the hills, and the sun was a promise of yellow warmth behind the mist. A few mourning doves sang their sweet, nostalgic stupid song behind the hedges. "Are you still working for the government?" he asked.

"No," Arthur said.

"They're not taking you all into Cheyenne Mountain or something like that? Putting you aboard a space shuttle?"

"No," Arthur said, feeling a twinge. *What do you hope is going to happen . . . ? Something not too far from what Grant is hypothesizing?*

"Are you coming back here this evening? Just going into town, and then . . . coming back?"

Arthur shook his head. "I don't think so," he said.

"You're going to drive, wander until . . . it happens?"

"I don't know," Arthur said.

Grant grimaced and shook his head. "I've wondered how long we could keep it all together. We are all going to die, aren't we, and we can't do anything?"

Arthur felt as if he were breathing shards of glass.

"We face these things our own way," Grant said. "If you're in a car, driving, maybe everybody can keep together. Keep going on. If we all stay at home, maybe . . . too. Also."

Please, you are powerful, you are Godlike, Arthur prayed to the Bosses at the top of the network, *take us all, rescue us all. Please.*

But the information already passed on to him made that prayer a hollow thing. And he had no assurance his family was going to be saved; no assurance at all, only a strong, living hope. He reached out for Grant's hand and clasped it between his own.

"I have always admired you," Arthur said. "You're not like me. But I want you to know that I've always admired you, and Danielle. You are good people. Wherever we are, whatever happens, you are in our thoughts. And I hope we will be in yours."

"You will be," Grant said, jaw clenched. Danielle and Francine came through the front door, Marty in tow. Becky did not come out, but watched through the front bay window, a small radiantly blond ghost.

Arthur sat behind the wheel again after making sure Marty was strapped securely into the station wagon's back seat. Grant held Danielle tightly with one arm and waved with the other.

Nothing so different about this, Arthur thought. *Simple family leave-taking.* He backed the station wagon out of the driveway and maneuvered on the narrow street, glancing at his watch. One hour to get where they had to be.

Francine's face was soaked with tears, but she made no sound, staring ahead, her arm hanging limply out the window.

Marty waved, and they drove away.

Winds from the ocean had driven the smoke of eastern fires inland, and once the mist had burned off, the air was fine and blue and clear. Arthur drove them across the heavy, gray-girdered San Francisco–Oakland Bay Bridge, almost empty of traffic, taking the 480 off-ramp to the Embarcadero and turning south for China Basin Street and the Central Basin.

"Do *you* know where we're going?" Francine asked.

He nodded; in a way, he did know. He was following directions, but he had a picture of a fifty-foot fishing boat. Twenty passengers sat in the sun on the rear deck, waiting for them.

He parked the car in the lot at Agua Vista Park. "We're walking from here," he said. "It isn't far."

"What about the luggage?" Francine asked.

"My toys?" Marty chimed in.

"Leave them here," Arthur said. He opened the tailgate and pulled out the box containing Francine's disks and papers. That was the only thing he would insist they bring. He let Marty hold it.

The excitement was returning; he could feel sad later about those left behind. Right now, it seemed certain what he had most hoped for was happening. The network was not blocking his way, or telling him to go back; he was being urged on. Only a few minutes remained.

"We're taking a boat?" Francine asked. He nodded. She lifted her purse, and Arthur shook his head: leave it. She slipped a plastic pack of family photos from her wallet and tossed the rest aside almost angrily, face contorted.

"Aren't we going to lock the car?" Marty asked. Arthur hurried them away, leaving the tailgate open.

You do not need possessions. Bring nothing but the clothes on your back. Empty your pockets of change, keys, everything. Bring only yourselves.

He tossed his keys and change, wallet and comb, onto the asphalt.

They walked through an open gate in a chain link fence onto a long, broad pier, lined on each side with the gently bobbing masts of fishing boats. "Hurry," he urged.

Francine pushed Marty ahead of her.

"All this for a boat ride," she said.

At the end of the pier, the boat he had visualized awaited them. There were indeed about twenty people standing and sitting in the back. A young woman in faded jeans and a windbreaker guided them onto the ramp and they boarded quickly, taking their places in the back. Marty perched on a smelly pile of worn netting. Francine sat on a winch.

"All right," the young woman shouted. "That's the last."

Only now did Arthur dare to let his breath out. He glanced around at the people on the boat. Most were younger than he; four children were in the group besides Marty. There were no passengers past late middle age. As he looked into their faces, he saw that many had been involved in the network, and yet they were not being rewarded for their labors. Otherson the network had been left behind; many not on the network, like Marty and Francine, were going along.

Still, nobody seemed to have any idea where they were headed. The boat pulled into the choppy bay waters and headed north. The sun cast welcome warmth, and the winds over the bay took most of it away.

The young woman came around to each of them and held out her hand. "Jewelry, please," she said. "Rings, watches, necklaces. Everything." Everybody handed over the valuables without complaint. Arthur removed his wedding band and nodded for Francine to do likewise. Marty surrendered his Raccoon wristwatch without complaining. He was very sober and very quiet.

"Do you know where we're going?" a young man dressed in a business suit asked the woman as he handed her a gold Rolex.

"Out near Alcatraz," she said. "That's what the skipper tells me."

"I mean, after that?"

She shook her head. "Has everybody turned in everything?"

"Will we get our things back?" a small Asiatic woman asked.

"No," the young woman in jeans replied. "Sorry."

"Is Becky and Aunt Danielle and Uncle Grant coming with us?" Marty asked solemnly, watching sea gulls glide over the boat's wake.

"No," Francine answered, taking the word from Arthur's lips. "Nobody else is coming with us."

"Are we going to leave the Earth?" Marty asked. The adults around him visibly cringed.

"Shhh," the young woman said, maneuvering her way past him. "Wait and see."

Arthur reached out and gently pinched Marty's ear between thumb and forefinger. *Smart boy,* he thought. He looked out across the water, feeling the bay's whitecaps thump rhythmically against the boat hull. Several people were becoming seasick. A nut-brown, gray-bearded man of about forty came down from the pilot house and passed out plastic bags. "Use them," he said gruffly. "Everybody. We don't need anybody sicker than they have to be, and we certainly don't need chain reactions."

Arthur surveyed the city's skyline, blinking at the salt spray. *All that work. Around the world. Thousands of years.* He could not even begin to encompass the enormity. Francine came to him and wrapped her arms around him tightly. He leaned his cheek against her hair, not daring to feel as optimistic as he wanted to be.

"Can you tell me what's going on now?" she asked.

Marty snuggled up to them. "We're going away, Mom," he said.

"Are we?" she asked Arthur.

He swallowed and barely moved his head, then nodded. "Yes. I think we are."

"Where?"

"I don't know."

They cut through the water under the San Francisco–Oakland Bay Bridge, Yerba Buena Island and Treasure Island to their right, tall mounds of dark green and brown on the slate-colored, white-flecked waters.

"See, Marty?" Francine said, pointing up at the bridge's maze of girders and the huge piers and tower legs. "We drove over that just a while ago."

Marty gave the wonder cursory attention. The sea was getting

rougher. Alcatraz, a desolate rock cluttered with ancient buildings, a water tower prominent, lay dead ahead. The boat slowed,
its motors cutting back to a steady chug-chug-chug. The young
woman passed among them again, examining everybody closely
for unnecessary belongings. Nobody protested; they were either
numb with fear, seasick, exhausted, or all three. She smiled at
Marty in passing to the rear again.

The boat stopped, drifting in the chop. The passengers began to
murmur. Then Arthur saw something square and gray rise beyond
the port gunwale. He thought immediately of a submarine sail, but
it was much smaller, barely as wide as a double doorway and no
more than ten feet out of the water.

"We'll have to be careful," the woman told them, standing on a
short ladder near the pilot house. "The water's rough. We're all
going to climb down through this doorway." An empty black
square appeared in the gray block. "There's a spiral staircase going
down into the ship. The ark. If you have a child younger than
twelve, please hold its hand and be very careful."

A burly fisherman in a black turtleneck sweater struggled to
extend a short gangplank to the block's entrance.

"We *are* leaving," Francine said, her voice like a girl's.

One by one, in silence, they crossed the none-too-stable plank,
helped by the fisherman and the young woman. Each person
vanished into the block. When his family's turn came, Arthur went
first, then helped Francine lift Marty across, and grasped her hand
firmly as she lurched over.

"Oh, Lord," Francine said in a trembling voice as they descended the steep, narrow spiral staircase.

"Be brave, Mom," Marty encouraged. He smiled at Arthur,
walking before him, their heads almost level.

After descending some thirty feet, they stepped through a half-
oval entrance into a circular room with three doorways clustered
on the opposite side. The walls were peach yellow and the lighting
was even and warm, soothing. When all twenty stood in the room,
the young woman joined them. The fisherman and other crew
members did not. The half-oval hatch slid shut quietly behind her.
A low moan rose from several in the room, and one man about ten
years younger than Arthur sank to his knees, hands clasped in
prayer.

"We're inside a spaceship," the young woman said. "We have
quarters farther down. In a little while, maybe a couple of hours,

we'll be leaving the Earth. Some of you know this already. The rest of you should be patient, and please don't be afraid."

Arthur clasped his wife's and son's hands and closed his eyes, not knowing whether he was terrified, or exalted, or already in mourning. If they were aboard a spaceship, and all the work he and the others in the network had done was coming to fruition, then the Earth would soon die.

His family might survive. Yet they would never again breathe the fresh cold sea air or stand in the open beneath the sun. Faces passed before him, behind his eyelids: relatives, friends, colleagues. Harry, when he had been healthy. Arthur thought of Ithaca Feinman and wondered whether she would be aboard an ark. Probably not. There were so few spaces available, fewer still now that the ships in Charleston and Seattle had been destroyed. A breeding population, little more.

And all the rest . . .

The younger man prayed out loud, fervent, face screwed up in an agony of concentration. Arthur could very easily have joined him.

67——

A loose group of ten took to the Four Mile Trail in the early morning, Edward and Betsy among them. They hiked through the shadows of Douglas fir and Ponderosa pine, pine pitch tartly scenting the still morning air. The climb was relatively mild at first, rising gradually to the vigorous Sentinel Creek ford some two hundred feet above the valley floor.

By eleven they were on the steep ascending trail cut into the granite façade to the west of Sentinel Rock.

Edward paused to sit and take a breather, and to admire Betsy in her climbing shorts.

"They used to charge to climb this," Betsy said, propping one well-made leg against a ledge to retie her hiking boot.

He looked over the edge at the distance they had already

climbed and shook his head. By noon, they had peeled out of their sweatshirts and tied the sleeves around their hips. They stopped for a water break. The ten, by now, were spread along a half mile of the trail like goats in a terraced-rock zoo exhibit. One young man a few dozen feet above Edward had enough energy to beat his chest and let loose a Tarzan cry of dominance. Then he grinned foolishly and waved.

"Me Jane, him nuts," Betsy commented.

Their good cheer continued as they stood at Union Point and looked down across the valley, leaning on the iron railings. The sky was only slightly smoky, and the air was warming as they ascended. "We could stop here," Betsy suggested. "The view's pretty good."

"Onward." Edward put on a valiant face and pointed to the goal. "One more heavy climb."

By one o'clock they had hiked over a seemingly endless series of switchbacks up the bare granite slope, stopping briefly to examine the manzanita growth. They then followed a much more reasonable, comparatively level trail to Glacier Point.

Minelli and his companion Inez had already pitched tents in the woods behind the asphalt paths leading up to the point's railed terraces. They waved at Edward and Betsy and motioned for them to come over and share their picnic lunch.

"We're going to take in the view," Edward called to them. "We'll be with you in a little bit."

Leaning on the rail of the lowest terrace, they surveyed the valley from end to end, and the mountains beyond. Birdsong punctuated the steady whisper of the breezes.

"It is *so* peaceful," Betsy said. "You'd think nothing could ever happen here . . ."

Edward tried to picture his father, standing by the railing more than two decades ago, waving his hands, clowning as his mother snapped his picture with a Polaroid camera. They had driven up to the point that time. An hour later, they had been on their way home, ending the last happy time of his childhood. The last time, as a child, he had felt he *could* have been happy.

He touched Betsy's arm and smiled at her. "Best view in the world," he said.

"Grandstand seat," Betsy agreed, shading her eyes against the high bright sun. They stood near the edge for several minutes, arms around each other, then turned and walked back to the tents to join Minelli and Inez.

The afternoon progressed slowly, leisurely. Minelli had bought a stick of dry salami in the store, and two loaves of bread; Inez had somehow come up with a large wedge of Cheddar cheese. "We had a whole wheel a few days ago," she said. "Don't ask how we got it." Her smile was tough and childish and sweet all at once.

Minelli passed around cans of beer, warm but still welcome, and they ate slowly, saying little, listening to the birds and the hum of the wind through the trees behind them. When they had finished, Edward spread a sleeping bag on the grass and invited Betsy to lie back and doze with him. The climb had not been exhausting, but the sun was warm and the air was sweet, and large fat bees were buzzing in lazy curves around them. They were well fed, and the beer had made Edward supremely drowsy.

Betsy lay beside him, head resting in the crook of his arm. "Happy?" she asked him.

Edward opened his eyes and stared up at white clouds against a brilliant blue sky. "Yes," he said. "I really am."

"So am I."

A few dozen yards away, other campers were singing folk songs and sixties and seventies tunes. Their voices drifted in the restless, warm air, finally melding with the wind and the hum of the bees.

68

Walter Samshow celebrated his seventy-sixth birthday aboard the Glomar *Discoverer,* cruising in circles a few kilometers beyond the zone where huge gouts of oxygen had once risen to the ocean surface. The bubbling had stopped three days before.

The ship's galley prepared a two-meter-long birthday cake in the shape of a sea serpent—or an oarfish, depending on whether you asked the cook or Chao, who had seen several oarfish in his time, but no sea serpents.

At five in the afternoon, the cake was cut with some ceremony under the canvas awning spread on the fantail. Bible-leaf slices of the serpent were served on the ship's best china, accompanied by champagne or nonalcoholic punch for those ostensibly on duty.

Sand silently toasted his partner with a raised glass of champagne at the stern. Samshow smiled and tasted the cake. He was trying to decide what flavor the peculiar mud-colored icing was—someone had suggested sweetened agar earlier—when the ocean all around suddenly glowed a brilliant blue-green, even beneath the intense sun.

Samshow was reminded of his youth, standing on the beach at Cape Cod on the night of the Fourth of July, waiting for fireworks and tossing his own firecrackers into the surf just as their fuses burned short. The firecrackers had exploded below the surface with a silent puff of electric-green light.

The crew on the rear deck fell silent. Some looked at their shipmates in puzzlement, having missed the phenomenon.

In rapid succession, from the northern horizon to the southern horizon, more flashes illuminated the ocean.

"I think," Samshow said in his best professorial tone, "we are about to have some mysteries answered." He knelt to put his plate and glass of champagne down on the deck, and then stood, with Sand's help, by the railing.

To the west, the entire sea and sky began to roar.

A curtain of cloud and blinding light rose from the western horizon, then slowly curled about like a snake in pain. One end of the curtain slid over the sea with amazing speed in their direction, and Samshow cringed, not wanting it all to end just yet. There was more he wanted to see; more minutes he wanted to live.

The hull shuddered violently and the steel masts and wires sang. The railing vibrated painfully under his hand.

The ocean filled with a continuous light, miles of water no more opaque than a thick green lump of glass held over a bonfire.

"It's the bombs," Sand said. "They're going off. Up and down the fractures—"

The sea to the west blistered in a layer perhaps a hundred meters thick, scoured by the snaking curtain, bursting into ascending and descending ribbons of fluid and foam. Between the fragments of the peeled sea—the skin of an inconceivable bubble—rose a massive, shimmering transparent mass of superheated steam, perhaps two miles wide. Its revealed surface immediately condensed into a pale opalescent hemisphere. Other such bubbles broke and released and condensed from horizon to horizon, churning the sea into a mint-green froth. The clouds of vapor ascended in twisted pillars to the sky. The hiss and roar and deep churning, gut-shaking booms became unbearable. Samshow clapped his hands to his ears and waited for what he knew must come.

A scatter of calved steam bubbles broke just a few hundred meters to the east, with more on the oppositeside. The turbulence spread in a high wall of water that caught the ship lengthwise and broke her spine, twisting her fore half clockwise, aft counterclockwise, metal screaming, rivets failing like cannon shots, plates ripping with a sound curiously like tearing paper, beams snapping. Samshow flew over the side and seemed for a moment suspended in froth and flying debris. He felt all that he was a part of—the sea, the sky, the air and mist around him—abruptly accelerate upward. A much larger steam bubble surfaced directly beneath the ship.

There was of course no time to think, but a thought from the instant before lingered like a strobed image, congealed in his mind before his body was instantly boiled and smashed into something hardly distinguishable from the foam around it: *I wish I could hear that sound, of the Earth's crust being spread wide.*

Around the globe, wherever the bomb-laying machines had infested the deep-ocean trenches, long sinuous curtains of hot vapor reached high into the atmosphere and pierced through. As the millions of glassy columns of steam condensed into cloud, and the cloud hit the cold upper masses of air and flashed into rain, the air that had been pushed aside now rushed back with violent thunderclaps. Tsunamis rolled outward beneath corresponding turbulent expanding concentric fronts of high and low pressure.

The end had begun.

DIES IRAE

69——

Below San Francisco Bay, hours after boarding the ark, the young woman who had guided them on the fishing boat—her name was Clara Fogarty—went among the twenty in the waiting room and spoke to them, answering questions, trying to keep them all calm. She seemed none too calm herself; fragile, on the edge.

Help her, Arthur was ordered. He and several others immediately obeyed. After a few minutes, he circled back through the people to Francine and took her hands. Marty hugged him fiercely.

"I'm going to visit the areas where we'll be staying," he said to Francine.

"The network is telling you this?"

"No," he said, looking to one side, frowning slightly. "Something else. A voice I've not heard before. I'm to meet somebody."

Francine wiped her face with her hands and kissed him. Arthur lifted Marty with an *oomph* and told him to take care of his mother. "I'll be back in a little while."

He stood beside Clara Fogarty at the middle hatch on the side opposite where they had entered. The hatch—little more than an outline in the wall's surface—slid open and they passed through quickly, before they had a clear impression of what was on the other side.

A brightly illuminated broad hallway, curving *down,* stretched before them. The hatch closed and they regarded each other nervously. More hatches lined both sides of the hallway.

"Artificial gravity?" Clara Fogarty asked him.

"I don't know," he said.

At a silent request, they stepped forward. They remained upright in relation to the floor, with no odd sensations other than the visual. At the end of the hallway, another open hatchway awaited them; beyond was a warm half darkness. They entered a chamber similar to the waiting room.

In the center of this chamber rose a pedestal about a foot high and a yard wide. On the pedestal rested something that at first examination Arthur took to be a sculpture. It stood about half as tall as he, shaped like a hefty square human torso and head—rather, in fact, like a squared-off and slightly flattened kachina doll. Other than an abstracted and undivided bosom, it lacked any surface features. In color it was similar to heat-treated copper, with oily swirls of rainbow iridescence. Its skin was glossy but not reflective.

Without warning, it lifted smoothly a few inches above the pedestal and addressed them both out loud:

"I am afraid your people will soon no longer be wild and free."

Arthur had heard this same voice in his head just a few minutes ago, beckoning them through the hatches.

"Who are you?" he asked.

"I am not your keeper, but I am your guide."

"Are you alive?" He did not know what else to ask.

"I am not biologically alive. I am part of this vessel, which will in turn soon become part of a much larger vessel. You are here to prepare your companions for me, that I may instruct them and carry out my own instructions."

"Are you a robot?" Clara asked.

"I am a symbol, designed to be acceptable without conveying wrong impressions. In a manner of speaking, I am a machine, but I am not a servile laborer. Do you understand me?"

The object's voice was deep, authoritative, yet not masculine.

"Yes," Arthur said.

"Some among your group might panic if exposed to me without preparation. Yet it is essential that they come to know and trust me, and come to trust the information and instructions I give them. Is this understood?"

"Yes." They answered in unison.

"The future of your people, and of all the information we have retrieved from your planet, depends on how your kind and my kind interact. Your kind must become disciplined, and I must educate you about larger realities than most of you have been used to facing."

Arthur nodded, his mouth dry. "We're inside one of the arks?"

"You are. These vessels will join together once we are all in space. There are now thirty-one of these vessels, and aboard twenty-one of them, five hundred humans apiece. The vessels also contain large numbers of botanical, zoological, and other specimens—not in most cases whole, but in recoverable form. Is this clear?"

"Yes," Arthur said. Clara nodded.

"Most of my early communications with you will not be through speech, but through what you might call telepathy, as you have already been directed by the network. Later, when there is more time, this intrusive method will be largely abandoned. For now, when you go among your companions, I will speak through you, but you will have the discretion of phrasing and timing. We have very little time."

"Has it begun?" Clara asked.

"It has begun," the object said.

"And we're leaving soon?"

"The last passengers and specimens for this vessel are being loaded now."

Arthur received impressions of crates of chromium spiders being loaded from small boats through the surface entrance of the ark. The spiders contained the fruits of weeks of searching and sampling: genetic material from thousands of plants and animals along the West Coast.

"What can we call you?" Arthur asked.

"You will make up your own names for me. Now you must return to your group and introduce them to their quarters, which are spaced along this hallway. You must also ask for at least four volunteers to witness the crime that is now being committed."

"We're to witness the destruction of the Earth?" Clara asked.

"Yes. It is the Law. If you will excuse me, I have other introductions to make."

They backed out of the shadowy room and watched as the hatchway slid shut.

"Very efficient," Arthur said.

" 'The Law.' " Clara smiled thinly. "Right now, I'm more scared than I ever was on the boat. I don't even know all the people's names yet."

"Let's get started," Arthur said. They traversed the curved hallway. The hatch at the opposite end opened and they saw a cluster of anxious faces. The smell of fear drifted out.

70——

Irwin Schwartz stepped into the White House situation room and nearly bumped into the First Lady. She backed away with a nervous nod, her hands trembling, and he entered. Everyone's nerves had been frazzled since the evacuation the night before and the rapid return of the President to the Capital. No one had slept for more than an hour or two since.

The President stood with Otto Lehrman before the high-resolution data screens mounted on the wood paneling covering the concrete walls. The screens were on and showed maps of different portions of the Northern Hemisphere, Mercator projection, with red spots marking vanished cities. "Come on in, Irwin," Crockerman said. "We have some new material from the Puzzle Palace." He seemed almost cheerful.

Irwin turned to the First Lady. "Are you here to stay?" he asked bluntly. He respected the woman, but did not like her much.

"The President specially requested my presence," she said. "He feels we should be united."

"Obviously, you agree with him."

"I agree with him," she said.

Never in United States history had a First Lady deserted her husband when he was under fire; Mrs. Crockerman knew this, and it must have taken some courage to return. Still, Schwartz had himself given long hours of thought to resigning from the administration; he could not judge her too harshly.

He held out his hand. She accepted and they shook firmly. "Welcome back aboard," he said.

"We have photos about twenty minutes old from a Diamond Apple," Lehrman said. "Technicians are putting them on the screens any minute." Diamond Apples were reconnaissance satellites launched in the early 1990s. The National Reconnaissance Office was very zealous with Diamond Apple pictures. Usually, they would have been reserved for the eyes of the President and Secretary of Defense only; that Schwartz was seeing them indicated something extraordinary was in store.

"Here they are," Lehrman said as the screens blanked.

Crockerman apparently had been told what to expect. Lines of glowing white rimmed in red and blue-green laced across a midnight-black background. "You know," Crockerman said softly, standing back from the screens, "I was right after all. Goddammit, Irwin, I was right, and I was wrong at the same time. How do you figure that?"

Schwartz stared at the glowing lines, not making any sense of them until a grid and labels came up with the display. This was the North Atlantic; the lines were trenches, midocean ridges and faults.

"The white," Lehrman said, "is heat residue from thermonuclear explosions. Hundreds, perhaps thousands, maybe tens of thousands—all along the Earth's deep-ocean seams and wrinkles."

The First Lady half sobbed, half caught her breath. Crockerman stared at the displays with a sad grin.

"Now the western Pacific," Lehrman said. More white lines. "By the way, Hawaii has been heavily assaulted by tsunamis. The West Coast of North America is about twenty, thirty minutes away from major waves; I'd guess it's already been hit by waves from these areas." He pointed to stacks of white lines near Alaska and California. "The damage could be extensive. The energy released by all the explosions is enormous; weather patterns around the world will change. The Earth's heat budget . . ." He shook his head. "But I doubt we'll be given much time to worry about it."

"It's a softening up?" Schwartz asked.

Lehrman shrugged. "Who can understand the design, or what this means? We're not dead yet, so it's a preliminary; that's all anybody knows. Seismic stations all over are reporting heavy anomalistic fault behavior."

"I don't think the bullets have collided yet," Crockerman said. "Irwin's hit the nail on the head. It's a softening up."

Lehrman sat down at the large diamond-shaped table and held out his hands: your guess is as good as mine.

"I think we have maybe an hour, maybe less," the President

said. "There's nothing we can do. Nothing we could have ever done."

Schwartz studied the Diamond Apple displays with a slight squint. They still conveyed no convincing reality. They were attractive abstractions. What did Hawaii look like now? What would San Francisco look like in a few minutes? Or New York?

"I'm sorry not everybody is here," Crockerman said. "I'd like to thank them."

"We're not evacuating . . . again?" Schwartz asked automatically.

Lehrman gave him a sharp, ironic look. "We don't have a lunar settlement, Irwin. The President, when he was a senator, was instrumental in getting those funds cut in 1990."

"My mistake," Crockerman said, his tone almost bantering. At that moment, had Schwartz had a pistol, he would have killed the man; his anger was a helpless, undirected passion that could just as easily leave him in tears as draw him into violence. The displays conveyed no reality; Crockerman, however, conveyed it all.

"We really are children," Schwartz said after the flush had gone out of his face and his hands had stopped trembling. "We never had a chance."

Crockerman looked around as the floor shook beneath their feet. "I'm almost anxious for the end," he said. "I hurt so bad inside."

The shaking became more violent.

The First Lady held the doorframe and then leaned on the table. Schwartz reached out to help her to a chair. Secret Service agents entered the room, struggling to stay on their feet, catching hold of the table edge. After Schwartz had seated the First Lady, he sat down again himself and gripped the wooden arms of the chair. The shaking was not dying away; it was getting worse.

"How long will it take, do you think?" Crockerman asked nobody in particular.

"Mr. President, we should get you out of the building and onto the grounds," said the agent who had made the most progress into the situation room. His voice quavered. He was terrified. "Everybody else, too."

"Don't be ridiculous," Crockerman said. "If the roof fell on me now, it would be a goddamn blessing. Right, Irwin?" His smile was bright, but there were tears in his eyes.

The display on the screen went out, and the lights in the room dimmed shortly after, to return with less conviction.

Schwartz stood. Time once again to be an example. "I think we should let these men do their job, Mr. President." He had a sudden heavy sensation in his stomach, as if he were in a fast-rising elevator. Crockerman stumbled and an agent caught him. The rising sensation continued, seemingly forever, and then stopped with a suddenness that lifted the White House a fraction of an inch from its foundations. The framework of steel beams that had been built into the White House shell in the late forties and early fifties squealed and groaned, but held. Plaster fell in clouds and patches from the ceiling and a rich wood panel split with a loud report.

Schwartz heard the President calling his name. From where he lay on the floor—somehow he had rolled under the table—he tried to answer, but all the breath had been knocked out of him. Gasping, blinking, wiping plaster dust from his eyes, he listened to a hideous creaking and splitting noise overhead. He heard enormous thuds outside—stone facing coming loose, he guessed, or columns toppling. He was forcibly reminded of so many movies about the demise of ancient cities by earthquake or volcano, huge blocks of marble tumbling onto crowds of hapless citizens.

Not the White House . . . Surely not that.

"Irwin, Otto . . ." The President again. A pair of legs walking with short jerks near the table.

"Under here, sir," Schwartz said. He saw a brief portrait of his wife in his mind, her features indistinct, as if he looked at an old, badly focused picture. She smiled. Then he saw their daughter, married and living in South Carolina . . . if the ocean had spared her.

Again the rising. He was pressed to the floor. It was brief, only a second or two, but he knew it was enough. When it stopped, he waited for the collapse of the upper floors, eyes scrunched tight. *Jesus, is the entire eastern seaboard going up?* The wait and the silence seemed interminable. Schwartz could not decide whether to open his eyes again . . . or to wait out the long seconds, *feeling* the sway of the building above.

He turned his head to one side and opened his eyes.

The President had fallen and lay faceup beside the table, ghost-white with dust. His eyes were open but not aware.

The White House regained its voice and screamed like a thing alive.

The massive legs of the table buckled and exploded in splinters. They could not withstand the weight of tons of cement and steel and stone.

71——

Quaint, Edward thought; quaint and touching and he wished he could muster up the emotion to join them; a group of twenty or more had gathered by now in a circle a hundred yards behind the Granite Point, singing hymns and more folk songs. Betsy clung to him on the asphalt path. Fresh tremors had subsided, but the air itself seemed to be grumbling, complaining.

Ironically, having climbed the trail to have a good vantage, they now stood well back from the rim. A foot-wide crack had appeared in the terrace stonework. From where they stood, they could see only the upper third of the opposite wall of the valley.

"You're a geologist," Betsy said, massaging his neck with one hand, something he had not asked her to do, but which felt good. "Do you know what's going on?"

"No," he said.

"It's not just an earthquake, though?"

"I don't think so."

"So it's beginning now. We just got up here."

He nodded and swallowed back a lump of fear. Now that it had come, he was near panic. He felt trapped, claustrophobic, with only all of the Earth and sky to move in—not even that, lacking wings. He felt squeezed between steel plates of gravity and his own puny weakness. His body was forcibly reminding him that fear was difficult to control, and presence of mind in the face of death was rare.

"God," Betsy said, placing her cheek against his, looking toward the Point. She was shaking, too. "I thought at least we'd have time to talk about it, sit around a campfire . . ."

Edward held her more tightly. He imagined her as a wife, and then thought of Stella, marveling at the fickleness of his fantasies;

he was grasping for many lives, now that his own seemed so short. Over his fear he thought of long years together with both of them.

The tremors had almost passed.

The hymn singers continued searching for a common key, hopelessly lost. Minelli and Inez came from the trees and climbed the hill between the close switchbacks of the asphalt path. Minelli whooped out loud and ran his hand through his hair. "Jesus, isn't adrenaline great?"

"He's crazy," Inez said, breathing hard, her face pale. "Maybe not the craziest I've met, but close."

"Does it feel warmer to you?" Betsy asked.

Edward considered that possibility. Would heat transmit itself before a shock wave? No. If the bullets were colliding, or had collided only a short time ago, deep in the center of the Earth, the expanding and irresistible plasma of their mutual destruction would crack the Earth wide before heat could ever reach the surface.

"I don't think it's warmer because of . . . the end," Edward said. He had never felt his mind racing so rapidly over so many subjects. He wanted to see what was happening in the valley.

"Shall we?" he asked, pointing to the terraces and the still-intact rim.

"What else did we come here for?" Minelli asked, laughing and shaking his head like a wet dog. Sweat flew from his hair. He whooped again and took Inez's plump hand, dragging her across the gravel to the terraces.

"Minel*liiii,*" she protested, looking back at them for help. Edward glanced at Betsy, and she nodded once, face flushed.

"I am so *terrified,*" she whispered. "It's like being high." They walked together toward the edge. "I pity all those folks who stayed home. I really do."

The two couples stood alone on the terrace, looking down into the valley. Not much had changed; there was no visible damage, not at first glance, anyway. Then Minelli pointed to a thick column of smoke. "Look."

The Ahwanee was on fire. Nearly the entire hotel was ablaze.

"I love that old place," Betsy said. Inez moaned and wrung her hands.

"How much longer, do you think?" Inez asked, her expression that of someone about to sneeze, or shriek. She did neither.

350 • Greg Bear

"It seems real close," he said. Betsy raised her arms with a moan and he hugged her tightly, almost squeezing the breath out of her.

"Hold me, dammit," Inez demanded. Minelli blinked at her, then followed Edward's example.

Ten minutes after the meeting, Arthur and Clara had assigned the members of their group to the new quarters along the curved hallway. Two of the younger children were crying inconsolably and all were emotionally exhausted; Arthur stood in the confines of the cabin he and Francine and Marty would share, pondering the common sanitation facilities accessible through the first door-way on the right of the sealed hatch where they had met with the robot. A few had already used the lavatory; some had gone in there to be sick. Clara was one of the latter. She came to the Gordons' cabin and leaned against the edge of the hatch, rubbing her eyes with one hand. "All settled, I think," she said. "What's next?"

Francine had said little for the entire time they had been aboard. She sat on the bed, clutching her box of disks and papers with one hand. Marty held her other hand firmly. She stared at Clara with a vacancy that worried Arthur.

Choose four witnesses. The restatement of the command in their minds was polite but unequivocal. *It is the Law.*

Clara jerked and stood upright. "You heard that?" she asked.

He nodded. Francine turned to look at Arthur. "They want us to choose four witnesses," he told her.

"Witnesses to what?" Her voice was small, distant.

"The end," he said.

"Not the children," Francine said firmly. Arthur briefly conferred with the voice. *Two must be younger, to pass on the memories.*

"They want two children," he said. Francine clenched her fists.

"I don't want Martin to experience that," she said. "It's bad enough if we have to."

"They want kids for what?" Marty asked, looking between them, wide-eyed.

"It's the Law. Their law," Arthur said. "They need some of us to watch the Earth when it's destroyed, and two of them must be kids."

Marty thought that over for a moment. "All the other kids are younger than me," he said, "except one. That girl. I don't know her name."

Francine turned Marty to face her and gripped his arms. "Do you know what's going to happen?" she asked.

"The Earth is going to blow up," Marty said. "They want us to see it so we know what it's like."

"Do you know who *they* are?" Francine asked.

"The people that talk to Dad," Marty said.

"He understands pretty well," Arthur said.

"I'll say," Clara agreed.

Francine gave her an angry glance, then focused again on Marty. "Do you want to see?" she asked.

Marty shook his head no. "It would give me nightmares," he said.

"Then it's decided," Francine said. "He—"

"But Mom, if I don't see, I won't know."

"Know what?"

"How mad I'm supposed to be."

Francine searched her son's face slowly, and then let him go, wrapping her arms around herself. "Only four?" she asked softly.

"At least four," he said. "All who wish to see."

"Marty," Francine said, "we'll share nightmares, okay?"

"Okay."

"You're a very brave boy," Clara said.

"Are you going to watch?" Arthur asked Francine.

She nodded slowly. "If you and Marty watch, I can't chicken out, can I?"

How much longer? he asked.

There will be a gathering in the common viewing cabin in an hour and ten minutes.

He sat on the narrow lower bed beside Francine and Marty. "We'll be leaving the Earth soon," he said. "In a few minutes, probably."

"Can we feel it when we take off, Dad?" Marty asked.

"No," he said. "We won't feel it."

Grant had followed the Gordons' station wagon to the bay, and waited a hundred yards away, engine idling, as they parked and walked to the pier. Then he had parked his BMW beside the wagon, slung a pair of binoculars around his neck, and followed at a discreet distance, feeling like a fool, asking himself—as Danielle had asked when he left—why he didn't simply confront them and demand answers.

He knew he wouldn't do that. First, he could not really believe that Arthur would be part of a government escape into space. Grant couldn't believe such an escape was contemplated, or even possible. Nobody could travel far enough away to survive the Earth's destruction—not if such destruction was as spectacular as what he had seen in the movies. And even if they could—traveling out beyond the moon, for example—he didn't think they would be able to live very long in space.

But he was curious. He believed as firmly as Danielle that the Gordons were up to something. In the curious kind of floating emotional state he now experienced, tracking the Gordons offered a possibility for diversion.

He was otherwise powerless. He could not save his family. He felt what billions of others—all who knew and believed—were feeling now, a deep terror surmounted by helplessness, resulting in a dopey calmness, not unlike what his grandparents must have felt as they were led to the death pits in Auschwitz.

This, of course, was vaster and more final than the Holocaust. Nondiscriminatory. Thinking such thoughts pressed him up against a wall of ignorance; he had never been particularly imaginative, and he could not conceive the means or motives behind what he nevertheless knew was coming.

He stood on the concrete seawall and watched them board the fishing boat. The boat, covered with people, sailed out to the north.

Then he sat on the concrete and rock, buttoning his coat and slipping on a cap to keep away the chill of the breezes off the bay.

Grant had no clear plans, or clear idea what he was doing. If he waited, perhaps an answer would come. Hours passed. He doubled his legs up on the rock and pressed his knees against his chest, chin on the new denim of his pants. The afternoon passed very slowly, but he stuck with his vigil.

The ground trembled slightly and the water level of the bay rose a foot against the seawall, and then fell until the rocks at the base of the wall were exposed—a drop of perhaps four or five feet. He expected—almost welcomed the possibility—that the water would rise again drastically and drown him.

It did not rise again.

Like a robot, he stood and walked through the unlocked gate to the end of the pier, where he leaned his elbows against the wood rail, staring north. He could barely see Alcatraz beyond the San

Francisco–Oakland Bay Bridge. The water just south of Alcatraz appeared rougher than usual, almost white.

A dark gray shape sat in the middle of the whiteness. For a moment, Grant thought a ship had overturned in the bay and was floating hull-up. But the gray bulk was rising higher in the water, not sinking. He lifted his binoculars and focused on the shape.

With a jerk of surprise, he saw that it was already out of the water, and that it had a flat bottom. He had an impression of something shaped like a flatiron, or like the body of a horseshoe crab, four or five hundred feet in length. It rose above the span of the bridge, lifting on a brilliant cone of blinding green. Across the bay came a teeth-aching high-pitched hissing, roaring sound. The object accelerated rapidly upward and dwindled against the late morning sky. In a few seconds, it was gone. How many others had seen it? he wondered.

Could the government really have had something in the works —something spectacular?

He bit his lip and shook his head, crying now, not knowing why. He felt a peculiar relief. Somehow, a few people were getting away. That was a kind of victory, as important as his parents surviving the death camps.

And for those still condemned . . .

Grant wiped the tears from his eyes and hurried back along the pier, bumping into an iron pole as he passed through the gate. He ran to his car, hoping he would be in time. He wanted to be home with his family.

The bridge was practically deserted as he crossed. He could not see the spot in the bay where the water had been white.

He did not know how he would explain this to Danielle. Her concerns would be more immediate, less abstract; she would ask why he did not try to find a way to save them all.

Perhaps he would say nothing, just tell her that he had followed the Gordons as far south as Redwood City . . . and stopped, waited a few hours, and turned back.

She wouldn't believe him.

72——

The ship, Arthur learned, contained 412 passengers, all boarded in secrecy during the morning and the previous night. The passengers had been divided into groups of twenty, and for the most part would not mingle until several days had passed, and they had grown used to their situation. The only exception would be the witnessing.

Out of their group of twenty, nine had volunteered, two children, three women, and four men, including Arthur, Francine, and Marty. The nine followed the stocky copper robot through the chamber at the end of the curved hall.

They walked along a narrow black strip in a cylindrical corridor. Arthur tried to make a map in his head, not entirely succeeding. The ship apparently had compartments that moved in relation to each other.

Passing through a hatch ahead of them, the robot rolled abruptly to take up a new vertical. They found themselves doing likewise, with a few moans of complaint and surprise. In a cabin about a hundred feet long and forty or fifty feet deep, they faced a broad transparent panel that gave a view of bright steady stars. Marty kept close to Arthur, holding his arm tightly with one hand, the other clenched into a fist. The boy had sucked his lips inward over his teeth and was making small smacking sounds. Francine followed, tense and reluctant.

Arthur looked down at his son and smiled. "Your choice, fellah," he said. Marty nodded. This was no longer a youngster playing patsy to a pretty blond cousin; this was a boy feeling his way to manhood.

More people entered through a hatch in the opposite side of the cabin in groups of four or five or six, children among them, until a small crowd faced the darkness and stars; Arthur estimated seventy or eighty. He seemed to recognize some from his time on the network, though that was hardly likely; all he had heard were their inner voices, which almost never matched physical appearance. He thought of Hicks's inner voice, robust and young and sharp, and of his white-haired, grandfatherly presence. *I'm going to miss him. He could have helped us a lot here.*

Arthur flashed on Harry, desiccated, decaying, buried deep in a coffin in the Earth; or had Ithaca had him cremated? That seemed to suit both of them better.

A tall young black man stood behind Arthur and Francine. Arthur nodded a greeting and the man returned the nod, cordial, dignified, terrified, his neck muscles taut as cords. Arthur examined the other faces, trying to learn something from the mix, how they had been chosen. Age? There were few older than fifty; but then, these were just the ones who had chosen to witness. Race? All types found on North America were represented. Intelligence? There was no way to tell that . . .

"We're in space, aren't we?" the tall young man asked. "That's what they said, I just didn't believe them. We're in space, and we're going to join with other arks soon. My name's Reuben," he said, offering his hand to Arthur. They shook. Reuben's hand was damp, but so was Arthur's. "This your son?"

"This is Martin," Arthur said. Reuben reached down and shook Marty's hand. Marty looked up at him solemnly, still sucking his lips. "And my wife, Francine."

"I don't know how to feel," Reuben said. "I don't know what's real and what isn't anymore."

Arthur agreed. He did not feel like talking.

Something flashed against the stars, turning in the sunlight, and then steadied and approached them. Francine pointed, awed. It was shaped like a huge, rounded arrowhead, flat on one side, contoured to a central ridge on the opposite side.

"That's Singapore," said a woman behind them. Not all of the network received information at once, Arthur decided; that made sense. It would have flooded them.

"Singapore," Reuben said, shaking his head. "I've never even been there."

"We have Istanbul and Cleveland," said a young man at one end of the cabin, hardly more than a boy.

The gray ship passed out of view above them. There was still no sensation of motion, nor any sound except for the murmurs and shuffling of the cabin's occupants. They might have been standing in an exhibit hall waiting for some spectacular new form of entertainment to begin.

The stars began to move all in one direction; the ark was rotating. Arthur searched for constellations he knew, and for a moment saw none; then he spotted the Southern Cross, and as the rotation continued, Orion.

The white and blue limb of the Earth rose into view and the occupants of the cabin gave a collective gasp.

Still there. Still looks the same.

"Jesus," Reuben said. "Poppa, Momma, Jesus."

Danielle, Grant, Becky. Angkor Wat, Taj Mahal, Library of Congress. Grand Canyon. The house and the river. Steppes of central Asia. Cockroaches, elephants, Olduvai Gorge, New York City, Dublin, Beijing. The first woman I ever dated, Kate—Katherine. The bones of the dog who helped me come to grips with the world and become a man.

"That's the Earth, isn't it, Dad?" Marty asked quietly.

"That's it."

"It's still there. Maybe we can go back and nothing will happen."

Arthur found himself nodding. *Maybe so.*

The woman who had known about Singapore said, "They're still in the Earth. They're the last of the planet-eaters. They can't leave because we'll get them."

Arthur glanced nervously at her, as if she were a dangerous sibyl; her face was pale and convulsed.

73———

"Rock of a-a-a-ges . . ."

The singing had taken a slightly frantic tone, sharper, higher, more disturbing. The column of smoke from the Ahwanee had risen above the Royal Arches; the hotel was almost consumed, and sparks from the blaze threatened to ignite the surrounding woods.

From their vantage, they watched park fire trucks spraying water on the flaming ruins.

Spend your last few minutes trying to save something, Edward thought. *Not a bad way to go.* He envied the fire fighters and park rangers. The fire took their minds away from the inevitable. Up on Glacier Point, people had nothing to do but think about what would happen—and sing very badly.

The rock beneath them shifted the merest fraction. Betsy returned from the rest room, sat firmly beside Edward on the lowest terrace, and placed her arm through his; they had not been separated for more than a few minutes the last hour. Still, he felt alone, and looking at her, sensed she felt alone as well.

"Do you hear it?" she asked.

"The grumbling?"

"Yes."

"I hear it."

He imagined the lumps of neutronium and anti-neutronium, or whatever they were, meeting at the center; perhaps they had already met, minutes or even an hour before, and the expanding front of raging plasma had just begun to make its effects known on the Earth's mantle and thin crust.

In high school, Edward had once tried to draw a scale chart of the layers of a section of the Earth, with the inner and outer cores, mantle, and crust outlined in proportion. He had quickly found that the crust did not shown up as more than the thinnest of pencil lines, even when he extended his drawing to an eight-foot-long piece of butcher paper. Using his calculator to figure how large the drawing would have to be, he had learned that the floor of the school gymnasium might suffice to hold a drawing that gave the crust a line equal to a width a third that of his little finger.

Hidden volumes and surfaces again.

Insignificance.

Geologists dealt with insignificance all the time, but how many applied it directly to their personal lives?

". . . cleft for meeee . . . Let me hiiide myself in theeee . . ."

"The air *is* getting hotter," Minelli said. The neckband of his black T-shirt was soaked and his hair hung down in black ribbons. Inez sat farther back, on the upper terrace, sobbing quietly to herself.

"Go to her," Edward commanded, nodding in her direction.

Minelli gave him a helpless look, then climbed up the steps.

358 • Greg Bear

"People are all that matter," he said softly to Betsy. "Nothing else matters. Not in the beginning, not in the end."

"Look," Betsy said, pointing to the east. Clouds were racing across the sky, not billowing but simply forming in streamers at very high altitude. The air smelled electric and was oppressive, tangible, thick and hot. The sun seemed farther away, lost in a thin milky soup.

Edward looked down from the clouds, dizzy, and tried to orient on the valley. He searched for a familiar landmark, something to give him a fixed perspective.

The Royal Arches, in slow motion, slipped in huge curved flakes down the gray face of granite onto the burning hotel. Tiny trees danced frantically and then fell on their own isolated chips of rock, limbs raised by the passing air. The roar, even across the valley, was deafening. The scythe-shaped flakes, dozens of yards wide, crumpled like old plaster on the valley floor, extinguishing the Ahwanee, the fire trucks, fire fighters, and tiny crowds of onlookers in a blossoming cloud of dust and debris. Boulders the size of houses rolled through the forest and into the Merced River. New slopes of talus crept across the valley floor like an amoeba's pseudopods, alive, churning, settling, striving for stability.

Betsy said nothing. Edward glanced apprehensively at the crack in the terrace nearby.

Minelli had given up trying to hold on to Inez. She fled from the rim, her breasts and arms and hips bouncing as she leaped up steps and over rails. He grinned at Edward and held out his hands helplessly, then descended to sit beside them.

"Some folks ain't got it," he said over the declining rumble of falling rocks. He looked admiringly at Betsy. "Guts," he said. "True grit. Did you see those concentrics come apart? Just like in school. Hundreds of years in a second."

"We aare chiiildren in youuur haaands . . ." The hymn singers were self-absorbed now, paying no attention to all that was going on around them. Entranced.

To each his own.

"That's how the domes are formed, that kind of concentric jointing," Minelli explained. "Water gets into the joints and freezes, expands, splits the rock away."

Betsy ignored him, staring fixedly into the valley, her hand still locked in Edward's.

"The falls," she said. "Yosemite Falls."

The upper ribbon of white water had been blocked, leaving the lower falls to drain what had already descended. To the right of where the upper Yosemite had once been, the freestanding pillar of Lost Arrow leaned several hundred feet of its length slowly out from the cliff face, broke into sections in midfall, and tumbled down the brush- and tree-covered slopes below. More rock spalled from the northeastern granite walls above the valley, obscuring the floor with disintegrating boulders and roils of brown and white dust.

"Why not us?" Minelli said. "It's all on that side."

A superstitious something in Edward wanted to shut him up. *Pretend as if we're not here. Don't let it know.*

The rock beneath them quivered. The trees beyond the hymn singers swayed and groaned and splintered, limbs whipping back and forth. Edward heard the hideous crack of great leaves of granite shearing away beneath the point. Three thousand feet below—he didn't need to look to know—Camp Curry and Curry Village were being buried under millions of tons of jagged rock. The hymn singers stopped and clutched each other to keep their balance.

"Time to get away," Edward said to Betsy. She lay flat on her back, staring up at the twisted, malevolent overcast painted on the sky. The air seemed thinner; great waves of high and low pressure raced over the land, propelled by the minute shifting of continents.

Edward reached under her arms and dragged her away from the lowest terrace, up the steps. The game now was to stay alive as long as possible, to see as much as they could see—to experience the spectacle to their last breath, which could be at any moment.

Minelli crawled after them, face wrapped in a manic grin. "Can you believe this?" he said over and over.

The valley was alive with the echoes of falling sheets of granite. Edward could hardly hear his own words to Betsy as they stumbled and ran down the asphalt path, away from the rim.

A scant yard behind Minelli, the rock split. The terrace and all that was beneath leaned away, the gap widening with majestic slowness. Minelli scrambled frantically, his grin transformed into a rictus of terror.

To the east, like the great wise head of a dozing giant, Half Dome nodded a few degrees and tilted into a chasm opened in the floor of the valley. In arc-shaped wedges, it began to come apart.

Liberty Cap and Mount Broderick, on the south side of the valley, leaned to the north, but stayed whole, rolling and sliding like giant pebbles into the mass of Half Dome's settling fragments, diverting, and then finally shattering and sending fragments through miles of the valley. Somewhere in the obscurity of dust were the remnants of the Mist Trail, Vernal Fall, Nevada Fall, and the Emerald Lake.

The silt of the valley floor liquefied under the vibration, swallowing meadows and roads and absorbing the Merced along its entire length. The fresh slopes of talus dropped their leading edges into snakelike fractures and began to spread again; behind them, more leaves of granite plummeted.

The air was stifling. The hymn singers, on their knees, weeping and singing at once, could not be heard, only seen. The death-sound of Yosemite was beyond comprehension, having crossed the border into pain, a wide-spectrum roaring howl.

Edward and Betsy could not keep balance even on their hands and knees; they rolled to the ground and held each other. Betsy had closed her eyes, lips working against his neck; she was praying. Edward, curiously, did not feel like praying; he was exultant now. He looked to the east, away from the valley, beyond the tumbling trees, and saw something dark and massive on the horizon. Not clouds, not a front of storm, but—

He was past any expression of awe or wonder. What he was seeing could only be one thing: east of the Sierra Nevada, along the fault line drawn between the mountains formed by ages of wrinkling pressure, and the desert beyond, the continent was splitting, raising its jagged edge dozens of miles into the atmosphere.

Edward did not need to do calculations to know this meant the end. Such energy—even if all other activity ceased—would be enough to smash all living things along the western edge of the continent, enough to change the entire face of North America.

Acceleration in the pit of his stomach. *Going up.* His skin seemed to be boiling. *Going up.* Winds blew that threatened to lift them away. With the last of his strength, he held on to Betsy. He could not see Minelli for a moment, and then he opened his tingling eyes and saw against a muddy blue sky filled with stars—the atmosphere racing away above them—saw Minelli *standing*, smiling beatifically, arms raised, near the new rim of the point. He receded through walls of dust on a fresh-hewn leaf of granite, mouth open, shouting unheard into the overwhelming din.

Yosemite is gone. The Earth might be gone. I'm still thinking.
The only sensation Edward could feel, other than the endless acceleration, was Betsy's body against his own. He could hardly breathe.

They no longer lay on the ground, but fell. Edward saw walls of rock, great fresh white revealed volumes on all sides—thousands of feet wide—and spinning trees and disintegrating clumps of dirt and even a small flying woman, yards away, face angelic, eyes closed, arms spread.

It seemed an eternity before the light vanished.

The granite volumes enclosed them all.

74——

From ten thousand miles, the Earth seemed as natural and peaceful and beautiful as it had over thirty years before, when Arthur had first seen it in full-frame pictures from space. That view—a clouded jewel, opal and lapis marbled with rich whorls of cloud—had entranced him, made him more than ever before feel a part of some cosmic whole. It had changed his life.

The witnesses were subdued. Nobody said a word or made a loud sound. He had never experienced such rapt concentration in a crowd. Marty stood by his side, having let go of his hand, a boy barely four feet eleven inches tall, standing alone. *How much does he understand?*

Perhaps as much as I do.

Nothing compared with what they expected to see. Not the burning of an ancestral house, or the sinking of an ocean liner; not the bombing of a city, or the horror of mass graves in time of revolution or war. The crime that had been committed against humanity was virtually total. Except for them—the occupants of the arks, and the records saved for transport in the arks—the Earth would be no more.

He could not wrap his thoughts around the totality. He had to take separate losses and mull them over. They were highly personal losses, things he would regret; but his single mind was not the holographic mind of humanity.

Essential things would be destroyed that he had never known. Connections, evidences, histories as yet uncovered, irretrievable. All the arks could save was what humans had so far learned about themselves. Hereafter, they would be refugees with no hope of ever returning to a homeland, no hope of recovering the thread of the pasts they had lost.

They would be dependent on the kindness, or whatever their motivations might be, of strangers, of nonhuman intelligences that so far had shown little evidence of being willing to reveal themselves; benefactors as mysterious as their destroyers.

Lives. Billions of human beings, their existence always fragile, sharing mutual oblivion. There was no way Arthur could encompass that. He had to deal in abstractions.

The abstractions were enough to sear him. Backed by the realization that what he saw was real and immediate, his soul burned. He had had months to come to grips with these facts and implications; those months had not done to him what the vision of the Earth, whole and bright, was doing to him now.

No explanations came from the network. Later, when each of the witnesses had faced their private griefs, perhaps the details of the end would be made clear, and a planetary postmortem would be conducted.

Strange images flashed through his mind. Television commercials from his childhood, smiling women in Peter Pan collars with tightly coiffed hair, images of motherhood tending perfect families. Faces of soldiers dying in Vietnam. Presidents standing one by one before the television cameras, ending with Crockerman, a very sad image indeed.

The 200-inch telescope at Mount Palomar. He had never worked there, but he had toured the historic site often enough. The 600-inch at Mauna Kea. His dormitory room at Cal Tech. The face of the first woman he had ever made love to, that first year in university. Professors lecturing. His joy on discovering the properties of a Möbius strip; he had been thirteen at the time. Equal joys on grasping the concepts of limits in calculus, and reading the first articles on black holes in the late 1960s.

Harry. Always Harry.

The first time he had seen Francine, in a skimpy black one-piece swimsuit, as voluptuous as a goddess from the sea, with long wet black hair, the backs of her legs and her inner thighs rough with damp sand, running to take a towel from her friend and collapsing on her back with a laugh not five yards from where Arthur sat. *Not all is lost.*

Marty touched his arm. "Dad, what's that?"

The globe did not seem noticeably different. But Marty pointed, and others among the witnesses were murmuring, pointing.

Over the Pacific, a silver-white mass grew like mold in a petri dish. Over the western United States and what they could see of Australia, similar blossoms of condensing moisture expanded.

Within minutes, the Earth blanketed itself in an impenetrable blanket of white and gray. Waves passed through the mass, ripples as visible as those in a pond, but moving with clockwork slowness. Above the north pole, frantic curtains of light played, guttering and re-forming like lines of candles in a breeze. They were aurorae. Something was wreaking havoc with Earth's interior dynamo.

Arthur pictured the explosion expanding through the superhot, highly radioactive inner core to the outer core, where the Earth's magnetic field was born. The dense molten material compressing even more highly on the edge of the expanding blast. Mechanical shock waves shooting out to the crust, shifting the ocean basins— already weakened by the chains of thermonuclear explosions— and shifting the continents, up to ten times thicker than the ocean basins, buckling them all, raising them a few hundred feet, or a few miles. Oceans receding, spilling out over the continents . . . All now hidden behind the masses of clouds.

The Earth's surface extremely hot, atmosphere sloshing like water in a bowl. Most of humanity dead already, destroyed by earthquakes, horrendous atmospheric storms or floods. Soon the rock below would compress no more, and the Earth would—

"Jesus," Reuben said behind them. Arthur glanced at him; the young man's face expressed both fascination and horror.

The clouds clarified. They glimpsed through smeared atmospherics a muddy, churning mass, lit in places with the hellish light of magma welling up through fractures hundreds of miles wide. Continental and ocean-floor plates drove together at their edges, fusing into solids no more able to keep their shape and character than gases or liquids, rippling like fabric.

Nowhere could he see any of the works of humanity. Cities—if any still existed, which did not seem likely—would have been far too small. Most of Europe and Asia were on the other side of the globe, out of sight, their fate no different from what they saw happening to eastern Asia and the western United States and Australia. Indeed, these landmasses could no longer be distinguished; there were no oceans or land, only belts of translucent superheated steam and cooler cloud and tortured basins of mud, shot through with dull brown magma and, here and there, great white spots of plasma beginning to burrow out from the interior.

"Is it going to blow up?" Marty asked.

Arthur shook his head, unable to speak.

Despite the growing distance between the ark and Earth, the globe visibly expanded, but again with clockwork slowness.

Arthur checked his watch. They had been viewing for fifteen minutes; the time had passed in a flash.

Again the Earth took on the appearance of a jewel, but this time a great bloated fire opal, orange and brown and deep ruby red, shot through with spectral patches of brilliant green and white. The crust melted, turning into basaltic slag adrift in slowly spinning patches on a sea of brown and red. There were no discernible features but the colors. The Earth, dying, became an incomprehensible abstraction, horribly beautiful.

Already, with the appearance of long spirals of white and green, intensely bright, the final fate became obvious. The limb of the world no longer made a smooth curve; it had visible irregularities, broad low lumps distinct against the blackness. From these lumps, jets of vapor hundreds of miles high lanced through the turbid remnants of the atmosphere and cast pale gray fans into space.

Such volcanoes might have been seen in the early ages of the Earth's coalescence, but not since. New chains of released fire and vapor emerged across the face of the distorted globe. Slowly, a spiraling snake of white plasma shot chunks from its interior coils outward, the projectiles traveling at thousands of kilometers an hour but still falling back, being reabsorbed.

No single piece of the Earth's crust had yet been flung out with a velocity equal to or greater than eighteen thousand miles per hour, orbital velocity, much less escape velocity. But the trend was obvious.

Countless island-sized bolides pocked the face of the Earth with a churning effervescence. These bolides rose hundreds, even thousands of miles, then fell, scattering broad trajectories of smaller debris. At the limb, the increased altitude of these molten projectiles was apparent. Energy rapidly built sufficient to toss them into orbit, and even to blow them free from the bulk of the globe.

Home. Arthur connected suddenly with all that he saw; the abstraction took on solidity and meaning. The stars behind the glowing, swelling Earth suddenly filled with menace; he imagined them as the glints of wolves' eyes in an infinite night-bound forest. He paraphrased what Harry had said on his tape:

There once was an infant lost in the woods, crying its heart out, wondering why no one answered, drawing down the wolves . . .

He was past tears now, past anything but a deep blunt suffocating pain. *Home. Home.*

Marty faced the panel with eyes wide and mouth open; almost the same expression Arthur had seen when his son watched Saturday morning cartoons on television, only slightly different: tighter, with a hint of puzzlement, eyes searching.

The Earth bloated horribly. Beneath the swelling crust and mantle, the spirals and fractures of white and green light widened into vast canals and highways running crazy random courses through a uniform dull red landscape. Huge bolides exited in long graceful curves, arcing thousands of miles—entire Earth radii—out in space, and not falling back to the surface, but tracing glowing orbits around the stricken planet.

Twenty-five minutes had passed. Arthur's legs ached and he had drenched his clothes in sweat. The room filled with an awful animal stench, fear and grief and silent agony.

Virtually everyone he had ever known was dead, their bodies lost in the general apocalypse; every place he had ever been, all of his records and the records of his family, all the children Marty had grown up with. Everyone on the ark was cut adrift in nothingness. He could distinctly feel the separation, the sudden loss, as if he had always known the presence of humanity around him, a *psychic* connection that was no more.

The brilliant highways and canals of the revealed plasma energy sphere now stretched thousands of miles, vaulting the molten, vaporized material of the Earth outward in a rough ovoid, the long axis at right angles to the axis of rotation. The tips of the ovoid spun away huge globules of silica and nickel and iron.

Against the dominant light of the plasma, the twisted remains of mantle and compressed streamers of the core cast long shadows into near-Earth space through the expanding dusty cloud of vapor and smaller debris. The planet resembled a lantern in fog, almost unbearably bright. Inexorably, the ovoid of plasma pushed everything outward, attenuating, blasting, diminishing all that was left, scattering it before an irresistible wind of elementary particles and light.

Two hours. He glanced at his watch. The moon shined through the vapor haze, a quarter of a million miles distant and seemingly aloof. But tidal bulges would relax, and even though the moon's shape had been frozen by ages of cooling, Arthur thought the relaxation would at the very least trigger violent moonquakes.

He turned his attention again to the dead Earth. The plasma glow had dimmed slightly. Distinct ethereal pinks and oranges and grayish blues gave it a pearly appearance, like a child's plastic ball illuminated from within. The diameter of the plasma ovoid and the haze of debris had expanded to well over thirty thousand miles by now. The ovoid continued to lengthen, spreading the new belt of asteroids into the stubby beginnings of an arc.

The transparent panel became mercifully opaque.

As if released from puppet strings, fully half of the witnesses collapsed on the floor. Arthur hugged Francine and gripped Marty's shoulder, unable to speak, then walked among his fellows, seeing what could be done to help them.

The copper-colored robot appeared at the end of the cabin and floated forward. Behind it came dozens more survivors, bearing trays and bowls of water, food, and medicines.

It is the Law.

The words echoed again and again through Arthur's thoughts as he helped revive those who had fallen.

It is the Law.

Marty stayed by his side, kneeling with him as he elevated a young woman's head and held a metal cup of water to her lips.

"Father," the boy said, "where are we going now?"

AGNUS DEI

The child, ravaged by wolves, falls quiet in the forest, and the long darkness is filled with an undisturbed silence.

PERSPECTIVE

New Mars Gazette, December 21, 2397; editorial by Francine Gordon:
The screen for today's edition is filled with news from the Central Ark. Four hundred more of us, most from the Eurasian arks, have been revived from deep sleep, and prepared for their arrival on New Mars by the Moms. (Does anybody remember who first called the robots Moms? It was Reuben Bordes, then nineteen, revived eight years ago and now on the New Venus Reconnaissance Mission.) Our population today hit the mark of 12,250; the Moms say we are doing well, and I believe them.

New Mars today celebrates its first year of autonomy. The Moms no longer exercise what my husband has called zookeeper's authority. Already we begin to factionalize and squabble; but these are the signs of a reborn planetism coming once again to maturity. Does that bring us much cheer? Not the politicians, bracing for the arrival of more Marxists.

But what we really celebrate, of course, is the four hundredth anniversary of the Ice Strike that began New Mars. This world has already become home to most of the human race. I feel a stronger connection to New Mars now than to Earth, blasphemous as that might seem; in our hearts I think we must acknowledge that the ten years since most of us came out of sleep have blurred the pain of Earth's death. Not banished, just subdued . . .

We cannot forget.

In four days many of us will celebrate Christmas. On Earth, that was a time of hope, of the promise of resurrection. Even the atheists among us must feel the power of this particular season and holiday, especially now, for like Christ, we carry the weight of billions on our shoulders; and more, we bear the responsibility of an entire planet's biosphere. We are like children dragged prematurely into parenthood, and the burden is frequently too heavy to stand.

Still, the suicide rate on New Mars has dropped precipitously in the last three years. We are finding our feet once again; we are desperately weak, but we are determined. We will not perish.

We will not forget our duties, nor will those who fly outward on the Ships of the Law to seek the home of the planet-eaters. My son is out there; what does he have to celebrate, on his equivalent of December 21?

For those of you who have supported this oft-times undisciplined, wandering little journal, on this day of celebration, my husband and I extend our heartfelt thanks. We hope that our philosophy-that New Mars and New Ve-

nus are and will be our true homes-has provided some comfort.

All of Earth has been reduced to one small
town. Whatever our differences, we are all extraordinarily close. We love you all, and welcome our newly awakened Eurasian brothers and
sisters.

Arthur put on his coldsuit and strapped a small tank of oxygen to
his belt. Even in the past year, the air had grown richer, and not
just in Mariner Valley, but on the green moss and lichen plains of
the highlands as well. Still, it was best to be safe; if he should need
to exert himself, the oxygen tank could save his life.

In the small individual air lock, he could hear the distant, tinny
sound of the celebration in the main hall of Geopolis. He had had
enough company for the evening; he needed solitude now, time to
think and reappraise.

The hatch opened and he stepped out onto a patch of ubiquitous
crisp lichen. The valley air at dusk was cold and still and the stars
steady as crystal.

The sky glowed a lovely, subdued mauve, edging toward blue at
zenith. To the southeast, the high valley walls caught the last
sunlight of the day, a thin irregular horizontal ribbon of intense
orange.

New Mars had recovered from its collison with the icy fragment
of Europa in the 390 years they had been in cold sleep, dropping
its mantle of cloud after two centuries of almost steady rain. Floods
had scoured the red and ocher terrain, and the increased temperature had released the frozen carbon dioxide of the poles, thicken-
ing the atmosphere. At that time, a century past, New Mars had
been ideal for primitive plants. Up and down the valley, the dust
and rock had been carpeted by lichens and mosses, and the new
small seas had been seeded with phytoplankton.

Oxygen soon returned in quantity to New Mars.

Farther north, the impacted remains of Phobos and Deimos,
rich in organic materials, supported highland farms of new wheat
strains, and the first experiments at Earthlike forests, chiefly coni-
fers. In a few decades, New Mars would have territories virtually
indistinguishable from Earth. She—New Mars had adopted
Mother Earth's gender—promised to be a planet of broad green

prairies, high semiarid forests, and deep, almost tropical oxygen-rich valleys.

Eight thousand were settled here, two thirds of the human race. The remaining third still lived on the Central Ark, some learning the theory of planetary management, some—a select few—waiting for their chance to ride more starships and carry out the judgment of the Law.

With virtually unlimited power supplies, no weapons, and resources sufficient for a hundred times their number already, their life on New Mars held promise of being idyllic. As always, only their own cussedness could change that.

He marched between the milky glass-walled greenhouses and up a low hill to a point where he could look down Feinman Rift. Far below, breeders tended the first range animals born out of genetic storage. It was warmer down there, and it rained far more often, and some complained that in a truly free society, that would be prime real estate, but the area was strictly reserved for the breeders. To give in to the community's baser instincts now might bring the Moms down on their backs again; it had happened once before, on the Central Ark, when human political authority had broken down into anarchy. Arthur did not wish to see it happen again.

Children do so hate to be disciplined.

Nobody knew who had sent these stern, dedicated robot guardians. Chances were they would never know. Arthur suspected that even benefactors had to be suspicious of their charges; it was best, for the time being, to simply stay hidden and quiet.

Arthur pinched his cheek and closed his faceplate against the cold. Then he looked to the east, above the pink haze of twilight, and saw the silvery point of Venus, still wrapped in a mantle of cloud.

Reuben Bordes was in command of the first exploratory and diagnostic mission to Venus. Twenty years ago, the now-moist Venerean clouds had parted briefly, and a decade-long rain had fallen, driving the planet's surface acids into chemical battle with molten rock thrown up by three centuries of fresh vulcanism. The clouds had closed again, and the reconnaissance expedition had been launched from the Central Ark.

Arthur did not envy Reuben his task. Venus was a hard case; it might be centuries more before humans could live in significant numbers on its surface.

What he was actually seeking was a clear view of the Milky Way, so that he could look at Sagittarius. He missed Martin deeply. To be cut off from the past was to cherish the future all the more; Martin was much of Arthur's future, though they would never see each other again, and hadn't communicated for a year and a half, by Arthur's time frame.

Martin had left on the seventh Ship of the Law, with fifty human crewmates, only eight years after Earth's destruction, before most of the survivors had been put into cold sleep. The ships had been traveling for centuries now, accelerating and decelerating, searching, refueling from dead ice moons.

He found Sagittarius, the Archer, between Scorpius and Capricorn. He lifted his gloved hand and pointed: *somewhere there.* Within the arc subtended by his trembling finger lay the solar system of Earth's killers.

How terrifying the sky was now. Arthur wished he could share Harry's vision of united solar systems forming vast "galactisms." Now, from what the Moms had told them, the galaxy was a vaguely explored frontier at best, a vicious jungle at the worst.

The galaxy, too, was young.

The planet-eaters had not come from such a great distance, after all. The first signs of their builders' interstellar dissembling, their protective coloration, had become evident less than a hundred light-years from the sun.

Martin, a quiet, solemn man who had grown to resemble his father, floated among a crowd of younger student-pilots on the observation deck of the kilometer-long, needle-thin Ship of the Law. All the Ships of the Law had been hewn from the material of the dead Earth itself. With the galaxy's center in view, still inconceivably faraway, he thought back to the debates he had had with the ship's Moms at the beginning of the journey.

"What if we find the civilization of the planet-eaters, and it's matured? What if it's beautiful and noble and rich with culture, and it regrets its past mistakes? Do we still destroy it?"

"Yes," the Moms had replied.

"Why? What good would that do?"

"Because it is the Law."

In fact, the builders of the planet-eaters had come very early on, thousands of years ago, to realize their mistake. They had laced the planetary systems around their parent star with dozens of false

civilizations, misleading beacons, even genetically engineered biological decoys, complete in every detail but one—the ability to
mislead a Ship of the Law.

Three ship-years before, Martin had walked the surface of one
such decoy planet, marveling at the creativity, the sheer expendi-
ture of energy.

The planet had revealed sophisticated defenses. They had
barely escaped the trap.

Now they were closing . . .

If they failed, others would follow, more informed, more aware
of the dangers and pitfalls of this neck of the galactic woods.

Despite his intellectual misgivings, Martin was committed. He
thought often of the age-old Law, and of the hundreds of mature
civilizations that had embraced it. In his heart, a cold, rational
hatred and hunger for vengeance echoed the demands of justice.

He knew, however strange and out of proportion it might be,
that one of his key subconscious motivations was to avenge the
death of a simple, uncomplicated friend: a dog. He vividly remembered those soul-branding hours in the ark's observation cabin.

Many of the humans aboard the Ship of the Law had been born
in the Central Ark and had never known their home world. They
were all dedicated to the search, regardless.

Silently, each day before the brief sleep of deep space, Martin
swore an oath he had made up himself:

To those who killed Earth: beware her children!

That is how the balance is kept.

ACKNOWLEDGMENTS:

Special thanks to Larry Niven, John Paul, Jonathan Post, John Anderson, and, as always, Karen and Poul Anderson. Beth Meacham, after she bought this book, lived part of it, as did her husband, Tappan King, my wife, Astrid, and Kim Stanley Robinson. The town of Shoshone is real, a lovely place, and I owe a deep debt of love and many fine hours to Susan, Charles, Maury, and Bernice Sorrells.